HIGHEST PRAISE FOR
JOVE HOMESPUN ROMANCES:

We at Jove Books are thrilled by the enthusiastic critical acclaim that the Homespun Romances are receiving. We would like to thank you, the readers and fans of this wonderful series, for making it the success that it is. It is our pleasure to bring you the highest quality of romance writing in these breathtaking tales of love and family in the heartland of America.

And now, sit back and enjoy this delightful new Homespun Romance . . .

MEG'S GARDEN
by Teresa Warfield

Meg's Garden

Teresa Warfield

JOVE BOOKS, NEW YORK

MEG'S GARDEN

A Jove Book / published by arrangement with
the author

PRINTING HISTORY
Jove edition / January 1997

The Putnam Berkley World Wide Web site address is
http://www.berkley.com/berkley

ISBN: 0-515-12004-9

A JOVE BOOK®
Jove Books are published by The Berkley Publishing Group,
200 Madison Avenue, New York, New York 10016.
JOVE and the "J" design are trademarks
belonging to Jove Publications, Inc.

PRINTED IN THE UNITED STATES OF AMERICA

10 9 8 7 6 5 4 3 2 1

March 20, 1996
Dedicated to the memory of Grandpa Robert,
who right now is building himself a tepee on
Grandma Dorothy's front yard in heaven

1

Eastern Kentucky, 1865

It took Meggie McBride the better part of an hour
to find her seven-year-old son and his friends this time.
They were in the habit of running off lately, as adventurous
boys were inclined to do. "Merely lads lookin' for excitement," her father-in-law, Edan McBride, would say—and
often did say. He'd remind her that the war was over, too,
that they were in no danger of encountering soldiers from
either side, that no one would grab their dear Ian and
squeeze him until he told where their last hog and bushel of
corn was hidden.

Still, Meg worried no less. While Kentucky had eventually joined the Union during the late war, Southern sympathizers abounded. The conflict between the states was too
recent—and the wife and son of a known Union officer
could not be too cautious. Southern sympathizers aside,
Meggie had seen her share of abusive Yankee soldiers, too.
Her skin crawled when she considered the things she, her
family, and friends had endured from both sides.

More recently, soldiers had started wandering home,
haggard-looking, tattered, edgy . . . and months ago Meg
had begun carrying a loaded revolver for protection. Right

now it rested in her left pocket, weighing down that side of her apron. She'd used the weapon only once, and although the experience still haunted her, she'd not hesitate to use the revolver again if she felt the need.

Sad how the war had divided relations and friends, as surely as it divided the nation. Edan had made no secret of the fact that he sided with the Union. Neither had Kevin, Meg's late husband—and the men's opinions had put them at odds with numerous people.

Meggie hiked her skirts, stepping through a tangle of brush on the edge of the Ohio River. She heard laughter up ahead, the gay sounds of playful children, and she quickened her steps. Sometimes she worried that she fussed over Ian too much. But then she also worried that he was far too independent for a child who'd suffered what he had suffered.

Perspiration dampened her face and the back of her neck, and still Meg pressed on, cutting between trees and more undergrowth. Summer was not two weeks old, and already it had dried much of the sogginess left by the spring thaw. Gentle hills cradled the river—and Meggie's heart. She'd been born atop a Kentucky mountain; she'd been raised here, she'd loved and married here, and she intended to bring up her son here.

She brushed by a glossy mountain laurel, decorated with rose-colored flowers. Azaleas had turned the hillsides scarlet. The sarsaparilla waved at Meg in the late afternoon breeze; she often dug up their roots and used them for flavoring. In the branches of the pines, hemlocks, oaks, and maples, robins fluttered, their breasts flashing red. Bluebirds sang *"cheery, cheery,"* and a killdeer dashed from tree to tree, his white breast crossed by bold black bands, his olive-brown back and cinnamon tail making him the prettiest creature in the branches, by far. A Kentucky warbler joined in the chorus from the low branch of a sweet birch, praising this glorious sunny afternoon.

Glorious indeed—but only if Meggie found Ian and his friends safe and sound.

She hurried on, drawing closer to the laughter, her heart racing.

At long last, she spotted four boys playing with the remains of a Rebel flag. It was dirty and tattered, as defeated as the Confederacy. They'd tied it to a long stick, and Ian himself lifted the flag and waved it around.

"General Lee of the Rebel forces, sir!" he said, deepening his voice, trying to make himself sound older and official. "We shall never surrender!"

"Then we'll burn until you do!" little Jefferson Parker announced.

Ian flapped the flag around, and when he stumbled a little, Meggie cried out, making a sound in the back of her throat. She rushed forward. "What the devil are ye doin', Ian McBride? Playin' at war. Have ye gone mad? An' wanderin' from the inn again. What am I to do with ye?"

A sheepish, guilty look flushed Ian's face. His fair hair, its golden highlights shimmering in the late-afternoon sunshine, lifted in the slight breeze. Jefferson's eyes widened. Russell Milan scowled and turned away, and Michael Willard stepped back, having felt the heat of Meg's temper more than once, and only as recently as last week when he chased one of her hens with a grass snake.

"We're playin', Mother, 'tis all," Ian said in their defense. "Russell found the flag an' brought it. It doesn't mean anythin'."

"Shoo—but doesn't it?" Meggie snatched the stick from Ian's hand and drove it into the soft ground. "I've no love of war, surely ye know that. But never mind, ye shouldn't be wanderin' where ye cannot be seen. Home now, all of ye! Playin' at war when so many died an' are still dyin'. When so much has happened!"

Ian and Jefferson looked meek. Russell's eyes flashed with anger. Michael sighed, probably wishing they could still play. But their game was over for the afternoon.

Ian shuffled his feet. Unfortunately the tragedies in his and Meg's family had touched him, had affected him, had scarred him. His limp was testimony to that. There'd been a day when Meg had feared he might never walk again. But her Ian had the courage of ten men, and he had determination enough for the world.

"I want my flag," Russell said sullenly.

"No," Meggie responded, and she yanked it from the ground and stood holding it, staring at it in disgust.

She turned the stare on Ian and his friends. "Playin' with such a thing! What a band of glorious Confederates the four of ye make. Wave this thing under the wrong Yankee's nose an'—"

Movement in the distance snared Meg's attention.

The sight of a man on horseback watching them made her heart, and voice, freeze. The man obviously hadn't shaved or bathed in weeks. He wore Union Blue, he was positioned not two hundred yards away—and she held a Rebel flag.

"He might shoot you before you can take your next breath," he said, finishing her sentence, his voice deep and cold. But the voice was nothing compared to the eyes. They were icy blue, as frigid as a January night.

Hesitation did not occur to Meg. She slipped her hand into her apron pocket, pulled out her revolver, and aimed it at the man. If his horse took one more step in this direction, he was dead.

The soldier tipped his head in an arrogant fashion and tightened his jaw. Seconds later he turned his mount and rode off.

Meggie waited until he was gone from sight, then she lowered her weapon and breathed again.

"Sweet Mother o' Mary," she swore softly. He might've killed them. Ian, her . . . Ian's friends . . . Killed them all and thrown them into the river to float away. She'd known people who had been killed during the late war for crimes far less serious than sporting a Confederate flag.

"'Tis all better now, Mum," Ian said in his sweet voice. "He's gone."

"What if he snatches us while we're walking home?" Jefferson's voice cracked.

"I'll grab a stick and wallop him!" Michael said with false courage.

While Meg glimpsed a flash of fear in Russell's eyes, he

laughed in the face of such danger, trying to appear brave as well as comical: "Why, don't you know the sight of this here flag's done scared him off? He won't be back. In no time at all he'll be some fifty miles upriver!"

"That'll take a good day," she informed him tartly. "We'll not wait around for such a thing to happen. We'll all be goin' home now. Scare him off? Shoo! Ye'd best remember who won the war, Russell Milan."

"Can I go with you and Ian, Mrs. McBride?" Jefferson asked. The boy had turned as white as new-fallen snow.

Meg ruffled his hair, her heart softening somewhat at the boy's frightened look. Then she scowled at him for good measure. "Ian an' I . . . we'll walk ye all to yer doorsteps. An' after t'day, ye'll not stray again."

Michael grabbed a nearby stick and started off on his own. "You'd better not cry, Jeff. You act like a girl sometimes."

"A little fear can be a good thing," Meggie told him. "A good thing indeed."

Michael continued on, shuffling and pouting. Meg knew he had fright in him that he wouldn't admit to; it was important to him to appear fearless no matter what. The boy had seven older brothers. He was the baby at home, but with his friends he often took charge, bullying and displaying courage Meggie knew he didn't really feel.

Walking each boy home would take some time. But with the soldier wandering the riverbank, she wasn't about to let the boys go off alone on their separate ways. True, the war had ended—finally. But resentments hadn't, and that Union soldier who'd just spotted her and the children with a Confederate flag had looked none too happy about it. At some point he might decide to turn back and . . .

Meggie shuddered. *Not again.*

"This," she said of the flag, "is a bothersome thing, indeed." She threw it into the river.

Russell's jaw dropped open at the sight, and Meggie shot him a severe look as she took Ian by the shoulders and turned him toward the line of trees Michael now neared. "Come along," she told Jefferson and Russell.

Russell cast another disappointed glance at the flag, which was floating down the river, and Meg's glare deepened. She'd deliver him home first. What a troublesome child he was today! He should've buried that flag when he found it.

MCBRIDE'S LANDING.

Richard Foster considered the words painted on the piece of wood nailed to a tree. The landing couldn't be far away; after all, signs were never posted far from businesses. One end of the sign had been carved to a point, indicating that the landing was northwest of here. And at any landing, there was always a ferry—in this case a means of crossing the Ohio River and entering his home state.

He broke into a sweat just thinking about crossing, and he grimaced as he shifted in the saddle. His leg ached, the one he had nearly lost at Gettysburg. He had to get off this horse soon. He had to rest. He'd slept on the ground last night in West Virginia because he hadn't wanted to be around people and because he preferred open spaces. But tonight he had to find a bed.

He dismounted and sat on a stump beside the water. Already he'd had one chance to cross, and he hadn't taken it. Back at Cox's Landing he'd sat and studied the water and the land on the other side for a good two hours, questions and thoughts going through his head in a mad rush, swirling, twisting, repeating . . . *And so I go home . . . What will they say? What will they think? How will they act?*

No one had thought the war would last as long as it had. Everyone had thought the South would lose quickly, that President Lincoln would effectively blockade Confederate harbors, preventing the importation of goods. Without imported goods, the South couldn't survive. She certainly couldn't support a lengthy war. Richard had entertained such thoughts himself, and he had left Ohio a hero alongside his brother—any man who enlisted in the army had been viewed as and treated as a hero—and yet he returned in shame.

If he returned. At Cox's Landing he'd turned away. And he very well might do the same at McBride's.

He thought of his family . . . his mother, his father, his sister, how proud they had been when he and Willy marched out.

He had promised to bring his brother home with him, and yet he was alone.

How could he face his family members? He didn't know what he should say to them, to his mother. Nearly two years now, and he still didn't know.

Upon spotting that Confederate flag a few miles back, he had frozen in place. Not another battle. Not more shooting. Not more screaming. Not more dying. During his time in prison, the battlefield memories hadn't faded.

Then he'd heard the woman who held the flag scolding the boys for playing with it, and his heart hammered in his chest. A Confederate flag didn't mean anything anymore. The war was over.

Still, resentments ran deep. To fly such a flag could be dangerous.

He had somehow overcome his initial shock and, like the woman, he wanted the boys to know the seriousness of what they were doing. Better still, he had wanted *her* to know the seriousness of what she was doing—even holding a Rebel flag might get a person shot by a jumpy Union soldier.

Presently Richard remounted and led his horse in the direction pointed out by the arrow. He had to keep going. Even if he chose not to cross at McBride's he had to find a comfortable place to rest for the night.

He soon rounded a bend in the river and spotted the landing. The ferry was just returning from the other side, drawing close to a wooden dock. A man stood on the deck, prepared to toss the mooring line, and another man, a burly-looking character who gave Richard a wary glance, watched from the wharf.

Richard expected to see a small house set back on the riverbank in which the ferry master no doubt resided. Instead he spotted what had to be considered a mansion for this part of Kentucky. A wide porch spanned two sides of the house, and on it sat a number of wicker chairs and tables. The house itself was clapboard and stood two stories high.

Richard thought he'd happened upon a well-to-do family—and if that were the case, he planned to make a quick decision about whether to cross or travel on. He reined in his horse near the dock and watched the ferry come in.

"Stoppin' for the night or crossin'?" asked the burly man, and Richard realized he was speaking to him. The man had quick eyes and a thick mop of reddish-blond hair.

Richard studied the Irishman.

The man studied him right back—rather, studied his Union Blue. "Goin' home?"

"Eventually." Stopping for the night . . . ? Was the man offering him lodging? "Do you let rooms here?"

The man chuckled, his eyes turning up merrily at the corners. "Do I let rooms . . . ? Why ye've just happened upon McBride's Landin' an' McBride's Inn, lad. I'm Edan McBride. B'lieve I do let rooms."

A friendly enough fellow.

A breeze rustled the tree branches. Water lapped at the sides of the ferry and the dock. An inn . . . a place to rest his leg—and his horse. Judging from the size of the inn, it must have numerous rooms.

"Busy place?" Richard queried.

The jolly face sobered. The merry eyes narrowed. "Well, now, I'd say last year at this time 'twas far busier than I prefer. This year . . . wouldn't be callin' it a busy place."

Richard shifted in the saddle. "I'd like a room facing the river. Do you have a stable?"

"Round on the other side," McBride said with a jerk of his head. "I've a man who'll tend that animal fer ye."

"I tend him myself."

Richard turned the horse away and tapped him into motion, heading for the inn and the stable. He felt Edan McBride's curious gaze on his back, but only for a moment. Doubtless the proprietor saw many a stranger come through here, and he'd surely learned long ago not to ask questions.

Richard was exhausted, but when an old Negro man in

the stable came forward, offering to take charge of his horse, Richard told him the same thing he'd told McBride— that he tended the animal himself.

The man eyed him. "I'll grab ya some oats an' a curry comb," he said with a jerk of his head. The fact that he'd had an education was apparent; he spoke better than most Negroes.

He went off, returning moments later with the items. Richard thanked him.

While the old man sat on a stool in a far corner of the stable and worked at whittling a piece of wood, Richard fed his horse. He combed him gently, taking special care with the animal's scarred neck and flanks. Like him, the horse was lucky to have survived the war. He'd been a cavalry mount, which meant he'd seen a lot of military action. Richard had bought the animal for a bargain price in war-ridden Richmond, and the gelding had been his companion for months now.

Now and then Richard glanced at the stablehand. Like the innkeeper, the Negro asked no questions, either. That was good—that was how Richard preferred his hosts.

The old Negro was doing more than whittling at that piece of wood. He was carving it, forming it into something. Richard suppressed the urge to walk over and have a look at the handiwork; these days he rarely engaged in conversation. One thing would lead to another. Conversations might lead to friendships, friendships to questions. He stayed to himself. He felt safe that way.

He looped the roped end of the curry comb on a nail just outside the stall and ran his hand down the horse's nose, gently assuring the animal that he'd be comfortable here— and that he would return in the morning to see him.

He rested against the gate of the stall before attempting to walk off. Damn if he'd use a cane. Bad enough to have an uncooperative limb and to think about returning home a cripple. To hell with hobbling around with the help of a stick. He wouldn't be gawked at like some traveling-show freak.

Richard tried to walk normally. But he'd stayed too long

in the saddle, and his leg ached like the devil. At the stable doors he grimaced, and halfway across the lawn he had to reach down and steady his quivering limb. The years he'd spent in that cramped, filthy prison hadn't helped. He'd get stronger from here. He had to get stronger.

He slowed his pace, suppressing the frustration that always welled up. He'd never had much patience.

He finally reached the inn. *Finally?* It wasn't such a great distance away. Before the war . . . before that shell had nearly blown off his leg, five hundred yards wouldn't have been a lengthy distance. He stepped up onto the porch with the help of the railing. A sign dangled from one of the columns, reading MCBRIDE'S.

Richard pushed open the front door and entered a wide hall flanked by rooms. Halfway down the hall, a staircase led to the second floor. The house smelled of stew or some other concoction, and when Richard's stomach growled, he realized he hadn't eaten since last night.

"Here," someone called from a nearby room, and Richard recognized McBride's voice.

The man sat behind a small desk in a modestly appointed room to Richard's left. Beneath his forearms rested a ledger in which he obviously had been working. Richard heard a door slam somewhere, then a woman's distant voice. He couldn't make out her words. Across the way, a stout woman dusted furnishings in a large room appointed with tables and chairs. A parlor of sorts. The keeping room.

"Ye must take fine care o' that animal," Edan McBride commented. "Had a horse once I considered me pride'n joy. Combed 'er four times a day. Even talked to 'er. Me pappy accused me o' neglectin' other things, an' I'd say he was right. I'd be combin' that horse when I should 'ave been mendin' fences or shearin' sheep. I—"

"You do have a room?" Richard asked. "One with a window facing the river?"

His brusqueness set the Irishman back. McBride studied Richard. Finally he jerked a nod and pulled open a drawer in the desk.

"Ye'll not be believin' what I'm about to tell ye, Poppa," a woman said, bursting into the room.

Richard instinctively turned at the intrusion.

"Of all the blessed—" She drew herself up short, freezing as her gaze fastened on him.

He wasn't accustomed to being interrupted, and the way he tipped his head and regarded the woman was more habit than arrogance. Richard recognized her immediately as the woman he'd seen holding the Confederate flag and scolding the group of boys for playing with it.

A pretty lady. He hadn't given her appearance much thought earlier because the flag had arrested his attention. But now . . . Her dress was modest and plain—dark green with a squared neckline and a white apron tied about her waist. Most of her auburn hair was restrained to one side in a long braid that fell over her shoulder and breast and ended at her waist. Wispy curls tumbled in disarray around the sides of her face, and a smattering of freckles across the bridge of her nose spotted her fair skin.

Her green eyes flashed at him. They narrowed on him at an angle, becoming decidedly hostile, something that didn't surprise Richard; after all, he still wore Union Blue and not long ago he'd come upon her holding a Rebel flag. Knowing she'd just wrestled it from those boys, he felt no animosity toward her, and he thought it important to let her know that.

Behind the desk, McBride scrambled to his feet. "Me daughter-in-law, Meggie," he told Richard, and he too narrowed his eyes—but on the woman he'd just presented to his newly arrived guest.

Richard swept his hat aside and dipped his head to Meggie in greeting. "I bear you no ill will, Mrs. McBride."

Her rosy lips snapped together. She made a show of noticing his sash, his shoulder scales, and the stripes of rank on his shirt.

Her chin came up in haughty defiance. "Lieutenant . . . We're not in the habit of boardin' soldiers," she said, and she tossed a questioning look at her father-in-law, then turned her glittering gaze back on Richard.

Her remark, her hostility, took him by surprise. He wasn't

quite sure how to respond. He'd damn sure encountered
enough animosity in Richmond and other areas to last him
a lifetime, but he didn't know what to think of hers. She had
been scolding those boys for playing with a Confederate
flag, so surely she harbored no Rebel sympathies.

"Meggie-girl, the war's over," McBride scolded softly.

Richard studied her, her truculent gaze, the color that had
risen in her cheeks. *"The war's over . . ." Had* these
people sympathized with the South? Perhaps Meggie McBride
still did.

"Never fear, I've nothin' against Union soldiers in particular," she said tartly, looking Richard straight in the eye.
She was a small thing, standing no more than five feet, three
inches, and weighing no more than one hundred and ten
pounds. But she had fight in her.

He wouldn't run from trouble—but he wouldn't encourage it.

"You'll hardly notice my presence, Mrs. McBride."

She tossed her head, giving a sarcastic laugh. "Oh, but
one always notices when there're soldiers about."

Edan McBride rounded his desk. He held out a key to
Richard and told him to turn left at the top of the stairs, that
his would be the room on the right at the end of the hall. He
received a glare from his daughter-in-law and he gave her a
reprimanding look in return.

Richard had never even offered the man his name, and
McBride seemed more eager to usher him off right now than
to know it. He knew, as Richard sensed, that Meggie
McBride intended to hold her ground. Obviously she had
encountered soldiers before—guessing that was not a
difficult thing. Whatever had happened during the encounter
had not been pleasant, and Edan was trying to defuse the
situation before she said much more to make their new guest
feel unwelcome.

He was nothing more than a weary soldier returning home,
exhausted mentally as well as physically. He had fought
people for years, and he wouldn't engage in conflict with
the pretty but insolent woman who had burst into the room
and made him feel unwelcome. No assurances on his part

would convince Meggie McBride that he'd come here in peace, and he didn't have the strength or a pressing desire to try to sway her opinion. He wanted quiet, a comfortable bed, and a warm meal.

Richard took the key from Edan McBride and quietly thanked the man for his hospitality. Then, keeping his limp as subtle as possible, he brushed by Meggie and left the room. Mounting the staircase wouldn't be easy. But comfort awaited him on the second floor, and he meant to reach it.

"War's over, Meg," Edan reminded his daughter-in-law again.

Dear Megan. The girl he'd come to know as his own daughter. She was usually a pleasant lass, except when the subject of the war and soldiers arose. Then Meggie's eyes lit with anger and fire, and she spat words as they occurred to her. Her devotion to those she loved always warmed Edan—he'd sensed it the day Kevin had brought her here to meet him—but he had little tolerance for her temper and her sharp words whenever certain subjects arose. Or whenever she encountered them face-to-face.

"I won't have it touchin' us again," she told him, drawing near to his desk. "Ye could've sent him on to Ironton or Havershill. There's plenty to be had in either direction."

"Meggie," Edan said, sinking down into his chair. "He's goin' home. He means no—"

"Ye're forgettin', Mr. McBride, that only a few months ago we boarded two soldiers who were goin' home, too. Well, Mrs. Clemons an' her girl'll not be forgettin' them for a good long while, an' that's the truth of it."

Edan rubbed his forehead. "Close the door b'fore he hears ye."

"Do ye think I care if he hears me?" she snapped.

Irritation bubbled in Edan. "*Ye're* forgettin' me own son, yer husband, was a soldier. If Kev'n had had the chance to come home alive, I pray to the Saints people would've taken him in along the way. 'Twas a long hard war for ever'one, Meggie, an' the sooner we forget, the better. Those men had evil in 'em or they wouldn't 'ave done what they did."

"An' the soldiers b'fore them?"

"Were fightin' for their lives an' existence. Ye don't understand war, or ye wouldn't question their actions."

That made her hesitate. She glanced off at the window, closed her eyes and breathed deeply. Then she looked at him again. "Ye're right. I don't understand war. I shall never understand it, Mr. McBride. Never."

She called him that—Mr. McBride—only when she was distraught or disapproved of something. Otherwise she called him Poppa, as Kevin had, or simply Edan. The war and the havoc it had wrought all over the nation was still too fresh, and on a personal level the events of two months ago had reopened healing wounds.

Unfortunately men would be drifting home from the recent conflict for months, perhaps longer, and many might stop at the inn. Meggie thought him heartless, boarding another soldier after the evil actions of those two. She did not know that he now kept several loaded revolvers in different places around the inn, that he had instructed the ferrymaster, Ryan Darrow, to keep a loaded revolver on him . . . that even old Mr. Sardis who minded the stable and the grounds and did odd work around McBride's also now kept a loaded weapon on his person. There wasn't a man within ten miles who hadn't been cautious for years and who wasn't even more cautious now.

Edan intended to board the homebound soldiers if his senses told him they were harmless. But in the event his senses were wrong, he meant to keep a good eye on any who slept beneath, or near, his roof.

"Ye didn't take a good look at his eyes, Meggie-girl, or ye would've seen he wants no trouble. Look at the way he doffed his hat an' remembered his manners upon seein' ye, lass. He's got a gentlemanly way about him. He'll be no trouble. The war took a lot from him, too, I'd wager. I'd say it took his spirit—an' almost took his leg. He means us no harm."

"Pray ye're right, Mr. McBride. Pray ev'ry mornin', noon, an' night," Meg said, and then she huffed off as she was inclined to do when angered. She had a way of gathering her skirts, squaring her small shoulders, and turning away, haughtily dismissing a person.

Edan listened to the fading click of her boots in the hallway, and when he heard the sound of a slamming door, as he knew he would, he set off for the kitchen to fetch a bowl of stew from Mrs. Hutchins. The soldier would be hungry, and he surely wouldn't venture downstairs for the evening meal after the greeting Meg had given him. Edan meant to take a bowl of stew up to the man himself and offer it to him along with an apology for his daughter-in-law's behavior.

2

"$\mathcal{W}$E WERE PLAYIN', Mum, 'tis all," Ian told Meggie again when she went off upstairs to see him after leaving her father-in-law. He was seated on the floor in his room, pushing around the wooden wagon his grandfather had made for him nearly a year ago. Meg shut the door with the heel of her boot and went to sit beside her son.

"Ye're very angry with me," he said, sounding far too grown-up for his age. "We didn't mean anythin' with the flag." His wide blue eyes, his father's eyes, clenched Meggie's heart and made her sorry she'd scolded him so severely.

"Ye mustn' wander off, Ian," she told him and then took his hand in hers. "Listen to me closely now. We've a new boarder . . . the soldier we saw earlier." She felt him start and she quieted him with a shake of her head and a gentle, reassuring smile. "All is well an' will stay well, love, but ye must listen an' do what I say. Ye'll sleep with me while he's here an' ye'll go nowhere without me, yer grandpoppa, or one of the others, not even to the henhouse." By "one of the others," she meant Mr. Sardis, other workers, and people she knew and trusted around the inn.

"He'll shoot us for the flag, Mum?"

"No, Ian. He'll not shoot us for anythin'."

"He looked angry. We were only playin'. We're not big enough to be soldiers!"

"Or foolish enough," Meggie said under her breath.

"Mr. Darrow said he'd ruther see a dead soldier if he has to see one 'tall."

Meg smoothed her son's hair. "Do not be repeatin' the things Mr. Darrow says. He can be a crude man when the notion strikes him."

"Ye feel the same way, don't ye, Mum?"

She shook her head. "No, Ian. I'm simply wantin' the soldiers to leave us alone."

"They're not all bad," he said. "Poppa was a soldier, wasn't he?"

Nodding, Meggie smiled sadly. Ian had scarcely known his father. He'd been all of two years old when Kevin had gone off to preserve the precious Union. There might have been daughters, perhaps more sons, if Kevin had stayed home and let the Confederate states go their own way. Now there was no hope of that. Kevin had been killed at the battle of Chancellorsville. Meggie's heart was still with him. She'd never marry again.

Ian patted her hand. "All will be well. The soldier . . . he'll be gone soon, an' I promise to never again play with a flag."

"Oh, love," Meggie said, "it was the *sort* of flag ye were playin' with." He charmed her at times. She loved him and adored him more than anything. "Are ye up to helpin' milk the cows, or should I take ye down to Mrs. Hutchins? Ye must be worn to the bone, all the walkin' we did."

He scowled a little. "'Tis all better. The leg doesn't pain me anymore."

She scowled right back at him. "Are ye tellin' me I worry for naught, Ian McBride?"

He smiled sheepishly.

She made a sound of exasperation in the back of her throat. Perhaps she did worry for naught. But after the fire in which he'd been injured, she'd spent many a day and night at his bedside not knowing if he would live or die—and she had spent many more days and nights wondering if he would ever walk again.

"The cows are waitin'," she said, getting to her feet. He started to do the same, and she started to help him up, as she usually did. But this time she stopped herself. He was growing weary of her fussing over him so much. She must learn to wait until he asked for her help, until he gave some indication that he needed it.

The milking did not take long. Mr. Sardis, old and bent, had already brought the cows in from the pasture and was milking one while the other cow munched noisily on a bundle of hay. Mr. Sardis had never been a slave, thank the good Lord. His parents had been free Northern Negroes who'd worked a farm in the Kentucky hills, and by the light of tapers at night his mother had made certain he'd learned to read and write. If Mr. Sardis had been younger during the Civil War, he would've joined the Union army, too, Meggie had no doubt. More than once she'd heard him express negative opinions about slavery.

He slanted a grin at her and Ian when they entered the barn through its creaking doors, and he promptly turned a nearby wooden bucket over on the earth floor.

"Young Master McBride," he greeted. "Somethin' tole me you'd be along. Take a seat. Lemme tell ya 'bout the time, a mighty long time ago, me'n my brothers set off down the river on a raft we made ourselves."

"It surely couldn't be *so* long ago," Meg teased. "Why, we all know ye're not yet thirty years old."

He had a good chuckle over that and he pulled back from the cow to shake a finger at Meggie. "Old 'nough I cain't promise to dance at Ian's wedding. Ya flatter an old man, Miss Meggie! I'd be in the ground already if ya didn't keep me on my toes."

Meg's grin widened. Ian used the cane Mr. Sardis had made for him, and he stumped his way to the overturned bucket.

There he settled himself and told Mr. Sardis he thought he'd already heard about his rafting adventures on the river, but that the accounts excited him so he should like to hear about them again.

Kind Ian. He'd heard about them dozens of times. Mr. Sardis loved to tell stories, but his entire collection consisted of only four stories at the most.

While Mr. Sardis started into his account of how he went about gathering just the right pieces of wood for his raft, Meggie took charge of milking the other cow.

Mr. Sardis finished before her, and then he went about brushing and feeding the horses they kept.

Meg was just finishing up her milking when she heard Ian ask about the scars on a particular animal. She knew of no scars on any horse of theirs and, her lantern in hand, she approached Mr. Sardis and Ian.

"I'd say he was a mite mistreated," Mr. Sardis said as Meggie neared the stall.

"We've only one boarder at present," she remarked. "I'm assumin' this animal belongs to him."

"He's a soldier," Ian informed Mr. Sardis. "Are ye thinkin' he did this?" Ian reached through the stall rails and ran his hand down a long scar on the horse's right flank. Other scars marked the animal's neck and legs. The horse skittered away from Ian, its eyes looking wild.

"Doesn't like strangers, that's for sure," Mr. Sardis said. "Cain't say who mistreated him."

"Well, we know who he belongs to," Meggie commented.

Mr. Sardis squinted an eye at her. "Army goes through a lot of horses, Miss Meggie. Doesn't mean that soldier's responsible for his condition. Cain't believe poorly of a man who takes an hour to comb 'n' feed his horse. Don't reckon he'd mistreat it like this."

"Ye saw him?" Meggie queried, tipping her head. Combing and feeding the animal, she meant.

"Yep. Plumb worn out himself, but he took care of this horse before he took care of hisself."

Meg considered that. What kind of man put the comfort of his horse before his own?

"A strange one, indeed," Meggie remarked softly as she

reached out to touch the animal's nose. He blew at her and jerked his head away.

"Doesn't do that with his soldier," Mr. Sardis said, squinting again. "Nuzzles all over that man."

Only an animal would, Meggie thought, as dirty and disheveled as the soldier had appeared.

"Let's take the milk to the well, Ian," she said, turning away.

"I'm wantin' to help Mr. Sardis," Ian told her.

Meggie turned back and gave him a stern look. "I said—"

"Please, Mum? He'll take me to the house when we finish. Won't ye, Mr. Sardis?"

"On my honor, Miss Meggie," Mr. Sardis said, looking entirely serious. "Wouldn't let anything happen to our Ian."

Nathaniel Sardis knew her well. He knew she was nervous about them boarding the soldier. He himself had pulled Ian from the burning barn after she'd tried to enter and the smoke had driven her back. She trusted him.

She smiled gently at the man. "I know." How well she knew. "Very well. But ye're not to venture from his sight," she told Ian. "I'll be waitin' in the kitchen."

Ian grinned. Mr. Sardis nodded at her.

Meggie almost bolted forward when her son jumped down off the railing. But Mr. Sardis caught him before he could land on the leg that had been injured when the barn had burned, and Meg shot Ian a scowl. "Ian McBride, are ye wantin' to scare the life from yer mother?"

"I told ye it was well," he said with a giggle. "I can run. I can do anythin'."

Meggie shook her head. She wished she could believe that. But it seemed like only yesterday that a fierce cracking had made her glance up, and in the distance she'd seen flames shooting up from the barn and had heard Ian's screams.

"Give it more time, Master McBride," Mr. Sardis said wisely.

Once outside the barn, Meggie lowered the two buckets of milk into the well to keep them cool, then she walked across the lawn and rounded the house to enter through the kitchen door.

Odd . . . A lamp had been left burning, and the kitchen was ungodly hot. Mrs. Hutchins had left a fire in the grate and a kettle of water dangling over it. She'd left the pot of stew on the cookstove, too, probably knowing Meggie and Ian had not yet eaten, along with a plate of yesterday's bread. Mrs. Hutchins always baked bread on Wednesdays. But why the water heating in the kettle at this hour?

Meg heard stirring in the next room—in the small bath room that extended off the kitchen. Had Mrs. Hutchins herself or Mr. McBride decided to bathe? Given the hour and what she knew of their habits, Meggie wondered at that.

Just as it began to dawn on her who might be in the room, the door opened, and the soldier, minus his shirt, stepped into the kitchen. He saw her and froze with his razor in hand.

Meg also froze. He wasn't naked, thank God, only stripped from the waist up. Clearly he'd been shaving; the dark beard was gone from one half of his jaw, and soap lathered the other half. The hair that curled on his chest was dark and generous, and his shoulders and chest were muscular.

All this Meggie glimpsed within seconds; it didn't take her long to spin on her heels and put her back to him. Sweet Jesus, but she was certain her face was the color of fall maple leaves—it felt as fiery!

"I . . . my apologies," he stammered. "Mr. McBride told me about the bath room. I waited until I thought most everyone had retired for the night. The kitchen was empty and dark."

For once, Meg was at a loss for words. The evening hadn't passed as it usually did. First she'd chased Ian and his friends down, then she'd walked every one of the boys home at the time she and Ian normally would be having supper with Edan, Mrs. Hutchins, and any boarders. By now she and Ian would have been reading together or doing something else, either in one of the front rooms or up in his room.

"Usually everyone has retired by this hour," she mumbled.

Was she trembling? She was not . . . she didn't like to think that she was. But she couldn't shake the thought that the man . . . the *soldier* was alone with her in the kitchen, and that he held a razor. A sharp one, too, she had no doubt. Edan felt the man intended them no harm, and Mr. Sardis certainly thought well of the stranger. But Meggie wasn't one to trust so easily.

"I was heating water for a bath," the lieutenant said. "You'll excuse me?"

From the corner of her eye, Meggie saw him start toward her.

She felt panicky inside. She could flee through the door that led to the hallway, or she could flee through the portal that led outside. Her mind reeled, remembering the last time she'd been caught alone with a soldier.

She wanted to flee the kitchen . . . Lord only knew how she wanted to flee. And yet the thought that she'd told Ian she would wait for him here made her stay. If she fled, Ian might walk in and find himself alone with the stranger, and Meg would not have that.

She was not without protection for herself.

She slipped her hand down into her apron pocket, and pulled out her revolver.

She'd started to turn back, intending to aim the weapon at the man. His hand caught her wrist. His other hand yanked the revolver away from her, and he twisted her around to face him.

If Meggie had been the sort to scream, she would have raised the roof. Instead she stared up into the man's glittering blue eyes. She felt the heat of his breath on her face, smelled the spicy scent of the soap on his jaw, and she caught her breath. She half expected the razor to be lifted to her throat. Then she saw that he'd somehow dropped it quietly on the nearby table.

The man might have an injured leg, but he'd moved quickly enough to defend himself against her.

"I'm unarmed," he said, his voice deep and low as he stared down at her. "I pose no threat to you or anyone else."

"But ye're not unarmed, Lieutenant," Meg responded smartly. "Ye held a razor, an' now ye hold my weapon."

He hesitated. Seconds later, he laid the revolver on the table and gave it a push to send it sliding out of reach.

His cold stare returned to Meg. "I plan to finish my bath if you don't mind, Mrs. McBride. If you do mind . . . I plan to finish it anyway."

Meg's brows shot up at that. Of all the arrogant . . . Typical of a soldier. Come in, take over, assume things . . . "We don't have enough water in the wells to wash all the dirt off o' ye," she retorted.

His eyes narrowed. "You have quite a tongue, madam. I don't know why you bother to carry a gun."

Meggie twisted her wrist out of his grasp. She eased away, putting the oak table between them. "Ye'll not be stayin' long, I presume?"

"Perhaps I'll stay until my money runs out." His eyes glittered with anger.

"Oh? Then perhaps *I'll* convince Mr. McBride to raise the nightly fee."

The man shook his head and gave a laugh of disbelief as he approached her. This time Meg did not back away. She'd not appear humble and meek and afraid.

When he stopped, perhaps a distance of a foot separated them. He was a fine-looking man, Meggie thought despite herself. He'd already washed some—his arms and face were fairly clean. His hair was black and wavy, tumbling to well below his shoulders. He stood two heads taller than she, which put Meg at eye level with his broad chest. That alone added to her nervousness, not to mention the fact that he was far too close for her peace of mind.

Silly lass. It wasn't as though she'd not seen a man's chest before.

She stared defiantly up into the lieutenant's eyes and she fought a tremble.

But only for a few seconds. Her temper flared again. If he touched her, Meg had her mind made up to kick him hard in his injured leg. That would no doubt put the man in

pain, and he'd think twice about ever trying such a thing
again.

"You don't like soldiers. You've made that clear, Mrs.
McBride," he said. "Considering that, it would be to our
advantage to avoid each other during my stay here."

"Gladly," Meggie retorted.

He studied her for another few seconds, his gaze dropping
to her mouth, then returning to her eyes. Meg again fought
the urge to step back, to put more distance between them.

The lieutenant finally moved first, limping past her
toward the hearth.

Despite her earlier embarrassment, Meggie turned and
stared at his strong back as he bent and lifted the kettle off
the hook. A long scar cut diagonally from his right shoulder
halfway to his waist. Surely such a wound would kill a
person, and yet here the man was, scarred and clearly
injured, but alive.

So they would avoid each other during his stay here . . .
And would he avoid all others? All those she loved and
cherished?

He was a remnant of the recent war, and Meggie would not
have the war upsetting the lives of her family and friends
again. She wouldn't let him take from their lives to suit his
needs, leaving them with nothing. She wouldn't listen to
his accounts of battles, his boastings of courage and prowess.

But perhaps Mr. McBride was right . . . the man meant
them no harm.

Regardless, his mere presence made her own war wounds
fester, and Meggie wanted the lieutenant gone as soon as
possible.

Richard felt Meggie McBride's stare on his back until he
stepped into the bath room and shut the door. He poured
the steaming water into the copper tub. Then he set the
kettle on the floor, lifted a nearby bucket and poured enough
cold water into the tub to cool the bath to a tolerable
temperature.

He had left his razor on the kitchen table. *Damn.* He
didn't have the stomach for any more of Mrs. McBride's

haughty resentment and sharp tongue tonight. If he hadn't already shaved off half the growth on his jaw he'd be inclined to say to hell with the razor.

He grabbed the shirt he'd shed a short time ago and started to slip it on. Then he thought better of it. Donning his shirt before stepping back into the kitchen, where Meggie might still linger, would be the gentlemanly thing to do. Then again, it might not. He remembered her hostile glance at his Union Blue, and he dropped the shirt. She might be more inclined to shoot him if he wore it.

Richard stepped back into the kitchen where he spotted her warming the remainder of the stew over the fire in the hearth. Her revolver was gone from the table; she probably had dropped it back into her apron pocket. He was curious to know where she'd come up with the British Tranter. It was a revolver used widely by the Confederates.

She tossed another fiery glance over her shoulder at him. From the corner of his eye, Richard watched her closely as he approached the table to collect his razor. Apparently she'd taken seriously his earlier actions and words concerning her weapon; she made no move to aim it at him again. Razor in hand, he retreated back into the bath room.

He finished shaving, then he stepped into the water and lay back against the end of the tub.

Presently he heard a child's voice in the kitchen: "Look what Mr. Sardis made fer me, Mum! He's makin' 'em fer Russell an' the others, too! He says we'll go fishin' one day soon, an' then we'll clean the fish an' fry 'em ourselves!"

"Will ye now?" Meggie queried. "Not if ye don't eat somethin' this minute. Why, if not ye'll surely blow away with the wind, Ian McBride."

"I'll not blow away," the boy said, and Richard heard the amusement in his voice. Ian's mother was spinning a tall tale, and Ian was not buying it. "Such a thing isn't possible."

"Oh, isn't it?"

"No." Ian giggled.

"Like a dandelion puff, ye will!"

"*No*, I'll not."

Meggie laughed with him. Then she told him to sit and eat.

Her voice lowered considerably after that, and Richard found himself straining to hear her next words to her son: "Mind ye now, no dallyin'! We've got company in the bath room. That soldier decided his toes needed scrubbin' at this hour. Imagine that!"

Richard's eyes popped open. His toes needed scrubbing? He stole a glance down at them and instantly had to agree with that. What a comical side Meggie McBride had.

Ian thought so—he giggled, then said, "I'll not dally, Mum." Finally all was quiet, and Richard assumed mother and son were eating.

Some five minutes later, as Richard was lathering his chest and arms, Meggie began humming a tune he recalled from the church services he had attended. Her humming was slower than the usual tempo of the song, and she paused occasionally, as if distracted by something. A number of times after the pauses, she picked up humming right where she had left off. He heard dishes clatter, water splash, a poker clank on the grate. And throughout the noises, Meggie hummed on.

When the sound of her voice faded, Richard knew she and her son had left the kitchen, hopefully for the night. Relief. He didn't want to sample Mrs. McBride's resentment again tonight.

He finished his bath and pulled the rag from the hole someone had made in the bottom of the tub. That started the water draining out through an iron pipe onto the ground below the inn. He donned the fresh shirt and trousers Edan McBride had provided him, and he collected his razor and shaving cup and set off for the room he had rented.

The room did indeed overlook the river, giving quite a view of the distant water, slopes, and treetops. The inn seemed like a quiet place, a haven where he could rest and think without being disturbed. Now and then the ferry would cross and he would watch it and deliberate on when and if he should go home.

Surely his family expected him, and yet he felt shame and

disappointment in himself. By now they had to know that William was dead.

Willy, who had joined up with fight in his eyes and spring in his step. Willy, who had gone down in front of him. And he, kneeling over his brother, feeling helpless, in a rage.

Would the scene never stop replaying in his head? Richard thought it would haunt him forever.

Earlier he'd pushed open the shutters on the two windows and tied back the curtains. He liked to sleep with the night air cooling him. But he wouldn't sleep for a while. He often stayed awake late, reading or writing in the journal he had started months after Gettysburg, months after he and Willy went down. Keeping the journal helped him sort his thoughts.

He sat at the small desk where he had arranged a number of items—the small leather-bound notebook, several books, pens, ink, and a blotter.

He opened the journal, turned to the next blank page, and wrote: *Today, just beyond the Kentucky border, I came upon a group of young boys playing with a Confederate flag. My first instinct was to pull my horse down with me for cover and start firing. Thank God I haven't gone completely mad. I might be a cripple, but I am no raving lunatic.*

He glanced off out the window, across the river, toward the state of Ohio . . . toward home.

Willy, he wrote. *I cannot bear the thought of looking upon our mother's face knowing how she loves him and expects him to come home. I often wonder if there might have been time to throw myself in front of him. Yet there was not. He was gone so quickly that even his own brother, who stood not ten yards away, had no chance to say goodbye.*

Richard rose. He walked to the window that faced the river, and there he dropped his head and rested it against the frame. He hated the grief that consumed him. Even more, he hated the guilt. He couldn't shake the thought that when Willy had joined the army, he'd followed the lead of the reckless older brother he adored.

Considering that, Richard had led the eighteen-year-old William straight to his grave.

3

SOMETHING WOKE RICHARD at the crack of dawn. Someone was singing below his window.

It was Meggie McBride's voice again, only this time she put words to her tune: "On many a winter's eve, young swains would gath-er there; for her father kept a social board, an' Charlotte, she was ver-y fair. Her father loved to see her dressed, fine as a city belle; for she was the only child he had, an' he loved his daught-er well."

Richard turned over in the bed. He tried to drown out the sunlight by putting a pillow over his face, and he tried to drown out Meggie's singing by pressing the pillow down around his ears. Doing that helped—it muffled the sound—but Meggie had a strong voice, and there was no drowning it out.

Well, strong as her voice was, she was surely only passing near his window; she'd move on soon, and he could go back to sleep.

"'Twas New Year's Eve an' the sun went down; wild looked her anxious eyes, along the frost-y windowpanes, to see the sleighs pass by. At a village inn, fif-teen miles round, there's a mer-ry ball to-night. The air is freezin' cold above, but the hearts are warm an'—

"Off there right now!" she shouted at someone, interrupting her song. "Ye're nothin' but trouble in here. Scat. Out!"

A few seconds passed, then Meggie McBride was after the person again. "Oh, that's a fine thing ye've done! Took a turn right through my vines. Look at them. Would ye just look at them! I've a mind to send ye off down the river on a raft. Ye don't like the water—that's surely no secret round here. An' look at ye standin' there givin' me such a face! I've a mind to do more than send ye off down the—"

Damn. Richard turned over in the bed and shoved the pillow away. Whoever had incurred Mrs. McBride's wrath this morning was getting a good dose of it. She was still scolding the person, reminding him or her that they had trampled through her vines last week also, and that she didn't make idle threats—she really would send the person off downriver on a raft if he persisted. And she might not include food and water!

Just about the time Richard thought she meant to carry on forever, she went back to singing: "An' while she looked with longin' eyes, a well-known voice she heard. An' dash-in' up to the cottage door, young Charley's sleigh appeared."

"It wouldn't be a fine morning without your singing, Meg," someone called to her.

"Mornin', Mr. Darrow!" Meggie called back. "Look at the blooms t'day. Why, have ye ever seen 'em so open an' colorful? I've not, I'll tell ye that."

"The prettiest one stands in the middle of them," the man responded.

Meggie shrieked. "*Caomh!* Ian, come now an' take him! Lovable . . . hah! *Foley* would be more like him. He plunders my garden like nothin' I've seen. Collect him now, Ian McBride, an' talk to him well or else ye've seen the last of him."

"Mum, ye'd not really set him afloat on a raft in the river, would ye?" the boy queried.

"I do what I say. Now get him."

Curiosity finally made Richard get up and go to the western window. Looking down, he spotted Meggie standing near a curved brick wall in a well-tended flower garden. Vines scaled the wall, and tiny blue blossoms decorated the greenery. Meggie herself wore gingham patterned in a green design, and her sleeves were pushed up to just above her elbows. Her hair was twisted and pinned to the back of her head, but more curls escaped around her face. The handle of a brown basket looped over her left forearm.

Several brick paths twisted off from a circular area in the center of the garden. Ian McBride, with the help of a small cane, limped hurriedly down one of the passages. "Come here, Caomh," he called. "Come now, else ye'll be sent away!"

Richard wondered what made the boy limp, and he wondered who Ian chased; he didn't see anyone besides Meggie in the garden area. Finally, when Ian hunched down beside a flowering bush and dragged a white cat out from beneath it, Richard guessed who, or what, had been attempting to destroy Meggie McBride's garden.

"Take him to Mr. Sardis in the stable," Meggie said. "There's a fam'ly of mice havin' their run of the place. Caomh gets the scent of them an' he'll surely not be back here. He'll be too busy feastin'."

That said, she turned toward her wall and began fussing over the vines there, rearranging them, smelling this bloom and that bloom, rearranging those, too. She plucked away wilting leaves and dropped them into her basket.

Ian tucked the objecting Caomh between his elbow and his body and stumped his way out of the garden. Meggie turned to watch her son, and she observed him for a good long while, surely for as long as it took him to reach the stable. Quite the attentive mother.

With the troublesome cat gone, Meggie would have no one to scold, and he might go back to sleep. Or so Richard assumed. But as soon as he laid his head on the pillow, she began singing again.

Since he couldn't drown out the sound of her voice, he was forced to listen to the tale of young Charlotte's courtship with Charles, how Charlotte's mother insisted that her daughter throw a blanket around her shoulders before she went off in the sleigh to the ball with Charles, and how Charlotte and her beau raced over the hills through the snow, braving the cold.

Surely Mrs. McBride knew he occupied the room above her garden. But then, given her rudeness of yesterday, her singing so loudly beneath the window didn't surprise him. She'd made it clear that she wanted him gone as soon as possible.

Richard got up and closed the shutters on the windows, pulling them so hard they banged against the frame.

For a moment Meggie's singing stopped. Childish of him to slam the shutters instead of informing her that he was still trying to sleep. He might have asked her to lower her voice or not to sing at all. But something told him Meggie would pay no mind to any request of his, and that she just might enjoy knowing she disturbed him. His slamming the shutters had let her know that—another reason he shook his head at himself for the show of temper.

She resumed singing, although the closed shutters softened the sound of her voice. Richard put the pillow back over his face and finally managed to fall asleep.

He was hungry when he woke. He'd been grateful to Edan McBride for bringing him up a bowl of stew last evening. This morning, however, no one attempted to bring up food.

It was just past ten o'clock, if Richard's timepiece was right. He again dressed in the clothes Edan had provided him, and washed his face over the basin that sat atop the room's small chest of drawers. Finally, he combed his hair and went downstairs, hoping to find Mr. McBride and inquire about meals.

Edan wasn't behind his desk or even in that room, and he wasn't in the other rooms—the large dining room, the keeping room, and a sitting room. Hearing voices that seemed to come from the kitchen, Richard elected to go that way.

". . . Sardis promptly gave the creature a bowl of milk an' made him feel welcome," Meggie was telling another woman, a stout, ruddy-faced woman with gray hair that sat atop her head in a tight bun. The very woman who had been dusting when Richard arrived yesterday. She now sat peeling apples in a chair near the back kitchen window. A bushel of apples sat at her feet, and a nearby bowl on a small table held apples that already had been peeled and cored.

"An' that's where Caomh will stay if he knows what's good for him," Meggie added. She stood with her back to Richard, facing a counter where she sorted through a pile of what looked like dried beans.

The other woman spotted Richard standing in the doorway, and her eyes brightened as she stopped her work. "Why, it's our new boarder," she said, placing a half-peeled apple and her knife on the table beside the bowl. She rose, beaming a smile at him. "I thought you might never wake. Let's see, I'm trying to remember your name and—"

"Ye can't possibly, Mrs. Hutchins," Meggie remarked, still sorting. "He hasn't seen fit to tell anyone."

Her sharp tongue again.

"Richard Foster," he informed Mrs. Hutchins.

"The *lieutenant* has been awake for some time."

"Oh." Mrs. Hutchins seemed rather nervous at Meggie's comment. She tossed a worried glance at Meg, then she smiled at Richard again. "You must be famished, Lieutenant."

"I prefer Richard or Mr. Foster."

"All right. Richard, then. What would you like—griddlecakes? Eggs? I can fry up some bacon."

Meggie turned around. "I'm sorry, Lieutenant. We don't serve breakfast after—" She froze with her mouth still open, her stricken gaze fastened on Richard. Rather, on the stitched clover that marked one shoulder of his shirt. "Where'd ye get the clothes?" Her voice sounded weak and strained suddenly.

Richard wondered at her reaction. "Mr. McBride lent them to me."

"They're not his to lend." she said and tossed down a bean. "Havershill's but a short distance away. Ye can purchase a set of yer own clothes there. Do it as soon as possible."

With that, Meggie lifted her skirts, tossed her head, and spun on her heels.

"Now, Meg," Mrs. Hutchins began, "surely Edan didn't mean a thing by—"

The door that led outside snapped shut as Meggie exited the kitchen, cutting off Mrs. Hutchins's last words.

The latter woman turned back to Richard and sighed. "That's Megan, if you haven't met her yet. I can't imagine that since Meg meets everyone nearly as soon as they arrive. She's a busy girl, that one, and she has a temper."

Richard wouldn't disagree with that. He'd experienced Meggie's temper several times yesterday.

Something about the shirt he wore had set Meggie off. Hell if he'd try to figure out her reaction. He had enough on his mind without worrying over why Meggie McBride was in a temper *again.*

He wouldn't subject himself to her tantrums. He'd go to Havershill as soon as possible and purchase civilian clothes.

"Do you serve breakfast at certain times, Mrs. Hutchins?"

"Usually only till nine," she responded, smiling again. "But if you're hungry, come here anytime and I'll feed you."

"I won't take advantage of your kindness."

Her smile widened. "Aren't you a mannered fellow! Have a seat, and I'll rustle you up some breakfast."

Richard pulled a chair back from the table and sat down while Mrs. Hutchins went about making coffee in a small pot she placed on the stove. She opened the door to the stove, tossed in several scoops of coals, and soon had a small fire going.

"In the summertime I do most of the cooking in the outside oven to keep from heating the inn too much," she said, putting strips of bacon in a skillet. "Otherwise, it gets a little toasty in here. Where're you from, Richard?"

"Ohio." The coffee was beginning to smell good. He couldn't wait to get a cup of it in his hands.

"Well, I'd say you're mighty close to home. I'm sure you won't tarry long here. Where at in Ohio?"

Richard rubbed his chin. *Questions.* Conversations with people always led to them. "Cleveland."

"About a week more of traveling and you'll be there."

He nodded slowly. "I could be."

She put the skillet on the stove and opened the back door, letting the morning breeze into the room. Then she moved to pour him a mug of coffee. "There you go," she said, setting it down in front of him.

Richard thanked her and took a drink from the mug.

Mrs. Hutchins wiped her hands on her apron. "Meg . . . She's really a good girl. We saw a few soldiers come through here during the war and then a few months ago, too. We usually have plenty here at McBride's, but every time after soldiers came through, we fought to get together meals for a while. The men hunted what was left, and Meg and Ian fished and got berries and pecans from the woods. Despite all that there wasn't always enough. That Meg . . . she'd hunt the woods all day for edible things rather than put her son to bed hungry at night."

Admirable. But Meggie McBride had been nothing but rude to him since his arrival yesterday, and Richard didn't care to hear about her better qualities.

He took another drink of coffee and thanked Mrs. Hutchins again for her consideration in fixing him a late breakfast. "I'll be down before nine from now on."

"Oh? Planning to stay around for a while?"

He rubbed his jaw again. That depended on when he got up the courage to cross over to Ohio on the ferry. "I might."

Questions gathered in her eyes. But Mrs. Hutchins, like Edan, had the good sense not to spill them.

As if knowing she'd asked enough, she went back to her stove and began turning bacon in the skillet.

"Meg didn't mean to be rude to you," she remarked. "That shirt Edan lent you . . . it's one Meg made for her husband before he went off to war. Meg stitched a clover like that onto every shirt she made for Kevin."

"She did mean to be rude," Richard said.

Mrs. Hutchins glanced at him, more questions in her eyes. "Meg's not like that."

"I was a Union lieutenant," he stated. Nothing more needed to be added.

"Well . . . you may be right in thinking that's what has her riled."

"Has he come home?" Richard asked against his better judgment. Curiosity could be a foolish thing.

"Kevin?"

"Yes."

"In a pine box after Chancellorsville."

Richard tipped his head, now listening closely.

"He's buried on the hilltop just west of here. It was his and Meg's favorite spot."

Mrs. Hutchins used a fork to put the strips of bacon on a plate. She took eggs from a basket on the table and cracked two over the skillet. The bacon grease sizzled and popped.

"Meg doesn't like war, doesn't agree with it. She's right, in a sense—if soldiers could just fight soldiers and not involve civilians, that'd be the best thing."

Richard narrowed his eyes. "Soldiers fight *for* civilians."

Mrs. Hutchins glanced sharply at him. "Not always. Some that came through here . . . they were fighting just to be fighting."

He'd seen that—men charging into battle, just wanting to fight, not necessarily caring which side they were on.

Why had he fought? For the sake of preserving the mighty Union. That had been the battle cry most of the time . . . *For the preservation of the Union*! Slavery aside, pride had driven the Union to war. How dare South Carolina and the other Southern states secede. How dare they try to dissolve the Union.

"Meg believes letting the Confederacy go might have been the best thing," Mrs. Hutchins remarked.

Not a bad thought.

Richard didn't know what he believed anymore. He'd once thought it vital to preserve the United States. Then he'd seen Death . . . The destruction caused by war . . . hundreds upon hundreds of bodies littering battlefields . . . sometimes thousands. He'd watched people die, had known he and his comrades in battle were starving out women and children by burning fields and taking or killing livestock and leaving the carcasses to rot.

He had dealt people some of the very hardships that the McBrides and the others at this inn had suffered. In the end, that had been the only way to defeat the South. Burn her, starve her out . . . control her. Even now, some Southerners might be starving. Lord only knew how many years it would take the Confederate states to rebuild. Richard carried around enough guilt for the entire Union army. No matter that a *Confederate* state had fired the first shots of the war.

"It's over," he said quietly as Mrs. Hutchins turned the eggs with a spatula. *Thank God.*

The room fell silent for a few moments.

She put the plate down in front of him on the table and remarked, "I think you're a tired soldier."

She was right. He was more tired than he'd ever felt in his life.

"I'm no longer a soldier," he responded and lifted the fork she'd provided him.

She took his coffee mug and went to refill it. "In other words, you don't want to talk about the war."

"That's right."

She returned to the table with the mug, giving him an understanding smile, a motherly sort of smile. Then she jerked a nod. "I'll heat some biscuits for you. Eat now." She turned away and went back to her stove.

Moments later she said, "I have a boy who hasn't come back from . . . you know, the fighting, yet. You look to be about his size. I'd be more than happy to lend you a few of his things until you can get your own. You know, so maybe Meg won't be angry about the shirt."

"I might take a ride into Havershill this afternoon," Richard said.

"All right. But if you change your mind . . ."

He nodded. Mrs. Hutchins was a kind woman.

After eating, Richard went to the stable to tend to his horse. There was Meggie's boy, his fair hair tousled but clean, seated on a pile of straw with his cat.

Caomh. What a strange name. Richard wondered who had come up with it. The tom cleaned his face with his paw, and Ian stroked Caomh's back. Nearby, Mr. Sardis sat on his stool whittling at another piece of wood.

Ian started when he saw Richard, his eyes suddenly filling with fear. Richard had no wish to frighten the boy, but he understood why Ian was afraid; he'd seen the same fear in the eyes of women and children whose homes his regiment occupied. Ian scooted back on the haystack, Richard took a step toward him, and Mr. Sardis came up off his stool.

"I mean him no harm," Richard told the stable man.

Mr. Sardis jerked a nod. "All the same, I reckon the boy'd ruther ya keep your distance."

Richard glanced at Ian, his jaw set with regret. He didn't want the boy to fear him. He really didn't. "I'm not a soldier anymore," he told Ian. "You've nothing to fear from me."

Ian caught his lower lip between his teeth and held tight to his cat.

Richard took several steps back, then turned and went off to the stall in which he had left his horse.

He brushed the animal again, smoothing his hands over the horse's many scars. He massaged the animal's right flank because he knew from caring for the horse that the once-injured flank tightened up now and then. He checked his shoes, and when the animal lowered his head to nuzzle him, Richard rubbed the side of the horse's face.

"Come on, we'll go out by the river," Richard said, and he reached for the halter he'd tossed over the top rail of the stall last evening. He slipped it up over the animal's nose, eyes, and ears, buckled it in place, then opened the gate and led the horse out.

He passed the haystack where Ian still sat holding his cat and looking apprehensive.

"How'd he get hurt so many times?" the boy ask timidly, surprising Richard.

"In battle," Richard answered. "We all have scars from the war . . . bad memories."

Ian studied him for a moment, then Richard walked on.

He led the horse in the direction of the landing, and he let him loose in an open area directly west of the inn. The animal lowered its head to graze, and Richard stared off across the river, at the land on the other side.

He wondered what sort of changes had occurred in the fifteen-year-old sister he'd watched wave goodbye to him one day more than four years ago. Mary was nineteen now. *Nineteen.* That hardly seemed possible. Of course, she'd given up her braids a good two years before he and Willy set out. But now . . . now Mary had to be a woman. Richard wondered if she had married. He'd received no letters in more than two years.

For all he knew, some letters might be floating around, still trying to find him. He hadn't exactly made himself accessible since Willy's death. He'd spent months in a Northern sympathizer's cabin, then more months in a Confederate prison. After Union forces arrived to free him and the others he'd silently gone off on his own. He'd not been ready to give anyone his name. Let the family think he was dead along with Willy.

He wondered about Jayne. She'd loved balls and parties and riding and gaiety. Jayne had had high expectations, but Richard had thought the match between them would be a good one. She was from a fine Cleveland family. He wasn't poorly off himself, and he'd been ready to settle and marry when they met. At the start of the war it had been fashionable to associate with enlisted men; it had been fashionable to support the war effort, too, even if that meant promising to wait for your soldier.

Jayne had eagerly done that, agreeing to marry him when he returned. But Jayne wasn't the type of woman to let herself become a spinster, so Richard doubted seriously that she was waiting for him.

A small group of people had gathered at the dock and were boarding the ferry. Once they settled, the ferrymaster collected money from them, and Edan McBride was there to loosen the rope from the mooring stump. The ferrymaster and another man took up poles and began guiding the boat across the river.

"So ye've decided to partake o' this fine day," Edan remarked, approaching Richard.

"'Morning," Richard greeted.

The Irishman chuckled. "Why, I'd say it's afternoon by now."

Richard glimpsed the sun, positioned squarely above them. "I believe you're right, Mr. McBride."

Edan pulled a handkerchief from his trouser pocket and wiped the perspiration from his brow. "Happens occasion'ly," he said, settling on a nearby log. "Business is good on the ferry. People from round here comin' an' goin', travelers . . . River's deeper than it looks. Most don't think o' swimmin' it for long. Then there's always the ladies done up 'n their bonnets an' dresses. Most don't want their skirts soiled." He wrinkled his brow and rolled his eyes. "Delicate things, most women. 'Course, Meggie's not so much that way."

Richard gave a dry laugh. "No, I wouldn't call your daughter-in-law delicate."

That remark cocked Edan's brows. "Had a few more rows with 'er, 'ave ye?"

"A few."

Sighing, Mr. McBride brought his hands down heavily on his thighs. "Meg speaks 'er mind, I'm afraid. Sometimes more'n she should. The lass has an Irish temper, that's fer sure, an' one she doesn't often keep rein on."

"This is her husband's shirt."

Edan nodded slowly, narrowing one eye at the garment. "Eh, I'll not be denyin' that. Had some words with ye about it, did she?"

"A few," Richard said, getting to his feet, not always an easy task anymore. "How far is Havershill?"

"Not far. Four miles west, maybe less. We go to socials up that way from time to time, an' church. Still here come Sund'y, ye can go along."

Richard nodded and thanked the man for the invitation.

McBride squinted an eye at him. "Goin' on to Havershill?"

"Only to find a store that sells clothing or someone to make me a few things."

"Now, don't let Meggie's sharp tongue drive ye to Havershill t'day. Ye still look in need o' rest, an' Meg needs to remember 'er 'usband's dead an' buried an' in no need of that shirt anymore."

Richard glanced off across the river again. Once he set foot on Ohio soil . . . Mrs. Hutchins was right—it might take him a week to reach home.

He watched the ferry approach the opposite bank, and he wondered at his cowardice in not forcing himself to cross over. He had faced down some of the meanest men in battle. He had run between gunfire, he had dodged sabers. But he couldn't bring himself to stand before his family and tell them that Willy was dead and that it was his fault.

"I'm not interested in helping her remember, Mr. McBride," Richard said, and he took his horse's reins and led him back toward the stable. There he meant to saddle the animal and head for Havershill.

Mr. Sardis and Ian were gone when Richard reached the stable. He saddled his horse, feeling relieved that Edan had told him the village wasn't far away. He didn't know if he could stand even two hours' ride in a saddle today. His leg still smarted from the abuse he'd put it through since leaving Richmond. He'd spent more hours on the horse than he should have and now he was suffering for it.

He traveled the riverbank, guiding his horse around fallen logs and scrubby undergrowth, smelling the sweet scent of the grass as the animal's hooves stirred it. Birds chirped in the branches of trees and fluttered through the air. Sunlight glittered on the waters of the Ohio.

Havershill was not unlike other villages Richard had been through. A main street cut through the more concentrated area, and scattered buildings flanked it. The barber had posted a hand-painted sign in his front window, offering haircuts, shaves, tub baths, and dental services, and several men stood before the shop, smoking and pausing in their conversation as Richard rode by. The blacksmith shop and livery were one, and the blacksmith himself stood off to the side of the stable alternately melting and shaping what looked like a horseshoe; Richard had heard the clanging some distance before he actually reached the village.

NEWELL'S BOARDING proclaimed a sign planted in front of a large, two story-brick house. Not far away the U.S. Post resided in a tiny gray shanty. Opposite that a gathering of buildings housed the mercantile and the Presbyterian Assembly. A few buildings sat apart from the cluster, and a short distance away small boats rocked in the water beside the wharf.

Richard reined in his horse before the mercantile, dismounted, and tossed the reins over the railing there. A woman watched him from one of the front windows, worry lines creasing her brow. A man stepped up beside her, looking somber himself, and another man exited the post office shanty, squinting against the sun and watching Richard.

Distrustful people. But then, according to the things Mrs. Hutchins had told Richard this morning, the people of this area had reason to be. Most likely people everywhere would be distrustful of strangers for a good long while.

Richard stepped up to the door of the mercantile and pushed it open.

4

$\mathcal{A}$T MCBRIDE'S THE evening meal was served in the dining room. The ringing of the bell outside announced it. Richard had smelled roasting beef as soon as he returned this afternoon, and his stomach had started rumbling then.

As he entered the dining room, Mrs. Hutchins placed a platter in the middle of the table. Other dishes filled with potatoes, corn, and bread surrounded it.

On the other side of the table, Ian told his mother that he had so washed his hands, and Meggie gave him a suspicious stare. Finally a guilty-looking Ian spilled the truth and his mother told him to go take care of the dirt on his paws this minute, before she had a chance to take up a switch. "I'll not be lied to," she said, turning him toward the doorway.

She spotted Richard and stiffened immediately. So did Ian, and the boy pressed back against his mother. Surely they had known he would be down for meals. But then, Meggie had hoped he wouldn't stay long, perhaps not past this morning.

"Mrs. McBride," Richard greeted, approaching mother and son. He held out to Meggie the folded shirt Edan had provided him yesterday.

He caught Meggie's eye, needing to let her know the depth of his sincerity when he spoke. He felt for the widows and grieving family members of soldiers killed during the war. "Before you told me, I didn't know it belonged to your late husband."

She hesitated. Then she took the shirt, pressed it to her chest, and said softly, "He's still alive in my heart."

Richard understood that, how someone could live on in your heart. But oh, the pain at knowing you could never share a conversation with that person again, never laugh and jest with the person, never embrace him. It was a pain he knew all too well, and as he stared into Meggie's emerald eyes he knew he had found common ground with her.

Not that he meant to ever strike up a conversation with any casual acquaintance about Willy. He talked to no one about his brother. Richard's every thought about Willy's death was hidden in the pages of his journal, and they _might_ be revealed to his family after he took the final step toward going home.

Richard nodded at Meggie, then he turned to Mrs. Hutchins and asked if he should sit at a certain place. Earthenware and silver had been laid out in all but five places.

"Edan sits at the head," she said, smiling. "Other than that, it doesn't matter where you sit."

Ian went off to wash his hands. Richard, having been raised with a certain amount of manners, waited for Meggie to choose a place at the table, then he planned to choose his own. But she decided to wait him out. See which place he chose, then possibly take the place farthest from him. The realization made Richard raise his brows. She stared at him, her eyes glittering.

"I would rather eat alone in my room than be seated before a lady," he told her.

Mrs. Hutchins gave him a look of utter astonishment.

Meggie tipped her head. "Oh, but ye'd parade round a room half naked b'fore one."

That set Richard back a mental step. The woman really did say most anything that occurred to her. "Unavoidable," he said. "You didn't seem willing to leave the kitchen, and I had water boiling and needed a bath."

"That ye did," Meggie agreed.

"You stared from hearth to bath room, Mrs. McBride. Hardly the act of a woman who minds the sight of a half-naked man." Unlike him to be so crass. But then, Mrs. McBride was itching for a fight.

Her eyes flared in insult and astonishment. She took a step toward him. "Why, ye arrogant . . . ! I've seen better, I assure ye."

A bark of laughter shot out of Mrs. Hutchins, and she clapped a hand over her mouth to cut it off.

Meggie's remark stung Richard—he was self-conscious about the scars that marked his back—but he wouldn't tell her so or give a hint that it did. "The food will soon grow cold," he said.

She continued to stare at him. He stared right back.

Finally Richard rounded the table and pulled out a chair on one far end. With a tip of his head and a lift of one brow, he offered Meggie the seat.

Holding his gaze with her own, she sauntered to the opposite side of the table and took the seat farthest away from him and the one he offered her.

Richard had never wanted to turn anyone over his knee, but right now he did. Meggie McBride was acting childish.

Edan entered the dining room. Within seconds the man's imploring gaze had taken in Richard, who still stood with his hand on the back of the chair; Mrs. Hutchins, who looked uncomfortable, as if she expected an explosion at any moment; and Meggie, who sat with a smug look on her face.

"By the smell of things, ye've outdone yerself this time, Mrs. Hutchins," Edan said, scampering to one end of the table where a setting had been placed.

Ian followed his grandfather closely, and when Edan pulled out his chair and commenced to settling himself in it, Ian did the same with the chair closest to his grandfather. Mrs. Hutchins thanked her employer for the compliment, then she sat in a chair on Richard's side of the table.

Out of respect for Edan and the fact that this was his

house, Richard decided to let the argument with Meggie go.
He took the chair he held for himself, his gaze still locked
on her. He'd never been put off so rudely—and after he had
nicely returned her husband's shirt.

He couldn't remember the last time he'd been in such a
temper. He'd felt lifeless for so long, since he'd been shot
down while charging after the Confederate who blasted
Willy. Maybe before that . . . ever since his last sparring
match with his brother.

There might be hope for him after all. He was tired, but
Meggie brought out the fight in him. Maybe, just maybe, his
conflicts with her would help bring him back to life. She
loathed him because he was an ex-Union soldier, and she
lashed out at him because of the things her family and
friends had suffered from soldiers during and after the war.
And perhaps even because the Union army had taken the
husband she obviously loved.

Whatever her reasons, her tantrums stimulated Richard in
a way Meg couldn't possibly realize; they provoked anger,
emotion, the urge to *do* something when he might otherwise
be unmotivated. Meggie, who would surely love to bury
him six feet under, instead might be helping him.

"The lieutenant was jus' complainin' about the food
growin' cold," she said with a mischievous tilt to her head.
"On account of ye, I'm afraid, Mr. McBride."

Edan's gaze snapped to Richard. "Lieutenant . . . ye'll
forgive my tardiness. I—"

"Mrs. McBride has a way with little white lies," Richard
said. He still watched Meggie closely—he doubted whether
he would take his eyes off her whenever they occupied the
same room. "As well as a way of calling me lieutenant after
I made it clear to her that I prefer Richard or Mr. Foster." He
looked at Edan. "No apologies necessary, Mr. McBride. My
remark that the food would soon grow cold was aimed at
Mrs. McBride, not at you."

"I left the carving to you, Edan," Mrs. Hutchins said,
obviously trying to create a diversion.

The innkeeper glanced once more from Richard to the
defiant Meggie, then sighed and turned his attention to the

cut of meat on the platter in the center of the table. He stood, took up the carving knife, and dug into the task at hand.

"I'm the only boarder?" Richard asked the man.

"At present. They wander through."

"Though they usually stop for only a night," Meggie commented.

Did the woman ever bite back a sharp remark?

No matter how badly she wanted him gone, Richard meant to stay for as long as it took him to decide to cross the river. Retreat had never been an easy thing for him to stomach.

"Meg," Edan scolded under his breath. Then in a louder tone: "'Twas a busy day with the ferry."

"Mr. Darrow let me cast off. Did ye see that, Grandpop?" Ian asked with wide-eyed excitement. "Did ye?"

"I did, an' I saw the fine job ye did o' it, too."

"Ye hold tight to the post when ye do it, Ian?" Meggie queried, looking concerned.

As Ian assured his mother that he *always* held tight to the post, Mrs. Hutchins reached for the bowl of potatoes sprinkled with herbs. "Here now, we can start these around while Edan's carving," she said, and she held the bowl out to Richard.

He refused it, saying he would be glad to take a share after the women served themselves. Mrs. Hutchins blushed at the kindness, and from the corner of his eye, Richard caught Meggie's disgusted look. His gentlemanly ways were making her ill.

To hell with her. He liked Edan, Mrs. Hutchins, and Ian, and he meant to be nothing but mannered where they were concerned.

Poor, poor Meggie McBride. If the beginning of this meal were any indication, she would have stomachaches for as long as he stayed on at the inn. Right now, Richard had no idea how long that would be.

Meggie barely slept that night. She tossed and turned. She dreamed . . . remembrances of soldiers demanding the last of their food, Ian crying that he was hungry.

She had nothing to feed him—they'd depleted even her herb garden—but she was determined to find something; she grabbed a basket and her son, and went off in the direction of the forest.

She found shriveled berries, the last of the wild summer fruit, some acorns old Mr. Sardis had told her could be ground into flour and the flour made into bread. Ian was thirsty. He tugged at her skirt and told her he wanted milk. But no one within five miles of them had a cow or goat anymore, and Meg cursed silently, wishing Ian were still a baby and she still had her own milk to give him. She would sit with him this very minute, open her bodice, and fill her son's belly.

Ian cried again, and this time Meggie realized that it was a cry of fear. She spun around just as someone grabbed her by the hair. She fought, but the man pinned her to a tree while Ian cried. The man was a soldier, and although Kevin himself was a soldier, Meg had seen and experienced enough cruelty to hate the sight of Blue and Gray alike. Meggie's head was jerked back; the cold steel of a knife blade touched her throat . . . She managed to bring the revolver around and fire it.

She woke gasping for air, still feeling the cold blade. Her hand was on her throat, and perspiration dampened her skin. Beside her Ian turned over and mumbled something. She placed a trembling hand on his brow, trying to soothe him back into deep sleep and calm herself.

Sweet Lord. Would that memory never stop haunting her? She thought it had, at least in her dreams. Then the lieutenant had turned up here, looking like the most sullen, angry man in the world, and her fears had risen to the surface again.

Her stomach and chest felt tight. She wondered exactly how long he planned to stay.

How many times had she wondered that since his arrival? Too many. Far too many.

Ian settled, and Meg rose and went to her window. She and Kevin had taken this back room after they married, and the view here was mostly of the forest. Silver moonlight outlined the trees, and Meg listened to the branches brush together. There sat her little garden shed where she kept her tools and where she dried herbs, onions, peppers, and flowers from time to time.

She leaned against the window frame and tipped back her head so the gentle night air would touch her neck. Like a lover's fingers, it caressed her skin, gliding over her and lifting her hair. Her breasts tingled, sore and heavy because her monthly time drew near. She'd been too long without her husband. Rarely a night had passed while Kevin was here that they did not make love.

She tried to remember the color of his eyes—for some reason she'd had a difficult time doing that lately. It shamed her that she couldn't remember, and she tried again with all her might. She recalled a pair of sky-blue eyes, glittering angrily at her, and knew instantly who they belonged to: Lieutenant Richard Foster.

Shame enveloped her again. She ran a hand up the side of her face and over her temple, as if trying to clear the image from her head. Why in the heavens would she remember the eyes of a man she despised, of a person she wanted gone from the inn as soon as possible?

He unsettled her, that's why. He concerned her. He worried her.

If she were truthful with herself, she might admit that he was a bit handsome without the scraggly beard and the dirt. She *might*. And the possibility of her ever doing that piled shame upon shame. She had the worst time maintaining eye contact with him—and Meggie had learned how important maintaining eye contact was in letting a person know you weren't afraid of him.

Mrs. Hutchins or Edan had told him she'd made the shirt for Kevin. That's surely how he knew that.

It had been rude of him to wear it for a second longer after *she* informed him that it belonged to her husband.

But, Meg had to admit to herself—although she would never tell him so—he'd returned the shirt to her in a kind way, despite her continual impertinence toward him. He'd returned it with a gentle, understanding light in his eyes, and that baffled Meggie.

Understanding? What did he know of her? Why was he kind when she was rude?

Mrs. Hutchins might have told him a few things pertaining to their lives here, but she was never free with details to the guests about the McBride family and friends. After all, everyone who lived and worked here had learned that once guests packed up and rode off, many would never be seen by them again.

"He's from Ohio," Mrs. Hutchins had told Meg, "so I'm sure he'll move on soon."

Well, Meggie hoped so. It wouldn't do for the lieutenant to stay here for long. He'd already overstayed his welcome as far as she was concerned.

And she . . . she had to put a stop to her passionate longings for her husband. She might visit Kevin atop their hill, but never again would he touch her as he had so many times.

Meggie turned away from the window and crawled back onto her bed. She listened to Ian's heavy breathing, and soon she began to fade into sleep herself.

She woke near dawn, as usual. Mrs. Hutchins would be in the kitchen already, and Meggie knew where *she* would soon be. She pulled her full shift up and off, and slid freshly laundered pantalettes on, securing them at her waist. She slipped a chemise on over her head and smoothed it down, then adjusted and tied the drawstring that would hold it in place just above her breasts. Over that, she laced a corset, and finally she stepped into a dress patterned with yellow and green flowers. Now to pull on her boots, lace them, and brush her hair.

It took only moments to do the last two necessary things, then Meg went off to her garden, where she knew the birds and a million lovely herbs, flowers, and sundry plants awaited her. Well, perhaps not a million. But plenty enough that Meg lost herself every morning in the place she loved more than any other.

The sweet william was a little droopy, and Meggie told it so. The foxglove stood fairly straight, and the pink and yellow hollyhocks that grew close to the edge of the house stood tall and proud, waving their sweet blooms. The yuccas were in bloom, a burst of yellow rising from a leafy base, and the crape myrtle clung to the edges of Meg's garden in purple splendor. She rose on her tiptoes to inhale the fragrance of a lower branch, and she closed her eyes, certain that for a few seconds she was transported to heaven.

The oregano, the basil, the thyme and rosemary . . . All bid her a good morning as Meggie walked the paths, speaking softly to them, telling them how lovely they were. The chives threatened to bloom, and Meg thought she might allow some of them to do so. Others would soon perfume the kitchen and the garden shed, where they would be hung to dry. Silver lavender leaves shimmered at her, the bright green santolina fairly danced in the morning light, and the Johnny-jump-ups, violas, and primroses greeted her with cheery colors.

Dew dampened everything, but it fairly saturated the pink phlox that grew near the wall scaled by morning glories. The latter were as bright and lovely today as they had been yesterday, and Meg approached them leisurely, tucking the vines here and there, carefully rearranging petals, taking time to assess her beloved garden. No new weeds today, or if there were any, they escaped Meggie's notice. She'd have plucked them without delay.

She went off to the garden shed to fetch her leather gloves and her tools, and on the way back, a song sprang from her. It happened just so every day. She could no more tend her garden without song than she could breathe without lungs. Mr. McBride often laughed at her belief that she sang life into her many plants, herbs, and flowers, but Meg persisted with the conviction.

> *"Do, do, pity my case,*
> *In some lady's gar-den;*
> *My clothes to wash when I get home,*
> *In some lady's gar-den."*

It was a spry tune; she didn't sing many that weren't. A pretty, interweaving dance that she, acquaintances, and friends performed at socials often went along with the song.

"Do, do, pity my case,
  In some lady's gar-den;
  My clothes to iron when I get home,
  In some lady's gar-den."

Her voice naturally grew louder as she sang and became absorbed in the tasks she so loved performing.

She trimmed away some of the lavender, dropping it into her basket, then she went on to the oregano.

"Bein' troublesome, again, I see," she complained at it. Troublesome indeed. As well as a pest to the other occupants here. Oregano loved to spread itself far and wide, and Meggie had no doubt that it would take over the entire garden if she allowed such a thing.

"Not t'day," she told it, and set to work clipping.

"Do, do, pity my case,
  In some lady's gar-den;
  My floors to scrub when I get home,
  In some lady's gar-den."

She went on with the tune. On and on and on. After all, it could last as long as one had lyrics to insert about her many tasks. Meg sang about baking bread; she sang about washing windows, sweeping the porch, clipping her garden, milking the cows, making butter, beating rugs, making beds . . . She sang and sang and sang because she so enjoyed the tune and because it insisted on bubbling from her. There was no holding it back. Not while she was gardening anyway.

She heard a creaking above her and then a voice: "Mrs. McBride, I'm trying to sleep."

She knew without glancing up just who the voice belonged to. But she glanced up anyway, taking note of the rumpled-looking man who peered down at her. She smiled pleasantly, because she truly felt rather pleasant at this time of day. She smiled a little mischievously as well, because she had found something more that irritated their new boarder.

"'Mornin', Lieutenant. What exactly are ye tryin' to tell me?"

He gave her an impatient look. "Your singing woke me. And it's keeping me awake. Since your garden happens to be located directly below this window, trim your weeds without singing."

Her *weeds*? "Why, did ye ever hear such an absurd thing?" Meg asked the oregano. "Ye're not so bad that ye deserve such a name.

"Ye could leave," she called up to the lieutenant in as sweet a tone as she could muster.

"*You* could stop singing at this ungodly hour."

"Impossible," she said without consideration.

His scowl deepened. "Why is that?"

"Because my herbs . . . all my garden occupants thrive on the singin'."

"Then sing to them in the afternoon!"

"Impossible. They love this time of day."

"Your singing woke me, and it's keeping me awake," he grumbled.

"Aye. Ye do look a bit frowsy. Dark circles beneath yer eyes . . . yer hair lookin' as if it just endured a fierce wind," Meg remarked wickedly. "An afternoon nap would do ye good. It'd be a fine thing indeed."

"Mrs. McBride."

"Somethin' else, Lieutenant?"

He slammed the shutters.

Meggie giggled a little, then she went back to clipping her oregano, and to singing just as loudly as before.

"Do, do, pity my case,
  In some lady's gar-den;
  A stranger looking frowsy-eyed,
  In some lady's gar-den."

She giggled again, wondering if the lieutenant would shove open the shutters and glare down at her again, this time more fiercely than before. But all was quiet on this side of the inn, and Meg moved on to the sweet basil.

"Do, do, pity his case,
  The lady loves her gar-den;
  The stranger's almost had enough,
  Of this lady's gar-den."

She laughed at the cleverness of the new lyrics. Then she cast a slanted look up at the shutters that guarded the window on this side of his room. He'd be gone soon, Meg felt certain of that.

And if not?

Why, she'd sing every morning until he did decide to leave.

5

$\mathcal{S}$HE AND EDAN had more words, this time about the fact that he'd invited the lieutenant to attend church with them in Havershill. Thank goodness the man hadn't taken her father-in-law up on the offer, another "harmless" gesture on Edan's part. Meggie might have taken ill suddenly, feeling too under the weather to attend service that particular Sunday morning.

Two more days slipped by, and still the soldier remained, despite more sarcasm on Meggie's part over evening meals, and despite her louder-than-normal morning singing. He went out of his way to be courteous at suppers, pulling out chairs for her and Mrs. Hutchins (although Meg always chose her own), and sharing conversations with Edan about the ferry business and the day's activities.

Meggie went about her business as usual, cleaning rooms in the inn, leading the cows and bulls with Ian's help to the river to drink, and sometimes herding in the small flock of sheep with Edan or taking the animals out to graze. They took Felan with them, their shaggy sheepdog who was a match for any creature that might think to trouble his charges. He drove the animals right and left, up through the hills, and he rested with his head on his front paws while they grazed. When shearing time arrived every year, Meggie and Mrs. Hutchins worked the wool themselves, spinning it into thread and then weaving the thread into cloth. When fall arrived and Edan drove sheep and calves to market in Ironton, Meg always sent cloth along with him.

She told herself that Richard Foster's niceness was merely an act, that he was trying to impress Mr. McBride and gain his trust. Why, she wasn't certain, and Mrs. Hutchins rolled her eyes at the suspicion when Meg related it to her.

"You have a hard heart, Megan McBride," she remarked.

Meggie tossed her a scowl, then took up a basket and went off to gather eggs. Mrs. Hutchins called her Megan only when she sorely disapproved of her conduct.

Most of the time the lieutenant watched the Ohio, either from his window that overlooked it, or from the riverbank where he occasionally limped along or sat while his horse grazed nearby. He watched the rafts and small ships that went by, and sometimes he watched the river when there was no activity at all.

What sort of strange fellow watched the water all the time? Meg wondered to herself. He appeared distant when he did, removed from this place, lost in his thoughts, and he rubbed the side of his head occasionally as if the thoughts were not pleasant ones.

Strange behavior, indeed. Even Ian remarked about it, asking his mother's opinion about why Mr. Foster watched the river so much. Was he expecting someone, perchance? Meggie answered Ian honestly: She didn't know.

If he wasn't watching the river, he was sitting beside it, busily writing in a black notebook. Two afternoons of watching him do that, and Meg itched with curiosity. He wrote, then stared off across the river, then he wrote more.

He penned his thoughts, she soon realized, and she itched even more with curiosity—this time to know the thoughts.

But that was not a wise urge. She didn't really want to know his thoughts. She wanted the soldier to go away. He and his black notebook and his horse and his fluttering blue shirt and broad shoulders . . . his wavy dark hair and sad but handsome eyes.

More days passed. She sang in her garden every morning, as always, and she smirked every time he slammed the shutters. Then she sang louder, knowing the shutters wouldn't block her strong voice.

The school in Havershill had recessed for the summer, and Meg had gone around to the parents and volunteered to help the schoolchildren stay up on their reading and ciphering once a week. It was something she planned to do for Ian anyway. In exchange for the lessons, some grateful parents occasionally brought her chickens or bags of flour or sugar or coffee, although Meg expected nothing for the tutoring.

Ian's friends usually came for the lessons—Jefferson Parker, the mischievous Russell Milan, the grumpy, sullen Michael Willard. Margaret Scott, Wilma Ridge, Heidi Roberson, April Nelson. Ordinarily the children might have been allowed to walk alone, both to the inn and back. But when the war began and the soldiers started coming, not many parents had let their children out of sight for long. The same was true even now.

Some parents brought their children, and Meg always went after Margaret and Heidi. Margaret's mother had died a few years ago and her father's farming work was rarely done. Heidi's father was ill and had been for some time, and Mrs. Roberson had her hands full taking care of her husband and their two-year-old twins. Meggie took the wagon as always, and she and Ian went after Margaret and Heidi. When they returned with the girls, there sat Jefferson and Russell beneath the huge oak on the front lawn, sheltering themselves from the sun.

The days were growing hotter, surely they were, Meg thought as she wiped her brow, and it was only June. By August they'd be able to sit and watch light steam drift up from the river. She'd get a pitcher of lemonade and bring it out for the children.

Just as the thought occurred to her, Michael came shuffling around the side of the house. The dark-eyed, dark-haired, fair-skinned Wilma came from the opposite side, a cup in her hand, and the outspoken April and her father approached in a buckboard.

"Don't ya wonder what smart thing April'll have to say today?" Margaret asked Heidi.

The two girls didn't like Heidi, and Meggie couldn't blame them—after all, who liked a person who thought she knew everything there was to know?—but Meg wouldn't condone their saying anything mean behind the girl's back. She shot Margaret and Heidi a severe look that told them exactly that. They promptly quieted.

"She's really smart," Ian commented. "April."

Yes, she was—and it was a nice thing of him to say.

"But not *that* smart," Heidi said rather quietly. "Otherwise, why would her pa make her come here every week?"

Good question. But Meg already knew the girl was right. April's father made her come *because* she was smart, because he didn't want her at a disadvantage when school began again during the fall. Precisely the reason other parents sent their children. Precisely the reason Meggie held the classes.

"She has feelin's just like the rest of ye," Meg said. "I'll not have them hurt."

Margaret and Heidi looked at each other. Whatever else they were thinking, they didn't say it—at least not in front of Meg. Of course, while they were out of her hearing range, she couldn't prevent them from talking amongst themselves about April, or even to April herself.

The lieutenant was seated on the riverbank staring across the water again. Odd man, Meggie thought. Odd, odd man. Edan and Mr. Darrow were minding the ferry, and Mr. Sardis was not far away, shodding several horses just outside of the barn. The men's presence safeguarded the children against the soldier, no matter that he no longer wore his military dress.

Feeling much peace of mind knowing that Edan, Mr. Darrow, and Mr. Sardis were close at hand, Meggie set off for the kitchen to make lemonade and to fetch a plate of the cookies Mrs. Hutchins had baked just yesterday afternoon.

*   *   *

Richard hadn't thought Meg McBride had a gentle side, a compassionate side—what compassionate person sang at the top of her lungs every morning, knowing her singing bothered someone? But as he sat on the riverbank, watching her dole out lemonade and cookies to the gathering of children, he thought differently.

She talked and laughed with the children. She read to them. She listened while they read, and when they appeared baffled by a word—and several times they did—she helped them with their sounds, patiently encouraging them to read the word themselves. She went through addition and subtraction with them, then she shooed them off to run and play on the lawn.

She brushed and braided the girls' hair. She tussled in the grass with the boys and tossed sticks for the sheepdog to retrieve. She even took the children on the ferry, once over and once back.

Watching her, Richard forgot to watch the river. Hearing her laughter, he forgot to dwell on Willy's death and his reluctance to go home. Seeing her smile, her bright face, her dancing eyes . . . he forgot how terrible he felt inside.

It wasn't long before he realized that he was smiling at her; *because* of her. Despite losing her husband to the war and despite her other personal struggles, Meggie had not lost her ability to be happy.

She read more with the children, then their parents began to arrive.

When all but two of the girls had gone, Meg loaded them and Ian in the wagon and set off on the road that twisted off behind McBride's.

"The lass has her good side," Edan said, snapping Richard from his staring.

Richard nodded, shielding his eyes from the late-afternoon sun. He had to admit that she did. He just wasn't quite sure why Mr. McBride felt the need to point that out to him.

He started to ask the man if Meggie would be all right taking the children home alone, and then he laughed at the absurdity of that. If a bear or mountain lion or a wandering stranger with evil intent took hold of Meggie McBride . . . well, Richard had no doubt that the woman would leave teeth and claw marks of her own. The animal would be sorry it had attacked her.

"Is there a maid or someone who cleans the rooms?" Richard asked Edan instead.

"Why, sure," McBride answered. "For the upstairs, that'd be Meg herself— Ye're not tellin' me she hasn't minded her duties . . ."

"The room hasn't been dusted or swept since I've been here."

Edan looked serious. "No need to worry. I'll make sure it's done."

Richard nodded. He had paid through today, and he was prepared to pay for another week's boarding. He imagined the man would be true to his word; Edan didn't strike him as being dishonest.

Mrs. Hutchins did the cooking and often cleaned the downstairs rooms, and several years before, Meggie had taken it upon herself to clean the upstairs rooms. But because the lieutenant seemed so distasteful to her, Meg had not ventured near his room. When Edan asked her about dusting and straightening it, however, she could avoid the task no longer.

"I know ye don't like him," Mr. McBride told her that evening. "But he's a payin' customer an' he's entitled to the same treatment as any boarder."

He was right, of course, and Meggie hated that. It seemed she was left with no choice but to dust and straighten the lieutenant's room, to place herself in a position of servitude to him.

Ooh, that thought certainly made her grumble some choice words under her breath! The next morning she even went so far as to ask Mrs. Hutchins if she might trade cleaning the downstairs rooms for the day.

"Meggie," the woman scolded. "I will not help you turn your nose up at that nice man."

Nice man . . . hah! Meg turned on her heels and stormed off.

"A very nice man who obviously wants peace in his life," Mrs. Hutchins called after her.

Meggie waited until the lieutenant appeared on the riverbank with his horse before she grabbed a broom and the basket that held her cleaning supplies. She started to trudge up the stairs, then she hurried on, telling herself that the quicker she cleaned the room, the better. She certainly had no wish to find herself alone with the man again.

The corner room he occupied had always been her favorite, because of the way one window overlooked her garden and the other overlooked the ferry and the river. A desk sat at an angle in the corner between the two windows, and the bed sat to the right of the window from which the lieutenant had grumbled at her the other morning.

To Meggie's surprise, the bed was made, and no clothes were strewn about anywhere. Upon investigation, she found them neatly folded in the chest of drawers—long underwear and socks in the top drawer and trousers and shirts in the second drawer. The third drawer held clothes, also. But a collection of personal objects occupied the fourth drawer, among them the journal in which the lieutenant had written these past two afternoons. Apparently he had written down enough of his thoughts for a time, as he'd gone down to the riverbank without the book today.

A locket caught Meg's attention, glittering at her from beside a set of saddlebags. Before she could even think that it was wrong of her to pry into another person's belongings, her hand reached down into the drawer for the locket.

She dropped it. It was surely not her business. No, it was not.

And yet, when the locket hit the bottom of the drawer and snapped open, Meggie stared down at the miniature likeness that was now exposed to her: a girl with hair as dark and wavy as Richard Foster's. She looked to be around sixteen, and Meg caught herself wondering who the girl was, if she was his sweetheart at home. If so, he was in no hurry to return to her.

She pushed the drawer shut and went about her cleaning. She dusted the desk, carefully wiping around the revolver that sat on one far corner of it. Then she cleaned around several books.

She dusted the windowsills, the chest of drawers, the headboard, the lamps. She swept the floor and cleaned the windows. She carried the ewer and basin of water downstairs, marveling beneath her breath that the lieutenant had apparently changed it himself at least once. He must have, otherwise by now it would surely reek and have mildew floating in it. Well, thank goodness he had changed it, because she wouldn't wait on him hand and foot.

She draped clean cloths over the handle on the washbasin in his room, all the while speculating on how Mr. McBride had discovered that she hadn't cleaned the man's room once during his stay. The dirty towels and clothes were a clue, since the lieutenant may have had to ask for clean ones. However Mr. McBride had discovered her neglect, he now would be on her about it every day that Richard Foster remained, Meggie felt certain.

She grabbed her cleaning supplies and her broom and went on to the next room, knowing that although there was no occupant, a thin film of dust covered the furnishings.

That evening, while brushing and feeding his horse, Richard was aware of Ian watching him from the haystack again, watching him as he held Caomh tightly and as Mr. Sardis began milking the cow he had brought into the stable moments before. Ian watched him every evening from the haystack, until his mother arrived to fetch him for bed or to help milk the cows, or both.

On the fifth day Ian had remarked that he surely brushed the horse a lot. On the sixth day he had said the horse wouldn't hardly let anyone else near it. On the seventh day he told Richard that he'd never seen anyone take such good care of an animal.

Today he became braver, trying to engage Richard in conversation by asking if the horse had a name.

"Never thought to give him one," Richard said, shrugging.

"He went to war a lot?" Ian queried.

Richard nodded. "I imagine, given his scars and skittish nature."

The boy petted his cat, which had apparently not made another appearance in Meggie's garden. Most of the time it was busy running from the long-haired sheepdog that always looked as though he'd like to have Caomh for an afternoon snack.

Meggie's garden . . . If that wasn't a subject that irritated Richard to no end. The *singing* she did every morning while gardening was actually what irritated him. She had become louder since the morning he had shouted down at her. After that day, he had slammed the shutters a number of times. She was trying to bother him, he realized. So he decided to make her think her singing no longer bothered him, that her defiant, impertinent behavior no longer exasperated him.

He refused to call down to her again. Instead, yesterday morning and then this morning he rose and calmly pulled the shutters. He went back to bed and tossed and turned. He covered his head with his pillow. He pulled the blanket up over his head. He tried to sleep and he couldn't—her voice was too loud.

She talked to her plants and flowers. Why in the world would anyone *talk* to plants and flowers? She told them how pretty they were, how tall they stood. She praised them for being so colorful, and for sharing their space with the others. This morning she'd told the mint that it was overpowering the basil—and that was a difficult thing to do, indeed.

Richard had yanked his blanket clean away from the tick and fought the strong urge to march downstairs and outside. If he ever got that far, he would gag the woman. He wouldn't be able to resist the temptation. He had never been a morning person, not even during his years in the army, and he didn't intend to change that personal habit for Meggie

McBride. *Damn* if he'd change *any* of his personal habits for her, a woman who clearly loved to cause him misery.

"Could I give 'im a name?" Ian asked timidly.

Richard stopped brushing. "I don't see why not."

"I like names," Ian said. "I've a book of 'em. Old Irish names. Do ye know . . . Caomh means 'lovable.' Because he is."

"I didn't know that. It suits him."

Ian smiled shyly. "Caith means 'from the battlefield.'"

"You've certainly been there and back, haven't you?" Richard asked the horse. The animal dipped his head to the bucket of oats Richard had put down for him.

"Could we call him that? Caith?"

Richard grinned. "We *will*. How's that?"

Ian's smile widened into a grin, too. "'Tis good!"

Mr. Sardis had stopped milking to glance over at them. Usually he squinted suspiciously at Richard. But this time his old wrinkled face looked free of distrust. He dipped his head to Richard, silently approving of what he'd just overheard, and Richard turned back to brush his horse more.

"Caith." He grinned at Ian again. "It suits him."

Ian sighed contentedly and scratched Caomh's head. A few seconds later, he asked, "What happened to yer leg?"

Now *that* was something Richard was not prepared to talk about. "The war," he answered simply.

More seconds went by.

"It'll get stronger," the boy said.

Richard remembered Ian's limp. He remembered the cane the boy used. He remembered Ian scrambling around the lawn, trying to keep up with his mother's other pupils as they played, and doing a damn fine job of it, too.

"I guess you know," Richard remarked.

Ian smiled, looking sure of himself. "I do."

6

*R*AIN BEAT EVERYTHING in sight that night. It flooded Meg's garden and her shed, and the next morning Richard woke to her fussing about the ravagement. Some of her plants and herbs would never be the same, she complained, and she apologized to them that such a thing had happened.

She was the queerest person Richard had come across. How interesting to hear her doing something in her garden besides singing. He caught himself listening, wondering when she would start a song.

That afternoon she tended the vegetable garden that was coming to life out back of the inn. Richard was walking across the lawn, and when he rounded a corner of the inn and saw her, he stopped short and watched her. He wasn't sure why. Maybe because she tended every plant delicately, with tenderness and affection. Maybe because her hair shimmered with copper highlights in the afternoon sunshine. Maybe because a smile occasionally brightened her face. She was pretty, very pretty.

Two more boarders arrived the next day, a Mr. and Mrs. Stottlemeyer. They had ferried over from Ohio on their way to visit relations in southern Kentucky. Their small carriage was unloaded at the landing, and when it pulled to a stop in front of the inn, Richard caught sight of Meg, her auburn curls bouncing around her face as she emerged from the front entrance.

The smile she offered the couple was one of the brightest he had seen; it lit her eyes and put more color in her cheeks and lips. He was struck by the notion that he would like to be the recipient of such a smile from her. But he doubted seriously that that would ever happen. Meggie seemed bent on despising him.

He wondered if she knew the couple. But an hour or so later he learned otherwise from Mrs. Hutchins, who emerged from the back kitchen door to toss away a bucketful of dirty water as Richard was on his way to the outhouse.

"The Meg you see isn't the Meg we usually see around here," Mrs. Hutchins said, "and she's not the Meg most boarders see. Pity you've shed your uniform and she's still rude to you." The woman shook her head.

She started back toward the kitchen, her bucket in hand. Then she stopped. "Mr. Foster, I have a question."

Richard's ears perked.

"Reckon your family's missing you?"

He flinched. "I don't know."

She set the edge of the bucket on her wide hip. "Well, I'll tell you this. I'm not trying to scat you out of here, but being the worried mother of a soldier, I sure hope my boy's not holed up somewhere taking his sweet time about coming home. You've been here more than a week, and you haven't said a word about when you plan to cross that river and go on home."

Her remarks caught Richard off guard. "I never say much."

She shoved the bucket up onto her hip more, like a mother pushing up a baby. "'Course, if you stay 'cause you're interested in our Meg, now . . . I'd understand that."

He had to laugh. "Meggie wouldn't let me within ten feet of her. Even if I were interested, she would thwart any advance on my part."

"That might be so," the woman said, twisting her lips and

considering the matter. Seconds later, the corners of her eyes crinkled with a devilish smile. "But like you said, she stared at you from hearth to bath room that night. At a half-naked man, mind you."

"Dear lady," Richard admonished, trying to look indignant.

She laughed, too. "Aw, you didn't mind! Now, my Zachary . . . if he comes bringing a bride with him, I'll understand the delay."

She sobered, studying him.

"Why don't you go home, Mr. Foster? You must want to—you look at that river every day like you want to."

"I can't yet," he said. "I can't."

She sighed. "There must be a mighty burden on your shoulders that's keeping you away. Well, one day soon, then."

She went on to the kitchen door, and Richard went on to the outhouse.

One day soon . . . Maybe. Perhaps.

Hell, right now he couldn't even bring himself to touch the water or to walk up onto the landing dock and help people disembark the ferry whenever it came in.

Several more guests took up lodging at McBride's that night. A Mrs. Jennie Schmezel, her fair-haired daughter Ingrim, and their driver, a Mr. Cutter who apparently came through quite often, accompanied by his fiddle and a spry tapping of his boot whenever he touched the bow to the strings.

Meggie greeted the McBrides' new arrivals with the same bright eyes and beaming smile with which she had met the Stottlemeyers. She appeared for supper that evening in a calico dress decorated with rambling green vines and trimmed with soft lace. A green ribbon caught her hair to one side, and the curls spilled over her shoulder, her breast, and tapered to an end just above her small waist.

Her eyes glittered in the lamplight, and several times Richard caught himself staring at her, thinking how extraordinarily lovely she was—and how gracious, displaying manners and courtesies that surprised him.

Meggie caught him staring, too, and each time she did, she tipped her head, lifted her chin, and narrowed her eyes. The loveliest eyes Richard knew he had ever seen . . . fringed with dark lashes, emeralds enhanced by the color of the design on her dress.

He wondered if Meg knew how pretty she was tonight, and he almost laughed aloud at the thought. She did, and she was teasing him with the fact, using yet another weapon to try to make him miserable. She didn't seem to realize that trifling with a man was not the way to make him go away.

"Mrs. McBride tells us you're a Union lieutenant," Mrs. Stottlemeyer remarked to Richard.

"I was," he responded.

"Oh?"

"Why did you leave the service?" her husband asked. "Heaven knows we still need our forces. Now that this nonsense with the South is over, we should send troops West to deal with the Indian problem."

"My enlistment was up," Richard said simply.

Mrs. Stottlemeyer worked at making a small pile of the snap beans still left on her place. "Not because of your injury?"

Edan coughed. Mr. Cutter's eyes widened. Even Meggie flinched at Mrs. Stottlemeyer's indelicacy. Mrs. Schmezel, her blond hair pinned in numerous loops and curls, eyed Mrs. Stottlemeyer. Ingrim Schmezel's jaw dropped open for a few seconds as she stared at the rude woman, then the seventeen-year-old gathered her shy composure and focused her attention on her meal. Mrs. Hutchins reddened and asked the Stottlemeyers if they had much farther to travel.

"Eight miles," Mr. Stottlemeyer responded.

"He wouldn't leave 'cause of his leg," Ian told the missus, guessing at her reference. "'Twill get better. Mine—"

"Ian," Meg scolded.

"Oh, no, I didn't mean he would leave, young man," Mrs. Stottlemeyer said. "I meant that perhaps the injury hampered him and he could no longer perform his necessary duties."

"Hardly anyone else's business," Ingrim commented, never once raising her lashes.

"My enlistment was up," Richard said again, this time with a quiet coolness that made Mrs. Stottlemeyer turn nearly as white as a freshly laundered sheet.

"He can still do anythin' he wants to do. Anythin' anyone asks him to do," Ian said.

Meggie scowled at him, silently warning him not to say another word.

"I know!" she said. "Shortly we'll move aside the furniture in one o' the front rooms an' dance to Mr. Cutter's fiddle. I know how ye love to play," she told Mr. Cutter.

He grinned at her. "I surely do. And I love the dancing that goes along with it."

Edan chuckled. "Our Meg . . . always snatchin' up the chance to dance."

She beamed at him. She told Mrs. Hutchins to hold dessert until later, after they all tired of dancing and wanted to sit and relax.

The meal was finished, and Meggie and Mrs. Hutchins began clearing away the dishes. Richard excused himself to go upstairs. No way would he make a fool of himself by trying to dance. He had experienced enough humiliation for one evening.

"Ye can dance, too," Ian told him. "I do."

Upon first meeting the boy, Richard had noticed his limp and the fact that he walked with the aid of a stick. He'd wondered what had happened to Ian's leg, but he hadn't asked. It wasn't in his nature to pry into such private matters.

Ian did seem to get around quite well. Richard had watched him from his window and from the riverbank as the boy helped cast off the ferry and even helped pole it over and back. He often played on the grass with his cat, tossing down his stick and limping as he ran. And then there was all that playing the other day on the front lawn with those other children. Ian didn't let the fact that he had suffered some sort of injury to his leg stop him from being an energetic boy.

"Ian, this's the last time I'll tell ye," Meggie warned him. "Once more, an' ye go up to yer room." She didn't want him talking to Richard about the subject, that was clear, and yet the boy's eyes shimmered with the desire to help someone with whom he felt a common link.

"He doesn't offend me," Richard told Meg.

"Ye can do it," Ian said softly, risking his mother's wrath. He stole a glance at Mr. and Mrs. Stottlemeyer, who were talking with Edan across the room while Mrs. Hutchins gathered dishes. "Don't be bothered by them. Most people don't say such things."

"I'm thinkin' the lieutenant wishes to be left alone," Meggie commented.

"It's all right," Richard said, smiling down at Ian. "When they do, what do you do?"

"Ignore 'em. But like with Georgie Sanfield an' his group . . . wouldn't leave me alone on the way home from school one day. I fixed Georgie . . . tripped 'im outside the next day. He took a tumble in the mud. I got in trouble . . . didn't mind."

Meggie rolled her eyes. "Ian McBride."

"After that, Mum walked me to school an' back ever'day. I minded *that*."

"Oh, an' those boys might've done more than tease ye all the way home after ye gave Georgie that tumble in the mud!" Meggie said, defending her action.

"Don't go, Mr. Foster," Ian pleaded. "Ye can watch, an' then if ye've the urge to join in, ye can."

The boy was really trying to reach out to him.

Ian's sincerity and his optimism were not without effect; Richard finally smiled and said all right—he would stay and watch.

While Meggie and Mrs. Hutchins cleared away the last of the dishes and food, Edan suggested that the men go move the furniture in the parlor. Mr. Stottlemeyer, Mr. Cutter, and Ian started out of the dining room behind him. Richard followed Ian. He had no reservations about helping move the furniture, but he did have grave reservations about taking part in something like dancing that required a certain amount of coordination.

Finally everyone gathered in the front room, and Mr. Cutter launched into playing a spry tune.

Meggie gave a yelp, said, "Old Joe Clark!" and urged everyone but Richard to "take positions."

The group soon had two lines formed, and when Mr. Cutter began singing the lyrics to the song, the dancers skipped forward, clapping and interweaving. Meggie sang along, too.

> *"Old Joe Clark, the preacher's son,*
> *He preached all ove' the plain.*
> *The highest text he ever took*
> *Was high, low, Jack an' the game.*
> *Round an' round, Old Joe Clark,*
> *Round an' round we're gone.*
> *Round an' round, Old Joe Clark,*
> *An' a by-by, Luc-y Long."*

Ian held his own, despite the quick movements required by the song, and despite his mother's worried looks as the tune went on and on.

For the most part, Meg was having too good of a time to fret over her son. She sang, clapped, laughed . . . Her eyes sparkled, her hair shimmered, color flushed her cheeks . . . She was the heart of the gathering.

Richard wondered if the song would ever end. When Meggie and Edan squared off against each other, taunting each other about who would be the first to collapse of exhaustion, Richard realized that was the idea, that the song went on as the dancers dropped off.

They were all having a gay time, and Richard couldn't help but smile at Edan and Meggie's antics as they clapped their thighs, lifted their legs high, and continued the interweaving and skipping. The others continued, too, but not with the same level of energy and enthusiasm displayed by Meggie and her father-in-law.

Mrs. Stottlemeyer was the first to drop off, clapping her

open hand to her chest and trying to catch her breath. "I can never last beyond Morgan Brown's horse with the huge teeth!" she said, plopping herself down in one of the chairs the men had moved to the edge of the room. She produced a handkerchief and waved it in front of her flushed face.

Mrs. Schmezel went next, encouraging her daughter to stay in. But Richard doubted that Ingrim would stay in much longer; her face was flushed, and she appeared short of breath.

> _"Peaches in the summertime,_
> _Apples in the fall._
> _If I can't get the girl I want,_
> _I won't have none at all."_

How Meg still managed to sing, as winded as she had to be, was beyond Richard. She went on and on. Mr. Stottle-meyer gave in, and soon after, Mrs. Hutchins collapsed in the chair next to Richard's. Minutes later, Ingrim slowed, then quit.

Amazingly, Ian kept going.

Just as he seemed to start slowing down, Edan skittered backward and said he was done in, that they'd gotten the best of him. Meggie bowed out moments later, obviously to let Ian be the triumphant one. Ian then pleaded with Mr. Cutter for a waltz.

"Ye can dance to this one, Mr. Foster," the boy said. "I know ye can. Come an' try it. Mum'll dance with ye, won't ye, Mum?"

The Stottlemeyers, Schmezels, and Mr. Cutter did not know about Meggie's animosity toward Richard, but Edan and Mrs. Hutchins did, and their apprehensive gazes shifted back and forth between Meg and Richard.

Richard shifted uncomfortably in his chair, and Meggie tried not to look too alarmed, although Richard could tell she wished she could decline without raising questions in the minds of their new guests. For all her temperamental ways, Meg did have an inclination toward politeness and manners in front of people she had no reason to dislike.

"Please, Mum," Ian pleaded. "He let me name his horse."

Meggie's brow shot up as if she were thinking, "Oh, so I'm supposed to repay him for the kindness by dancing with him?"

"Ingrim will dance with him," Mrs. Schmezel said, looking far too eager, a case of a mother searching for a suitable match for her daughter.

Ian turned his big pleading eyes on Richard. "Ye'll dance the waltz if Mum agrees to dance with ye?"

How could he deny the boy? If he took the floor and stumbled, making a fool of himself, only his pride would be hurt. And pride in the overall scheme of things meant little. Ian's desire to help him meant more.

Richard started to say, "I'll try," then he thought better of it. "I will," he said instead, and he couldn't deny to himself that the thought of dancing scared him.

Mrs. Hutchins made a little sound in her throat as Mr. Cutter started a slow waltz, closing his eyes as he strummed the strings. Mr. Stottlemeyer took his wife's hand, now that they had both caught their breath, and led her out again.

"Mum?" Ian pressed.

"Very well," Meg said finally. "But mind ye, Ian McBride, I'll not get in the habit of repayin' yer debts."

Ian clapped his hands together as Richard stood and made his way over to Meggie. In the early days of his injury, he hardly had been able to move the limb without pain. Now it was occasionally uncooperative, and he cursed it. On cold and rainy days it was worse.

He strode toward Meg, who suddenly looked as uncomfortable as he felt. She clasped her hands in front of her, and her lashes dropped and lifted several times. Warmth filled him, something he'd not felt in a long time. He found Meggie pretty, beautiful at times; impetuous, fiery, temperamental. She glittered with life, and that, more than anything, was what attracted Richard to her.

A grin twitched one corner of his mouth. Aside from their encounter in the kitchen that night, he hadn't seen Meg appear so uncomfortable. The new guests might not recognize the way she felt, but he was beginning to know her looks.

"Careful, Lieutenant," she warned in a near whisper, "lest I change my mind."

"You're without your revolver, I trust?"

"Ha! Fortunately for ye. Did ye put Ian up to this?"

He couldn't help but laugh softly. "Hardly. Your son came up with it himself. Being close to me might not be as detestable as you think."

She tipped her head. Ah, there it was . . . her temper gathering in her eyes! "Arrogant man," she seethed, though she wore a smile for the sake of the guests.

His grin widened as he slipped his fingers beneath hers and lifted her hand.

She started at the touch, and he might have also, if his experience with women and his years spent in the military hadn't trained him in maintaining control of his outward reactions. Of course, he hadn't been in an intimate situation with a woman for more than two years now. The war had heated up, becoming a matter of day-to-day survival. Then Willy's death and his injury. Truth be known, since then he'd had no interest in women or in much of anything else. But then, some things, once learned, were not forgotten.

Richard placed his other hand on Meggie's waist and stepped closer to her, silently cursing the sensations roiling through him. So tiny, her waist, and the flare of her hips just below it . . . the smoothness of her skin with its light sprinkling of freckles . . . the rich color of her eyes . . . the shape of them—and that of her small nose . . . the rosiness of her lips as they parted in breathlessness . . . the impetuous tilt to her jaw . . .

"Ssh," he said to settle her.

She glanced down to gather her wits, treating him to a tempting view of her long lashes. Then she turned a sugary smile up at him, and they started into the waltz.

There was no way to keep from putting weight on his injured leg as he danced, and although he tried to maintain a pleasant look, his jaw tightened with every twinge of pain. They twirled and dipped, although there was no graceful way to do either, and despite the pain, Richard enjoyed the dance. He'd always liked to dance, and he couldn't remember the last time he had.

"It hurts ye," Meg said with a gasp at one point.

Richard managed a smile. "You're not enjoying yourself, Mrs. McBride?"

"Don't be absurd. I don't enjoy causin' others pain!"

"Oh, you would have shot me in the kitchen that night."

"I'll not have another soldier try to force himself on me or threaten those I love. I'd have killed ye quickly, with little pain an' sufferin'."

He laughed; he couldn't help himself. "A comforting thing to know."

"Ye continue to dance for Ian's sake, so ye won't hurt his feelin's, don't ye?" she asked, giving him a wondering look.

"That's part of it."

"An' yer other reasons?"

"Only one."

She rocked her head in exasperation. "Ye're not an easy one to converse with, I don't mind tellin' ye."

He laughed again—once again, because he couldn't help himself. There was something extraordinarily charming about this woman. Something adorable. Something exceptional that he wanted to gather against him.

"Come now, Mrs. McBride, you know my other reason and you enjoy teasing me with it. You like to dangle it under my nose."

If she had been an upper-crust belle, she might have batted her lashes at him. Instead she stared up at him, and Richard felt an urge to kiss her. Right here, right now . . . To touch his lips to hers and drink of the life bubbling from within her.

He dipped his head closer to hers and said softly, "Because I enjoy being near you."

Meg gasped, and Richard whispered another "Ssh" to calm her. He didn't want her tearing away from him, embarrassing herself in front of the McBrides' guests. "You've known that, Meggie," he said. "You've teased me this evening."

She withdrew slightly. "Best remember what I said about makin' sure ye don't suffer."

He smiled. "You have nothing to fear from me. I'd never try to force myself on anyone."

Mercifully the waltz ended. Letting Meg's hand slip away from his had to be one of the hardest things Richard had ever done.

Ian clapped, saying, "Hurrah, hurrah! I told ye ye could do it, Mr. Foster. Mum, ye've helped him, like ye helped me so many times!"

"Aye," Meggie muttered under her breath, "but I have my limits."

Edan had drawn Ingrim Schmezel out to dance, and she kept glancing at Richard.

Later, when another waltz drifted from the strings of Mr. Cutter's fiddle, Richard bowed before the girl and asked if she would care to dance with him. Ingrim smiled shyly, and Mrs. Schmezel looked pleased.

Meg watched from the opposite side of the room as Richard drew the girl out and pulled her into the waltz. Did Meggie's eyes narrow on him again, this time with a spark of jealousy, or was that only his imagination playing tricks?

Richard couldn't be certain. He smiled and dipped his head at Meg, then he swept Ingrim around just as Edan took his daughter-in-law's hand and led her out.

7

MEGGIE WAS IN her garden shortly after dawn the following morning. It was still recovering from the heavy rain of last week, and all the plants and herbs looked much better finally.

As she thinned the oregano and the basil, she sang of a courtship, of a young man who was stricken with love at the sight of a certain beauty. Upon offering her gold and silver, houses, lands, and ships, the woman informed him that she cared little for such material things—all she wanted was a nice young man.

> "There she stands, a lovely creature,
>   Who she is, I do not know;
> I have caught her for her beauty,
>   Let her answer, yes—"

"Are you dreaming, Mrs. McBride?" Lieutenant Foster called down to her.

Meg froze with a clump of basil in her right hand. Dreaming? Considering that she was perfectly wide awake, why would the foolish man ask such a question?

She didn't wish to talk to him—heaven only *knew*, after that dance last evening and the conversation they'd shared during it, she had no wish to talk to him. The way he'd looked down at her . . . the way he'd pulled her close to him . . . He'd been wearing some spicy scent, as sweet and piquant as fine rum. Why, the cologne alone had made her want to draw closer to him.

And his eyes! She couldn't always look him straight in the eye. He had a way of looking at her . . . Sometimes his eyes danced with laughter. Sometimes they flickered with desire. Sometimes they showed no emotion at all, only a vast hollowness that made Meg wonder all the more about the man, why he stayed on here; if some occurrence during the war had taken part of the life from him.

One thing was certain: she'd enjoyed their closeness during that dance. That thought troubled Meggie. It troubled her a lot.

"What makes ye think such a thing, Lieutenant?" she called.

He'd nestled himself on the windowsill and was smoking a cheroot. He shrugged. "The lyrics. Offers of gold and silver, houses, lands, and ships. Do you dream of a man coming along and offering you those things, Mrs. McBride?"

"Hah!" Meggie couldn't help herself—she scrambled to her feet and said it again: "Hah! I've no need to dream of such things. I'm content at McBride's. This is my life, an' 'tis a life I love, too."

Watching her, he drew on the cheroot. "An observation. You sing often about love and courtship. Hidden desires, perhaps?"

She scoffed again. "I've no need to pine for love an' courtship. I've had them—I'm still very married to my husband."

"A dead man?"

Meggie stared up at him. What did he hope to accomplish with such questioning? Did he assume, because she was a war widow, that she was a lonely woman? That all women yearned for courtship and love?

Truth be known, she never thought of those things. She simply sang the songs because they were the songs she knew.

"Aye," she answered simply. "There's not a man alive who could take my Kevin's place."

"Have any tried?"

"A few."

"The coldhearted Meg McBride," he said from his perch. He drew from the cheroot again. "Her real love is her garden."

She wrinkled her brow. "Can't say I've heard ye talk so much at one time since ye've been here, Lieutenant."

He chuckled. "Can't say I *ever* talk much in the morning. You woke me again—I suppose you know that? You woke me the way you do every morning."

Meggie couldn't help a grin. "I suppose I do. But for some reason, this mornin' ye've decided to have a conversation with me instead of slammin' the shutters."

"A new strategy."

Her gaze went to his hand as he flicked at something on the windowsill. So strong, his hands . . . Meg recalled the warmth of the one as it lifted hers, as his fingers curled around hers, and she recalled the sparking warmth of the other hand as it came to rest gently on her waist. She watched the smoke drift up from his mouth and nose, and she recalled the warmth of his breath in her hair, how it nearly made her gasp, how it made her heart thump.

What the devil was the matter with her?

The man attracted her!

She who'd pledged herself eternally to Kevin McBride. She who had never been interested in another man. She who wanted Lieutenant Richard Foster gone as soon as possible and had from the moment of his arrival.

She couldn't possibly be attracted to him! She couldn't afford to be. If he realized she was, he might stay longer, and she couldn't have that. She couldn't risk it.

She didn't just *want* him gone, she *needed* him gone.

Only she and Ian knew what terrible secret she harbored, Ian because he'd been there when the event occurred. The others . . . she hadn't told the others because she wanted to involve no one else.

Meg made no comment about the lieutenant's new

"strategy." She went back to thinning her oregano and basil, placing select portions of each in small pottery bowls. She'd take the herbs into Havershill this afternoon and see if Mr. Dickson would display them in his store and try to sell them for her. He often did that with her dried herbs, and she could think of no reason why he wouldn't do that with the thinnings.

"I didn't thank you for the dance," the lieutenant said.

Meggie's hand froze for a second around a clump of basil. She quickly busied herself again, not wanting to give the man even a hint that he unsettled her. "No need," she responded.

He was quiet for a time, though she felt his gaze on her. Saints alive! Did the man have to stare? Why didn't he pull the shutters and go back to bed the way he usually did?

Another song began in her head, and soon she began singing it aloud. She would have bitten it back if it had been a song of courtship or love. Fortunately it wasn't. It was a riverman's song, one she'd heard many times during her childhood years.

"Thank you for the dance, Meggie," he called down to her.

She stopped working again. Irritating man! She'd told him there was no need to thank her!

Meg scrambled to her feet again, determined to set him straight about where they stood exactly, that he shouldn't count on getting too friendly with her because she wouldn't welcome his advances; that he shouldn't read anything into the dance. Ian had suggested it, after all. He had encouraged it, in fact. The dance certainly hadn't been her idea. It had been Ian's, and Richard Foster hadn't run the other way when the proposition had been put to him. *She* would have, if McBride's hadn't had other guests and if Ian wouldn't have been sorely disappointed. That thought alone had made her accept the dance.

Meg lifted her hand and opened her mouth, ready to tell the Union officer just how things were.

The shutters closed.

"Lieutenant?" Meggie tipped her head, waiting for the shutters to open. They didn't.

"Lieutenant, don't assume somethin' ye shouldn't! 'Twas only a dance. Don't think it meant more! If not for Ian, it wouldn't've happened! I know ye can hear me—ye hear me singin' ev'ry mornin'. Take note of what I'm sayin'!"

Ingrim Schmezel chose that moment to round the corner of the house and approach Meg's garden. Meggie caught sight of the girl from the corner of her eye, and she clamped her mouth shut. How embarrassing to be caught calling up to the lieutenant. Someone might think she *was* pining—and for him, of all men.

Once again, she went back to her basil and oregano. She might get done with the thinning sometime today. Might.

"Was that Mr. Foster?" the quiet girl asked.

"Indeed it was."

"Mrs. Hutchins said he sleeps late every morning."

"He tries."

"Does he always speak to you from the window?"

"He usually growls. Says my singin' wakes him."

Ingrim looked baffled. "Growls? Mr. Foster? He seems like a nice man. A very handsome one, that's for certain." She blushed at the admission.

A thought occurred to Meggie. The girl was pretty enough, her pale hair pinned and arranged in ringlets that just brushed her shoulders, although her eyes were rather dull.

Another thought occurred to Meg, this one that Mr. Foster would never be interested in anyone with dull eyes. A strange thought since she knew little about his likes and dislikes.

Anyway, the idea of matching the lieutenant with Miss Schmezel was a good one. Such a match would take his concentration off *her,* and it might even lead him away from McBride's by his nose.

"Have ye a beau, Miss Schmezel?" Meg queried quietly, waving the over girl to settle herself on a nearby wooden bench. She'd talk a little more softly so her voice wouldn't carry up to the lieutenant's window.

Ingrim blushed. "A few at home."

Tipping her head, Meggie smiled. "But surely none that can compare to the lieutenant. Such an upstanding gentleman. An' from such a fine fam'ly!"

Ingrim had just settled herself. She clasped her hands together. "Oh, none!"

"He's lookin', y'know."

"Looking?"

"Aye. For someone to settle down with. To court. To marry. To offer gold and silver, houses, lands, and ships."

Now that was a lie if Meg had ever told one. Several lies now. Or they could be; how was she to know? She had no knowledge of his financial means, of his family, or of his worldly possessions. But her last remark sounded clever considering the song that had brought him to the windowsill.

"Really?"

Ingrim was so addled by the prospect put before her, she didn't think to question it. She wasn't from these parts or she might know the song from which Meg had drawn the words.

"Really," Meggie said.

"Oh, but he didn't look twice at me last evening."

"He danced with ye. Besides, we'll make him look twice. More than twice."

Ingrim frowned. "Whatever do you mean?"

"The right look, the right smile, the right arrangement of a dress's neckline . . . a fallen handkerchief . . . Why, such things bring a gentleman to a lady's side in a second! Ye an' yer mother . . . ye're leavin' soon?"

"I think so, yes."

Meg affected a worried look. "He's ripe for pickin'. Have ye given much thought to acquirin' a husband?"

Ooh, she'd never in her life set about doing such a mischievous thing! Tellin' such blatant untruths about a person. But then . . . to just about any unmarried woman, the lieutenant really might seem "ripe for picking."

The girl shifted uncomfortably. "A little."

"An' yer mother, has she thought of it?"

Ingrim sighed. "All the time. But her choices!"

"Mortifyin', hm?" Meg asked, placing a hand over the girl's. She sat beside Ingrim on the bench. "The lieutenant *is* handsome though, isn't he?"

"Oh, yes, very!"

"What about suggestin' him to yer mother? Givin' her a hint that he's interested won't hurt a thing. A hint that *ye're* interested, an' he may follow ye to the end of the earth! A man like him, fresh from the war, no wife, no children . . . He has means, I'm tellin' ye."

Well, means enough to stay on and on at McBride's, and that alone was enough to make Meg tell a few harmless lies about him. Ingrim was pretty enough; if the lieutenant was a lonely man, well, here was a woman who wanted a man.

In her mind, Meggie did nothing wrong, and that was that. She'd feel no guilt over the matchmaking.

Ingrim soon went off to talk to her mother, and Meg went back to her gardening. She hummed the tune about the lady's garden, occasionally glancing up and smiling at the lieutenant's window. Ingrim might be shy, but with a little encouragement . . . Well, soon Richard Foster might stop troubling her—Meggie. The day Ingrim and her mother left with their driver, the lieutenant might be close behind them.

Mr. Cutter and the Stottlemeyers left the inn shortly after noon. Ingrim and her mother stayed on, despite Mrs. Schmezel's original plan to move on today. Meggie knew why.

Ingrim had taken her seriously. This morning, Mr. Sardis had taken the sheep up into the hills to graze, something Meggie and Ian often did, and Meg was just beginning to load her herbs in the back of a wagon when the girl appeared outside. Ingrim was dressed in a pretty yellow gown trimmed with soft lace and a few flounces on the skirt, a little overdressed for the afternoon. But then, Meg had that figured out, too: Richard Foster had taken up his usual place on the riverbank while his horse grazed nearby.

Ingrim walked back and forth, wearing a delicate bonnet that matched her dress. It was tied in a wide bow beneath her chin. She looked like a flower walking the riverbank, one that was sure to get the lieutenant's attention.

It wasn't so easy. She walked and walked. She appeared deep in thought, but Meg saw her glancing at Mr. Foster now and then. Men coming and going on the ferry certainly noticed her; not one failed to stare until Mr. Darrow either called for them to load or unload, or until their wives elbowed them good and hard.

And Mrs. Schmezel? Well, Meggie felt positive that the woman had taken up some strategic location where she could view the happenings.

Sure enough, when Meg ventured around to the side of the house there was Mrs. Schmezel, staring down from the window of her room. Meggie snickered a little, then went back to loading her herbs.

A new strategy.

Richard laughed to himself. Perhaps Meg McBride would see fit to stop singing in her garden every morning if she wished to avoid having conversations with him. He knew he was the last person with whom Meggie wished to speak, and he had decided that if she insisted on waking him so early every morning, well, he would insist on discoursing with her. He would open the shutters, perch himself on the windowsill, and think of things about which to talk with her. If Meg didn't like that, she shouldn't sing and wake him. Simple as that.

The Schmezel girl was making a play for his attention. It didn't take Richard long to figure that out. She walked back and forth along the riverbank in a dress that was more evening wear than day wear, and she occasionally paused to smile at him.

She was pretty enough, but Richard had no interest in her.

He watched the water and thought of home, of the house on Euclid Avenue, of Mary nearly plowing him down as she tore through the upstairs hallway, trying to escape her nursemaid; of Willy coasting with him along the avenue in the frigid Ohio winter; of the lake with its ice floes and its way of pounding the shore with fierce winter storms.

His mother was the most compassionate person he knew, always taking in strays and trying to find them homes—and that included orphaned children. His father was a stoic man with a sharp business sense—he'd taken his family far these past twenty years, from a shanty to the fashionable avenue, from being snubbed to being respected. His sons were growing into fine young men, and he was proud, Richard had once overheard him say. They had his knack for business, particularly Willy, who all too often wanted to tag behind his older brother. Against their father's better judgment.

An older brother who was often wild and reckless, who had led Willy out onto the icy waters more than once. Willy should have listened to their father.

"Damn you, Willy," Richard seethed at the river. "You had to follow me this time, too. *Damn you.* Look where my hunger for adventure and heroism led you."

He snapped a blade of grass and threw it. It didn't go far. It didn't weigh enough to go far and it didn't catch the air in the right way.

A breeze whipped a patch of tall grass not far away. The ferry was coming back this way. A village sat not five miles off the opposite bank, Edan had told Richard yesterday. Despite all the coming and going of people on the ferry, McBride's was a serene place. The inn itself was quaint, set back from the river, cradled in the arms of Meg's garden.

She was still loading her pots in the back of her wagon. Ian had appeared to help. She laughed at him about something, and her laughter drifted across the grass and down the gentle slope, teasing Richard's ears. Edan drifted by the wagon, made as if to snatch one of her pots. Meggie swiped at him, flashing him a sly smile, telling him that if he dared, she'd toss him in the soup kettle tonight. Her hair appeared coppery in the afternoon sunlight. Her smile was a force of its own.

A pretty smile. No, more than pretty . . . fetching, mischievous, full of life and energy, reminding him of how he had once felt. The war and its events had made a serious person of him, made him prefer a place like this country inn to the city, a woman who seemed content to garden as opposed to fussing over what gown she should wear and how she should style her hair.

And yet the spunky Meg reminded him of his old self, of the way he'd been before sadness and guilt had gripped him, before the war had injured him in so many ways. That wild recklessness hadn't been all bad. Tempered some, there might have been a bit of good in it.

"You find the river peaceful and relaxing?" Ingrim Schmezel asked from not far away. Richard had been so engrossed in thought and in watching Meg and Ian load the wagon that he hadn't noticed Ingrim's approach again.

"I've always had a fondness for water," he responded.

She clasped her hands in front of her. She was young and pretty in a fair sort of way. But she seemed too naive for him to express true interest in her. Of course, until Meg, he'd had no interest in any woman for years. He'd been too busy surviving, then wallowing in depression and guilt. He'd be polite to Ingrim—he was almost always polite—but he wouldn't express interest he didn't feel.

" 'By thirty hills, I hurry down, or slip between the ridges; By twenty thorps, a little town, and half a hundred bridges.' " She quoted Tennyson, verses from a poem Richard himself had studied a few times back in school.

"You like the water, too," he said, getting to his feet and dusting his trousers.

She smiled. "Always. My father has an interest in shipping." She switched her hands, clasping them behind her back this time.

"Would you care to walk?" he queried.

Her smile widened. She nodded. Then she looked uncertain. "Your—your leg . . . It will be all right?"

He hated when people asked that, or asked something similar. He hated having the subject come up at all. He hated pity.

"It's fine," he said.

He left his horse grazing; he didn't imagine they would walk too far.

Directly in front of the inn, most of the undergrowth had

been cleared away. A short distance off, however, it thickened. Here and there were low-lying bushes and fallen branches. Miss Schmezel walked on, saying nothing.

"Mrs. Hutchins says your mother woke up ill this morning," he commented, for lack of better conversation.

"Yes. Our reason for not leaving this morning as planned." Her face pinkened. Her lashes fluttered up and down several times, not as if she were playing coy, rather as if she were nervous.

He would make certain they didn't stray beyond sight of the inn. A girl so young—she couldn't be more than seventeen—was usually watched closely by a parent or chaperone. If Mrs. Schmezel peered out a window, trying to catch sight of her daughter, Richard wanted her to see Ingrim. He wondered if the mother knew her daughter had been walking the riverbank, trying to get his attention.

"A little stomach illness," Ingrim said, smiling prettily at him.

"She'll be better tomorrow," he suggested.

"Yes, surely."

He nodded, and they walked on.

"Where did you say you were from?"

He thought back to last night. "I didn't."

"Oh."

"Cleveland."

"Returning from the war?"

He nodded.

"My brother was in the war," she said. "He was sent home with an injury shortly after the fighting began. We're from near Columbus."

"You've traveled a good distance already."

"Yes, but the weather has been beautiful."

"We should turn back," he said, offering his arm. Their conversation bored him.

She glowed, smiling, her eyes suddenly not appearing so dim, and Richard fought the urge to withdraw his arm, he felt such uneasiness inside. Something told him she had something different in mind for them than he did.

She placed her hand on his arm, and they turned back.

The sound of fabric tearing halted them. Ingrim glanced down, gasped, and tugged at her skirt. The material, caught on the small branch of a bush, tore more. Her tugging didn't help.

Richard knelt and worked at freeing the fabric.

Ingrim gasped again when it ripped more. She tugged at it a second time. "Mother will be furious! It's one of my best."

"Don't pull on it," he said. The fool girl. Common sense should tell her that if she pulled it would rip more.

She let go of her skirt, and he freed the hem.

As he stood, Ingrim was waving at someone. Richard turned and caught sight of Meggie and Ian headed off in the wagon. Apparently Meg had finally loaded the last of her pots, and she and Ian were taking them away. To where, Richard had no idea.

Meggie waved to Ingrim, and her smile froze in place, then faded when she saw that Richard had taken note of her. She turned her attention back to putting the wagon on the road leading away from McBride's.

Richard laughed under his breath. Nothing like the sight of him to sober Meg.

"She looks rather sour suddenly," Ingrim commented.

"She usually is where I'm concerned."

The girl studied him, looking baffled. "That's odd. Only this morning, Mrs. McBride was telling me what a fine gentleman you are. She truly likes you."

That raised his brows. "Really?"

"Yes. I would say so. She said you're from a fine family, too. She called you an upstanding gentleman."

Richard leaned heavily on his good leg. His conversation with the Widow McBride hadn't gone *that* well this morning. In fact, she had caught on to the fact that he might have more than just a passing interest in her, and for several moments after he pulled the shutters, she'd called up to him, saying he shouldn't read anything into their dance last night. It was only a dance, after all, and he should assume nothing.

She wouldn't even have considered dancing with him if not for Ian's encouragement, she said. Or implied—he couldn't remember her every word. But he knew the dance hadn't even bruised her dislike of him. Oh, it had made her aware of the attraction between them. Meggie had been married, after all. She was no naïve, virginal girl.

From the moment Richard lifted her hand, she had breathed a little faster and intermittently glanced away from him in a way that was not like her. Meggie was bold and brassy. Meggie met things head-on. Meggie lifted her chin and stared a person in the eye.

He didn't just chuckle under his breath this time. *He laughed.*

Ingrim gave him a queer look.

Richard couldn't imagine why Meg would tell Miss Schmezel such things, unless she was simply trying to be polite. Unless she wanted to appear a gracious hostess. Maybe Ingrim had asked her about him, and Meggie had bitten her tongue to keep from saying the things she really felt, that she didn't like him because he was an ex-soldier and because he represented the very thing that had taken her husband—the war.

Or . . . maybe Meg was more nervous than he realized about the questions he'd put to her this morning: *Do you dream of a man coming along and offering you those things, Mrs. McBride?* The gold and silver, houses, lands, and ships of which she sang. He'd asked if she still considered herself married to a dead man. He hadn't asked the question in so many words, but she'd known that was the question on his mind. Had any men tried to take her husband's place? he'd wondered aloud. And then he had shocked her by thanking her for the dance last evening.

"Well, Mrs. McBride is right," Richard said, half grinning. "I am an upstanding gentleman." Of course, she had spoken sarcastically, he felt certain, and Miss Schmezel hadn't realized.

He meant to perch on the windowsill and have quite a conversation with Meggie tomorrow morning. Yes, indeed. About all of her good remarks and comments concerning him.

Ingrim smiled. "From a fine family."

A slur, that's what *that* was from Meg. She thought so poorly of him, she surely didn't believe he was from a fine family. First, attack with sarcasm his reputation as a gentleman, then attack his family, something she knew absolutely nothing about.

Richard gave another bark of laughter. He saw her dancing green eyes in his head. How he'd love to tangle his hand in Meg's curls and give them a yank. The imp! Doubtless she'd made the comments to Miss Schmezel, then walked off laughing at her wittiness.

In fact, the fiery little leprechaun probably had been laughing off and on all day.

Well, he might just decide to catch her soon. And according to Irish folklore, when one caught a leprechaun, weren't treasures usually revealed?

8

*I*NGRIM WAS ALL smiles for Richard that evening. She apparently had heard Meggie's remarks about him not as sarcasm, but as truth, and the girl was clearly out to catch a man.

She wore a shimmery blue gown for supper, one that dipped a little low at the neckline, revealing her ample wares. Shy she might be, but Ingrim either had been taught or was learning quickly how to use her assets. She took the seat opposite Richard, and she bent over her meal more than necessary, giving him a stimulating view of her finer qualities.

He lost count of how many times she gazed at him from beneath her lashes and engaged him in conversation. Did he ride for fun? Did he row? She had been to Cleveland a time or two herself—ungodly cold up there, but the city had its fine points. A hotbed for abolitionists during the late war, or so she had heard; the last step of the journey to Canada and freedom for fugitive slaves in the decades preceding the military conflict.

Edan took up that line of conversation, saying that he and several of his friends had provided cabins deep in the surrounding woods for fugitives during those tense years.

"Thank the Lord it's over," Mrs. Hutchins said. "Now if my boy would only come home."

Meg gave the woman a sad look, and Richard wondered if she'd given up on Mrs. Hutchins's son ever coming home.

"At this late date, one wonders why he hasn't," Meggie said softly. Her unspoken words were the really sad ones—she didn't have the heart to tell Mrs. Hutchins outright that she didn't think her boy was coming home. Meg thought he'd been killed in the war; Richard read the thought as she shifted positions in her chair and avoided meeting Mrs. Hutchins's gaze.

"He'll be here. Mr. Foster has given me hope that he's simply being slow about it," Mrs. Hutchins said.

Richard flashed her a smile. "Men will trickle home for some time."

"I pray ev'ry night," Meggie told Mrs. Hutchins, suddenly reaching across the table to take the woman's hand. She gave the older lady a meaningful look. "I pray hard."

God above, Meg McBride had feeling in her! Of course, Richard had known that. She was a fine mother—he'd seen that—and she seemed to be a fine person as far as everyone but him was concerned. Mrs. Hutchins had related to him how Meggie had never once put Ian to bed hungry during times when most everyone in these parts had had little or no food. He'd seen her interact with her pupils. And her garden . . . certainly Meg tended it with more compassion and feeling than Richard had ever seen. He was feeling caustic himself because he was still smarting from Meg's sarcastic remarks to Ingrim about him being an upstanding gentleman and about his family being so fine.

Of course, Meggie didn't, and couldn't possibly, know the real truth of her words—that he *was* an upstanding gentleman. Well, perhaps not upstanding. Neither he nor anyone of his acquaintance had ever applied such a descriptive term to him. But a gentleman, yes. From an upper-crust family, schooled in manners and decorum, even if he hadn't always practiced them. Willy had adhered to them mostly, while he, Richard James Foster, had been the rebel. But he had at least learned the manners and proper behavior put to him—that was the important thing—and he might decide to astound Meggie McBride by utilizing them.

While Miss Schmezel was giving a fine display of her goods, Richard's attention inevitably drifted to Meg. Other than her few remarks to Mrs. Hutchins, Meggie sat quietly through most of the meal, eating more slowly than usual, eating hardly anything. She sat beside Ingrim, wearing a rust-colored, modestly cut dress. The neckline was trimmed with lace, and it dipped only low enough to give a hint of its hidden treasures.

If Meg had thought to look drab beside the elegantly dressed Miss Schmezel, she'd made a huge mistake in her thinking. The lamplights danced, casting just the right combination of flickering shadow and light on her skin. Each time she shifted her position, her hair, the top half of the unruly curls swept up and caught in a clasp at the back of her head, appeared to change colors; first gleaming red, then deep copper.

Her lips appeared darker tonight, duskier, her eyes lighter, and the latter baffled Richard. He wondered if it was an effect of the room's lighting, too, and he tried to catch her gaze with his so he might study her eyes.

He did once, but Meg quickly glanced away. He swore more than the usual amount of color stained her cheeks suddenly. But that could have been another illusion.

She appeared uncomfortable for a few moments; eyes on her plate, she pressed her napkin to her lips, then lowered it to her breasts, as if hiding that part of her from his perusing gaze. Finally she lifted her lashes and stared boldly and defiantly straight into his eyes.

Richard grinned. The Meg he knew. Anything but a proper drawing-room lady. She was full of defiance and stubbornness. Put her on a battlefield, and she'd slay the enemy single-handedly. Or die trying anyway.

"I—I've heard Cleveland has fine theaters," Ingrim remarked, her gaze shifting between Richard and Meggie.

"An' surely the lieutenant has attended ev'ry one, bein' the fashionable man he is," Meg decided to comment, tilting her head in her haughty way.

Sarcasm again. Did she really think he was totally unrefined? That, like her, he'd been brought up in the backwoods somewhere, learning to butcher hogs or some other such thing instead of learning politeness and proper behavior? She didn't really believe that. She was taunting him, again trying to irritate him in whatever way possible.

"Have you, Lieutenant?" Miss Schmezel asked.

"I prefer to be called Mr. Foster," he told the woman— while still looking at Meggie. "Yet Mrs. McBride persists."

A slow grin turned up one corner of Meg's mouth. Her hair flashed copper again, and her eyes danced like the Devil's. He swore shards of orange floated in them.

Well, not even the Devil frightened him. He'd faced the Devil on the battlefield. He'd faced the Devil when Willy died. He'd faced the Devil in that Confederate prison. And here he was, still alive.

Richard leaned forward, staring at Meggie, suddenly wanting more than anything to stand above her, sink his hands into her hair, and turn her face up to his. It was her bite that vexed him more than anything. Her razor-sharp bite that pierced his skin and drove to the bone.

He suddenly realized in those seconds, while their eyes flashed at each other, while her breasts rose and fell a little more rapidly, and while everyone else in the room quieted with shock, that Meg had more passion in her than any woman he'd ever known. He hadn't touched her in an intimate way. He hadn't tasted her dark lips, caressed her skin, felt the blood pulse through her neck, pushed his hands up into her thick explosion of hair. But if he ever did those things . . . Lord God, Meggie would be hotter than the blaze that ignited Atlanta. She was that full of life.

He adored her passion.

The woman loved sarcasm . . .

Edan cleared his throat. "Perhaps, Mrs. Hutchins, you could bring the pudd—"

"Your garden may be your court, the bench there your throne . . ." Richard told Meggie, his voice low. "Your crown may be a vine of the flowers that scale the wall; your subjects may be the other flowers and certain people around this inn . . . If you insist on calling me lieutenant when I've requested otherwise, I'll have to call you Queen Meg. In the most caustic manner, mind you. Remember who looks down on whom every morning."

The room had fallen deathly quiet. Ingrim Schmezel's jaw dropped open. Mrs. Hutchins's face reddened. Edan raised both brows to the point of looking almost comical. Ian went back to eating as if he wished to blot out the entire skirmish—his mother had not taunted a guest and the guest had not finally retaliated.

Meggie's grin faded.

One instant she looked as if she might shoot fire across the table at Richard, and the next instant she laughed and congratulated him on his cleverness. "To compare my garden to a queen's court! A crown of mornin' glories! Ye've attended all those theaters, haven't ye, Lieutenant? An' taken them to heart, too!"

He lifted his water glass in toast to her. "Without doubt, you compare to every devious monarch in the history of the world, Queen Meg."

She laughed again. Then she lifted her water glass and touched it to his. She was teasing him, taunting him in a different way this time, flashing her eyes and smile at him. Dangling before him what she never meant to let him taste.

"And every troublemaking leprechaun," he muttered.

More laughter.

Ingrim had produced a fan and was waving it beneath her chin. "My, it's rather warm in here." She glanced at Edan. "If you'll excuse me? I believe I'll go walk outside."

"Certainly," he responded.

"Wait, I'll go with ye," Meg volunteered, setting her glass on the table. She'd had enough of the heat herself, it seemed.

As she stood, gathering her skirts, Richard watched her closely. Not a tremble. Not a flutter of lashes. Not even a flush to her cheeks anymore. Perfectly composed.

Damn the woman.

Yet he admired her strength, her stubbornness.

"Well!" Mrs. Hutchins said, once the other two women

had left. "Our Meg may have met her match. She's really not so bad as she seems."

Chuckling, Edan wiped perspiration from his brow. "Her scepter," he said. "You forgot her scepter."

Richard laughed.

"Could I 'ave some puddin' now?" Ian asked.

Mrs. Hutchins scrambled to get up. "Dear boy, you certainly can. I'll bring it straightaway."

"Might I interest ye in a game o' chess?" Edan asked Richard.

Now that sounded inviting. He hadn't settled down to a game of chess in a long time. "Are you any good?" he asked Edan.

The man grinned. "Might give ye a fair game." Mrs. Hutchins had gone by this time, and Edan tipped forward. "Got a bottle o' spirits that's been temptin' me fer a time, too."

Richard grinned. "By all means, Mr. McBride, lead the way."

"Now don't be tellin' Mrs. Hutchins or yer mother what ye jus' heard," Edan told his grandson.

Ian beamed. "*I* know the bottle's a secret!"

"What a good lad ye are," Edan said, rounding the table. "Trained 'im well, that I did."

Richard followed the man as he scampered from the room.

What a ninny of a girl! To run at the first sign of trouble. A little playful bickerin' back an' forth over the fact that I keep callin' him lieutenant when he asked me not to.

Ingrim Schmezel had no stamina, no determination. She should have been dropping a handkerchief for him to fetch, knocking over her glass, inviting him to go walk with her in the moonlight.

But then, not every woman was as bold as Meg.

"Ye heard him," she told Ingrim shortly after the girl fled. "He's attended most ev'ry theater in Cleveland. He's no doubt been other places, too—Chicago, New York. He's got means, that's certain."

That was what primpy girls such as Ingrim wanted, and what their mothers wanted for them—financial means, social standing. Meggie had seen such women before. Heaven only knew they came by McBride's in droves, flickering their fans, batting their lashes, making certain the sunlight didn't ruin their fair skin.

"He did not pay an ounce of attention to me," Ingrim said.

Saints. A whiner. Meg couldn't stand a whiner. "He did so."

"For a few seconds. Then he turned to you!"

"Only because I insist on callin' him lieutenant."

"I didn't know he does not wish to be called lieutenant."

"He doesn't. So if ye're still thinkin' to get his attention, don't be callin' him that."

"How am I to do it?" Get his attention, that was.

"I've a plan for tomorrow, see," Meggie said, leaning close. "The extract of a certain flower makes the object of yer affections fall madly in love with ye. I have it. I'll slip it to the lieutenant somehow. But mind ye, ye're the first person he's got to see when he wakes in the mornin'. Ye'll have to knock on his door an' wake him—he's not an early riser."

"Really?" Ingrim stared at her in amazement and disbelief. "Where did you hear of such a thing?"

"Never mind. But I can tell ye, it works. My husband . . . he didn't look twice my way till I slipped the extract in his drink one evenin'." Meg's father had run a tavern some five miles south of McBride's, and her mother had been full of superstitions and tales, some of which Meggie still scoffed at. She'd had her eye on Kevin for months, and then one day her mother pressed a tiny bottle into her hand and told her to try the contents in Kevin's drink and to be near him when he woke. Kevin passed out some time later, her father had a few men drag him to their barn, where he could sleep the night away, and Meg made certain she was right there with him when he woke.

"Wasn't six months later, Kevin an' I married," she told Ingrim.

"I suppose it is worth a try," the girl responded, still looking skeptical.

"Remember what I said about knockin' on his door in the mornin'. How else will ye be the first one he sees?"

Ingrim nodded. "Such an indecent thing to do!"

"Forget decency right now," Meg said, her impatience growing again. "Do ye want the man?"

"Yes, of course, but—"

"None of that. Now, off with ye. Sleep early tonight so ye'll be sure to wake early tomorrow."

Meggie didn't give Ingrim a chance to object to that. She turned her by the shoulders and gave her a little push toward the house. Off Ingrim went, with only one uncertain glance backward.

Now to figure a way to get the lieutenant to drink whatever she put the extract in.

Moments later, Meg entered the inn not far behind Ingrim. She heard Edan's booming laughter and she knocked lightly on the sitting room door, thinking the laughter came from that room. It died suddenly, and Meg knew Edan McBride well enough to realize that he was up to something. She turned the doorknob and gave the portal a little push.

There he sat across a game table from Richard Foster. They were playing chess, although they didn't seem to be playing too seriously, given the fact that Edan had been laughing so. When he played chess seriously, he didn't laugh. He concentrated on the game.

The lieutenant rubbed his chin, glancing at Meggie as she entered the room, a funny look lighting his eyes. He was about as good as Edan at hiding guilt. They were up to something, the two of them. And she knew her father-in-law well enough to guess at what it was.

She sauntered around behind him and leaned over his right shoulder. "Been spiritin' away the spirits again, haven't ye, Mr. McBride?"

His heavy brows came together in a thick, crooked line. "Now, Meg, I'm a grown man an' I know me own mind. G'on about yer bus'ness an' leave me be."

She laughed. "I'm not the one ye have to fear. Mrs. Hutchins . . . *she's* the one who'll raise the roof."

"As soon as ye leave here, ye'll go off an' tell her," he grumbled. "The two o' ye . . . ye'd best remember who runs the place. I'm McBride, an' I'll tip a bottle when I please."

"He likes his whiskey," she told the lieutenant. He half smiled at her. She ran her hand along the back of Edan's chair as she moved away from it. She wandered around the table, loving to tease her father-in-law.

For years Mrs. Hutchins had been in the employ of this inn, and for years she had tussled with Edan about his spirits. Whenever she got wind that he'd somehow gotten more into this establishment, she usually turned the place upside-down until she found his bottle, or bottles. He had a number of Irish friends in various locations in this part of Kentucky, and they were all too eager to make the whiskey and supply Edan with it.

"Meg, ye've got the look of the Devil t'night," Edan said, watching her closely.

The lieutenant laughed. "Precisely my thought over supper."

She'd reached the back of Mr. Foster's chair. "Who supplied ye this time, Mr. McBride?"

Edan gasped. "Close the door if ye're meanin' to discuss it! Damned woman's still cleanin' from the meal."

Meg ran her hand along the back of Richard's chair, too, and without meaning to, she grazed his back. "Ye know why I tell her, don't ye?" she asked Edan.

When seconds ticked by and he didn't answer, she smiled as she walked around to the other side of the table. "Ye're selfish with yer contraband. Ye've shared with me once, Mr. McBride. Only *once* in all these years." She knew why it had been only once, and that thought made her chuckle.

It made Edan redden furiously.

Richard Foster laughed again. He sometimes found Meggie more amusing than she did herself.

Edan scrambled up from his seat and scurried to the door, reminding her of a rat trying to protect his cheese.

"Never mind with that," she said, referring to the door. "I'm off to help Mrs. Hutchins. But, mind ye, when I return, I expect a sample."

He scowled at her. "Ah, Meg. Ye're not meanin' to put me to shame in front of this nice gentleman, are ye now?"

She cackled. Once, a good two months before she and Kevin married, she literally drank Edan under the table. She'd met him glass for glass, and he'd been the first to slump in his chair.

"Just a sample, Mr. McBride. Just a sample."

Meg loved the robust Irishman with her entire heart. They had their spats—Lord only knew they had their spats, because she was so headstrong. But, despite the times she grated his nerves raw, she suspected he loved her in return, as if she were his own daughter.

"I'll be back," she said and moved away from the table.

She flashed him an impish smile just before she reached the door. Edan clapped a hand to his head and groaned. The lieutenant chuckled.

True to her word, she helped Mrs. Hutchins clean up the supper mess. Next, she delivered Ian to Mr. Sardis in the barn, where her son always spent the better part of his evenings lately. Then Meggie fetched one of many little bottles from her room and dropped it into a pocket in her dress. Handy things, pockets. She sewed them into just about every article of clothing she owned. Finally she hurried back downstairs to join Edan and the lieutenant in the front room, taking care to lock the door behind her this time.

"Look, Mr. McBride," she said, "I've even brought my own tin." She pulled it from her pocket and flashed it before him. He and Mr. Foster hadn't bothered to hide their cups this time around; their tins sat boldly on the edge of the game table.

"Behind that cabinet," Edan grumbled at her.

"Drain yer cups," Meggie told the men. "I'll refill them."

They did, and she took the tins and carried them off with her.

She found Edan's bottle exactly where he'd said she

would. "A clever place, Mr. McBride. But Mrs. Hutchins is a thorough cleanin' woman. Better to hide the bottle upstairs."

"I've hidden many a bottle from the sharp eyes o' that woman," he snapped. "I'm not needin' yer advice."

Meggie smiled as she poured whiskey into the cups. They were concentrated on their game now, Edan and the lieutenant. She watched them from the corner of her eye as she trickled extract into Mr. Foster's tin, recorked her bottle, and dropped it back into her pocket.

She carried the men's cups over and replaced them from where she had taken them. Then she settled with her own on a settee.

The whiskey was potent. It wouldn't take much of the brew to put a big man on the floor. After taking a drink, Meggie blew air in and out of her mouth to cool her throat.

"Saints alive, Mr. McBride!" she said "'Twas Renegade Tom who brewed this batch, I know it. He likes kick to his whiskey."

The lieutenant laughed at her.

"'Twas Tom, indeed," Edan said, "an' that's a secret ye'll carry to yer grave, too."

"Oh, never ye fear! Ye know how I can be trusted."

Both men shook their heads at her.

"Lord God, I've never met such an outrageous woman," Richard remarked.

Edan shot him a scowl. "Ye've not seen the worst of her."

Meggie laughed and swigged back the last of the brew in her cup. Indeed he'd not.

The next morning, Richard woke with the worst headache he'd ever had. In his thirty years, he'd drunk a variety of liquors, beers, and concoctions, and his head had never hurt so much. It pounded, pulsed, drummed, hammered. It felt as if a herd of buffalo galloped through it.

He rolled over in the bed and groaned when someone knocked on the door. Just a knock, but it sounded as though someone ignited a stick of dynamite. What the hell was in that Irish whiskey anyway?

Another knock, and this time Richard scrambled from the bed to put a stop to it. One more pound might make him rave like a lunatic.

He jerked the door open, trying to clear his blurry vision by blinking. Another pain tore through his head, and he groaned and sank back against the door frame.

"Mr. Foster, are you well?"

It was Miss Schmezel, and why she asked such a damn-fool question was beyond him. He'd just risen from bed. His hair was tousled, and a day's growth of whiskers darkened his jaw. And he had a headache that made him feel like death warmed over. Worse. He wished he could fall back into the grave. He wore trousers, and that was that. His state of undress had to shock Ingrim.

"No, I'm not well," he growled, unable to employ manners at the moment. "Do I look well?"

She stared at him, expecting . . . Expecting what? She was dressed, thank God. Otherwise, if Mama decided to poke her head out of her room, he might be in one hell of a position. Such as standing before a minister in a church by noon.

What possessed Ingrim Schmezel to knock on his door at this hour? The sky was just beginning to lighten, for the love of God.

He had to put a stop to her infatuation with him before it went any further.

"Miss Schmezel, what exactly are you hoping to gain by your association with me?" he queried, mustering as much politeness as he could.

She was taken aback by the question; her eyes flared. She hoped for something, that was clear. She stood expectantly in the doorway, staring at him. "Why, I . . . Did you have something to drink last evening?"

The question baffled him. "More than I should have."

"From . . . from Mrs. McBride's hand?" she asked rather reluctantly.

He considered that. "How did you know?"

"And you feel nothing?" Her voice grew softer, more timid. "Nothing at all for me?"

He blinked. His head hammered again. He winced. "Am I supposed to?"

She continued to stare. Seconds passed.

"Miss Schmezel, I have a headache," he said impatiently. "I'm going back to bed."

"She's made a fool of me," Ingrim whispered, obviously in shock. "A fool. It's not working! I'll wake Mother, and we'll be on our way."

She turned away from the door and started to walk away. Something was going on here, something involving Meggie and last night's drinking. Richard's hand shot out and pulled Ingrim back.

Her eyes widened. "Mr. Foster, I—"

"Explain, Miss Schmezel. Why you had to know if Meggie McBride gave me something to drink. Why you think she made a fool of you. If she convinced you to do something that concerns me, I want to hear about it. Now."

Ingrim hesitated.

Then she told him about the extract.

She backtracked occasionally, saying that when Mrs. McBride had told her what a fine gentleman he was and that he was from a fine family, she also had encouraged her to flirt with him to try to win him.

That was astounding enough—trying to match him with this girl. But the part about Meg putting something in his drink, a love potion, made Richard's eyes narrow. The little conniving . . . He had half a mind to . . .

"You say I was supposed to fall madly in love with the first person I saw when I woke?"

Ingrim nodded.

He laughed, a thought suddenly occurring to him. A clever thought.

"Then I will. Go back to your room. Pretend you overslept. Don't mention a word of this conversation to Mrs. McBride if she asks if you came to my door."

The girl nodded again. "What do you plan to do?"

"Turn Meg's game on her," he said, and his grin widened.

This would be fun. And God only knew, he hadn't had fun in years.

9

WEEDS WERE TRYING to take hold of Meg's Johnny-jump-ups and violas, something she wouldn't stand for. She spread a small cloth on the ground to protect her dress, as she usually did, and set to work. It was just past dawn, and she'd spotted the weeds the minute she stepped into her garden.

> *"As I was lumb'rin' down the street,*
> *Down the street,*
> *Down the street;*
> *A handsome gal I chanced to meet,*
> *Oh, she was fair to view."*

She pushed the Johnnys out of the way and snatched away the greenery that threatened to choke off her flowers. She worked in a circle around the violas, stealing looks up at the lieutenant's window now and then.

Hah! By now Ingrim had surely paid him a visit—the girl was eager to get his attention. And by now, surely the lieutenant was smitten with Miss Schmezel. Next Meggie meant to convince the lass that she had to lead him away, that there was another girl just down the way, perhaps?—interested in him and that he had to leave the inn as soon as possible if Ingrim wished to keep him.

"Buffalo gals, can't you come out tonight?
Can't you come out tonight,
Can't you come out tonight;
Buffalo gals, can't you come out tonight,
And dance by the light of the moon?"

"Good morning, Queen Meg!" a voice called down to her.

Meg stopped dead in her plucking. The lieutenant. But why did he sound so cheery? He was always grumpy when her singing woke him.

Unless . . . unless Ingrim had paid him a visit, and he considered himself wildly in love.

Meggie got to her feet and brushed off her skirt. She smiled up at him—he'd settled himself on the windowsill once again.

"Why, good mornin', Lieutenant," she called, watching him curiously. "How're ye feelin' t'day?"

"Fine. I—"

Sobering, he stood suddenly, leaned over the sill, and stared at her, as if struck by something about her. "Your hair, Mrs. McBride. Did you do something different with it?"

Meg reached up and touched her hair. She'd brushed it, pulled it back, and tied a ribbon around it in the usual manner; most of the time that was exactly how she wore it. "No. Can't say that I have."

He continued to stare.

"Lieutenant, did ye—"

"Your eyes . . . What have you done to make them appear so bright and pretty?"

She wrinkled her brow. "Not a thing. I've—"

"Why, it's your entire face! I've never seen prettier skin. And your mouth . . . I don't recall that dress. You look . . . stunning in it."

Meggie had grown nervous. He'd been a little taken with her after their dance. But now he stared down at her with wide, glassy eyes, looking as though he'd never seen anything like her. The dress was one she'd worn several times since he made his appearance at the inn. Nothing was different about her hair, her face, her skin, or her mouth. So what in the blazes was wrong with—

Meg clapped a hand to her face. Oh, Mother o' Mary!

"Lieutenant, did ye have a visitor earlier this mornin'?"

He appeared baffled by the question. "A visitor?"

"Yes, a visitor."

He thought for a moment. Then he shook his head. "If I did, I don't recall."

"No one came to yer door an' woke ye?"

"No. Was someone supposed to?"

Meggie cursed under her breath. So she was the first person he'd seen upon awakening. Why hadn't Ingrim gone to his door? Had she overslept?

Meg fought the urge to tear into the inn, fly upstairs, and jostle the girl awake.

That would do her no good now. No good at all. Her singing had awakened the lieutenant, he'd appeared at the window, looked down, spotted her—and now he was smitten by her. Under the spell of that extract.

Meg groaned. To her knowledge, there was nothing she could do to reverse the effect.

"Would you like to ride along the riverbank with me this afternoon, Meggie?" he asked.

She laughed nervously. "Lieutenant, ye can't think to be taken by me. Go back to bed now, an' when ye wake, yer head'll be clear. Ye won't be half mad, thinkin' yerself sweet on a-a rude, temperamental Irish girl. Go. Off with ye. Back to bed."

He laughed down at her. "My head feels clear already!"

"Impossible, considerin' the amount of whiskey ye drank."

"I'm telling you, I feel—"

"Back to bed. Ye're not well. Really, ye're not."

"Will you sing more, Meggie?" he asked in a pleading tone. "If I lie back down, will you sing more?"

Saints. He reminded her of a lovesick pup! But if her singing was the only way to make him go back to bed, she'd sing. It wasn't true that when he woke, his head would be clear. But she needed time to think, and she couldn't think clearly with him standing at the window pining for her!

Meg sang more of "Buffalo Gals." She plucked more weeds. She twisted her lips and went over in her mind every note her mother had left about her gardening and about how to use various plants and herbs for treatments and for other things, such as making a person fall in love with another person. She had to reread the notes. Perhaps she'd missed something. Perhaps there was a cure for the lieutenant's love-struck state and she just didn't realize it.

Richard had pulled his shutters, afraid he would burst out laughing and that Meg would hear him. The look on her face! Nothing had done him more good in a long time. Shock, dread, exasperation, frustration . . .

His head still hurt, as it had never hurt in his life, and it had pounded with each word he'd uttered to Meggie. But the pain was worth the laughter and the knowledge that he'd gotten the better of her. The conniving Meggie McBride! How dare she pretend to want a taste of Edan's whiskey so she could put a love potion in his cup. All to make him fall in love with Ingrim Schmezel.

Meg didn't have a clue that Ingrim had come to his door and spilled the milk. And she wouldn't either. Ingrim was embarrassed enough that she wouldn't tell Meggie—Richard felt certain of that.

He'd go back to bed. But he'd wake just as smitten by Meggie—and just as determined to make a nuisance of himself.

Over their whiskey, Edan had hinted that he needed another man to help with odd jobs, that Mr. Sardis was getting too old and bent to be expected to do some of the more difficult tasks. Richard had made an arrangement to work out his boarding fees in exchange for helping Edan with the tasks, and today they intended to split wood and repair a section of the porch roof. So Richard went back to bed, but not for long.

When he awoke the second time, he wondered if the whiskey or that love potion caused his headache. At least it had abated some. Upon rising, he was so thirsty he drank two full glasses of water before heading downstairs in search of coffee.

Mrs. Hutchins greeted him with a smile and a mug, as always. The kitchen smelled of cinnamon, of herbs and spices. Several piles of vegetables—carrots, onions, potatoes, celery—sat on the table, waiting to be chopped, Richard presumed. A slab of what looked like beef sat nearby. Not far away the table was sprinkled with flour, and there sat the largest mound of dough he had ever seen. As a boy, he'd invaded the kitchen at home and watched the cook many times. If he had seen such a sight as that huge mound he might have run off scared half to death.

Mrs. Hutchins had fired up the cookstove, and Richard wondered how she tolerated the heat pouring from it. The back door stood open, so that helped. Still, the kitchen was uncommonly hot, and Mrs. Hutchins appeared flushed as she poured his coffee, then went back to kneading the mound of dough.

"I don't know what to make of you and Meg lately," she remarked.

Richard sipped coffee. "Neither do I."

She eyed him. "Now, why is that?"

"I'm smitten by her. But she can't seem to stand me." If he meant to pull off the scheme he'd concocted concerning Meggie, he had to convince Mrs. Hutchins, also, of his lovesick state. She and Meg talked, he knew that. He meant to bother Meggie to death for days, follow her around like a lovesick boy . . . and he wanted no one to give her a hint of what he was up to. That included Mrs. Hutchins.

"I've figured out Meg," the woman told him. "At least, I think I have. Of course, sometimes a person can't know about her, what she might be up to next. But you know what I think?" she asked, glancing up from her dough.

Richard smiled. If he didn't give some indication that he was interested in what she thought, he had a feeling she meant to tell him anyway. "What?" He sipped more coffee. For some reason it tasted uncommonly good this morning.

"I think she's sweet on you and just won't face it."

He choked. He coughed. He sputtered. He plopped his mug down on the table. "Meggie, sweet on *me*?"

She laughed, a jolly sound that filled the kitchen with more morning light. "Why, sure. Even a girl like Meg, hard tempered and difficult as she can be, can get sweet on someone."

Richard gave her a serious look. "Mrs. Hutchins, she's still in love with her husband."

She twisted her face into a frown. "That may be. That may well be. If it is, Megan's got to get over him sooner or later. Lord, the man's been dead and buried for a while now. There's no bringing him back, no matter how often the girl stands on that hilltop and talks to him. She's young and pretty. And she's good with young'uns. Don't you agree?"

He nodded.

He drank more coffee, growing nervous suddenly with this conversation. What was the woman driving at? Throwing hints his way . . . He had unfinished business in Ohio. He couldn't become a candidate for the position of Meg McBride's second husband.

"She could have a houseful of her own, provided she gets past Kevin and goes on with her life."

"Getting past someone's death doesn't happen overnight," Richard said.

Mrs. Hutchins kneaded the dough more. "Sounds like you're speaking from experience."

He was that obvious. He laughed at himself, a short laugh filled with regret and bitterness and disbelief and dread. "I might be."

"Could be the reason you're holed up here."

"I don't need another mother, Mrs. Hutchins," he said. His "reason for being holed up here" wasn't a subject he wanted to discuss with anyone.

She didn't flinch. "No, but maybe you need a friend."

He drank more coffee. She kneaded the dough. He stared out the back door, watching the swaying tree branches in the distance, thinking of Willy and home, of his sister and his parents; wondering if his mother and father could or would ever forgive him for leading Willy off.

He wanted to go home. He needed to go home. Even if only for a while. He'd have no peace until he did, even if going home meant facing the parents who might not want to see him again. He at least had to know how they felt. And he had to face up to what he'd done.

He was scared.

"Maybe," he said, and then he drained his mug and put it back down on the table. He shot Mrs. Hutchins a mild smile. "I told Edan I'd help him with chores today."

He headed for the door.

"Don't you want breakfast?"

"Thanks, but no. Not today." He'd been hungry upon first coming downstairs. Now he seemed to have lost his appetite.

"Meg's going into town this afternoon to pick up some supplies," Mrs. Hutchins said matter-of-factly. "She'll be taking Ian with her—she always does. But I reckon she could use some bigger help."

Richard turned back, grinning. "You're too obvious."

She laughed, her cheeks round and blooming, like roses. "Well, you said you're smitten by her. And since I think she's sweet on you . . ." She shrugged. "Sure won't hurt to encourage things along."

"Do you encourage every stranger who stops at McBride's?"

"Lord, no! See, you're not a stranger anymore."

That warmed him. But he shook his head. "I'm going home one day, Mrs. Hutchins. I must."

"You can always come back."

She'd considered the matter apparently, him and Meggie and how she wanted things to work out.

He had no serious thoughts in mind. He liked some things about Meg. In fact, if he considered her and the events that had occurred since his first day here, he had to admit that he liked some things about her a lot. Whether that meant he'd ever think about really falling for Meggie . . . How could he do that when he didn't know what the future entailed, especially with regard to his family in Ohio?

He had to think about what he wanted to do with his life

now that the war was over. Pick up where he'd left off in Cleveland or start anew somewhere?

He didn't know yet what he wanted to do. For that reason, he shouldn't seriously involve himself with a woman. Since he had no stability, he felt he had nothing to share with her.

"Thanks," he told Mrs. Hutchins. Then he finally made it out the kitchen door.

He found Edan out back already, just approaching the pile of wood he and Mr. Sardis had gathered from the forest the day before. The two men had spent most of one day last week felling trees, sawing them into pieces that were small enough to haul back here in a wagon.

"How're ye feelin' this fine mornin'?" Edan asked, beaming as usual.

Richard managed a grin. Splitting wood would be hell on his headache. "Like I won't be drinking any more Irish whiskey for a while."

Robust laughter spilled from McBride. "Got ye, did it?"

"You might say that."

"It did. Ole John's brew's got a mean kick. There's a spare axe if ye're still of a mind to do this."

He meant if Richard felt good enough to split wood. He didn't, but he damn sure wouldn't admit that to his drinking partner of last evening. If Edan felt good enough to split wood, male pride dictated that Richard should also.

He hadn't split logs in several years, however, not since he'd taken a detachment out to gather firewood for an army encampment. He hadn't done any type of hard labor in quite some time now, in fact. He thought he might tire easily. He thought his leg might ache after only a short time.

He grabbed the spare axe and concentrated on taking his mind off his physical weakness. He grabbed a section of log, set it up on a tree stump, and went to work.

Hours later, he and Edan had split a stack of wood nearly the size of Meg's garden shed before Richard felt the first pang in his injured limb. He took a short break, settling himself on the tree stump for a few minutes.

He'd just picked up his axe, preparing to get back to work, when he saw Meggie bring a wagon out of the stable.

He split more wood, aware that she was searching around outside the inn for Ian. The boy had been helping Mr. Darrow with the ferry, then he'd gone around to the other side of the inn, toward the outhouse. Come to think of it, that was the last time Richard had seen him, and that had been hours ago.

"Did you find him?" he called to Meg when she came from the direction of her garden.

She looked ready to spit nails. "No. An' I tell ye, he'll not be able to sit for a while when I find him this time. I told him not to run off again."

"He's not with Mr. Darrow?"

"No."

"Where would he have gone?"

"Off with Russell 'n' Michael, most likely," Edan said, heaving his axe into another piece of wood. He left the axe there and began unrolling his shirtsleeves.

"Friends?" Richard asked.

"Trouble's what they are," Meggie said, approaching, her eyes filled with worry.

"We'll find him," Richard told her. He followed Edan's example, leaving his axe stuck in a piece of wood. "I'll saddle my horse."

"I was makin' butter," Meg said, kneading her hands together. "I should've had him stay with me."

"We'll find him," Richard assured her again.

"Take Meggie an' go west," Edan told Richard. "I'll take Nathaniel an' we'll search east o' here. If ye find Ian an' his friends, fire a shot into the air."

"I have my revolver," Meg said, lifting it from her apron pocket.

Richard didn't especially like the sight of that thing, and he told her to put it away until they needed it. He expected a defiant reaction from her. Instead, without question, she lowered the pistol back into her pocket. Edan had an odd look on his face—as if he wondered where she'd come up with such a weapon.

"Mr. Dickson sold it to me," she told him. "Ye didn't think I'd go unprotected, did ye?"

Shaking his head, Edan headed toward the stable. Richard and Meggie followed.

Mr. Sardis was repairing a rail on one of the stalls. He glanced up as Edan told him that Ian was missing and that they needed to search for him.

"He couldn't have gone far," Richard said, thinking of Ian's limp and of his age. "Does he know the area around here? The forest?"

"He knows it," Meggie said sharply as Richard headed for Caith's stall. "I've no doubt he could find his way home. It's what might be lurkin' in the woods that troubles me."

Richard could see it in her eyes, what she thought might be lurking in the woods: stragglers coming home from the war; soldiers.

"No one wants any more trouble, Meggie."

"Ye weren't here months ago, Lieutenant."

She was right. He grabbed Caith's saddle from the rail, asking Meg, "What happened a few months ago?" Something, surely. Something involving soldiers; something that made Meggie tense and nearly frantic now.

She didn't answer him. She grabbed Caith's bridle from a hook on a nearby wall and followed Richard into the stall.

He stopped her with a shake of his head. "He won't let anyone but me saddle and bridle him."

Meggie dropped the bridle over the top stall rail. "I'm goin' on, then," she said. "On foot. Ye can catch up."

They should go together. She wouldn't have long to wait while he prepared his horse. But Meg had her mind made up, and he refused to waste time by arguing with her.

She turned and hurried off, a frantic mother. Nothing would delay her from finding her son.

Edan and Mr. Sardis were saddling horses, too. McBride shook his head, looking at Richard. "God help the person that stands between Meg an' Ian."

Richard dropped the saddle on Caith's back and buckled and cinched it. The horse nuzzled him, and Richard, while pulling the bridle up over Caith's nose and ears and adjusting it, explained softly that Ian was missing and that they had to help find him. As skittish as Caith was with most people, he was a military horse and Richard had never had trouble with him following commands. He'd been mistreated by someone, and that accounted for his nervousness. But Richard could think of no other companion with whom he'd rather go into a tough situation. Caith wasn't gun-shy—and he was loyal.

Richard grabbed his canteen from where it dangled from another hook. Then he brought Caith out into the open.

They walked outside together, and Richard filled the canteen from the well near the left side of the inn. He tied the canteen onto Caith's saddle just as Edan emerged from the stable with his own horse.

"Ye might need this," McBride said, and he tossed Richard a rifle, a Springfield. Impressive. Springfields were the best. Edan didn't intend to miss what he shot at, and he intended to make damn sure he could reload and get off more shots quickly.

Next came a pouch of bullets, and Richard asked no questions; as a soldier he'd learned to follow commands. He wondered again what had happened at the inn months ago—something that had scared Edan as much as it had scared Meg apparently. Edan didn't strike Richard as the type of man who would take up arms without good reason.

Gripping the rifle, Richard dropped the bullet pouch into his trouser pocket. He swung up onto Caith, set his boots in the stirrups, and tapped the horse into motion.

He soon entered the coolness of the forest.

The ground was soft, so it didn't take him long to track Meggie down. His sharp eyes noted grass that had been pressed down, bushes and foliage that had been pushed aside, strands of auburn hair caught by the thorns of a wild rosebush. His sharp ears listened for sounds, twigs crunching, the brush of boots on undergrowth. Beneath him, Caith behaved as he'd been trained to do, falling still and quiet whenever they stopped, whenever he sensed Richard was listening or watching or waiting.

Meggie's voice drifted their way, calling for Ian. Richard turned Caith in her direction. She'd made good progress on foot, driven by motherly instinct.

She heard him coming. She whirled around, her revolver in hand, twigs caught in her hair.

"I might have shot you," she gasped, slumping a little.

"If I'd meant you any harm, you wouldn't have had time," Richard told her. Odd. Not two weeks ago, she wouldn't have balked at the idea of shooting him. "Like the day I came upon you with that flag."

She stared at him, registering his point.

"Are there specific places where Ian and his friends play?"

She nodded. "A few. Up ahead."

Richard glanced off, listening. He heard only the trees and the birds and something scurrying not far away, scrambling through fallen leaves and undergrowth. A rodent.

"Come here," he commanded Meggie.

Her brows furrowed. "Why?"

She shouldn't be questioning him right now. Her timing was bad. But he didn't suppose Meg ever gave thought to that when she decided to argue. He didn't suppose she ever gave thought to *whether* she should argue, either. She did it naturally.

"So you can swing up behind me and we can look for Ian," Richard said, narrowing one eye at her. He didn't like having to explain himself. Not when he had a job to do.

She considered that. Then she said, "I'd rather walk."

Damn the woman. Defiant, rebellious, argumentative . . .

He nodded. "I'll be behind you." Guarding her rear when he ought to *kick* her rear.

She walked on, leading the way. Her boots brushed through the forest floor, pushing aside fallen leaves and occasionally crunching twigs, making it harder to listen for abnormal sounds. Stubborn woman. Haughty even when he tried to help her.

They passed through an area where the undergrowth had been cleared away not long ago. An animal had been digging at the ground. Fresh dirt sprayed the lower trunks of nearby trees, and there was a fresh hole the size of a large bowl. Leaves had been brought to cover the earth here; more leaves were concentrated in this area than on any other part of the forest floor.

Meggie gasped at the sight of the hole, but she missed only one step.

Richard glanced at the disturbed earth, wondering at her reaction, why the sight of a hole in the ground would startle her.

From the corner of his eye he caught her using the toe of her boot to push leaves over something on the ground. She didn't take long to do that, either. He'd bet she missed only two steps this time.

He continued to follow her, silently noting this place and its location.

They traveled on, between sweet birches and scrub pines, between sugar maples and white oaks; among the sooty caps of pinecone mushrooms and the white, waxy stems of Indian pipe where decaying vegetation covered the forest floor. Wood frogs abounded here, some flesh-colored, some as brown as the dead leaves, changing colors with their environment. In swampy areas they might be green or black.

Impressions in damp beds of leaves and then in places where the ground was softer than others began catching Richard's eye. He made other observations, too: a turned leaf . . . a broken branch . . . slight tracks made through the ferns, some now broken and twisted, that grew abundantly between trees . . . The last gave the boys away. The trails through the ferns revealed two or three small people traveling together.

"They came this way," Richard told Meggie.

Her head twisted around. "How do ye know?"

He told her.

When her eyes widened slightly with newfound appreciation, he fought the urge to ask if she minded having a soldier with her so much right now.

They continued on, Richard following Meg. She looked for the signs of travel through here now that he'd pointed them out to her, and she followed the signs fairly well. Now and then she turned back to look at him, as if silently asking if she was going in the right direction, and every time he nodded her on.

She trusted him in this. Of course, who else did she have to trust at the moment? If she'd been thinking clearly at the time, she might have raised a loud objection about Edan appointing them as partners in this search.

Her face was flushed. The curls on her forehead and along her hairline were damp. She stopped when she sensed him halt behind her, and when she glanced back, she gladly accepted the canteen of water he offered.

Richard took advantage of the moment—he listened. He spotted several deer, poised and alert, watching them from the thicket to their left. The deer flicked their tails, then bounded off when Richard turned his head their way.

He heard sounds. Foreign to the forest. Light. Almost musical. Birds didn't make such noises.

Meg heard the sounds, too. Her head shifted to the right. "They're there! Not far!" she said, breathless with excitement.

"Get up here, Meggie," Richard said, extending his hand to her.

This time she didn't argue. Caith would take them to her son faster than she could get to him on foot. She took Richard's hand, swung herself up, and settled behind him. Her hands rested lightly on his back.

A flick of the reins and Caith was off again, this time going right.

The noises grew louder, more distinct. They changed. No longer musical. No longer those of young boys having fun. Someone shouted. Cried.

Behind Richard, Meggie tensed. "Hurry. Please hurry!"

A short distance from the noises, Richard stopped Caith and told Meg to get down. She did—no argument this time, either—then he slid down, still gripping the Springfield in his hand.

"Stay here," he told her.

He crouched as well as he could considering his injured leg. He assessed the area ahead for the best coverage, then he stole off that way.

He spotted a clearing and a small pond where the boys had been swimming. There was Ian, his hair wet and matted, wearing only his trousers, his skin white against the brown material. Richard recognized the two other boys backed up against the huge trunk of a sugar maple as boys he'd seen with the group of children Meggie taught. Ian's playmates.

A bigger boy, almost a man, stalked the three younger ones, poking at them with a sharpened stick, drawing yelps and cries. He was man enough to have a day's growth of whiskers on his chin and hair curling beneath the vee of his shirt. Man enough to find someone his own size to taunt and hurt, too. He jabbed the pointed end of the stick at Ian's face, and Richard came out of hiding.

He had just raised the rifle, intending to fire off a shot near the bully, when a crack sounded behind him. A bullet whizzed by his ear, making Richard duck. The bully howled, grabbed his foot, and hopped around.

"Yeah!" shouted one of the younger boys.

"That'll learn ya!" said another.

"Mum?" Ian said, paling even more. Forget that Meg had just saved him from having his eye put out. He was in trouble with her and he knew it.

It was a good, clean shot, Richard had to admit. Meggie had hit exactly what she'd aimed at.

Still, Richard spun on her and glared. "I told you to stay there."

"I'm not accustomed to takin' orders, Lieutenant," she retorted.

She dropped her revolver back into her apron pocket, grabbed a good-sized stick off the ground, and stripped it of leaves.

When she hiked her skirts and her green eyes flashed, Richard thought she meant to tear off after Ian. Ian apparently thought so, too. He began stammering, telling her that he was sorry he'd wandered off again, that he promised not to do it ever, *ever* again. His playmates stood looking wide-eyed, possibly wondering if Ian's mother meant to take the switch after them, too.

She tore off after the bully, surprising them all.

"Tim Willard, pick up that stick an' fight fair! Ye think to poke these boys with it? Ye want a fight? I'll give ye a fight!"

She went after the bully, brandishing her stick and screeching at him like a mad person. Her face flamed with anger. Her flashing eyes alone might have made the bravest of men turn tail and run.

Which was exactly what Tim Willard did. He was not a brave man. Forget his injured foot. He took one look at the angry mother coming after him, his mouth widened into an O, and he tore off yelping into the woods.

Meggie chased him into the thicket.

How far she meant to go after him, Richard didn't know. He laughed at the sight of her going after the half-grown Tim and he laughed at the sight of Tim tearing off. He laughed so hard he had to sit down on a fallen tree.

"'Tis not so funny," Ian scolded.

Richard tried to be serious. Poor Ian. He probably would like to have his mother chase Tim the rest of the day. And tomorrow. And the next day.

"From your point of view, I don't imagine it is," Richard said.

And he laughed more.

10

$\mathcal{M}$EGGIE WOULD SURELY be back soon. She surely wouldn't chase the bully halfway across Kentucky.

Then again, she might.

Richard fired a shot into the air, as Edan had told him and Meg to do if they found the boys. Maybe one shot too many, Richard thought immediately after he pulled the trigger. If Edan and Mr. Sardis heard two shots, they might think someone was shooting at him and Meg. They might tear through the forest, trying to find them instead of going back to the inn and waiting for them to return with Ian and the other boys.

During Meggie's brief absence, Ian had managed to find his shirt, and he and his friends had plopped down on the ground and were now looking at each other. Ian and one of his friends had pretty long expressions. The other boy muttered smartly, "Pop'll be after her for getting after Tim like that."

"Ye're takin' up for him?" Ian blurted out.

"I know he's your brother 'n' all," Ian's other friend said, "but he was gonna *cream* us. Turn us upside down in the swimmin' hole mebbe. 'Member when Tim did that b'fore?"

Ian nodded earnestly. He remembered well, apparently. He stood up and stomped over to glare into Tim's brother's face. "Yer pop thinks about comin' after my mum, I'll be waitin' for him. So will my grandpop."

As fiercely protective of his mother as Meggie was of him. Richard fought a grin, feeling a surge of pride in Ian.

The bigger boy shoved Ian and sent him sprawling backward. "Freak! Don't threaten me!"

Ian scrambled to his feet and charged the boy, giving a fine effort for someone with a crippled leg. He knocked Tim's brother over, and the boys rolled on the ground, fists flying.

The boy still seated glanced at Richard as if expecting him to do something. Richard shrugged. Boys had to fight out their differences. Nature dictated that. Ian and Tim's brother were too small and too young to do any real damage. So one of them might end up with a blackened eye or a bloody nose. Getting either sooner or later was a consequence of being male.

After a few minutes, Meggie emerged from the trees, a smile of satisfaction on her face. She'd chased that Tim Willard off good. So good, in fact, he'd never get within a hundred yards of Ian ever again. Now she had to get rid of her smirk and go after Ian. She meant to give him a good licking with her switch, so good he'd never again think of running off.

She was so shocked when she saw Ian and Michael fighting on the ground that it took a few seconds for her brain to register exactly *what* she saw. Two bodies entangled, twisting and grunting and heaving in the grass and mud beside the water. Swinging arms and legs. And there sat Richard Foster, enjoying the fight!

"Enough!" Meg shouted, running toward the boys. She meant to break them up, even if that meant using her switch on both of them. "Get up. Get up right now!"

They continued fighting.

"Ian McBride, stop this minute!" She itched to use the switch. But the boys rolled and tangled and she didn't know what she'd hit. A few good blows to their rears would stop them, she felt certain. But she couldn't be sure she'd hit their rears.

"All right, Ian, get up," Richard Foster said from nearby. He'd left his seat, apparently deciding to help her break up the fight.

Decent of him, Meg thought caustically.

He stepped forward, reached down and grabbed two arms, somehow figuring out which belonged to whom. He pulled the boys to their feet.

Ian was still swinging, or trying to. The lieutenant lifted him as if he weighed little more than a small bag of flour, and he set Ian apart from Michael another six inches. "Enough damage for one day," Richard told Ian.

Enough damage for one day? What kind of thing was that to say to a seven-year-old? . . . *For one day?* That implied that tomorrow Ian could decide to do more "damage" and that would be fine. The soldier mentality was showing its ugly colors.

Meggie stepped between the lieutenant and her son, facing Ian. "Ye shame me, Ian McBride! Scufflin' on the ground like a wild animal. Fightin' with Michael! Fightin's not the answer to yer problems!"

Ian hung his head. Shame worked with him better than any other discipline. Better, even, than the switch. But Meg worried that shame might be losing its effectiveness. Twice within two weeks now he'd run off, not telling her where he was going, not even asking *if* he could go.

"It may not be the best answer, but sometimes it's the only option," the lieutenant remarked.

Meggie spun on him. How dare he interfere while she was disciplining Ian! How dare he challenge what she'd told her son. How dare he differ with her on this in front of Ian—after what she'd told the boy.

Anger threatened to crack her voice. "If ye're wantin' to debate the topic, Lieutenant, do it another time. I told Ian fightin's not the answer."

Meggie watched him stiffen, saw anger gather in his eyes. "What were you doing when you went after Tim?" he demanded, his voice low.

She caught her breath. Instinct told her to say something more, to lash out verbally . . . to fight. Just as she did when she'd gone after Tim. The lieutenant had made his point and made it well. If anything, Ian was just like her in temperament. Actually, calmer.

Michael grabbed around them for Ian. Richard snared his arm, then backed him up. He glared down at the boy, whose chest was heaving and whose face was bright red with anger. Well, except for the darkening area just beneath his left eye. Ian had walloped him a good one.

"How far do you live from here?" the lieutenant demanded of Michael.

The boy said nothing. He glared right back. At least Ian had the good sense to hang his head. Michael Willard . . . he didn't know when to stop being defiant.

"Not far," Meg told Richard. "We're closer to his home than we are to the inn. We should take him—"

"Go home," Richard told Michael. "The next time you think about calling names and striking first, think again. Especially if you're faced with Ian."

Meggie couldn't help herself: "We shouldn't be lettin' him—"

Richard turned the glare on her, and it was so intense, Meg stopped short.

He faced Michael again, who didn't look quite as belligerent anymore. "Can you find your way home?"

The boy glanced down at his dirty feet. "Yes, sir."

Meggie's brows shot up. She'd never heard Michael call anyone sir.

Effectively humbled, Michael went off to gather his shirt and boots, not taking the time to stop and put them on. He walked away, between trees, into the thicket, growing smaller and smaller, soon disappearing into the forest.

"We should follow him," Meg said. "Make sure he gets home safely."

"He's gathering his pride," Richard responded. "I wouldn't follow him."

"Ian, you *whupped* him," the other boy said, jumping up and down. "You really whupped him!"

Meggie scowled. "'Tis nothin' to boast about."

"Has he bothered you before?" Richard asked Ian. "Called you names? Been a bully like his brother?"

Ian nodded.

"I don't imagine he'll do it again."

The lieutenant went off to gather his rifle, muttering something about boys being allowed to be boys, being allowed to settle their own differences. He said he was going to get Caith from the woods and then headed in that direction.

Meg stared at his back as he walked off. She still didn't like the fact that he'd challenged her parental authority, and in Ian's presence. But she had to admit, to herself, of course, that he had some wisdom about him. He'd dealt with bullies before, that was obvious. And as he'd pointed out to her, her going after Tim was really no different than Ian's going after Michael.

She didn't know what had happened to make Ian angry enough to want to do that, and she'd always taught him to walk away rather than fight. But she didn't always do that herself.

"Can ye wait till we get home?" Ian asked her, glancing at her switch.

She'd forgotten about it. Meggie looked down at it. Ian was safe, and there'd been enough fighting for one afternoon. His nose was bleeding. She wanted to pull out her handkerchief and wipe it, draw him against her and hug him tight, tell him how glad she was that he was safe. He felt the blood, and he smeared it when he tried to wipe it away with the back of his hand.

Meg dropped the switch, started to pull out her handkerchief . . . remembered what Richard had said about boys being allowed to be boys.

Ian's first fisticuffs . . . Ian's first nosebleed . . . Meg imagined there would be more. She had to stop mothering him so much. Smothering him was more like it. He was growing up, going through some of the trials all boys probably endured.

She didn't imagine he'd like having her wipe his nose in front of Russell. She moved her hand away from her pocket.

"Yer poppa's dead, Ian," she said, looking her son in the eye. "Ye know how I grieved when he came home in that box. I'd hate to grieve for ye. Get yer things an' let's go home."

She walked off, refusing to lecture him again, refusing to coddle him. But, oh, how she wanted to do the latter! Her heart clenched, and she squeezed back tears at the thought of her boy maturing, distancing himself from her, someday growing up and away from her. No one had warned her that motherhood included the heartache of loosening the reins and then finally letting go one day.

Despite her fight against them, a few tears slid down her cheeks as she started through the trees. She wondered if Ian and Russell were coming. She thought about looking back, and she fought the urge to do even that. Perhaps they wanted to walk together, away from her.

More tears slid down her cheeks. She swiped at them. "Ye're bein' silly, Meg McBride," she scolded herself. "Ye're overreactin'. There's no stoppin' him from growin' up."

"His independence isn't a threat to how much he cares about you. You'll always be his mother," the lieutenant told her softly. He had his horse now, and he had approached on her left while she was chastising herself.

The man had a tender side. A gentle side. An understanding side. A side Meggie didn't want to see. A side she wished didn't exist. For various reasons, she didn't want to like him.

But she was afraid she was beginning to.

Late that afternoon, out of curiosity, Richard rode back out to the section of forest through which he and Meg had tracked the boys. He rode to the spot where the earth had been disturbed by an animal's digging, where leaves had been piled; where Meggie had booted leaves over something on the ground when she thought he wasn't looking.

He dismounted and dug around in the leaves. His fingers touched something hard, something metal.

What he came up with surprised him: the buckle off the

strap of a .69 caliber cartridge box, standard Union issue to a "Billy Yank." The buckle was round and imprinted with an eagle. It was unmistakable.

The hole where the animal had been digging was larger, more dirt thrown here and there. Something protruded up from the bottom of the hole.

The toe of a boot.

Richard brushed away leaves from the small clearing and contemplated the entire area, where the grass had been interrupted, where the breaks in the ground began, where they ended, where the dirt was slightly sunken in, more settled . . . the fact that the interrupted grass and the sunken dirt formed a rough three-by-six-foot rectangle. The dirt had been tamped down at some point and had settled more since.

Someone was buried here, and not very far down, either, judging by the size of the hole that revealed the toe of that boot.

Richard stared off at nothing in particular. All around him the trees whispered; the birds sang and chirped. The forest smelled of earth and of decay, of pine and a hundred other scents. He and his detachment had buried men during the war. Too many.

Maybe just boots were buried here.

Not likely. The hole was too big for just boots. And— wild animals dug for a reason, namely to eat. Most had a keen sense of smell, even if a food source was buried.

Turning the buckle over in his hand, Richard wondered if he should question Meggie about the area, about why she'd felt the need to hide this buckle from him; about what—or who—was buried here. His first inclination was to corner her and drill her until she spilled the truth, as unpleasant as he suspected the truth might be.

If he did that and he got the truth out of her—what he already suspected—what would he do with it?

Someone was buried here, and he suspected that someone was a Union soldier.

He'd been a soldier for a number of years. He'd sworn allegiance to the United States military. He'd fought along-side many a man who carried the .69 caliber box. If he questioned Meg and got the truth out of her, wouldn't he feel obligated to report what he'd discovered to the proper authorities?

He already felt that way. Provided his suspicions were right.

A sense of outrage raised the hair on the back of his neck.

A grave had been dug here, and a body occupied it, no doubt. Meggie knew about it. He'd bet his life Meggie knew about it. Why else would she hide the buckle from him?

A Union soldier occupied the grave, minus the buckle from his caliber box.

Damn.

Had Meggie killed the man? Had she been unable to control her dislike of soldiers when this one passed through? Upon Richard's arrival at the inn, she'd made no bones about the fact that she disliked him because he was a soldier. Had her dislike once driven her to murder?

An even bigger question troubled him: Did Edan know? Had he taken part in the killing?

It had to have been murder. Had to have been . . . Why else would someone try to keep a death secret? Why else would Meg have hidden the buckle from him as they passed by? She hadn't wanted him to know a man was buried here. A Union soldier.

Richard's thoughts were jumping ahead; he was making assumptions he shouldn't be making. In the back of his mind was Mrs. Hutchins's voice, telling him about the hardships the McBrides and others at the inn had endured at the hands of soldiers from both sides. Perhaps this soldier had come through with malicious intent also.

Maybe it hadn't been murder. Maybe it had been self-defense.

"Damn," Richard muttered, and he dropped the buckle into the knapsack that dangled from one side of Caith's saddle. He didn't like going back and forth, thinking maybe this and maybe that. He needed facts. He needed the truth.

He needed to confront Meggie with what he'd found.

He buckled the knapsack, closing it securely, then he began searching the woods for large stones or heavy items to lay across the grave. The least he could do for a fellow soldier was protect his body from scavengers.

He meant to carry through on his scheme to make Meggie think her "potion" had backfired on her, and he meant to do it as lightheartedly as possible. But at some point, he and Meg would have a conversation about what he'd discovered here. And she had better not lie to him.

She'd better not even *think* about lying to him.

He couldn't sleep that night. He kept seeing images in his head: bodies on the battlefield, tattered gray uniforms coming at him, muskets a few feet from his face, sabers gleaming in the sunlight; the smoke of battle clouding for as far as one could see . . . .

He heard noises downstairs, not loud noises, but enough to keep an edgy ex-soldier from sleeping even when he finally settled down.

Richard pulled on his shirt and went downstairs to investigate.

Meggie was in the kitchen, stirring something in a kettle that sat on the stove. The back door stood open, and the coolness of night tempered the heat in the kitchen. A burning lantern sat on the mantelpiece above the hearth, and another sat amid the jars that cluttered one end of the table. The kitchen smelled of sweet berries.

Meg still wore a red and white gingham dress. Her hair was tied back with a red ribbon, and it curled and twisted all the way to her waist. She seemed absorbed in what she was doing.

Not wanting to startle her, Richard knocked lightly on the door frame.

She spun around after the second knock. He'd startled her anyway.

Upon seeing that it was him, she relaxed a little. That was surprising since she didn't like to be around him. She hadn't objected too much this afternoon in the forest only because her mind had been on finding Ian.

"Sorry," Richard said. "I didn't mean to spook you."

"Ye're awake late," she observed.

He nodded. "Couldn't sleep."

"Oh?" A question lingered in her eyes. The lamplight softened them. Usually they sparkled and appeared full of fight and mischief. Tonight her eyes looked like green velvet, inviting, almost alluring. Her lips appeared darker, too. Richard wondered if she'd been eating the berries in her pot.

"War memories," he said.

She emitted a short, bitter laugh. "I know about those."

A moment of quiet passed between them.

"I hear it was hard to find food after soldiers came through," he remarked.

She arched a brow at him.

"Mrs. Hutchins told me. Besides, I was a Union soldier. We starved and burned out the South, remember? Even if we hadn't, we were in constant need of supplies and food. The difference was, the quartermaster almost always paid for what we took."

"Hah! No one ever paid us a penny."

She turned back to the stove, went back to stirring the contents of her pot.

Richard strode to the pitcher that sat atop a cabinet across the room and poured himself a cup of water. "What are you cooking at this hour?"

She shot him a brief smile. "I couldn't sleep, either. Berries for jam. Mr. Sardis picked them yesterday. He knows I love jam."

Cute. Richard couldn't help but smile back at her. "At least you don't sing while you cook."

"It's not quite the same as tendin' my garden."

She was smiling again. He couldn't believe it. Meg hadn't smiled at him so much at one time, at least not with good intentions, in the nearly two weeks he'd been here.

"You have a pretty smile, Meggie McBride," he said.

Their eyes met with intensity this time. With meaning.

Seconds later she glanced away, obviously feeling awkward. He'd seen Meg turn red when she was angry, but he hadn't seen her *blush* the way she did now.

She focused on her pot again, stirring a few more times

while Richard leaned back against the cabinet, the cup still in his hand, and watched her.

Her flush deepened. "Ye're starin', Lieutenant."

"Not very gentlemanly of me," he remarked. Still, he continued to watch her.

"Ye were nice this afternoon, helpin' me find Ian."

"That surprises the hell out of you, doesn't it? That I can be nice."

"I've reason to be mistrustful."

"Not of me. You never had reason, Meggie."

She glanced at him again, and this time her eyes sparked. "How am I to determine whom to trust?"

Good question. He wasn't sure there was a good answer. He nodded. "Point well taken."

"I was turned over my father's knee many times for my stubborn ways," she admitted.

Richard chuckled. "Somehow that doesn't surprise me."

She tossed her head. "As well it shouldn't."

The kitchen fell silent for a few moments.

"Ye're right about lettin' boys be boys," Meggie said. "I'm always afraid somethin'll happen to Ian. Somethin' did once. Since then I don't like lettin' him out of my sight. To see him fightin', actually *fightin'* with another boy! Why, Michael might've hurt him!"

"In Russell's words, Ian 'whupped' him."

"Shoo! To think Ian could do somethin' like that!" Meg clearly grew more surprised the more she considered the skirmish between the two boys. She sighed. "I know, he's a lad."

Richard nodded. "A bloody nose . . . getting one is part of growing up."

Meggie sighed. "I'm protective, I know it. Mrs. Hutchins is always tellin' me I'm *overly* protective. I don't want Ian to ever dread the sight of me."

"He has at least once already," Richard said. "When you picked up that switch today. I've never seen a boy look so relieved as Ian when you went after Tim instead of him."

"Hah! That must've been a funny sight. How'd ye keep from laughin'?"

"I didn't."

She shook her head at him. A moment later, she sobered again. "I've reason to be protective, too. Once some soldiers bullied Ian into tellin' where we hid some of the animals. Ian felt bad about tellin', but what was he to do?"

"A boy his size, faced with a man—"

"Men," she corrected, going to the table. "An' Ian was smaller at the time, nearly two years younger than now. The Kentucky Guard needed food, an' they meant to have it. Why, Ian might die of fright alone if another soldier ever takes hold of him." Meggie propped one jar between her elbow and side and picked up two more, one in each hand.

Speaking of soldiers, he should ask her about the grave.

He didn't want to right now. These were some of the most peaceful moments he and Meggie had shared. He didn't want to ruin them.

"Have you been eating those berries?" Richard asked, eyeing her mouth, curiosity getting the better of him as he changed the subject. He didn't like dwelling on the war, on the atrocities that had happened during it. It was over, and everyone had to go on. Southerners weren't the only ones piecing their lives back together. Certainly they were rebuilding their homes and businesses . . . entire cities. But in the end, Northerners and Southerners alike had suffered, physically and emotionally. Some families were in ruin. While their men were gone, no one had taken care of the farms, businesses, finances . . . Richard knew men who had enlisted in order to have Union pay to help support their families. The pay had been slow in coming, however, and in the meantime, the families had lost everything to banks and other creditors.

Meg wiped at her jaw on both sides. "I have it on me?"

Grinning, Richard stepped forward, toward the stove— and Meggie. "No. Your lips are stained."

She put the jars down on the table. "Probably my entire mouth," she said, wiping at it. "An' it's surely other places.

It's never just on my lips." She meant the juice from the berries, the stains it usually left.

"Let's see. Look at me." Richard tipped his head this way and that way, trying to find evidence on the sides of Meg's face and under her jaw. She tipped her head, too, helping him with the inspection.

"Only one other place," he said finally.

"Where?"

"Be still."

With the tip of his right index finger, he began wiping at one corner of her mouth.

Meggie flinched, stepping back, nearing the stove again.

Richard shook his head at her. "Think about it. If I wanted to hurt you, wouldn't I have tried this afternoon while we were alone in the woods?"

She stared at him.

"Pretty eyes, pretty hair, a pretty smile . . . Gone right now. But something tells me it's a common occurrence when nothing's bothering you, Meggie McBride."

He wiped at the smudge again. This time she stood still.

"Ye don't call me Mrs. McBride anymore," she said.

"You do seem more comfortable with that." Richard frowned. "How long ago did you have a taste of that jam? This is dried on." He grabbed a damp cloth from the table and used one corner of it to wipe at her mouth. "You're comfortable with Mrs. McBride because it keeps distance between us."

"Not such a terrible thing. That's what ye wanted . . . remember?"

Had she become breathless? He thought she had.

"I remember," he said, his voice lower now. "You tell yourself the distance is not such a terrible thing. As if you're trying to convince yourself, Meggie."

He let his thumb slip around the cloth to touch her lower lip, to graze it . . . to tease her. Being close to him could be nice, as he had proven during that waltz. He meant to prove it to her again. Meg was so determined to feel uncomfortable with him, to keep a safe distance between them . . . that it drove him mad.

She nearly jumped out of her skin.

He calmed her with a slow shake of his head. "You know enough about me by now to know I mean you no harm, Meggie McBride. Is it good?"

Her eyes flared. "What?"

He fought laughter. She thought he was talking about his touch. "The jam."

"Aye. I make the best this side of the Ohio." She withdrew a little. "Ye're finished?"

"No. Meggie, you're skittish. Don't be afraid of me. You have no reason to be."

She tipped her head. "I'm not afraid." Say anything to her that even remotely sounded like a challenge, and she'd rise to the occasion. The defiance so inherent to this Irish girl was back in her eyes.

"Yes you are."

"Ye could get as close as ye wanted, an' I wouldn't be afraid."

"Really?" he queried, his voice suggestive. Her stubbornness, her rebellious nature was making her forget that as recently as this afternoon, she hadn't wanted him close to her. She hadn't even wanted to be on the same horse as he. "Now, Meggie, you know that's not true."

Her head tipped a little more. Her eyes narrowed. Her face . . . her lips were turned up to him. He stared down at them, feeling a twinge of the hunger he'd felt several times since meeting her, a hunger he'd not felt in several years.

Their eyes met, and he fought the urge to pull her close, to wrap his arms around her and feel the warmth and the excitement of her. He had to take this slowly. Meggie was indeed skittish, as skittish as Caith when Richard had first approached the horse. Her pride might not let her turn tail and run, but she would want to if he went too fast.

Right now, she was fine, warming to him. He had enough experience with the opposite sex to know that the haze settling in her eyes meant she wasn't as indifferent to him as she pretended. Or as cold.

Should he pursue that look? Investigate it?

In the back of his mind was the thought that he could get

entangled with Meggie, seriously entangled. He liked her far too much. And he wasn't sure he wanted such an entanglement; he had unfinished business in Ohio.

She hadn't responded to his last comment.

He lifted his other hand to her face, slow and easy so she wouldn't spook. Her hair tickled the back of his hand as his fingers touched her jaw, then dropped to her neck.

She felt incredibly good to touch.

Too good.

His plan was to have her come willingly into his arms, then he'd tell her that he knew about her scheme, about the fact that she'd laced his whiskey with her potion with the hope that he'd fall madly in love with Ingrim.

But he had to be careful, more careful than he'd ever been.

Meggie looked good and felt good, and if he weren't cautious he might really end up smitten.

11

*M*EGGIE SWALLOWED.

God, oh God, what was he doing? Touching her so, taunting her so, tempting her so. He'd been kind this afternoon, and that had melted her cold heart some. Now here he was again, conversing with her, being sweet on top of kind, teasing lightheartedly about the jam she'd tasted and the evidence the taste had left on the side of her mouth. Wiping at the dried jam and looking down into her eyes. Obviously wanting her.

Thawing her resolve, that's what he was doing.

The potion was still working on her. She had to find a way to stop it. There had to be a remedy. Something.

He'd become serious. That, and the way he looked down at her made Meg realize he meant to kiss her. Any minute now, any second . . . Oh, Lord. Although her mind chanted that she ought to break away and flee out the back door, she had no intention of doing so. She didn't have the willpower to do so. She looked at his lips, and she was shocked at the thought that she wanted to feel them on hers.

Their eyes meeting, that's what had done it. She had known exactly what he wanted as soon as her gaze met his, and she didn't doubt that he knew he crumbled her last shred of resistance when he stared down at her and then brought his hand up to touch her jaw and neck. The man had done this sort of thing before, touched women, courted them, romanced them right into his arms. She wasn't immune to his charm. She came alive whenever he neared her. Her every muscle tingled, her breath came faster, and her heart jumped and hammered.

Yet she *shouldn't* feel this way. How could she when she loved another man . . . her husband?

She winced at the thought.

"Don't, Meggie," Richard whispered. "No guilt."

She started. Saints, the man had read her mind. At her wince, he'd known exactly what she was thinking. He was good. He was very good.

His head dropped down closer to hers, slowly, and then slower still. Meg thought she would die with wanting him to kiss her. She knew he was going to. She knew she wanted him to. So why was he taking such a blasted long time about doing it?

"For God's sake, kiss me," she said.

He laughed. "Meggie."

She stomped her foot. "Well, ye're teasin' me!"

"No. Only trying to take it slowly."

"Ye go slower, we'll see the turn of the century b'fore the deed's done."

He was still grinning. "That jam should be good and done by then."

Meg turned her head slightly, nuzzling his hand, wanting him to turn serious again. Never mind the bubbling jam behind her. Never mind anything. He'd made her believe he was going to kiss her, and now she meant to make certain he did.

He sobered. It didn't take much.

His hand slid up, into her hair, behind her ear, taunting the back of her neck, pressing her closer to him. And finally, oh finally, his lips touched hers, lightly and sweetly.

Then he lifted his head and studied her.

He brushed the hair away from her face, touched it as if in awe, murmured that it was the softest thing he'd ever felt.

Meggie melted more.

Her gaze went to the vee of his shirt, where his chest hair grew in abundance, curling and peeking out. His shirtsleeves were full, the linen resting lightly on his broad shoulders. So far she'd not touched him except to welcome his kiss.

She lifted her hands to his upper arms, felt the strength of him, became all the more excited. She was sometimes too bold for her own good.

Her heart was still loyal to Kevin, so what were these feelings engulfing her? Was she just hungry for a man? Wanting to be with one? Wanting to feel desired again? Wanting to be touched and made love to?

Her loyalty to Kevin aside, she'd thought she had moral convictions, having been taught that a man and woman should marry before developing intimate relations.

He dipped his head and kissed her again. More of a kiss this time, his lips lingering on hers. Meggie couldn't help herself; she parted her mouth beneath his, inviting him deeper.

He groaned softly and swayed against her.

So they were both caught up in need. How long had it been for him? She didn't know anything about him, really, only that he was from Ohio, a wounded Union soldier on his way home—and that for some reason he was in no hurry to get there.

His tongue slipped into her mouth, caught hers, tangled with it, danced with it.

Meg opened wider to him, and she heard the low whimper that escaped her. Sweetness . . . Lord, had she ever tasted such sweetness? Had she ever felt such growing need? He was a virtual stranger who had helped her find her son today, a stranger she had not liked or trusted. Yet she felt consumed with want for him. Scared that, after drinking that potion, he might want more than she did—namely marriage. But even that didn't stop her from sharing this intimacy with him.

Richard had never expected Meggie to melt so easily in his arms, to become so ready and willing to let him touch her and kiss her. He tangled his hands in her hair, drank the

nectar of her mouth, stepped closer to her. He dipped and
touched his hips to hers.

She made that sound again, that low whimper in the back
of her throat that threatened to drive him mad, that fed his
desire. Fiery, passionate Meggie . . . he didn't know why
her coming so alive in his arms surprised him.

This little interlude was going further than he'd planned.
He had no desire to stop it.

He traced her lips with his tongue, caressed her neck,
lowered his head to taste it, to explore the soft heat. More
whimpers came from Meg, and she tilted her head back,
giving him full access, wanting his kisses and touches.

She stiffened suddenly and glanced around. "Something's
burning."

Richard couldn't help himself: "I know."

She rolled her eyes. Then she yelped and batted at
something behind her.

When Richard saw the flames licking at her apron strings,
he thought he'd split his belly laughing.

Meggie grabbed the damp towel he'd used to wipe the
corner of her mouth and she batted at the flames, turning
around and around.

Richard strode over to the water pitcher and grabbed it.
Seconds later he'd soaked the back of Meg's skirt, putting
out the fire.

"Too bad," he said, looking at the charred strings.

"What?" she demanded, hands on her hips. "That my
apron caught on fire? It's not so important to me. I'd rather
it was the apron than—"

"No, too bad the fire's been put out."

It took her a second to grasp his meaning. Her face
flamed. She turned away, her hands catching the edge of the
table as she fought for composure.

"Has it, Meggie?"

She laughed a little, not genuine laughter. Nervous
laughter more than anything.

The ribbon that had bound her hair in the back had
loosened, slipping down through her curls, trying to work its

way to the end. Richard helped it along, reaching out and
tugging it loose, setting Meg's hair free.

She glanced at him, the shyness and embarrassment of a
first encounter in her eyes. The look was unlike her, but he
found it stimulating regardless. A new side of Meggie
McBride.

He fluffed her hair, enjoying the feel of it. She didn't
flinch from the touch. God, how pretty she was . . . her
tiny nose, her long lashes, her strong jaw, both sides
meeting in a perfectly rounded chin . . . Her eyes, so deep
when she glanced up at him, a hazy green, restraining her
passionate nature.

"Tend your jam, Meggie," he said softly. "If you take a
notion to seek me out when you finish, you know where to
find me."

She caught and held her breath. He swore she did.

One last caress of her hair, and then Richard mustered
willpower and limped toward the door. At some point
during those intimate moments, he'd meant to tell her that
he knew about her scheme. He'd missed that chance. He
ought to tell her now.

He couldn't. He wouldn't. He wanted Meg in his arms.
Telling her he knew about the potion and that he'd been
playing her for a fool would make her hit the roof, perhaps
make her explode as no one had ever seen her explode. He
didn't want that to happen—at least not tonight.

Meg felt both relieved and regretful when he left the
kitchen. She could think more clearly, or at least try to.

She sank down onto a stool beside the back door,
gathered her apron in her hands, and lowered her flaming
face onto it. She was like a freshly lit candle in Richard
Foster's arms. What the blazes was the matter with her?

Untouched for too long. Her body was feeling deprived,
that was all.

She was capable of more self-control than that.

That potion had worked well, too well. Why had that
foolish Ingrim overslept? And then she'd left without even
fussing about the lieutenant not falling for her, about the

potion not working. She'd wanted so much for him to like her, to become sweet on her, but she'd left without making much of a play for his affection. Of course, by that time he'd had his sights set on Meggie.

Meg managed to finish the jam. She poured the bubbling berry liquid into jars and left them sitting on the table so the jam would settle overnight.

She wondered if she should even try to go upstairs. Would the lieutenant be waiting for her? Expecting her in his room?

Shoo! Wasn't he full of himself? Thinking he could kiss her a few times and she'd be eager in his arms. Eager to tumble around the bed with him!

As much as she'd enjoyed his kisses, she didn't like the thought that he assumed he had her in the bag. One day last summer Ian and his friends had somehow bagged a squirrel and brought it home for dinner. Well, she had more fight in her than that squirrel, and she didn't intend to be anyone's dinner—or late-night treat.

She had a little something in mind that would deflate Richard Foster's swollen ego. It would give her a good laugh, too—and it might just make him angry enough to pack his things, tuck his tail between his legs, and take the ferry across the river to his home state.

He might not even wait on the ferry, Meggie thought, giggling to herself.

She covered the jars to keep flies out of the jam, then she grabbed her cloak from where it hung on a peg near the door.

She giggled again as she stole out into the night, intent on visiting Mabel Vail. Mabel was sixty-something years old. She'd been widowed for some ten years now, and she loved a good prank. She was also a friend of Meg's. Meggie meant to promise Mabel several jars of the blackberry jam in exchange for her help. But she knew Mabel would offer her services whether or not she promised the jam.

Upstairs, Richard still couldn't sleep. Now, instead of being haunted by war memories, he lay awake waiting for Meggie, almost hoping she wouldn't come.

He'd light the lantern and talk to her if she did, explain that he hadn't meant for things to go so far, that he was even ashamed of himself that he'd extended such an invitation to her.

What had he been thinking? Not about the fact that one of these days he'd leave the inn and go home, and where would that leave Meggie? She wasn't a harlot; she wasn't a woman a man might sleep with and then leave.

Matters had gotten out of hand down there in the kitchen.

He thought about her apron strings catching on fire, and he had another good laugh. "Something's burning," she'd said, not intending a double entendre. It had been the best laugh he'd had in a long time, and that included the laugh he'd had this afternoon when she'd gone after Tim Willard with her switch.

Meggie . . . who knew what to expect out of her next? If she didn't find mischief, mischief found her.

He tossed more. He got up and smoked a cheroot. He drank a glass of water. He went back to bed and couldn't get comfortable. He listened for her boots in the hallway.

She wasn't coming.

He felt relieved—and yet disappointed. Not that he had any intention of taking her into his bed now that he'd put some distance between them and had had time to consider the matter, to ponder it.

He somehow managed to drift off. Then the squeak of the door hinges startled him wide awake.

He propped himself up on his elbows, saw a caped figure push the door shut and then turn toward the bed. Even the person's head was covered.

Earlier, Richard had opened one set of shutters, allowing moonlight and a cooling breeze into the room. The figure crossed the room and closed the shutters.

It was Meggie, Richard felt certain. Come to take him up on his offer.

The memory of their heated kisses down in the kitchen made him tingle again. The thought of Meg in his arms, in his bed, responding to his touches and caresses in her passionate way . . . Lord God, how in the world would he muster the strength to explain to her that he didn't want to take advantage of her? How would he turn her away?

"Meggie?" he queried softly as she approached the bed. "Hm?"

God. He twisted, meaning to get up and light the lantern that sat on the desk. Why was she draped in that damn cloak? It wasn't that cool in this room, or anywhere in the entire inn.

She grabbed his arm and pulled him down.

Of course, his resistance was weak. He didn't really want to light the lantern. He didn't really want to talk to her right now. He didn't really want to turn her away. He wanted Meggie McBride in his arms. He wanted her on the bed, beneath him. He wanted to taste her again.

He was naked. He always slept that way when he slept indoors.

She stretched out on the bed beside him and tugged him toward her, whispering his name. He couldn't see well; when she'd closed the shutters, she'd cast the room in darkness, and his eyes hadn't yet adjusted to the change.

But then, he didn't need to see well. He recalled the hazy look to her eyes earlier, her flushed cheeks, her lips, parted in breathlessness, stained by the berries and opening beneath his lips, inviting him. He recalled the silkiness of her hair falling between his fingers, the fact that she'd *wanted* him to kiss her. Her body language and her response had indicated she wanted much more.

Richard remembered all these things from several hours ago, and it suddenly didn't matter that he couldn't actually see Meggie right now. He saw her in his mind, and when he put his hand on the curve of her hip, he felt her.

She whispered his name again, and this time her voice sounded raspy, probably from her state of arousal. She pressed close to him. He spoke her name, feeling a surge of desire, and slid his hand up over the cloak to her breast.

Odd. He'd thought her breasts were fuller, more rounded; he'd expected them to feel firm.

It didn't matter. He dropped his hand down to her buttocks and pulled her hips to his. He meant to get rid of the cloak and anything she wore underneath it as soon as possible.

He pushed the hood from her head, the cloak from her shoulders . . . realized she was naked beneath the garment. God, that excited him all the more. She'd stripped before coming to him, pulling the cloak on for cover until she was safely in his room.

He kissed the corner of her mouth, slid one hand up into her hair, the other up the side of her face.

There he stopped cold.

This wasn't Meggie.

The hair was too thin. The skin was wrinkled. The breath smelled of decay.

A cackle issued from the body pressed against his, and Richard shot up off the bed.

"What the hell . . . ?" he bellowed. "Who the hell are you?"

"Meggie, without the fixin's," the crone said, still laughing. She was sitting up on the bed now, and she'd let the cloak fall away.

Richard fumbled around on the desk. He found the matchbox, and had the lantern lit a few seconds later. It brightened, casting the room in a glow. But the orange flames did little to soften the harshness of the creature that had claimed his bed.

Scraggly gray hair hung well past her drooping shoulders. Her face was mottled and wrinkled, and the skin beneath her chin swayed in loose bags with her every cackle. One blackened tooth occupied the top gum, and the teeth on the bottom were brown and broken and looked as if they might fall out at any time. Her breasts were dried peaches, the pits sunken and shriveled. Her belly hung in layers. Below that . . .

Ugh. He couldn't look lower. He couldn't bring himself to look lower.

"Evenin' there!" she said. "I hear you was wantin' a woman for the night."

"Get out," Richard said evenly. He would kill Meggie. String her up by her ankles from some tree branch and torture her slowly. She was responsible for this. This scheme reeked of Meggie.

The crone cackled more. "Ah, c'mon. We'll have fun. We'll tear this bed up! My, you're looking mighty good. Mighty good to taste!" She licked her lips, feasting on the sight of his nakedness.

Richard grabbed his trousers from the back of the desk chair. "Get out," he said again, this time with more force. He pulled the trousers on.

"If I ain't good 'nough for you, I got friends who'd like t'give it a go. You can take your pick!"

"Get . . . *out*!"

She snapped her flabby lips together. Ugh. To think he'd almost kissed them. The loose skin on her neck swayed back and forth. Richard grabbed the cloak and tossed it at her.

Someone rapped on the door.

"Richard, are ye well?" It was Edan. Richard damn sure didn't want Edan knowing about the old woman in his bed.

She shrugged, then cackled more. "Ain't like I can fly out the window."

If she had a broom, she could. She looked enough like a witch.

"Get that cloak on," Richard ordered her. "I'm all right, Edan."

He spun away, raked his hand through his hair, rubbed his jaw. He had to think this out. How to get her out of here without Edan knowing she was here.

When he turned back, she'd draped the cloak over her shoulders. She also had moved off the bed and made her way to the door.

"Wait," Richard said, starting that way.

Too late. She yanked the door open and greeted Edan with her monstrous grin. His brows shot straight up.

"Mr. McBride!" she croaked. "How are ya this fine night? I'm ready to dance. Had me a good tussle, an' now I'm ready to charge!"

She started down the hall, kicking up her heels in what had to be a jig, singing and going on about what a fine man Edan had staying under his roof.

Several doors opened farther down the hallway. Mrs. Hutchins appeared in her nightcap and gown. Ian poked his head out into the hall, trying to figure out what was going on. And then there was Meggie in her nightdress, slanting Richard a grin. Good thing they weren't alone. He'd take her neck in his hands and . . .

Right now he had to deal with Edan. He had to explain himself and this predicament.

Richard rubbed his jaw. Hell, he wanted to hide his face. "Edan, my apologies," he said rather quietly. "I assure you, I didn't bring her—"

"M'boy, ye have odd taste in women," the man said, loud enough that everyone in the hallway surely heard him. He rubbed his jaw, too, and turned away, shuffling up the passage, mumbling to himself and shaking his head.

"If I were of a mind, I'd demand marriage," the crone told Richard from where she stood near the top of the stairs.

Richard knew he turned as white as freshly fallen snow; he felt his face drain of all color and warmth. He retreated into the bedroom and slammed the door. If there were a bolt, he'd slide it into place.

He heard the crone cackle again. Then Meggie's laughter joined hers, loud, robust, irritating, aggravating, maddening.

Richard tossed himself back down on the bed and stared up at the ceiling.

What would she think of next?

He wouldn't contemplate that. He absolutely would not.

12

HE WOKE BY himself the next morning. The sun had already lightened the sky, but Meggie wasn't singing.

She wasn't in her garden, in fact, when Richard looked down on it. He was stunned. She was always in the garden by this time, tending her plants and singing.

He didn't know how to feel. He could go back to bed and sleep a little later this morning. That was, if Meggie didn't turn up down there in a few minutes and disturb his peace. He didn't even have to close the shutters. He could leave them open, letting the morning air into the room. He could go back to bed without having to toss and turn. He wouldn't have to put a pillow over his head to try and drown out her voice.

He went back to bed. He tossed and turned. He plopped the pillow over his head. Why, he didn't know. There was no voice to drown out.

He rose and closed the shutters, thinking maybe the morning light was bothering him, keeping him from going back to sleep.

He still tossed and turned. He still plopped the pillow over his head.

He missed Meggie's singing.

The realization made him sit up and laugh.

Sure. He missed her singing. The singing that irritated him. The singing that woke him when he'd rather sleep. The singing that made him close the shutters when he'd rather have them open.

Where the hell was she? She was *always* down in her damn garden singing at the same time every morning.

Not that he wanted to see her today. Not that he had any desire to see her. Not after the mischief she'd pulled last night. She'd probably laughed in her sleep, seeing him chase that old crone off, listening to the woman cackle and say she ought to demand marriage.

He'd expected Meggie to be in her garden laughing up at him this morning.

Or at least singing.

He lay back on the tick and made a sound of exasperation in his throat. He couldn't sleep *with* Meg singing, and he couldn't sleep *without* Meg singing.

Damn.

Meg had gone out to the forest to find the buckle she'd hidden from the lieutenant yesterday. She figured finding it and burying it, disposing of it, was more important than tending her garden this morning. Her herbs and plants would miss her, as she would miss them, but she'd slept little last night because she'd worried about retrieving the buckle.

So here she was, pressing through the forest scrub, walking between the pines, maples, and oaks, plucking berries from wild vines and dropping them into her apron pockets, if not popping them into her mouth. She paused to inspect a fascinating bloodroot, its unfolding leaves almost enveloping the plant's milk-white blossoms. Sumac and sassafras grew in clumps, and a nearby spice bush threatened to overpower the blue cohosh and the wild ginger.

She caught sight of a Virginia snakeroot and committed the spot to memory; the roots smelled of camphor and turpentine and could be used in a variety of ways. Then came the river birch that grew, oddly enough, a distance from the water, and Meg knew she was close to the place where she'd dug with a spade for what had seemed like hours and then rolled the dead soldier into the grave.

She shuddered, remembering. She shuddered too at the thought of approaching the grave again.

She neared the clearing. She'd grab the buckle, drop it into her pocket, and leave. No dallying over the spot where she'd buried the man she'd killed.

She stopped cold, staring at the gravesite.

She'd taken great care to pile enough leaves on the area to hide it from detection. But since yesterday, since she and Richard Foster had passed through here, someone had come along and cleared the leaves away. They'd piled rocks on the area, as people did when they wanted to deter animals from digging up a grave. And an animal *had* been digging at the site. She'd noticed that yesterday.

Foolish of her to pile leaves on the site. No grass had grown back.

Who had brushed away the leaves and piled the rocks on the grave? The buckle was gone, too, she quickly noticed.

Meggie's heart pounded.

Was it coincidence that she'd passed by here yesterday with the lieutenant and that today the leaves were gone and the rocks were in place?

Had he noticed her hiding the buckle?

Surely not. He'd been concentrating on tracking the boys. Surely, surely not.

He had to have noticed. Who else would have taken the buckle? And so soon after the incident. Had he come back here after they'd returned to the inn? Or had he come back here last night?

She hadn't seen him much after they'd returned to the inn. She hadn't seen him until suppertime. He'd had time to return and make the changes she had noticed.

Meggie's palms perspired.

If he'd come back here after they had returned to the inn from finding the boys, had he taken the buckle? And if so, if he'd seen her covering it up and he'd gone to the trouble to return for it, why hadn't he questioned her about it? He could have questioned her in the kitchen last night.

But then, he'd had other things on his mind when he found her in the kitchen.

He had the buckle. She felt certain of that.

He must have suspicions, too; questions. One being why would she hide what was obviously a Union buckle?

If he'd figured out that this was a grave . . .

The stones piled on it suggested that he had. And if he'd guessed, because of the buckle, that a Union soldier was buried here, then the stones also suggested he must feel loyalty toward the dead man. Which meant he'd question her sooner or later.

Maybe she'd spot the buckle the next time she cleaned his room. But even if she took it, he might still question her. In fact, the buckle suddenly disappearing might make him question her all the more.

Saints. She was in a lot of trouble.

Provided he was the one who had taken the buckle and piled the stones here. She might be letting her mind run away with her. Perhaps she was jumping to conclusions. Perhaps someone else had taken the buckle and piled the stones on the grave.

In the back of her mind, Meggie knew she was kidding herself. *Richard* had found the buckle. *Richard* had piled the stones on the grave.

She didn't walk back to the inn as spryly as she'd come here. On the way to the site, she'd skipped, she'd sung, she'd taken time to admire the dewdrops on the leaves and the grass. Now she twisted one corner of her apron. Her eyes took in the entire forest, but her mind was on the grave and the soldier buried there; it was on the lieutenant and that buckle, on the fact that he'd surely piled the stones and had suspicions.

She'd have to lie if he asked her about the grave and the buckle. She'd have to pretend innocence. If he told her he'd seen her hide the buckle in the leaves, she'd have to look him straight in the eye and tell him she'd done no such thing, that he must have imagined seeing her do it.

Would he leave things at that?

Probably not. He already was spitting angry with her for

the trick she'd pulled last night. He was probably glad for a reason to cause her trouble.

Meg laughed as she thought of Mabel coming out of his room. Mabel, in only the cloak, her hair stringy and wild, and Richard standing in the doorway, a stricken look on his face. Mabel saying she ought to demand marriage, and Richard unable to slam the door fast enough. Edan looking at both of them as if they were mad. Well, he already knew Mabel was. But now he surely thought the lieutenant was also. Hah.

Her mirth lasted for only a few minutes. The thought of Richard finding that buckle, perhaps guessing that it belonged to a soldier, and then realizing that the site was a grave, was too serious a matter for Meg to laugh over anything for long.

Instead of going back to the inn right away, she went to Kevin's grave. She plucked weeds away from the small headstone Edan had made to go here, and she sat on the grass beside her husband. She told him how big Ian had become and how much stronger he was since the accident. She'd already told him about shooting and burying the soldier—she'd told him that when it happened. Now she told him she feared that what she'd done had been discovered. If it had, and the lieutenant intended to cause her trouble, she might have to take Ian and go away.

She shed a few tears over that. This was home. Her husband was buried here, and she didn't want to stray far from him.

"I wish it had been yer arms around me yesterday, love," she whispered. "Yer lips on mine."

What a glorious life they might have had together if he hadn't had such an adventurous spirit, if he hadn't felt such a need to join the fighting.

Meggie stretched out in the morning sunlight beside her husband. The grass was damp, but she didn't care. She thought of being in Richard's arms last night, and because of that she wondered if she had the right to be here, to lie beside Kevin like this. She had betrayed him, dishonored the vows they had spoken.

Stillness and quiet pervaded the morning and the hilltop.

She still loved him. She might always love him. As long as that was so, she couldn't allow herself to feel excitement in the arms of another man.

But the truth was, she already had. She'd wanted Richard to kiss her. She'd wanted to feel his hands in her hair and on her skin.

Brazen woman.

Disloyal wife.

She shouldn't be lying beside her husband, thinking of another man.

She rolled over on the grass and propped her chin in her hands.

She couldn't shake the thought that the lieutenant had made her feel utterly desired.

At the inn, Richard was reluctant to go downstairs and get breakfast. Mrs. Hutchins had come out into the hallway last night when that old witch had burst out of his room, and surely she either would be laughing at him this morning or slanting him curious looks, barely restraining the desire to ask questions.

He wondered again where Meggie was, why she wasn't in her garden, then he headed downstairs.

There was Mrs. Hutchins, ready with a cup of coffee for him, as usual, looking at him with a twinkle in her eye as if she might burst out laughing.

"Thank you," Richard mumbled, taking the mug from her.

"You're mighty welcome. What I wanna know is—"

"I don't want to talk about it."

"Of course you don't. But you know we're all curious to know how—"

"Mrs. Hutchins."

"All right. I won't ask." She was still smirking when she turned away. "Have a seat. I'll get breakfast."

He did. For some reason the coffee tasted uncommonly good this morning. He drained the mug and rose to pour himself more coffee. Mrs. Hutchins spread bacon in a skillet.

"Have you seen Meggie this morning?" he asked.

"Sure I have."

"Would you mind telling me where she is?"

She cast him a curious look.

"I have a matter to discuss with her," he said and did not intend to elaborate.

"I bet you do, and I bet it has something to do with—"

"Mrs. Hutchins . . . *Meggie.*"

She jerked her head to the right. "On her hilltop."

Richard considered that. "At her husband's grave?"

The woman nodded.

That explained why Meg hadn't been in her garden.

It struck Richard wrong that she should be at her husband's grave this morning after they had been in each other's arms last night. What was she doing? Sitting on that hilltop feeling guilty? Her husband was dead, for the love of God. Dead and buried. While part of Meggie might always love him, she was now a widow, a single woman. She shouldn't feel guilty about the fact that she'd enjoyed herself in another man's arms. And she *had* enjoyed herself. Richard had no doubt about that.

"You can see the hilltop from here," Mrs. Hutchins said.

Richard finished pouring the coffee and returned to the table.

"The soldiers who came here with trouble in mind . . ." he said, wanting to see her reaction to what he was about to say. "Did anyone ever threaten them if they didn't leave?"

She put the skillet on the stove. "Megan did, plenty enough times. They usually laughed at her, like they didn't take her seriously. They didn't know Meg's temper. They didn't realize Meg would have shot them in their sleep rather than look at them. Took her a while to get to that point, mind you. Meg doesn't go around waving weapons and threatening people over just anything. She gets protective when someone or something threatens the lives of the people she loves."

"They always left peacefully?" Lord God, his mind

imagined a dozen or more graves dug in different places in the forest, all by Meggie's hand. *Meg would have shot them in their sleep rather than look at them.*

Mrs. Hutchins gave a sharp laugh, one of bitterness. "Left with their packs and horses heavy with our food and supplies. Usually some of our animals tied behind the horses, too. Funny thing . . . one time, oh, just months ago, a soldier took several hogs. They came wandering back the next day. Meggie was hot about him taking those pigs. Edan said she must have said a prayer that the gates of hell would open and swallow that man—Edan found the soldier's horse grazing in the forest a few days later. No sign of that soldier anywhere."

That arrested Richard's attention. "Did any other incidents like that ever happen?"

Mrs. Hutchins thought for a moment. Then she shook her head. "Not that I recall."

"Do you recall things well?"

That drew a sharp look from her. "I'm not as old as I look. My mind's sharp. I recall things pretty well."

He sipped coffee. A few more moments passed.

"You ask me, Meg should move on. She should stop feeling like she still needs to devote herself to Kevin. He went off to fight the war. He knew what he was doing. Now he's dead, and Meg's still young and pretty. She ought to find her a good man and marry again, that's what she ought to do."

A faint smile turned up the corners of Richard's mouth. "I'm sure you're right, Mrs. Hutchins. I'm also sure Meggie's capable of making that decision for herself. When she's ready."

"At the rate she's going, she might never be ready," the woman complained, cracking eggs over the skillet.

True, Richard thought. Just as if he might never be ready to go home.

After breakfast, he went to feed and brush Caith.

He saddled and rode the horse along the riverbank for a time. Then they rode through the forest, and Richard turned Caith in the direction of the grave. It still troubled him. It would until he questioned Meggie about it. It might do so even after that, depending on the circumstances surrounding the man's death. And then there was the gnawing question of whether she'd killed other soldiers and buried them in the forest.

He and Caith rode between the many trees, and Richard realized he was searching the ground for evidence of other graves.

He found none. Thank God.

He returned to the inn around mid-afternoon. Ian was fishing a short distance from the ferry, and when Richard approached, the boy complained that nothing was biting.

"The ferry stirs the water and frightens the fish," Richard said, dismounting. "You won't catch much this close to it."

Ian pouted. "Mum won't let me go off downriver. Grandpop'd take me, if he weren't busy helpin' Mr. Sardis clean the deer they shot this mornin'. No one has time for fishin'"

"I do."

Ian squinted against the sun. "Mum might not let me go with ye."

"Where is she?"

"Back o' the inn, makin' butter."

"I'll go talk to her."

Ian scowled. "She'll not be lettin' me go. Grandpop calls her stubborn."

"She's definitely that," Richard said, chuckling. "I'll talk to her and see what happens." He eyed the tin can that sat beside the boy on the grass. Ian had covered it with a cloth. "What's in the can? Bait?"

Ian's head bobbed. "Crickets. Grandpop made me hooks. They catch the fish. When there's fish."

Richard nodded. "I'll be back."

Ian sighed and went back to studying his fishing stick.

Out back of the inn, Meg was leaning over a butter churn, stirring with the big handle, mixing what was probably cream. A yellow ribbon secured her hair in the back, but as usual, curls escaped around her face. Her face itself was flushed, and the hair falling around it was damp with perspiration.

She started when she spotted Richard. She looked ready to run inside.

"Mrs. Hutchins's skirt isn't big enough to hide you if I want to find you," he told her, fighting laughter. "No one's would be. Settle down."

"Don't ye be touchin' me, Richard Foster," she warned, eyeing him.

"We both know you liked the way I touched you, Meggie." Angry with her as he still was, the act was still on; he was still supposed to be under the spell of her potion.

Her scowl deepened. "I didn't."

"Don't lie to yourself," he said. "You spent the morning up at your husband's grave, feeling guilty. That doesn't change the fact that you liked being with me."

"Shoo! Aren't ye a conceited fool!"

"You liked being with me enough that you elected to send someone else in your place."

She drew back slightly. "Why would I do that if I liked bein' with ye?"

"Because you were *scared* of liking it. Scared that being with me might make you forget your husband for a while." He hadn't come here with the intent of provoking her, and he had to stop before he made her too angry. Before she refused to let Ian go fishing with him because she was angry with him.

"Nothin' could make me forget him," she whispered, paling.

"Meggie, you're young and pretty, and he's dead." Richard's voice had turned soft, almost tender.

She glanced away, and he was glad she did. He didn't want to see her eyes glass over, as if she fought tears. But he already had, and the strong urge to enfold her in his arms and hold her surprised him.

He cleared his throat. "I'd like to take Ian fishing."

She went back to churning. "He's already fishin'."

"He won't catch anything, fishing by the ferry."

"That's as far as I'll be allowin' him to go."

"He'll be safe with me, Meggie."

She stopped working and fixed an impatient stare on him. "When will ye be leavin'?"

That made him laugh in disbelief. She wouldn't even pretend to be polite. "I don't know. Meanwhile, let me take Ian fishing somewhere where he'll catch something."

She went back to churning. She stopped again, sighed, fastened another impatient look on him. "Leave soon. Tell me ye will."

"No."

She leaned against the churn handle. "Ye don't really like me." Shaking her head, she glanced up at him. "I've somethin' to tell ye. Somethin' that'll make ye look the other way."

"Really?" he queried. Was she about to tell him she had killed the Union soldier and buried him in the woods? Did she want to destroy her character in his eyes? He'd found no evidence of other graves, and he strongly suspected that if Meg had killed the soldier, she'd done so to retrieve the food—the inn's last two hogs—the man had stolen from her family and friends.

"The night I drank with ye an' Poppa . . . I put somethin' in yer drink. Somethin' to make ye fall in love with the first person ye saw upon wakin'," she said. She released the churn handle and stood twisting one corner of her apron. "I thought that'd be Ingrim. But the fool girl overslept. Then I was singin' in my garden, an' there ye were suddenly at the window, an'—"

"You were the first person I saw upon waking," Richard said, careful to flavor his voice with surprise. "Thank God Edan and I didn't pass out. *He* might have been the first person I saw upon waking."

He battled a grin. He battled laughter. Nice to see Meggie meek and regretful for once.

"So ye're not really as sweet on me as ye feel," she said, watching him. "It's the potion workin'."

He widened his eyes. "You mean I don't really feel like chasing you around that churn? I don't want to catch you and kiss you?"

She shook her head nervously, a series of jerks as her face reddened. "No."

He edged closer to her. "And I didn't really want to invite you up to my room last evening?"

More jerks. She stepped back.

"I didn't really enjoy our kisses in the kitchen?"

"No," she said, her voice lower now, trembling a little.

"I didn't really enjoy the softness of your skin?"

Another step back. "Lieutenant . . ."

"The silkiness of your hair?"

"'Tis the potion, that's all."

"The sweetness of your lips?"

"No! None of those things! 'Twas all the potion workin' on ye."

He didn't plan to let her off so easily. She had played several tricks on him now, and he meant to follow through with his own.

He grabbed her arm and pulled her close to him. She gasped and stared up at him.

"I beg to differ with you, Meggie McBride," he said, his voice low. "This urge I feel to kiss you right now is real." It was, too. Very real. "But, since it's broad daylight and anyone could be watching, I'll wait. I'll take Ian fishing and save the kiss for later."

He let go of her arm. She scrambled to the other side of her butter churn.

"What've I done?" she whispered, and Richard fought a wide grin.

He turned away to walk off. Then he thought of something else and he turned back. "Thank you for not singing beneath my window this morning."

He had taken four steps toward the side of the inn when her voice reached him: "I wasn't feelin' well this mornin', Lieutenant. T'morrow I'll be back, for certain."

He smiled. Good. He had missed her lilting songs, the sound of her fussing at her plants, telling one it was overpowering another.

13

$\mathcal{R}$ICHARD AND IAN went downriver, found a suitable spot, and there Richard fashioned himself a pole.

They caught more crickets, hooked them on their lines, and within only a few hours, they had snared a bucketful of fish. Ian was delighted, bright-eyed and hobbling as fast as he could back to the inn to tell his grandfather and everyone else the news.

Edan caught the boy up in his arms and swung him around, telling him how proud he was. He and Mr. Sardis were hanging salted venison in the smokehouse not far from the stable. Edan gave Richard a curious look, and Richard immediately knew the man was still wondering about the old woman in Richard's room last night.

"I won't talk about it," Richard warned Edan.

Grinning, Edan said, "Wasn't plannin' to ask."

"You'd like to."

"Aye. Strange taste in women, indeed."

"You know my taste in women had nothing to do with it."

Edan scratched his temple. "Thought ye wouldn't talk about it."

Richard shot Edan a playful glare, then went off to fetch several stools from the barn.

When he returned with the stools, he and Ian sat and

cleaned the fish. Afterward they took them to Mrs. Hutchins, who later breaded and fried them.

During the rest of the afternoon and early evening, Richard helped Edan split more wood and start building another hog pen. He occasionally caught Edan grinning at him, and once Richard tossed a stick at the man. When he thought of touching that old woman, of almost . . . If he'd been drinking, if he'd been drunk, he might never have realized she wasn't Meggie. God help him.

"Marriage, eh?" Edan said at one point.

"My hammer might decide to slip," Richard warned.

Edan cackled as he scampered off to get more boards.

He held his tongue over supper that evening, thank God. But he couldn't seem to wipe the grin off his face.

Richard suffered through the grin for a time, then he decided to laugh at himself along with Edan. He imagined the sight of that witch coming out of his room and him standing in the doorway with his hair tousled and a look of shock and fright on his face *had* been funny. Now that he was over the initial surprise and outrage of the incident, he saw the humor in it.

Meggie was tense. She hardly ate a bite. She kept looking at Richard when he knew she thought he wasn't looking. He had her believing he really thought the potion had nothing to do with how he felt about her. He imagined Meg would sing tomorrow morning, and loudly, too.

She did.

Meg sang at the top of her lungs. She didn't care if she woke everyone in the inn. She sang so loudly that Ryan Darrow, the ferrymaster, came over to tell her she could be heard clear across the river. He didn't mind. Hardly a soul did. He just thought it was amazing that her voice was so pretty and carried so far.

She had just plowed into her fourth round of song when Richard threw his shutters wide and perched himself on his windowsill. Meggie thought about glaring up at him. Instead, she continued singing. Poor, poor man. Couldn't sleep. He'd surely leave soon, if for no other reason than to have undisturbed rest.

He didn't go away. He sat on the windowsill the entire time she tended her garden, irritating Meg, making her wonder what was wrong with him. He didn't like her singing. It normally made him grouchy. He didn't like to be awakened early.

This morning he didn't seem to mind.

There had to be some remedy that would cancel the effect of the extract. This evening, Meggie meant to study her mother's notes again.

She and Ian had missed going into Havershill the afternoon he disappeared with his friends. So shortly after the noon ferry started across the Ohio, Meggie brought the wagon from the barn and hitched the horses. She'd take Ian with her to help gather supplies from Mr. Dickson's store, and they'd be home again by mid-afternoon.

"Let me help with that," the lieutenant said, taking the harnesses out of her hands.

The initial surprise of having him take over made Meggie freeze for a minute. He was slipping the harness on the first horse when she snatched the leather back.

"I'll manage fine by m'self, thank ye," she said smartly.

He made a sound of exasperation in his throat. "Stubborn Meg McBride. All right. You do that one, and I'll do the other one."

"I'll do them *both* m'self."

"Meggie."

Irritating man. She wished he'd go away. She spun and faced him. "When did I give ye permission to call me anything but Mrs. McBride?"

His eyes narrowed. "I didn't ask for your permission."

Rudeness on top of his other aggravating traits. Meg glared at him, then went back to harnessing the horses.

"I'm going to town with you," he said, walking around the animals and slipping a bit into the mouth of one.

Meggie stopped what she was doing and leaned her head against the neck of the horse closest to her. She closed her eyes. Could she *wish* the lieutenant away? *Think* him away?

She raised her head and met his gaze across the horses. Such striking blue eyes . . . why did he have such striking blue eyes? "Is there something ye're needin' from town? If so, I'll be glad to get it for ye."

"No. Mrs. Hutchins told me you had a long list of needed supplies, so I thought I would offer to help."

Such sweetness. First tracking Ian and those boys the way he had, then fishing with Ian, putting the biggest smile on her son's face she'd seen in a long while. Letting Ian name his horse . . . helping Edan with odd jobs . . . sharing conversation with Mrs. Hutchins almost every day. While the lieutenant had no way of knowing, the latter helped Mrs. Hutchins. She looked fondly upon him, as fondly as she'd looked upon her own son and upon Kevin; that and the fact that Richard Foster was a Union soldier like her Zachary helped fill the void Meggie suspected the woman felt, an emptiness left by the fact that Zachary had not yet come home.

Why did he have to be so sweet?

"I'm not needin' help," Meg told him.

He studied her. Then he asked softly, "How long will you be content to lie beside Kevin on that hilltop, Meggie? He's dead and buried."

She felt the color drain from her face. She drew a deep breath. "Forever."

"Not contentedly."

Her eyes began to burn. Weakness. How she hated it in herself. She didn't have time for it, just as her mother hadn't had time for it. She had no *tolerance* for it. This was the second time she had almost cried in front of the lieutenant. She wouldn't do it.

He walked around the horses, and Meggie never had a chance to realize what he intended to do. He lifted a hand and caressed her cheek.

Was the man never predictable? She had expected fighting anger from him today over the incident involving Mabel night before last. And when he'd left the horse a minute ago, she'd expected him to stalk off in a temper. Instead, he was being sweet again.

She knew she ought to step away from him, away from his touch. But it felt so good, so warm and comforting, so reassuring. She leaned into the touch just as he pulled away.

Surprise flickered in his eyes that she had intended to let him continue the caress. Seconds later he walked away, approaching the front entrance of the inn.

She sensed a good man in Richard Foster. A decent man, one filled with integrity and honor, one who would devote himself to the important people and friends in his life. She liked him entirely too much.

She wouldn't involve herself with him. Like all guests at McBride's, he'd travel on one day. There also was the matter of the buckle. And then there was still Kevin . . .

"How long will you be content . . . ?"

She wasn't content. He was right about that. She ached. She'd come alive in the lieutenant's arms the night before last, and part of her was beginning to want to take Mrs. Hutchins's advice, to take the advice offered by almost every close friend and family member: that she should go on with her life.

She'd hurt Richard's feelings by not allowing him to help her with the horses or to go to Havershill with her. Part of her felt bad about that. But another part of her felt it was the best thing. Perhaps it might help dissuade him from perching on the window ledge tomorrow morning and staring down at her with lovesick eyes.

He still did. He perched on the sill every morning for the next two weeks, leaning against the frame, sometimes trying to engage her in conversation. He never failed to tell her how pretty she was, how her hair glowed like copper in the soft sunlight, how she tended her plants with more gentleness and compassion than he had ever seen.

More guests stopped at McBride's, a variety of people with different destinations. Some arrived in the afternoon, shared the evening meal, then traveled on the following morning. Edan played the harmonica, and he often entertained their guests with his instrument. Some travelers arrived late at night, and, as always, Meggie rose to turn down beds for them. Hours later, Mrs. Hutchins greeted them with breakfast.

Richard had taken to doing odd jobs around the inn, and he could be found in the study most evenings, talking to Edan and looking over the ledgers with him. He seemed to be settling in at McBride's, Edan seemed to enjoy having him about, and both things troubled Meggie: If Richard became too comfortable here, would he ever go home? And why didn't Edan encourage him to go home? From the bits of their conversation she overheard one evening, she gathered that Edan and Richard had worked out some sort of arrangement, that Richard was helping with tasks to work off his boarding fees.

On the days Meg brought the children together for their lessons on the grounds in front of the inn, she was aware of Richard watching her from the riverbank. Later she always grumbled at him that she didn't know why he elected to watch her and the children all afternoon instead of the water the way he still did much of the time.

She didn't understand him—why he stayed, why he didn't go home. Summer would pass; in fact, July would soon blaze into August. Just how long did he intend to stay here? She put the question to him several times, and he never answered her.

She'd cleaned his room every day since Edan scolded her about not doing so. She usually cleaned while he helped Edan and Mr. Sardis with tasks or while he sat by the river. For a time, she fought the urge to meddle in his belongings, looking for the buckle. She told herself she had just missed finding it near the gravesite, and that the longer Richard remained silent on the subject the less she had to worry about—his silence must indicate he suspected nothing. One morning she went back to the forest and searched the site again. She turned up empty-handed and then began worrying all over again.

The worry finally got the better of her. She finally forced herself to search his room for the buckle.

She searched around the desk, beneath papers and books. She pressed down on the tick, knowing she'd feel the buckle through the feathers if, by chance, he'd slit the material and hidden the buckle in the tick.

Finally she searched the chest of drawers, underneath his neatly folded clothes, through the haversack in the second drawer, under more clothes in the third drawer, and between the pages of a book. In the fourth drawer she rummaged through a knapsack, then pushed aside a neck stock and a cap box. When she moved Richard's sack coat, her hand fell on the leather-bound notebook in which he had spent so many afternoons writing.

Meg wondered about the man, as she had for weeks now. She wondered about his thoughts. She wondered if he'd written anything in the journal about finding the buckle and piling the stones on the grave.

She opened the book, and her gaze fell immediately on the sloppy, distorted handwriting on the first page: *Willy, dead. I may as well be. I miss him.*

Willy? Who was he?

She read another passage, an inch or so down on the page: *Left Willy dead on the battlefield. Blown apart. Led him in. Couldn't lead him out. My leg looks bad. Hurts. God willing, may die yet. Pray to. Mother, if ever you read this, you will never know the depth of my own sorrow in knowing I have caused you such grief.*

Meg reread the last sentence several times, her breath catching in her throat. Such emotion in the passage! What had he done to cause his mother grief?

Led him in. Into battle? Had Richard been Willy's leader? His commander? *Couldn't lead him out.* Because of his— Richard's—injury? That, and the matter of Willy being dead on the battlefield?

Meg closed her eyes for a few seconds. She had heard some of the casualty figures of the various battles. Still, her mind couldn't grasp the thought of thousands of dead men scattered around fields and in woods. Incredible. Horrible, the things soldiers had seen. The wounds they themselves had inflicted.

Another passage, another inch or so down the page: *Woman here fussing over me. Bothers me until I eat.*

Changes dressings. Keeps them clean. Keeps me clean. Tried to get out of bed, out of here. Go off alone. Leg won't hold me. Made it to the door. Man carried me back.

Yet another passage followed that: *Will not leave me alone. She says I will keep my leg and that it will be strong again one day. Says not to mope about it. Does not know my brother is dead, that I killed him. I never knew just how much I loved him.*

Meggie glanced off at the window, seeing nothing in particular. *Killed him?*

Meg wondered how long ago the diary entries had begun. She wondered how long ago Richard had been injured. She turned the pages and read more.

I walked some today. Leg still painful. Mrs. Radford wonders why I do not talk. Mr. Radford saw the battlefield and said he knows why. I almost asked him about Willy. Thought better. Said he saw me stirring among the mess of bodies and pulled me out. Knew the Rebs would collect the wounded for prisoners soon. Is there a reason why I am still alive? There must be. I have not yet discovered it. Surely it is not to go home. Mother will blame me as much as I blame myself for my brother's death. I miss Willy. I write in this book to loosen my thoughts, as my guilt is too deep to share those thoughts with anyone.

Willy was his brother, the brother he said he'd killed. But Willy had died in battle. So why did Richard blame himself?

Led him in. Couldn't lead him out.

He blamed himself for Willy's death because he'd led him into battle? Again, Meg wondered if Richard had been his brother's commander.

What guilt Richard bore. What heartache! What misery.

His handwriting and his sentence structure had improved toward the end of the last passage. Meg wondered if his initial physical pain had caused his handwriting to be so sloppy and his sentences to be so brief when he first began the diary.

The handwriting and the sentences improved even more during the next few pages, as he told about reading books Mrs. Radford, the woman who cared for him, lent him. He also told of helping Mr. Radford with odd chores when his leg didn't pain him too badly and he didn't tire too easily.

Meg turned yet another page and read: *I was reported to the authorities by a suspicious man in the nearby village. A band of Rebs came along one afternoon. I was questioned and taken when my uniform was found in the Radfords' house. My patriotism had not diminished. I told the officer in command I was proud to serve President Lincoln and the Union forces. I was sent to Libby Prison in Richmond . . .*

There was more to that passage, quite a bit more. But footsteps and Edan's voice out in the hallway jolted Meggie from her reading. She snapped the journal shut, put it back where she'd found it, shut the drawer, and resumed her dusting.

She'd forgotten about looking for the buckle. She didn't care. Her mind was filled with thoughts of Richard and the things she'd read in his diary.

So his brother had been killed in the war, and he blamed himself for the death. He feared his mother's grief, the sorrow his brother's death would cause her.

That must be why he was camped here at McBride's, why he stayed and stayed, why he didn't go home. Why he sat and stared at the river—at Ohio on the other side. He didn't do that as much as when he first arrived. But he still did it occasionally. Such as this afternoon.

He'd loved his brother, that was apparent in his notes. His heart was heavy with grief over Willy's death, over his feeling that he'd caused it or at least been responsible for it; over the fact that he knew his brother's death would cause his mother much pain.

He was afraid to go home. He was afraid to face his mother's grief.

What of the rest of his family? Had he written to them to notify them that he, at least, was alive? Had the military listed him as missing in action when they failed to find his body on the battlefield? Had the Federals liberated him from Libby Prison when the war ended? Months ago?

Meg had heard about the prisons on both sides, North and South; that the death rate at Andersonville in Georgia alone had been around three thousand a month. Starvation, dysentery, typhoid, and other diseases killed the men. Thousands were housed in a handful of rooms. Meggie could only imagine the filth and the lack of food. Thank God Kevin had not suffered so. Thank God he'd died quickly.

The lieutenant had endured his share of grief. No wonder, upon his arrival at the inn, Edan had seen a great sadness about Richard. Meg hadn't cared to notice, she'd been so outraged that Edan was letting a room to another soldier.

Reading that first part of Richard's diary made Meggie view him differently when she saw him at supper that evening. He'd never been capable of acting like the other soldiers who had come through here. She'd realized that as soon as she read his notes about his stay with the Radfords. They'd taken him in, taken care of him, and although he'd not wanted to live at first, he'd eventually gained enough strength to help Mr. Radford in various ways, repaying the man's kindness and helping with the upkeep of the Radfords' home. He wasn't one to take advantage.

She wanted to read more of the diary, but she was frightened to do so. What perspective that little bit of it had given her! Richard had been as hurt, even more hurt, by the war as she'd been. He'd lost someone he loved deeply, too. And he bore guilt over the loss. He blamed himself for his brother's death, and he hadn't gone home because he feared facing his mother's grief.

When Meg met Richard's gaze over supper that evening, she did so with compassion and understanding. She wanted to ask why he blamed himself so for Willy's death. A part of her wanted to take his hands in hers and tell him she understood his grief, that he would heal, that the passing of time would help.

Her situation was precarious.

She felt for Richard; she now wanted to comfort him. But could she risk such closeness? He might have the buckle. He might have discovered the grave. He might alert the proper officials.

Perhaps he already had.

As he tipped his head and regarded her curiously, Meggie

knew too that if she let go of even a little part of her reserve, that if she tried to soothe his pain and help him through his grief and his fear, she might be in danger of falling in love with him.

She was still healing over Kevin's death. When his body had been delivered home she'd felt disbelief and anger. Then rage—at him, at the people who had shouted for war, who had claimed it was the only solution. She'd felt pity for herself and for Ian, longing for the other children she and Kevin might've had together.

Only during the last six months had she begun to feel a calmness start to settle over her where Kevin was concerned. She'd learned to deal with his death without crying so much and without exploding in anger. That was good.

She wondered how far the lieutenant had come in dealing with his own grief. Surely he'd made progress since those initial diary notes. She wondered if he thought of Willy and of his mother when he stared across the water. He must. His brother's death and his mother's grief still troubled him greatly. Meggie sensed that.

Edan initiated a conversation with Richard about the sheep and the calves, how he drove some to market in Ironton every fall and sold them there for shipment to Eastern markets. If Richard was still at McBride's come the end of the season, he was welcome to go along on the drive if he wanted to. In fact, Edan would welcome the company.

"If I'm still here then, I'll go," the lieutenant responded.

For some reason he chose that moment to look at Meg. The lamplight softened his eyes. His hair had grown since his arrival, and it curled gently at the ends. He always dressed for supper. Not lavishly. But he was in the habit of going upstairs, washing, putting on clean clothes, and fastening a stock around his neck or tying on a neckcloth. It gave him a polished look, one Meggie found stimulating.

She smiled at him again, a tender, gentle smile.

He gave her a look of suspicion and wonder—and then he smiled back.

Hours later, when Richard undressed and placed his boots near the foot of his bed, he noticed a folded paper on the floor. When he picked it up, he knew immediately what it was—the paper on which he had written the names of the soldiers he had tried to commit to memory before leaving Libby Prison. Soldiers who, knowing they would never make it out of the hellhole, had told him their names and asked if he would write or visit their families and tell them where they had ended up or that they loved them. Once liberated from prison, Richard had written the names down, fearing that he might forget them. He'd already written to several families. But a dozen more names and addresses appeared on the list.

He kept the paper between the back binding and the last page of his journal. While it was possible that it had fallen out the last time he took the journal from the bottom drawer, he was suspicious. He took special care of the paper. He was always aware that it was there, and he would have been aware if it had fallen out when he removed the journal from the drawer.

Meggie cleaned his room every day. Had she intruded in his private belongings? Meddled with his journal? Read his thoughts, his feelings about the things that had occurred in his life during these last years?

If so, then she knew about Willy.

A blatant invasion of privacy. *Damn her.*

He might be a boarder beneath her roof, but that didn't give her the right to raid his belongings. She had opened a drawer she had no business opening, picked up a book she had no business picking up.

Good God. He hoped she hadn't read his notes, his thoughts about Willy's death and their mother. His guilt. Those were things to be shared only with his family once he reached home. He'd written them down because doing so helped him. He had become withdrawn and introspective since Willy's death, and the writings had provided an emotional outlet.

He hadn't written as much this past month, he suddenly realized. His guilt didn't seem as severe as it once had. Maybe because there had been other things on which to concentrate—namely, Ian, Edan, Mrs. Hutchins, and Meggie. The guilt was still there, however, roiling around, if he stopped to think about Willy and the war and Willy's death.

If Meggie had read the journal entries, what did she think of him? Did she view her newfound knowledge as ammunition to be used against him during a moment of anger?

She was unpredictable.

She hadn't liked him in the beginning. In fact, she'd disliked him enough to pull a revolver on him, and she might have shot him if he hadn't grabbed the weapon.

But since the afternoon they tracked Ian and his friends, her dislike had seemed to settle into uneasiness. He didn't think she feared him so much anymore that she'd try to do him bodily harm. She played pranks instead . . . Ingrim, that potion, the old crone.

Still, Meggie was Meggie, and Richard had to wonder if she might use his guilt against him if she became angry with him. Despite her warm smiles over supper, he didn't trust her. Those smiles might be another game being spun out by her mischievous mind.

He didn't know why he worried over what Meggie thought of him if she had read the journal entries. She'd always thought poorly of him anyway because he had been a soldier.

The shutters were open. He'd left them that way. He strode to the window, loosening his neckcloth, trying to decide what to do about Meggie and her invasion of his privacy.

He stared out at the shimmering water as he pulled the cloth free. He unfastened the top button on his shirt, wishing it were morning, wishing Meggie were singing right now. No matter what else she did, he'd grown fond of her singing. Remembering how he loathed it in the beginning, he chuckled at himself.

He should go to sleep. He was tired. He'd played chess with Edan for hours after the evening meal.

He spotted a figure walking beside the water, wearing a flowing dress, looking like a spirit drifting along.

Meggie.

Richard leaned a little closer to the window. Surely his

eyes were playing tricks on him. When did she ever walk outside after supper? She usually helped Mrs. Hutchins clean, or she went off to the stable to help Mr. Sardis with chores, or she visited with boarders, or she and Ian went upstairs.

No mistake—it was her. She wore the same dress she had worn to supper: short-sleeved, buttoned high up on her neck, flaring temptingly over the curve of her hips. The material itself appeared different in the moonlight than in the lamplight; it had a silvery glow. He knew from having seen it earlier that it was decorated with tiny yellow flowers with green stems against a beige background. The skirt flowed around Meggie as if it caressed an angel. Her loosened hair curled wildly around her face.

She obviously couldn't sleep. He wondered why.

She looked beautiful. He couldn't drag his eyes away from the sight of her.

She felt his stare; she glanced around, her gaze finally settling on his window. She stared back at him. No turning away. No hurrying on.

She smiled.

Did he imagine that? *Another* smile from Meggie? He didn't think so. Another inviting smile.

Or was it a smile of satisfaction that she knew his darkest secret?

He perched himself on the ledge and lit a cheroot. Meggie walked on.

He smoked, watching her, remembering the fiery passion of her while she was in his arms that night in the kitchen.

He ought to go down and confront her about the journal.

To hell with that notion. As inviting as she looked, smiling those smiles, she'd end up in his arms, and the invasion wouldn't be discussed.

She smiled again . . . *again.*

Did she want to be with him?

Surely not. He'd invited her up to his room once, and she'd sent that hag in her place. And when he tried to get close to her the next morning, still playing the game, she'd been stiff and reserved. He'd given up since then. He'd kept his distance. Discovering her secret in the forest had taken the fun out of the game.

She'd kept her distance, too. An invitation from her now was a strange, suspicious thing. For all he knew, she might turn cold again if he went down to walk with her. She definitely would, because he'd muster resolve and bring up the subject of his notebook. He'd tell her that he suspected someone had been reading it—that he suspected *her*.

Not exactly a conversation to have with a woman in the moonlight.

She looked his way again. Smiled again. Damn her . . . what was she doing? Teasing him?

Meggie, Meggie . . . They had their differences, but damn if he didn't want her in his arms . . . in his bed.

Getting her there would lead to nothing but trouble. Despite her defiant, mischievous nature, she wasn't the type of woman to bed and then leave. If he made love to her, his sense of honor might make his conscience trouble him.

He damn sure wouldn't feel comfortable falling asleep beside her, either. He'd wonder what he might wake up to—Meggie reading more of his journal, if she hadn't read the entire thing already, or that old crone in the bed, taking her place. Or both. Would he wake to questions about his brother's death? Or, if he managed to sleep, would he dream about Meggie killing soldiers in the forest and burying them?

He didn't want to confront her about that business, but he would. He planned to set her mind at ease, tell her that if she'd killed and buried the man, he understood what had driven her.

Things were getting too complicated where Meggie was concerned. More than anything, Richard didn't like the suspicion that she knew about Willy, the fear that she might mention Willy's death one day.

Maybe it was time to move on, even if he didn't go home yet. Farther upriver, he'd surely come across another inn or a boarding house in a small town or village.

To move on would be to run.

Had he left his courage on the battlefield?

Grimacing, Richard drew deeply from the cheroot, surprised by the thought that he would miss Meggie a lot if he left the inn. He'd miss her singing, the way she fussed over her plants; he'd miss her flashing eyes, the impetuous tilt of her head, the sprinkling of freckles across the bridge of her nose . . . He'd miss her laughter, even the saucy sway of her hips during her haughty moments. Meggie was so alive—and he'd miss that *life* more than anything.

Damn if he hadn't grown attached to her. He was fond of her, of her temperamental ways, her mischief, her compassion, her stubborn devotion . . . For each of her trying attributes, there were good qualities to compensate.

He was making himself miserable, tearing himself up inside.

He moved away from the ledge.

He strode to the bedstead, sat down, unfastened a few more buttons on his shirt. He snuffed out the cheroot on a tin tray that rested on the table beside the bed, and he pulled his shirt off and folded it.

He was wide awake now. Another long night lay ahead of him. a night filled with thoughts of Meggie, of longings for her, of misgivings about her.

She wouldn't walk beside the river all night. She'd come inside sooner or later. And he'd hear her when she did. The floors were uncarpeted, and the sound of boots on them was unmistakable. She had to come up the stairs, and certain steps creaked—the third and the tenth. Ian had informed Richard of that one evening, making conversation.

Richard swore at himself.

He'd lie awake listening for the sound of her boots on the stairs and in the upper hall. And when he heard them? Would he don his shirt and venture to the door . . . to the hallway?

He was fighting a losing battle, something he rarely admitted. To avoid deepening this thing with Meggie, he'd have to leave the inn tonight, right now. He'd have to run.

It was time he stopped being a coward.

He lay back on the bed—and he listened.

14

*N*O GUILT, *RICHARD* once had told her.

Meggie scowled. Who was he to advise her about guilt?

He was right in this respect, however. Her husband was dead . . . she was a widow, a single woman. When she spoke to Kevin, there was no response. When she touched the ground where he lay, it was hard and unresponsive, unfeeling.

She walked along the riverbank for a while longer, carrying a lantern to light the way, feeling the evening breeze lift her hair and caress her skin. She unfastened the top buttons on her dress so she could feel the air on her neck.

She deserved happiness.

She was developing feelings for Richard. She suspected they'd been there before she'd read the diary. Reading it had made her more at ease with them, had made her realize he was an honorable man, a caring man, a tender man. Not at all the monster of a soldier she'd assumed him to be.

She was scared of the things he made her feel. More scared that he'd leave one day and her heart would be broken.

She should have called up to him, asked if he wanted to come down and walk with her.

If he'd figured out that she'd killed and buried that soldier, what must he think of her?

She walked more, trying to tire herself, never wandering beyond sight of the inn. She hadn't slept well last night, or the night before. Which was why she'd decided to walk tonight. A little fresh air and exercise might help her sleep.

She finally decided to go inside. She had a book upstairs that Mrs. Hutchins had lent her. She'd read part of that, feed her mind a little. That might make her sleepy.

Once upstairs, she dared a glance toward Richard's end of the hallway.

Everything was quiet. Everyone had gone to bed. No light glowed beneath his doorway, which meant he'd gone to bed, too.

Meggie turned in the direction of her room, feeling a heavy sense of disappointment.

A door opened behind her, creaking softly but briefly.

She froze. If she turned around and saw him standing there, she was doomed, she knew it. To heaven or hell, she wasn't sure which. If she met his gaze, if he looked at her the way he'd looked down on her from his window, she would go to him.

"We're both having trouble sleeping," he said, his voice soft but rich.

Meggie's heart lurched. *God, oh God.* She could hardly catch her breath. Her stomach twisted.

"Aye. But I'm off to do exactly that. Sleep," she said, and she forced her feet to resume their steps toward her room.

"Good night."

Again she froze. Saints alive. He plundered her resolve. Just the sound of his voice made her want to turn and go to him.

"Meggie."

She glanced over her shoulder, met his gaze.

Such emotion in his eyes, glinting desire. Such an imploring look: Would she come to him? Take his hand? Let him tempt her beyond the boundaries she'd given herself?

His dark wavy hair fell over his left brow, hiding that eye a little, giving him a rakish look. His shirt was untucked, and his feet were bare. He'd freed his shirtsleeve buttons, and the sleeves were full and loose.

Sweet Mary, this was the end, the blessed end of her strength where he was concerned. He looked too good. He wanted her, and she wanted him. To fight the pull between them seemed hopeless.

Her breath came fast. Meggie glanced down at the floor, at her hand that held the lantern, at her skirt. "What . . . what if 'tis only the potion workin' on ye?"

"It's not. I've known about the potion."

Her head snapped up. "Ye've . . . ?" He'd *known* about the potion? How?

"Ingrim," he said, without her asking the question. He shifted his position, leaning against one side of the door frame.

"Ye already knew when I told ye about it?" she asked, her temper rising. If so, he'd made a fool of her. How much *more* of a fool had he made of her? All the lovesick attention he'd shown her . . . All an act? What about now?

"I knew." He narrowed his eyes. "Before you blow up, Meggie, remember who put the potion in whose drink. Who meant to play a trick on whom."

She tilted her head, thrusting up her chin. Of all the dirty . . .

"Your hair is beautiful down like that," he said, and he smiled. "No potion."

He'd better not start with the compliments. She was angry, and there was no stopping her anger once it got going. Compliments wouldn't soften her.

"Your skin really is pretty."

Ooh . . .

"That dress makes you look like an angel in the moonlight."

The man had a way with words.

"I often wish I were one of your plants, that you would touch me and talk to me the way you do them."

Lord . . . She couldn't stand this—more plunder. "An' sooner or later ye'd be cut an' dried," she retorted.

He laughed.

They quieted again.

"Meggie."

She closed her eyes and whispered, "Why do ye say my name like that?"

"How would you have me say it? Should I shout it? Growl it? Formalize it? Megan McBride," he said, deepening his tone, becoming dramatic. "I find you devastating to the senses. Good sense, bad sense . . . every sense."

She laughed. She couldn't help herself.

They soon grew serious again, assessing each other, she giving him covert glances, he staring openly at her.

Who would take the first step? Who would dare bend a knee, stretch out a leg, plant a foot closer to the other person?

They were both frightened. Hidden fears . . . simmering emotions, sparking passion . . . pride. Everything was at stake.

Perhaps not. Perhaps tonight would be about passion only, about meeting physical needs.

Meggie closed her eyes again. It had gone beyond that for her. She'd started caring. To nurture and help heal was in her nature, but this feeling she had for him was even more than that. She wanted to hold his hand. She wanted to gather his head to her breast. She wanted to assure him that his brother's death was not his fault—when she didn't even know the details. But she knew *him,* and she didn't think him capable of leading anyone to his death. Beyond all of that, she adored his gentleness with Ian, his easiness with Mrs. Hutchins, his companionship with Edan. Before her stood a gentle man, a caring man, a man she cared about.

She wouldn't stand in the hallway all night while they silently debated who should take the first step.

She opened her eyes, tilted her head, fixed an impatient look on him. "Are ye tryin' to decide if ye're goin' to kiss me again?"

Laughing, Richard shook his head. "No. I'm wondering if we might wake someone with our conversation. And I'm wondering if *you're* going to kiss *me.*"

Blazes. A challenge. He knew her well. Knew she would

meet a dare head-on. She ought to play him, turn away just to show him she could resist a challenge.

She was gone if she joined him in that doorway. But she had no more patience for this game. She wanted to lose herself in his arms, in the sweetness of his kisses and caresses, even if that meant forsaking her pride for the time being.

She strode toward him, and when she reached him, she rose up on the balls of her feet and kissed him.

Their eyes met as their lips touched. For a few seconds—the longest of Meggie's life—Richard stared down at her.

She trembled with want, with need, with aching desire. "I don't have so much courage that I won't turn tail an' run if ye don't do something. Kiss me . . . turn me away . . . something."

"You're not playing games with me, Meggie?" he asked, his voice thick. "You're not teasing me? You won't change yourself into a witch in the middle of things?"

The question made her laugh.

His lips twitched into a slight grin. "I can't help but wonder."

She became serious again. She lifted a hand to his shoulder, felt the strength of him beneath her touch. "I'm not teasin'."

He considered that.

Once again, Meg closed her eyes. Impatience, impatience, impatience . . . "If ye're thinkin' to—"

His arm slid around her waist, and he pulled her close to him.

Meggie's eyes popped open. She found his face not two inches from hers, his eyes scanning her face, settling on her mouth. She felt the warmth of his breath, felt the heat of his body against hers.

She made a little sound, gave a little cry, and then his lips came down on hers, crushing, tender, demanding, sensitive.

His tongue skimmed her lips, and Meggie instinctively opened beneath him, inviting him in, giving a soft cry; one of relief and excitement this time, not of torturous anticipation.

Their tongues met, tentative at first, circling, touching, dancing, caressing. And when he lifted his head, Meggie wasn't anywhere near ready to let him go.

His hands slid up to her shoulders, pressing slightly, then to her neck. His fingers found their way up into her hair.

She stared up at him, her breath quick and uneven as he again searched her face, measuring her reaction, perhaps wondering where he stood with her. Meggie stared back at him, not trying to hide anything she felt. He'd stripped away her resolve, peeled it back slowly but surely, weakened it little by little.

Reluctance . . . doubt . . . flickered in his eyes. "Absolutely no games, Meggie," he said. "No trickery."

She shook her head. He thought she was still playing with him. She whispered: "No . . . none. I'm wantin' to be with ye."

Inhaling deeply, he tugged her with him into his room.

He pushed the door closed with the heel of his boot, then reached back and turned the key in the lock.

Meg pivoted away, nervous suddenly. A little late for such a thing. Here she was, in his room alone with him, and the door locked. *In the wolf's lair.* Exactly where she wanted to be. But the danger of it! The possibility of losing her entire heart to a man who might be gone from her life soon. Who was a danger to her in more than one way.

She had to forget all of that for tonight. She wanted to be with him without fears between them.

Richard felt her sudden withdrawal; she tensed, and her breath caught. Was she teasing him? Did she plan to turn and leave soon? If she was teasing, he meant to give her the opportunity to run before things progressed very far.

If she wasn't teasing . . . if she was just momentarily skittish . . . If they made love, he wanted no doubts, no reluctance, no feeling on her part later that he had seduced her. He wanted no blame. He wanted to be with Meggie tonight only if she wanted to be with him.

He squeezed her hand and eased forward behind her. He lifted her hair and kissed the back of her neck. So soft.

Scented with a wild, flowery fragrance. Her hair smelled fresh, like the night breeze. He moved away from her and went to sit on the window ledge.

She appeared confused that he would bring her into his room then leave her standing alone.

Richard smiled at her, trying to reassure her. "Stay only if you want to, Meggie. If you have doubts, leave."

She tipped her head, her eyes flashing suddenly. She scuffed her boot on the floor. "I want to stay. I told ye that."

He laughed. He adored her—and yet she could frustrate and anger him more quickly than any woman he knew.

"Ye don't trust me," she said.

Another laugh. "Observant of you. Tell me why I should."

"Because ye can trust me t'night—I'm tellin' ye that."

She seemed sincere. But then, one never knew about her.

He extended his hand to her. She stepped forward, her skirt and hair flowing around her. He had thought earlier that she looked like an angel. She still did. But in looks only. A mischievous leprechaun hid behind her beauty, a character that excited him and made him cautious at the same time. He still wondered if he'd be able to sleep beside her. He'd have to take a deep breath and put aside his mistrust for tonight.

Their fingertips touched, skin on skin, warmth on warmth.

Instead of taking her hand fully in his, he lowered his thumb and made circles on her nailbeds and just beyond, to the first joints. He turned his hand over and rubbed the underside of her fingers with his thumb. Next he brought her hand to his mouth and kissed the back of it, marveling at the softness of her skin and her delicate bone structure. How odd to think of anything about Meggie as *delicate*. But there was a definite femininity to her.

She sat beside him on the ledge, and he leaned over and kissed her. On the side of her mouth at first, his hand stroking her jaw. Her eyes slitted and her head tilted back, and those movements were almost Richard's undoing. He almost lifted her right then and took her to the bed.

Instead, he parted the material at her neck, where buttons had been loosened, and he dipped his head to taste the vulnerable flesh. He felt her pulse throb against his mouth, heard the quick breaths she inhaled and exhaled. He lifted his hand to stroke the underside of her left breast.

She whimpered and arched toward him. *Meggie, fiery Meggie.* Holding back until just the right time would take a lot of restraint, maybe more than he'd ever had to employ.

Richard brushed his forefinger over the outer roundness of her breast, over her nipple, and Meggie gasped and lifted her hand to the back of his head, pressing him against her neck. She was eager, as aroused as he.

His fingers found more buttons on her dress as his lips caressed her neck and jaw. His mouth found hers, and this time she required no urging to open to him, no primal hint. His hand slid beneath the material of her bodice, beneath her undergarments. His fingers toyed with her hardened nipple. As another gasp issued from Meggie, Richard again fought the urge to lift her and take her to the bed as fast as possible.

Meg arched her body toward him. His touch was exquisite. Only now did she realize how much she'd longed for it these past weeks, realize what she would have missed had she chosen not to offer herself to him.

His hair was soft, his chest hard. She ran her hands down to caress his chest, letting her fingers pause in the curly hairs that rose between the vee formed by the unbuttoned part of his shirt. He breathed nearly as fast as she, and his heart pounded as hard, she felt certain.

He pulled her closer to him, and Meggie eased her way between his thighs, settling on his lap, her arms falling around his neck.

She felt her skirt being pulled up slowly, slipping to just above her knees and then farther up, and more excitement surged through her. Her stockings were bunched around her calves and ankles—the way she always wore them—and Richard touched her thigh. She gasped with pleasure.

His arm slid beneath her thighs. The other dropped loosely behind her upper back. He lifted her, kissing her at the same time, and carried her across the room.

Meg clung to him, kissing him back, feeling tension in her every muscle, wetness gather in her most intimate female place. She was ready for this joining, had been ready for some time.

She lifted one side of his shirt, touched his strong back, caressed it with her fingertips, with her entire hand. He smelled and tasted faintly of Irish whiskey and, more strongly, of tobacco. Male scents . . . arousing scents. Beneath those was his own—the muskiness of his skin. Early whiskers darkened his jaw, giving it a rough feel as Meggie kissed it and ran her fingers along the hard plane.

He placed her on the bed, her head on the pillows, and he sat, lowering her boots onto his lap.

He began unlacing the boots, and Meg thought she would burst with want, with frustration at the slowness of his movements.

"Faster, Lieutenant, or I'll undo them myself," she said, her voice low and breathy.

He laughed, a deep rumbling sound in the back of his throat. "Meggie McBride, you shatter any seriousness we might have during such a time."

He went faster, though not fast enough to suit her, dropping the boots onto the floor long moments later. He worked on her stockings next as Meggie finished unbuttoning her dress. He seemed calm and cool; she was anxious and hot.

She couldn't get the dress off fast enough. As she worked at pushing it off her shoulders and down across her waist and hips, he grinned at her, a lazy, seductive grin that threatened to unravel her modesty all the more. She rolled her eyes at him as she lifted her hips. He laughed. But at last he pulled the dress free. He draped it across the foot of the bed, and Meggie rolled her eyes at him again.

"Neatness, at such a time!"

"It's a pretty dress. One of us should take care with it," he teased. "Crumpled on the floor, it will get—"

She grabbed the hem of his shirt and pulled him down to her, moving her feet off his lap and putting her legs on either side of him.

His head touched just below her breasts, bringing him nose to nose with her corset stays. He smiled, and then he

pulled the tie, glancing up at her as did. Meggie groaned.
How he tortured her with his slow teasing!

He unlaced the stays just as slowly, grinning all the while.

The heat of his belly pressed against her crotch threatened
to drive her wild. Meggie arched her hips toward him just as
he opened the corset and took her left nipple into his mouth
through her chemise.

He suckled, lifting his head now and then to have a look
at her face, to tease her. Meggie wanted to box his ears, he
exasperated her so!

She untied the drawstring on the chemise as he watched,
a serious look on his face. Finally.

He moved up to her, kissed her, pushed the linen down
over one shoulder, following the movement with his mouth,
and then the other. His lips skimmed their way over her
skin, spreading heat, sparks, fire . . . He kissed her neck,
and then the kisses turned into heavy nipping all along her
neck and shoulders. He freed her arms from the chemise and
pushed the material down to her waist.

Her breasts were his feast, his banquet, and Meggie could
not stifle the soft cries of pleasure that tore loose from her
as he began his sweet pillage. Kissing, biting gently,
suckling, licking . . . Tugging her nipples into the heat of
his mouth and swirling his tongue around them, sending
shards of pleasure straight to her belly and below.

She pulled his shirt up, pushed it off as he raised his arms
and helped her along. She gathered him to her, running her
hands up and down his taut back. He pressed his hips down
against hers. She whimpered with pleasure, feeling his
hardness, wanting it free, touching her, inside of her.

She worked at his trouser buttons as he worked at her
drawers. Their remaining clothes were unfastened, untied,
pushed, and flung away. No more worry about wrinkles.

Naked finally, Richard whispered her name as he brought
himself down to her. His erection brushed against her wet
flesh, and Meg caught her breath.

She looked up at him, into the smoky heat of his eyes,
pleading silently as she arched. And when he thrust, sinking
into her, she cried out, wrapped her legs around him, and

drew him in even more. She had him now. He couldn't hold back, couldn't be composed.

More thrusting. More cries. His breath hot in her ear, in her hair. His hands on her breasts. Her hands on his firm buttocks. Intimate whispers— *You feel good, Meggie. Ah, you feel so good.*

She caressed his hair, kissed his mouth, his jaw, his neck. She loved him with fiery intensity.

He moved his hips forward and backward, side to side, stroking her in different ways. She felt a fullness that increased with his every movement, and she parted her thighs and drew him in more, rocking her hips. He slipped his hands beneath her buttocks and brought her up, going deeper.

Meggie became lost in sensations. She panted, rocked, whispered, perspired . . . A tightness grew in her womb, drawing together, then bursting open to welcome him . . . this mating. Meg pressed her face into Richard's shoulder, crying his name as her world exploded in pleasure.

Still, she welcomed him. His movements grew frantic. Small groans issued from him with each thrust. He tilted his body to one side. Tensed. Caught his breath. He thrust again, this time flowing into her, filling her with his seed, with liquid warmth. How sweet he was! Sweeter than anything she'd known.

When he finished, he lowered his head to her breast, and Meggie stroked his hair. They slept enfolded in each other's arms, moonlight spilling into the room, the night breeze caressing them.

15

MEGGIE WAS SINGING when Richard woke, the song about the lady and her garden—and she wasn't in the bed.

He rubbed a hand over his eyes. He'd fallen asleep? Apparently.

Had he dreamed the night?

No. He smelled her on him, and when he rolled over he smelled the flowery scent of her hair on the pillow. Images came back to him—her head tossed back, her flushed face, her parted lips. He remembered the softness of her body snuggled against his, how warm she was. He must have drifted off then.

He wondered how she felt this morning, if she had regrets, if she had risen, dressed as fast as possible, and fled the room.

He rose, pulled on his trousers, and strode to the window. Spreading his arms wide, he braced his hands on the ledge as he leaned over it.

Meggie wore the dress patterned with green vines this morning, and she hovered over a wide, thick patch of sprawling plants right beneath the window, lifting sections of the flora and working the ground, pulling out weeds.

Richard almost called down to her, almost said good morning. Instead he stood watching her, not wanting to disrupt her singing. He watched and listened as he remembered their passion, their whispered words, the exquisite feel of her hands on his back, the excitement of her opening beneath him.

He doubted if he could ever get enough of her. He wanted her with him again right now, back in his arms, back in his bed.

> *"Do, do, pity my case,*
> *In some lady's gar-den;*
> *My chicks to tend when I get home,*
> *In some lady's garden."*

He went after a cheroot. Once he had it lit, he returned to the window and settled himself on the ledge, his legs stretched out and crossed at the ankles in front of him, his back resting against the frame. He smoked, and he listened to Meggie sing. He watched her, and he marveled at the beauty of the morning.

Her hair was braided to one side today, and it was pretty. But hadn't it been glorious last night? Loose and flowing, curling wildly down her back, around her shoulders and face, brushing his skin, making him mad with excitement. The memories aroused him.

He laughed at himself. He felt like a schoolboy raging with excitement over his first sweetheart.

But he wasn't a schoolboy and he wouldn't even venture to call Meggie his sweetheart—he didn't know how she felt this morning about their activities of last night.

He was never sure how she felt about him in general. Except that she was as attracted to him as he was to her. He'd known that before last night. Covert glances here and there . . . kisses in the kitchen that night . . . heated words over the butter—

"Good morning, Lieutenant!"

Richard had been daydreaming. The sound of Meggie's voice jolted him, and his jump was startling enough to send him sprawling over the narrow ledge, tumbling through the air toward Meggie and her herb patch.

She screeched. But at least she had the good sense to leap out of the way.

Richard instinctively put out his hands to catch himself. The move did little good; he landed on his back. While the fall was cushioned by the thick patch of soft plant, it knocked the breath out of him.

"Saints alive!" Meggie swore, closing in quickly. "Are ye all right?" A second later, she hovered over him, pushing away the plant.

A nearly overpowering spicy scent hit Richard, and he sat up in the patch, trying to catch his breath. The cheroot . . . he'd had a cigar in his hand when he fell. He glanced around for it, not wanting to see Meg's garden go up in flames.

He spotted smoke rising, a thin swirl in another herb patch on the other side of the nearby brick path, and he scrambled that way. He must not be hurt. He could still move fast, and nothing smarted.

Meggie followed, reaching him just as he snatched up the cheroot. He snuffed it on a brick while she looked on, her face at first pale, then suffusing with color.

"Perched on that ledge!" she scolded, hands on her hips. "Ye should hold on. I wondered if such a thing would happen. *When* it would happen! Now ye're smartin', an' so is my oregano! It'll never be the same."

Richard stared at her. He was reminded of the first morning he'd heard her singing in her garden, the morning she'd run Caomh out of her herbs.

"Never, ever be the same!" she fussed.

She was worried more about her plant than him? He'd just fallen two stories!

"Blast the oregano," he muttered, dusting his trousers.

"Ye already did," she said smartly. She snatched up the cheroot he'd left on the brick, grabbed his hand, and plopped the cigar in it.

The end of the cheroot was still hot, and Richard yelped when it singed his palm. He grabbed the cigar with his other hand.

"None o' that, either!"

"What?"

"Ye were plannin' to leave that where ye snuffed it."

"I was not," he said indignantly.

"Don't flap yer wings at me, Lieutenant. Ye were an' ye know it."

They glared at each other. She was right—he had been planning on leaving it. But he hadn't committed some hideous crime. She didn't need to scold him as if he were a child.

She turned away and fussed more over the ruined patch of oregano. "Droppin' down on ye. Half dressed, at that," she muttered.

"I expected at least a good morning from you, Meggie," Richard said. Was that too much to ask? A simple good morning? After they'd made love and slept together?

"I said good mornin', an' look where it got me! I'll not be sayin' it again. Off with ye now. Half dressed," she grumbled again. "If Mrs. Hutchins sees ye, she'll surely have a heart spell."

"'Morning, Miss Meggie!" someone called. "What's that you're growing there today? A man?"

Meg shook a fist in the direction of the landing. There stood the ferrymaster, leaning leisurely against the railing beside the dock. No ferry business this morning, it seemed. "Never mind ye now!" she warned. "Ye're bein' idle, Ryan Darrow, an' ye know what the Good Book says 'bout idleness."

He bellowed laughter. "Why, Miss Meggie! I was standing here minding my own business, enjoying your singing, as always. It stopped of a sudden, and then a man came up out of your garden. Idleness has nothing to do with curiosity."

She glared at him, then turned the glare on Richard again. "Off with ye now! See what ye've done? By noon, he'll have half o' Kentucky goin' on 'bout me growin' men in my garden."

"Perhaps you should," Richard said, smarting. She would sleep with him, but she didn't want to be seen with him? She obviously wanted no one to know that they liked each other, that they just might have a mutual romantic interest. "You could bury them easier, Queen Meg."

She flinched, went pale; turned her back on him and began nursing her oregano again. Her hands trembled. "Ye don't know much o' what went on round here. I did what I had to do." She glanced up at him, giving him a fierce look. "I'll tell ye this—I'd do it again to protect us."

She thought he'd made a reference to her burying that man in the forest. He hadn't. She'd been acting as though nothing intimate had occurred between them. He'd been hurt by that, and he had meant she'd have an easier time getting rid of him if she'd grown him. Chop him down, mix him with the soil . . . he'd be gone.

"Meggie, I didn't mean—"

She spun away. "I won't talk 'bout it more here."

"All right. But we have to talk, Meggie. We need to clear the air of some things."

"There's nothin' to talk 'bout," she said, the fear in her eyes unmistakable.

He wouldn't let her do this—run from him in her mind. He wouldn't run, and damn if he'd let her.

"After last night, there's nothing to talk about?" He shook his head. "Yes there is. I'm as frightened as you are, Meggie, for different reasons. We *do* need to talk."

He walked off, feeling her stare on his back.

Edan emerged from the inn just as Richard stepped onto the porch. He tipped his head, regarding Richard in a queer way. "Been tumblin' in Meg's garden?"

That stopped Richard cold. Now how would Edan know that just by looking at him? Unless . . .

"Ye're wearin' oregano in yer hair, lad," the innkeeper said, chuckling.

Damn. He was a laughingstock again. How odd that when people ridiculed him, Meggie was always involved in one way or another.

Richard brushed by Edan, intending to go back to bed for a time.

He definitely knew about the buried soldier. What else could his remark "You could bury them easier," mean? He knew.

And while he'd been tender last night, holding her, making love to her, whispering sweet words, Meggie couldn't be sure what he intended to do with his knowledge.

If he intended to report her to the proper authorities, wouldn't he already have done so? Why would he even want to discuss the matter with her?

It was surely what he wanted to discuss with her. The reference to burying men easier, then telling her they had to talk. Ha! About her hiding a buckle from him in the forest, about him finding a grave and piling stones on it to keep animals from digging up the soldier buried there.

Why hadn't she confided in Edan after she killed the soldier? Instead, she'd taken the frightened Ian home and left him with Mrs. Hutchins in the kitchen. Then she'd returned to bury the body.

Lord only knew, things would be much harder for her family and friends at the inn if anyone associated with the Union or sympathizing with the Federals found out she'd shot dead one of their fighting men.

A sympathizer already knew. A Federal soldier. A comrade-in-arms to the man she'd murdered.

Meggie tamped down the panic she felt, and remembered exactly why she hadn't told her father-in-law or anyone else about the soldier, why she'd told Ian it was their secret: If no one else knew, no one else could be accused of the murder if the terrible secret was discovered.

What did Richard think of her? The Union lieutenant, the patriot, the Yankee undoubtedly born and bred to hate the Southerner . . . After all, the conflict between the states had started a long time before the North and South engaged in military skirmishes and battles. The differences went clear back to shortly after the turn of the century, after the purchase of the Louisiana Territory from France, when more and more territories became states and the states came into the Union. There was always a fight about letting one free state in for every slave state, and resentments accumulated. Why, the entire battle over whether or not to allow the Republic of Texas into the Union had been about slavery, about unbalancing the scales. Surely many children born into Southern homes heard how evil Northerners were, and surely many children born into Northern homes heard how evil Southerners were.

The only peaceful solution would've been to let the Confederate states go. No war. No suffering and death. No rebuilding lives. No soldiers mourning for brothers, blaming themselves . . . not wanting to go home.

Richard did want to go home. Meggie sensed that. She sensed a love of family and roots in his notes, and in him in general. Yet he didn't go home because he felt responsible for his brother's death and because he was afraid to face his grieving mother.

If he confronted her again about the dead soldier, if he made the man sound like a victim . . . she'd let him have it with both barrels. She'd blast him with facts about what the soldiers had done. Their entire herd of sheep had been taken; the storehouses had been cleaned out; soldiers had helped themselves to anything and everything in the cupboards; the spring box in which they preserved milk, butter, and cream had been raided; the smokehouse had been stripped of hocks and other meat; and she and other women had been threatened. The soldiers had eventually taken all the food, even hunting the forest almost clean. They'd left not a morsel for Ian. They'd raped, too. Lizzie Milan right now had an infant whose father had worn Confederate Gray.

Richard need not talk to her about the dead soldier as if the man had done nothing wrong. Meggie didn't care how faithfully the soldier had served his country. She didn't care if he'd only been teasing, intending to set the hogs free in the forest, as he'd claimed when she aimed the revolver at him. He'd turned the tables on her somehow. She'd ended up with that knife at her throat and—

She shuddered, as she always did when remembering the events of that day. She didn't want to remember them.

If Richard thought poorly of her for taking the man's life, she'd regret that. But she'd feel no regret for actually doing the deed. And if he thought she *should,* then their relationship would go no further.

It might not anyway.

He had to go home one day. *Needed* to go home. He had to reconcile matters in his head and with his family. He'd have no peace until he did. And there was no guarantee that he'd be back once he left.

Meggie had known that when she went into his arms. She'd known it and she wouldn't feel distressed over it. What she'd done last night, she'd done because she wanted to. She had no regrets.

Well, perhaps one. Perhaps more than one. That she'd risen so early, washed, dressed, and come down to her garden. That she'd startled him and made him fall off the ledge into her oregano. That she'd snapped at him because she was worried about him. That he assumed she was more worried about her oregano.

One thing had led to another, and she'd been considering an apology until he'd made the statement about her burying men in her garden.

Whenever possible, Meg avoided Richard during the next few days. She went about her tasks, helping take the sheep to graze, bringing in the cows for milking, gathering eggs, cleaning the upstairs rooms (avoiding the temptation to read more of Richard's diary), teaching her children, and helping Mrs. Hutchins prepare the meals as time allowed.

Several more guests stopped at the inn that week, but they were stuffy elderly people who went to bed with the chickens. No singing or dancing for these travelers.

Of course, there were times when Meggie couldn't avoid Richard or ignore him, even times when she didn't especially want to but forced herself to—at evening meals and when he looked down on her while she tended her garden. August arrived, bringing stifling days, and most every morning he sat on his ledge without saying a word, simply smoking and watching her. Interesting that he didn't exactly perch on the sill since his fall—he sat a safe distance from the outer edge of it.

She dared not initiate conversation with him. She longed to be close to him as much, if not more, as she had the night she'd shared his bed. But given the fact that she suspected he wanted to question her about the grave in the forest and the buried soldier, she kept quiet.

Meggie soon realized he didn't mean to press the issue of them needing to talk, and she began to relax. She even occasionally chuckled to herself about his tumble. About Mr. Darrow's comment too that she was growing a man in her garden. After all, no one knew exactly what she might grow next. And the incidents of that morning really were funny when one looked back on them. It hadn't taken her oregano much time to recover, and she had to admit that the sight of Richard tumbling over the ledge and landing on his back, a startled look on his face, was comical once she knew he wasn't hurt.

She laughed off and on one entire morning, remembering him fighting his way up from the patch, half dressed, stems and leaves clinging to his hair. Remembering him looking so indignant that she seemed more interested in her injured herb plants than in him. Poor, poor man. Pity *his* case.

She missed him. Their playful banter. His glares. His grumbling about her singing. Why didn't he grumble at her lately? She wished he would.

Finally she could stand the silence no longer. One morning she couldn't resist the temptation to change the words to the lady's garden song:

"Do, do, pity his case,
in some lady's gar-den;
From his perch, he tumbled off,
in-to some lady's gar-den."

She snickered at her cleverness and stole a glance up at his window. He hadn't appeared there yet. Perhaps he was still sleeping.

She sang louder:

"Do, do, pity his case,
landing in her gar-den;
His clothes to dust when he got out,
of the lady's gar-den."

Hah! Clever, indeed!

"Sweet william, ye're lookin' a little frowsy this mornin'," she complained. She did her best to straighten the drooping leaves, then she moved on to the yucca, inspecting the ground beneath its base, humming as she went.

She resumed singing when yet more lyrics, newly created, popped into her head:

"Do, do, pity his case,
    in some lady's gar-den;
He plunged into the oregano,
    in the lady's gar-den."

"Are you having fun, Queen Meg?"

Ah. She'd known she could count on him to appear at the window sooner or later. And being sarcastic, too! She knew he couldn't sit peacefully up there while she ridiculed him.

She'd taunted him into appearing, shameless as she was, and she'd taunted him into being grumpy. If he didn't appear at the window every morning to at least watch her tend her garden, she didn't feel quite right anymore. And if he didn't grumble at her, she didn't feel quite right, either.

She smiled up at him, still fearful that he knew her deepest secret and wondering what he planned to do with the knowledge, but glad to see him. So very glad to see him—the frowsy, grouchy Richard Foster. "Ye know I am."

He nodded. "I know. You woke me once again, Meggie. I was sleeping heavily, dreaming of—"

"Do, do, pity his case,
    in some lady's gar-den;
His hair to comb when he gets home,
    from the lady's gar-den."

She snickered. "I'd apologize, Lieutenant, but ye know I wouldn't mean it."

He tipped his head. "Meggie . . ."

"Hm?" she asked, breaking up the ground around the rosemary.

"You're a scoundrel."

Interesting. "Goodness! I've gone from a queen to a scoundrel in a matter o' moments."

"You have no trouble doing that."

What had that night meant to him? Anything? Meg couldn't help but wonder as she glanced up at him in the morning light. His pretty blue eyes glowed with the softness of recent sleep. He hadn't bothered to comb his hair yet, and he had his usual cheroot in hand. A definite morning habit.

Before rising and dressing the morning after their love-making, Meg had quietly observed him, his tousled hair, his peppered jaw, his strong features, his broad chest . . . And she'd wondered then too what the night meant to him. If it meant anything. She hadn't had the courage to wake him and ask him. It had been too early to do such a thing anyway. And it wasn't a question that should be asked. She'd gone into his room with her eyes wide open, knowing that he'd go away someday, that he might not want further involvement.

She hummed a little more of the tune, sang more, finished tending her garden. Mr. Darrow called over to her, asking if she'd heard that the Parkers planned to have a play-party next week. Word of it was traveling up and down this part of the river, and all were invited, provided they brought a little something to eat. Such gatherings had been scarce in recent years, since the war had divided people.

"Ye surely can't attend, Mr. Darrow," Meg teased. "McBride's ferry's got to run day an' night."

The man looked crestfallen, utterly dejected. "Aw, Miss Meggie, surely not. Mr. McBride won't torture me so. He won't make me mind the ferry whilst you're dancing your heart away at the Parkers'. I've been wanting to dance with you for nigh on two years now, since the last play-party. Yonder at the Newells'. Remember that one, Miss Meggie?"

"Aye." And well she did, too. She'd still been in mourning, refusing to dance with anyone. She'd attended the event, wanting to see people she didn't often have the opportunity to see. But she'd sat in her somber black, and she felt certain her face had looked about as cheerful.

"You'll dance with me, *Miss Meggie*?" Richard asked from his window.

She shot him a playful scowl. She tapped her chin. "First I was a queen. Then I was a scoundrel. What am I now, Lieutenant? A lady? *Me*?"

"Of course," he said, grinning.

"Ha—an' ye're still feelin' that potion."

He laughed. "Never fear. That fall knocked out what remained. I have no delusions."

Her look changed to one of curiosity. "Delusions?"

"Yes. About us."

"What 'delusions' did ye have?"

"That you might care about me."

The remark made her catch her breath. She did care about him. The fool man didn't realize that after the intensity of that night? Or had he been with so many women he simply hadn't noticed the intensity? He hadn't felt what she'd felt . . . Why should he care if she cared anyway?

"That you might want to see more of me."

"I see quite enough of ye ev'ry mornin,' thank ye," she retorted. Who was she calling a fool? She'd sung him to the window this morning because she'd wanted to see him, because she'd missed his grumbling—and because she'd feared that he might not appear today. She'd practically ignored him for several weeks, after all. She was safeguarding her heart. Pretending indifference when indifference was not what she felt. She was the fool.

He was gone from the window. Meggie stared up at the hole, wanting to call up to him, wanting him to come back. Her and her smart mouth! It forever got her into trouble. She forever used it to get herself in trouble. She opened it, thinking to speak his name. But she snapped it shut instead.

She wouldn't. She couldn't. She suspected he already had part of her heart. She didn't want him someday taking the whole of it to northern Ohio with him. She wanted it to stay right here with her, in the Kentucky hills, in her garden.

16

THE FOLLOWING AFTERNOON Richard went into Havershill with Edan right about the time Meg started upstairs to clean rooms. Since the one day she read his diary, she'd resisted the urge to do so again. Today, however, that seemed impossible. It called to her from the bottom drawer.

Meggie kept turning her head that way, interrupting her dusting, interrupting her sweeping, questions running races in her head: How exactly had his brother died? Why did he blame himself so? How had he gotten out of that Confederate prison in Richmond? How long had he been out? The questions had been in her mind for a while.

"Saints alive, Meg McBride," she finally swore at herself. "Ye'll have no peace till ye've nosed through the whole of it."

Which is what she spent the better part of the next hour doing.

She read quickly, and sometimes she skimmed the words and sentences. In prison he'd met numerous dying men and promised to deliver messages to their families. Upon being liberated by Federal troops and hearing that General Lee had surrendered, he'd bought his horse with part of the money he'd been given in officer's pay, money that had accrued during his time in prison. Then he returned to the

Radfords' to collect what personal belongings he'd left there.

It had taken him a while to decide to head home. During the liberation, he'd been asked by a superior officer about sending notification to his family that he'd been imprisoned but that he was alive and well. Richard had told the man he didn't want his family members notified—that he planned to go home and notify them himself. *Cowardice,* he wrote. *It was an attempt to avoid having them know I was alive. When will I initiate the plan to return home and notify them myself? I might at least write to Mother.*

Directly below that passage appeared a scrawled address, as if Richard had been thinking of it and had scribbled it in the process. It was a Cleveland, Ohio, address. Meggie assumed it was his parents'.

She stared at the address, a wild thought going through her head. She couldn't do it . . . If he ever found out—and he would—he might not ever speak to her again.

But she thought of Mrs. Hutchins, how the woman waited every day for Zachary, her son, to come home. Wouldn't a woman who had two sons be thankful if at least one of them returned alive? All over the country, mothers, wives, sisters . . . had waited, were waiting still, and Meggie felt for them. In Ohio, Richard's mother waited. The woman had a right to know that her son was alive and well, that he'd survived the war.

Meg took the journal and went to the desk. There she found a piece of paper and a pen and ink. She wrote the address down, waited for the ink to dry, then folded the paper and put it in her apron pocket.

She sat on the floor with the diary again. He'd traveled through Virginia, West Virginia, and down into Kentucky, trying to work up the courage to go home; the courage to face his parents.

I was the daring one, he wrote, *the reckless one. From the time Willy could walk, he followed me. I often took him swimming in the river in cold temperatures, or we harnessed a sled to a horse and glided down the steep slopes near the lake. Willy wouldn't have enlisted if I hadn't. He wouldn't have gone to battle if I hadn't. I led the way. I led him to his death.*

"Lord," Meggie whispered. "Oh, sweet Lord. How he blames himself!" The blame went deeper than she'd realized.

She read about his decision to head toward home. He followed that with his concern over whether he would make it to Cleveland, whether his fear of facing his mother's grief would stop him. She read about him reaching the Kentucky–Ohio border, about him coming upon a group of boys playing with a Confederate flag, and she realized that he was writing about the day he'd discovered Ian and his friends, and her.

His next passage made Meg's eyes burn with tears: *Willy. I cannot bear the thought of looking upon our mother's face knowing how she loves him and expects him to come home. I often wonder if there might have been time to throw myself in front of him. Yet there was not. He was gone so quickly that even his own brother, who stood not ten yards away, had no chance to say goodbye.*

She read the passage over and over. She cradled the journal in her lap. She cried for him, for *them.* She cried for Richard and for Willy and for their mother, who doubtless had cried a river of tears by now. Had Willy's body not been shipped home? Did Mrs. Foster not even know her youngest son was dead? Did she wonder about both of them?

Richard had to write to her at least.

Meggie read about him meeting her—how she turned her sharp nose up at him, how she took one look at his Union Blue and seemed to loathe him. How he found her pretty, impulsive, irritating, temperamental—but full of life. In his wanderings, he'd met a lot of people whose spirits were dead or defeated by the war, including his own. *But Meggie McBride's remains, despite the death of her husband and despite her family and friends having to scrabble for food during the war years. She is bitter, but she is, for the most part, bright and gay. The sprite has fight in her, a spontaneous mischievousness, a rebelliousness that is both exas-*

perating and stimulating. Meggie is inspiration. Meggie is life.

She sat back on her haunches and smiled in wonderment. Now, that was sweet. He'd apparently written it not long after his arrival at the inn; other passages followed that described Mrs. Hutchins and Edan and Ian. He'd written about everyone shortly after meeting them.

I look at the river and know that when I cross it, I will not look back. I will go on from there. The Ohio presents the last barrier, no matter that there is still land to travel on the other side on the way to Cleveland. I am afraid to cross it.

Meggie realized that she was holding her breath. She knew Richard well enough to know that he'd never say that to anyone— *I am afraid to cross it.* He'd had to write it because he couldn't speak it.

His fear of crossing the river was why he sat sometimes and stared at it, why he had such a distant look on his face when he did.

She was crying again. Silly lass. So emotional.

She snapped the journal shut, aware suddenly that the light in the room had changed. Only slightly, but it was different enough to make her wonder how long she'd been reading. Part of the beam that had slanted across the floor now touched the foot of the bed, and the shadows in the room had shifted. Meg curled her hand around a bedpost. Such sweetness she and Richard had shared here.

She turned away, scowling at herself. She wouldn't allow such sentimentality. Pining. Remembering. Wondering if and when they'd be together again.

Her skirt and apron swished as she walked around the room, deliberating far more than she should. She should simply put the matter from her mind. Being with him again wouldn't be a smart thing to do. She could end up with a bellyful of child and no husband.

She might already have a bellyful of child.

Her hand wandered down, partially covering the area just below her waist. Her time was due soon. Surely it would come.

She replaced the diary in the bottom drawer and gathered

her duster, her bottle of oil, and her cloths. She placed everything in her basket, and then she took up the basket and left the room, closing the door behind her.

She had to convince Richard to write to his mother. And if she couldn't convince him to write? Why, she'd write to the woman herself.

It wasn't beyond her to take matters into her own hands.

Late the next morning, Meg decided to pick more berries and whatever nuts she could find. She collected Ian from the stable, knowing he liked to spend time in the forest, and they took up buckets from near the back steps and set off.

They ended up collecting more than just berries and nuts. Ian robbed the blackberry vines while the creeping wintergreen caught Meg's attention. She cut enough leaves to make several good batches of "mountain tea," and she stuffed into her apron pocket several cuttings from the rich orange-yellow plant. She used the juice of the plant to do away with the flies that always appeared in the kitchen during warm weather. The raspberry bushes were plentiful this year; Meggie filled a bucket halfway with the berries, then moved on to dig up some wild ginger.

It was a steamy afternoon, and when Ian spotted the river, Meggie saw the eager look on his face and laughed. "G'on," she said, wiping perspiration from her neck. "I might think o' joinin' ye, hot as it is."

He yelped, handed her his bucket, and raced off, going as fast as a crippled boy could go between trees and brush. He broke through the last of them, his shirt pulled halfway off already, and when he reached the water's edge, he plopped down on the ground and tugged at his boots. He pulled and yanked, working up more of a sweat trying to keep from getting poked by a stingy bush. Meg laughed again, and he let loose a grunt of exasperation just as a boot went flying.

A patch of mushrooms grew alongside a fallen, rotting tree. As Meggie began plucking mushrooms and dropping them into one of the buckets, Ian splashed into the Ohio.

The sound of the water was her undoing. She had to get

in. She had to get wet. Her mouth was dry, her skin clammy with perspiration. Her face felt hot, and her neck itched. She turned her back on the sooty mushrooms and picked up the buckets.

She made her way between the trees and scrub, and dropped the buckets near the base of a tree trunk on the grassy slope. There she shed her boots and dress, and when she splashed into the water she wore only her pantalettes, camisole, and corset. She and Ian always swam together, and she always swam in her undergarments.

"Watch me!" Ian shouted from a little upriver, his hair plastered to his head. He dived beneath a log tangled in the overhanging roots of a birch and came up on the other side. He was a strong swimmer, Ian; one day he'd wanted to see how many times he could swim to the opposite bank and back, and Meg had watched him do it three times, with only a brief rest after the second round.

"Ye should've been born an otter, Ian McBride!" she called.

"Pooh," he called back. "Born a boy instead."

Meggie laughed. She ducked her head into the coolness of the river, relishing it.

She swam out a ways, moving smoothly, pushing her hands and arms through the water, then drawing them back against it, pulling her body forward.

When she emerged, she stood shoulder-deep in the blue-green river, admiring the way the sunlight created tiny diamonds that glittered a far distance up the Ohio. There more trees overhung the bank, and the river deepened in color.

She dipped her head, went smoothly into the water, and swam out more. She came up, then went down again, scattering the fish and other creatures.

". . . comin' in, too?" Ian was saying when she broke through the surface.

Meg glanced around, thinking he was talking to her, that he hadn't seen her go under. But he wasn't talking to her. He was talking to Richard Foster, who walked along the bank near Ian, his hands tucked into his trouser pockets, his white shirt doing little to disguise the fine breadth of his shoulders. Enhancing them instead. The white was striking against his dark hair and black trousers.

Now where had he come from? She and Ian had wandered a good distance from the inn. He had to have followed them to know where they were. His appearance here was too much of a coincidence.

"Not today, Ian," he told her son as he stooped and picked up a twig. He broke it in two, then he stared out at the river, at the opposite bank, and all the sadness Meggie had glimpsed several times before was back, tightening his handsome features and putting a distant, sorrowful look on his face.

Now that she'd read more of his diary, she understood his look. He wanted to go home so badly, and yet fear held him back. He'd come this far, from the prison in Richmond to the Ohio River. If he ever made it across the wide waters he'd go on home; he wouldn't look back again.

She didn't want him to cross the river. If he did, she'd lose him forever.

Silly, silly Meggie McBride. She disgusted herself. Thinking she had him when she didn't. Even wanting him completely when he could shatter her world, when he had knowledge that could make her quiver with fear and send her running. He hadn't broached the subject of that dead soldier anymore, but she was always scared he would. Except for the one morning she'd antagonized him at the window, she hadn't gone out of her way to talk to him.

Whether or not she wanted him to cross, he needed to cross. It would be better for both of them if he did.

"Why not?" Ian asked Richard.

"Come in, Lieutenant," Meg urged, treading water. "The water's cool."

"I don't need cooling off," he responded.

Bother. This wouldn't be easy. She wished she could say something about having shed her dress. That might get him in the water. But the young ears of her son were perked, and she had to mind her words.

Ian began diving under the log again, and Richard settled

himself on the riverbank, in the shade provided by a drooping willow branch.

Meggie swam toward Richard. When her feet touched bottom, she swam in more. Ian busily came up with things from the riverbed that he placed on top of the log and inspected. He continued doing the same, occupied for the time being, having lost interest in Richard since the lieutenant had declined the invitation to swim with him.

Meg rose up out of the water, her back to Ian, aware that Richard was watching her. She pushed her hair back from her face and twisted it to wring it out. The water reached to just below her breasts, and she knew the linen of her camisole was nearly transparent when wet. Her nipples were hard from the coolness of the water; surely Richard saw them through the material. She smiled at him.

He reached down to his boot, produced a cheroot, brought it his mouth, and lit it. He smoked calmly, seemingly unaffected by her wanton display.

He couldn't be unaffected. Impossible. If she'd done such a thing the night he'd ushered her into his room, he'd have come to her in a heartbeat. So what the blazes was the matter with him today?

"Can ye swim, Lieutenant?" she ventured. If a wantonly display didn't affect him, perhaps a sting to the pride would.

He blew smoke above his head. He grinned.

"That means nay?"

His grin widened. "Miss me, Meggie?"

She stiffened. Why, of all the conceited . . . She stopped herself. It would help neither of them if she became angry. She had to play along.

She smiled. "Ye know I have. How could I not? Ye're a fine man. I'd be a fool if I didn't miss ye."

He took another long draw from the cheroot. He blew smoke again and studied her. "From a fine family, too. Oh—and I have fine manners and fine friends, and a fine knowledge of every theater in Ohio."

She couldn't help herself—she scowled at him. "I never said all *that*."

He laughed. "Not to me anyway."

She clicked her tongue. "I really never said all that."

"Of course not."

"Richard." She wanted to stomp her foot like an angry child. He laughed again. "What do you want, Meggie?"

Ian let out a yelp, and Meg spun toward him, sinking down into the water, preparing to swim his way.

He grinned sheepishly at her. "Turtle got away. He flopped 'imself back in the water."

"He didn't want to be caught," Richard remarked.

Ian said, "I know," and he sounded mighty disappointed.

Meggie swam off toward the center of the river again, annoyed at Richard, annoyed at Ian's interruption, annoyed that her plan to get Richard into the water hadn't worked.

Well, she didn't give up easily; she didn't often admit defeat. She'd get him into the Ohio somehow . . . someway. Venturing across it seemed to be the only thing holding him back from going home.

She had been reading his notes again. Richard knew . . . he'd found smeared ink, several blotches. One on the page where he'd written that he'd often wondered if there had been time to throw himself in front of Willy. Several pages later another blotch had smeared the ink on the page where he'd written that the Ohio River presented the last barrier to his journey home. Not his exact words. He couldn't remember the exact words he'd written. But his sentiments had run deep at the time he'd expressed those thoughts.

Last night he had sat and stared at the pages on which the blotches appeared. She had read far. She knew most everything. He felt violated. He felt naked.

He felt relieved.

Upon first discovering that Meg had been reading the notes, he'd considered hiding the journal. He'd told himself then that he wouldn't hide his belongings—that she could just stay the hell out of them. But if she'd read the notes once, she'd read them again. He knew that—and yet he'd taken no action to prevent her from doing so.

Why?

Relieved . . .

Strange that he should feel relieved that someone had
read his thoughts, that someone knew about Willy and his
guilt, his shame. Particularly when the reader was Meggie,
when he'd wondered if she planned to use his guilt against
him. She hadn't wanted him to stay here. She hadn't wanted
him here for even one night. She'd wanted Edan to turn him
away.

Given her initial loathing of him, her rudeness and her
trickery, Richard hadn't trusted her. He'd even feared falling
asleep beside her.

But he *had* fallen asleep beside her, with her, and there
had been no trickery from her. No replacing herself with an
old hag. No telling Edan later that she'd been taken
advantage of; no trying to drive distance and resentment
between him and her father-in-law. She hadn't expressed
regret. In fact, she had said nothing about the night they had
spent together.

Nothing. Which sometimes said everything.

She said nothing to him about that night whenever he met
her in the hallway, whenever their paths crossed in the
kitchen, whenever they spotted each other out in front of the
inn . . . She greeted him politely but distantly. She always
smiled then went about her tasks.

What the hell was she thinking? What was going through
her mind? She hadn't expressed regret, but her silence on
the matter troubled him. And God only knew he already had
enough to be troubled about.

He'd thought again about leaving the inn, about moving
on . . . about *running*. And he'd been just as angry with
himself over the thought as he'd been before. Running wasn't
the answer. He meant to face Meggie. He meant to draw her
aside at some point and talk to her. He meant to pull words out
of her about the night they'd spent together. He needed to hear
how she felt about it. He needed to hear how she felt about
what she'd read in his notes.

That was the real issue . . . what she thought about him
now that she'd read his notes.

He watched her swim. He watched her surface, the linen
becoming her second skin. He watched her wring her hair,

and he longed to wring it for her, to gently twist it and watch the water run down between her breasts.

He stood and neared the edge of the Ohio.

She went still and watched him. Surely she'd read the note about the river being his last barrier; the smeared ink was evidence that she had at least opened the journal to that page.

Her look, worry mingled with urging and fear, sealed his suspicion. She'd read the note, and now she silently bade him come into the water. And yet, the fear . . . her startled look . . .

Did she not really want him to go home?

He bent and scooped water into his cupped hands. He stared at it. He raised his head and looked across the river.

"Come in," Meggie urged, nearing the bank, her voice soft. "'Tis not so hard."

Insensitive of her.

"I'll help ye to the other side," she said.

The muscles in his jaw tightened. "Why? Because I know about a grave in the forest?" His voice was low enough that it wouldn't carry. "Because I know what's buried in it? Is that why you've avoided me, Meggie? Is that why you want me to cross? I'll more than likely go home from there, and you can stop fearing that I might do something with what I found."

She had frozen in place. Ian was still diving; from the corner of his eye, Richard watched the boy, not wanting him to hear this conversation.

"Why did ye go back?" she asked in a near whisper. She meant back to the forest the day she'd hidden the buckle from him.

"Curiosity."

She swallowed. "I . . . ye don't understand. They were camped somewhere in the hills, a group of 'em. He came an' took our—"

"I know why you did it," he said gruffly.

He reached into his trouser pocket and pulled out the buckle. He'd polished it. He ran his thumb over it, then turned his gaze on Meggie again.

She watched him closely, breathing rapidly.

Richard reared back and threw the buckle out into the middle of the river. It made a splash, and then the river swallowed it in one neat gulp.

Someday someone might find the buckle. But not today, and not for a while. Perhaps never. Maybe mud would wash over it. Maybe the Ohio would bury it forever—and Meggie's secret, too.

"I don't give a damn," Richard told her. "The war is over. It was waged in a lot of ways, on many fronts. We all did what we had to do."

She closed her eyes. She crossed her arms and hugged herself.

"I don't want you to regret that night, Meggie," he said, and then he took a deep breath. He didn't do this well, express his emotions in words.

"I don't," she said in a rush.

He studied her, saw that she was telling the truth. "I fell asleep with you. I didn't think I could." He tossed back his head, the hair from his forehead. He rubbed the back of his neck. "You've been reading my notes."

Another startled expression passed over her face. Her mouth parted slightly, the lips he wanted to taste again.

"Thoughts meant for no one but me."

"I—I make no excuse," she said, stumbling over her words, looking even more alarmed now. Meggie, who seemed to never lack confidence in speech. "No apology." She paused. Swallowed. Color had rushed to her face. "Ye must despise me for my curious nature. I—"

"Would it please you if I said I did?" He couldn't help but ask that. He had to know something about what she felt. He couldn't hold himself back much longer.

She shook her head. "No . . . oh, no."

He studied her more. She was sincere about that, too. He nodded and started to walk away.

"There's a play-party tonight," she said hurriedly, sounding breathless. "Music . . . games . . . food."

He hesitated, looking back at her. "Edan told me about it."

"Did he? Are ye goin'?"

"Are *you* going?"

"Aye . . ."

"Then I'll go."

"Ye'll dance with me?"

He'd been afraid she had no feelings, one way or the other, about their lovemaking that night. She must have feelings for him—why else would she be asking him to a social event, asking him to dance?

He meant to have fun with her: "Of course not. I'll dance with everyone but you. You're brazen, Meggie McBride."

Her chin shot up. Her eyes flashed. "Humph! Well, if ye didn't find something good in that, ye wouldn't bother with me."

"I'll tell you exactly what I find good in it," he said, his eyes feasting on the sight of her nipples, pebbles just beneath her wet camisole.

"Ikes!" She sank down, hiding her breasts in the murky waters.

Richard laughed.

He settled himself beneath the tree again. He kicked back against the trunk, closed his eyes, and took a peaceful rest, his first in days, while Meggie and Ian went on swimming.

17

$\mathcal{M}$EG HAD MADE herself a new dress for the event. The background was peach, and sprays of tiny blue flowers decorated the material. She tied a green ribbon at her waist and wove wildflowers throughout her hair. She made a little bracelet of vines from her garden and fastened it around her wrist. Excitement flushed her cheeks and darkened her lips as she laced her boots.

Richard knew about the soldier she'd killed and buried in the woods. He knew, and he'd said he didn't give a damn. Oh, he cared that the man was dead and buried—he was a compassionate person and he'd care about anyone being killed. But he understood why she'd done what she'd done.

Ian became impatient, calling up to her to hurry. He, Mrs. Hutchins, Grandpop, and Richard were ready and had been for some time. He'd see his friends again tonight, and Meg knew they'd play their own share of games and eat and have a merry time, same as the adults but in their own gathering. When the dancing and singing commenced, the youngsters would mingle with the adults, and everyone would swing and skip and clap and bounce to the fiddler's tune.

When Meggie finally started down the stairs, Ian was cradling a large basket covered with a cloth and no doubt filled with bread. Mrs. Hutchins had spent the day baking for the play-party, and the smell of her work filled the inn. She herself came up the downstairs hallway, toting the pot in which Meg had made rabbit stew this afternoon.

When Mrs. Hutchins spotted Meggie, she stopped dead in her tracks, and a smile broke out across her face. "Why, Megan McBride, I've never seen you look prettier!"

Blushing, Meg thanked her.

Ian looked mystified. "Ye're wearin' yer garden."

He could say the funniest things without trying to be humorous. Meggie shook her head at him. "Beggin' yer pardon . . . not my *entire* garden."

"I agree with Mrs. Hutchins," Richard said from Edan's study door. He leaned against the frame, his arms folded, his eyes bright as they surveyed Meggie.

She flashed him a smile of embarrassment. Then she hurried forward, intent on taking the pot of stew from Mrs. Hutchins. "People fussin' over me! Give me that pot. Ye worked most o' the day bakin' that bread."

"Megan doesn't take to compliments well," Mrs. Hutchins informed the lieutenant. Then she told Meggie: "You do look pretty. You should thank the man."

Meg's back was to Richard now so he couldn't see her face. She huffed at Mrs. Hutchins and took the pot handle out of the motherly woman's hands.

Mrs. Hutchins was getting up in her years. Although no one knew exactly how old she was, Meggie would venture to guess she was just past sixty. She'd been in the Kentucky hills for years, and everyone knew her. She'd started working at McBride's shortly after her husband died some ten years or more ago. She had the one boy, and when Edan offered her the position of cook and maid, she accepted it the next day. Zachary lived with her at the time, and they resided in a little cottage tucked back in the woods about half a mile. But when he enlisted and went off to the war, Edan didn't like the idea of her staying in the cottage alone, so he offered her free board at the inn. She promptly took him up on that, and not long afterward began acting as Meggie's self-appointed mother.

For the most part Meggie didn't mind the mothering. She

only minded when Mrs. Hutchins's affection became smothering.

"Simmer down now, Meg," the woman said. "Would you rather have him tell another girl that?" She brushed by Meggie, wondering aloud where she'd put her shawl. The evening promised to be cool in the hills, she told them all, just as Edan appeared beside Richard.

Meg started to say that it was hot outside, that the temperature would have to drop quite a bit for the evening to turn cool. But she didn't doubt that Mrs. Hutchins, a mountain relic, knew the signs of impending weather change as well as she knew when an expectant mother would give birth. She made a habit of predicting such things, and she was rarely wrong.

Deciding she should fetch a shawl, too, Meggie handed the pot to Richard and hurried off upstairs, while Ian groaned behind her. He was anxious to see his friends. The little elf would just have to be patient.

Moments later, the group set off out the front entrance. A wagon waited there, the horses already harnessed and hitched, blankets padding the bed. Mr. Sardis sat in a chair on the porch, whittling, as always. He'd stay behind in the event travelers arrived wanting to rent a room.

Mr. Darrow, already mounted on his horse, waited nearby. He looked like a dandy in his finely cut trousers and embroidered vest. He grinned at Meggie, and she wondered how long he'd saved to afford such clothing. But then, given the fact that he was a bachelor, he didn't have much else to spend his money on.

Edan handed Mrs. Hutchins up to the wagon seat while Richard lifted Meggie and Ian to the bed. They arranged themselves, finding a comfortable spot on the blankets, as he went off to climb up onto the seat and settle himself beside Mrs. Hutchins.

The group traveled for the better part of an hour up through the hills. Half the time Edan sang spry Irish tunes in his rich baritone with Meggie joining in occasionally in her smooth alto, and half the time Ryan Darrow bothered Meg, wondering aloud if she meant to dance with him and how often. Ian snickered, and Richard shot Meggie a questioning glance when she finally told the man she'd dance with him as often as he wished—if he wasn't otherwise occupied.

"Means he will be," Edan told Richard under his breath. Mr. Darrow didn't hear because he was going on about the songs he meant to request. "Meg'll find a way, ye can be certain of that."

Ian snickered again, and Meggie couldn't help but laugh a little herself. Edan was right. In the light of the lamps dangling from the front corners of the wagon, Meg saw Mrs. Hutchins smile stiffly; the woman didn't often approve of Meggie's mischief. Dusk had settled in, heavier in some places than in others, depending on the thickness of the forest trees that flanked the dirt road.

"Hush!" Ian said suddenly. "Listen!"

Everyone quieted, and Meg heard it faintly at first: music. Moments later, the wind shifted, and the sound became louder, the distinct chords of a fiddle. Ian grew restless, hovering over the railing to the wagon bed, and he soon spotted torchlights in the distance and tried to point them out to his mother.

Meggie had lost a few wildflowers out of her hair; they'd fallen onto her lap. She picked one up and twirled it beneath her nose.

"You're not wilting, are you, Miss Meggie?" Mr. Darrow asked. He apparently thought his question comical—he brayed, sounding like an obnoxious ass.

"I'll never wilt, Mr. Darrow," she responded as sweetly as possible. "Not now, not when I'm ninety years old. Not ever."

"Somehow I believe that," Richard commented, his blue eyes flashing laughter at her.

"Mum, can I go ahead?" Ian dared to ask, leaning out a little farther. "It's not far. See . . . there's the first wagon."

"No. Sit back now b'fore ye fall out."

His excitement was great, too great for him to mind his mother at the moment.

Meggie grabbed the back of his shirt and pulled him

down. "Ian McBride, ye'll settle yerself away from the others for a time when we reach the Parkers'."

"Oh, Mum." He flopped back against the railing and pouted, his elbow propped on his drawn-up knee, his chin resting heavily in his cupped hand.

Ian could pout better than any child in Kentucky, Meggie felt certain. And while she hated to see him pout, she knew he'd be having a grand time soon. She knew he'd play so hard he'd fall asleep in her arms on the way home later. He'd sleep half of tomorrow, too.

She started to reach across and tousle his hair. She stopped herself. They were moments away from reaching the gathering, and he wouldn't take well to such a show of motherly affection in front of his friends when he arrived at the play-party.

Meg smiled at him instead, which deepened his pout. Then she turned the smile on Richard, who was watching her and who seemed to know that she had to muster restraint to keep her hands away from Ian. Tousling his hair wasn't all she wanted to do. She wanted to hug him and kiss him.

The fiddling grew louder. The torchlights became unmistakable. Laughter and shouts reverberated. Ian gave up on pouting and perched his head just above the railing, watching as the wagon crept closer to the gathering. They passed other buckboards, positioned two by two, horses dipping their heads and whickering low.

One of the McBrides' horses snorted, and then someone rushed out of the darkness alongside the road, a lantern in hand.

"Edan!" the man greeted. "Bring that wagon on over here, an' let's see who ya've brought with ya. I've been wanting to get over that way and visit ya. Haven't had time till recently."

It was Moses Clemens, Meggie saw when he lifted the lantern up close to his face. She hadn't seen him in a good year, not since she and Mrs. Hutchins had come calling on Lizzy Clemens, his wife, after the birth of their eighth child last summer. Shortly afterward, he and Edan had had words about whether the Union should crush the Confederacy or simply cripple her. "Crush 'er," Edan had said, and Moses had scowled and looked sullen. Moses appeared friendly enough tonight. Meg hoped he and Edan would avoid the subject of the late war. It was over, after all, as both Edan and Richard had told her.

Once the wagon was settled among the others, Meg prepared to climb out of the bed. Edan would be around to help her down, but she half hoped she'd find herself looking down into Richard's face.

Mr. Darrow dismounted, tethered his horse, and scampered around the wagon before Edan or Richard could take a step in Meggie's direction. She fought to keep from scowling at him. Ridiculous man. She really would make certain he was kept busy this evening.

The fiddler, most likely Mr. Dickson, the owner of Havershill's mercantile, was playing the spry "Walking on the Green Grass." He played at almost all the local play-parties and gatherings. Meggie's feet itched as she glanced over the tops of heads and spotted the dancers. The men had already promenaded, and the men and women had formed their respective lines. The third man and woman in each line danced out toward each other, swung around, arm in arm, then danced back into their places.

"Let's go join them," Ryan Darrow said, pulling on Meg's arm.

"Bonnie Jane!" Meggie called in a hurry, spotting a good friend. Thank the sweet Lord—she had to get away from Mr. Darrow before the urge to kick him in the shin overcame her. Pulling on her arm that way!

She twisted her limb free and started off, telling Ian to stay close to Mrs. Hutchins until he spotted his friends. Once he did, he wasn't to leave the clearing.

"You said you'd dance with me, Miss Meggie," Ryan Darrow called.

"Later," Meg told him, carrying the pot of stew. She rolled her eyes—her back was to him.

Bonnie Jane spotted her, too, and her eyes brightened. She hurried toward Meggie, her brown curls bouncing. No doubt she was full of news about this person and that.

Bonnie kept up on everyone and everything in this part of Kentucky.

Meg embraced Bonnie, telling her how pretty she looked and wondering aloud where her little ones were. Bonnie had three children, a lad and two lassies. The youngest girl was ailing—her stomach, Bonnie said—and she was staying the evening and night with Bonnie's mother, who didn't take to such gatherings. The other two, six-year-old Dodie and eight-year-old Hubert, were in the middle of the dancing. Meggie spotted them weaving in and out between the dancers, disrupting the lines, Dodie in her ribbons and frills. The golden-haired children giggled and so did most of the dancers, and Meg couldn't help a little laugh herself. The little ones were so cute.

Bonnie's news was never all good. She included the bad with the pleasant, giving Meggie news of people she hadn't seen in a while. Eva Larkins, just married this past spring, was expecting, and Comfort Bergh's husband had caught his arm in a mill wheel recently and nearly ripped his limb off.

"He's back to using the arm a little," Bonnie said as she and Meg approached the table of food. "Comfort was distraught, as you can imagine. She still fusses over him."

"Like I fuss over Ian," Meggie remarked.

Bonnie smiled understandingly. "Well . . . yes."

Meg placed her pot on the table with numerous other dishes and pots of food. People had been eating already; portions of food were gone from most of the dishes.

Had Meggie heard that old Elsie Giles had finally passed on this morning? Bonnie wondered. Meg hadn't, and she wondered just how old Mrs. Giles had been. She'd outlived her husband by a good twenty-five years or more, and when she became feeble, she hadn't taken to anyone trying to care for her.

"Annie found her this morning. She was sitting in her rocker, looking as if she were asleep," Bonnie said. Annie was Mrs. Giles's great-granddaughter.

Meggie commented that she was sure Elsie Giles had died content—why, every time someone went to visit her, she could be found in that rocker. Surely a rocker just like that one had been waiting up in heaven for Mrs. Giles for some time.

Effie Thompson approached from the left, laughing behind her hand about something. Meggie hadn't seen her in probably five months, and although she was hungry, she turned her back on the food. She hadn't seen a lot of other friends in at least that long, either, and her stomach could wait. She hurried toward Effie and hugged her.

"Ryan Darrow's here," Meggie informed Effie, and when Effie's eyes brightened, Meg felt certain hers did, too. Effie had had an eye for Mr. Darrow for some time, and Meggie didn't doubt she'd keep him busy for the rest of the evening. Effie could be bold and forward.

Effie soon wandered off, and Meg found more friends, one right after the other. Several men who'd been trying without success to court her this past year found *her,* and before long she joined the dancing with Ned Morgan. She liked him well enough. He was always polite and courteous.

Lines formed again, one of men and one of women, and Ned and Meggie skipped to the foot of the men's queue. Leaving her there, he skipped his way over to the ladies' line. Meggie turned once with each gentleman while Ned turned once with each lady. They worked their way up the queue, and once they reached the beginning of it, they turned together and fell back into place. Then the next couple skipped out and began the same sequence while Mr. Dickson sang:

> *"All up and down, my hon-ey,*
> *All up and down we go.*
> *That lady's a-rockin' her sugar lump,*
> *That lady's a-rockin' her sugar lump,*
> *That lady's a-rockin' her sugar lump,*
> *Oh, turn, cinnamon, turn."*

Ian and one of the Bergh girls joined the lines, and they were followed by Edan and Mrs. Hutchins.

Torches burned around the edges of the clearing, flickering light on the gathering. People sat on tree stumps and in chairs with plates on their laps, tapping and stomping their feet to the lively music. Some sang along with Mr. Dickson.

When the sugar lump song ended, Meggie thanked Ned for the dance, then she found Bonnie by the table of food.

"Land sakes, there's too many verses to that song!" Bonnie said. "I couldn't last through them all if I tried."

Meg laughed. "Ye could. Ye just don't try."

Bonnie started toward the end of the table. "There's punch in a barrel down this way."

Someone touched Meggie's elbow. Richard spoke behind her: "I took the liberty of bringing you some."

Meg turned and found him standing right near her, holding out a tin cup filled with the dark liquid. Almira Parker had probably made the punch with forest berries, as she usually did whenever she decided to have such a party, and Meggie loved the brew.

She thanked Richard as she took the cup from him. Such gentleness, such longing in his eyes! Eyes as blue as a clear sky. Meggie felt a tremble as her fingers touched his.

"He brought you some!" Bonnie whispered behind Meg. "Who *is* he?"

Meggie could predict what would happen after she introduced Richard and Bonnie: Bonnie would make certain everyone in this county and the next three knew Meg had a new suitor. Meggie sometimes wished Bonnie didn't keep people so informed of other people's doings.

Chuckling, Richard introduced himself to Bonnie while Meggie was still gathering her wits. She sipped from the cup, then licked her lips. Almira had done as good a job as ever with the punch.

"Nice to meet you," Bonnie told Richard. She turned her gaze on Meg. "I'm off to see how Effie's progressing with Ryan Darrow."

Maybe so—Bonnie was always curious about how things were progressing—but her eyes said she wanted to give Meggie and Richard a little time to themselves, too. Meg knew Bonnie would be hunting her down before too long to see how things had progressed here.

Meggie gave a quick nod of her head, and then Bonnie was off, heading across the clearing.

"Have you eaten?" Richard asked.

Smiling, Meg shook her head.

"Would you like to?"

"That's why I came this way. My stomach's turnin' flips, threatenin' to leap out if I don't feed it soon."

He laughed. "Your sense of decorum, Meggie . . . one of the things I enjoy about you."

A grin twitched her lips. Sarcasm. He was almost as good at it as she.

She finished the punch and plopped the cup down on the table. Then she flipped her skirt around and tossed her head at him. "Between the two of us, we might come up with a full set of manners."

That drew more laughter from Richard. Meg was glad. He seemed happy lately, not the cold, reserved man he had been when he arrived at McBride's.

They found a stack of tin plates on the end of the table, and he followed behind her as she began serving herself. She took a little of this and a little of that, filling her plate with roasted venison and creamed duck, with potatoes and cornpones and pickled tongue. She found bowls beside the stacked plates and filled two with the rabbit stew she'd made earlier in the day. Richard slanted her odd looks, as if wondering if she could eat so much.

She handed him a bowl of the stew and told him she planned to eat every last morsel. "Dancin' so much, I'll need the stores," she said.

"You haven't danced much yet."

"*Yet*. Ye're plannin' to dance a bit this evenin'?" They moved away from the table in search of seats.

"I'm not sure."

His doubt made her impatient. "Ian showed ye ye could."

"Do you want me to dance, Meggie?"

She gave a little scowl as they found several stools on which to settle themselves. "If I'm askin' ye about it, I do. If it doesn't pain ye," she added.

"Dance—or play a game?" He mused over that. "Drop-Glove. Hunt the Squirrel. Itisket, Itasket."

Meg had just taken a bite of venison. She swallowed hard. "Who told ye about that game?" All three games he mentioned were different versions of the same.

"Edan."

She slanted him a look. Just what was Edan up to? "Did he now?"

Richard nodded. "If I drop you a handkerchief, you can catch me easily."

"Ha! Ye'll make it so!" Meggie nearly choked. In all three variations of the game, a circle was formed, and an appointed person took a knotted handkerchief, dropped it, and traveled around the outside of the ring, finally tapping someone on the shoulder. The tapped person then picked up the dropped handkerchief and chased the other person around the outside of the circle, both players trying to secure the open spot. In Itisket Itasket and Hunt the Squirrel the variations included curtsys and weaving in and out of the ring. But in Drop-glove, if the appointed person caught the tapped person, he or she was entitled to a kiss.

"Ye're thinkin' I want to catch ye an' kiss ye in front of ever'one?"

"Would you prefer to kiss me in private?" The man grinned from ear to ear.

Wouldn't Bonnie have great fun with this business! A virtual stranger to everyone shows up at a play-party, drops a handkerchief behind Meggie McBride during a round of Drop-Glove, and she chases him down, entitling herself to a kiss.

"If you prefer, you can drop the handkerchief, and I'll catch you," Richard said.

"Ye're a presumptuous one. Providin' I want to be caught."

The man was still grinning, having fun at her expense, at the risk of breaking her heart when he left McBride's.

Unless he'd decided not to return to Ohio. Unless he'd decided not to face his family. Saints! How she wished she could know what he was thinking!

"You do," he said smartly. Which irritated her all the more.

"Ye know what I'm thinkin', Richard Foster?"

"No. But, as irritated as you look, I'll soon find out."

"I'm thinkin' yer mum's hurtin'. She'd surely love to know if ye're alive or dead. I won't be a reason to keep ye from goin' home. A dance is far safer than a kiss."

That sobered him. He stared at her. Meggie wondered if he even breathed during those moments. He didn't seem to. She'd read the diary, and she saw no reason, now that he knew she'd read it, not to state her opinion.

"If that hurts ye, I'm sorry," she told him softly. "Truly, I am. I've watched Mrs. Hutchins all these months, the pain she's felt not knowin' 'bout Zachary. I've watched her, an' I'm thinkin' yer mum's pain must outweigh yer guilt."

"You're not the reason, Meggie. You don't understand—"

"I understand more than ye know. I understand yer feelin' sorry for yerself. I understand I'd be waitin' an' watchin' the road ever'day if I didn't know 'bout Kevin."

She glanced off, gathering patience and resolve.

She looked back at him. "Yer brother walked into the war with his own two feet, Richard. Ye didn't pull him into it. He didn't have to follow. Ye plan to carry the guilt with ye forever? It hurts ye, but it hurts yer mum more. I'd wager my life it hurts her more."

"This isn't a good time or place to discuss this, Meggie," he said, anger tightening his features.

"There'll never be a good time or place. Not while ye're hidin'."

He didn't respond. He stared at her.

"Drop me a han'kerchief later," she said. "Kiss me, but don't hide behind me. Don't think I'll make it easy for ye."

The words had been brewing for some time. She didn't want to be another reason why he didn't go home.

She stood and walked away.

He didn't drop her a handkerchief. He didn't even involve himself in the game. When Mr. Dickson began the Drop-Glove song, Richard hung back, leaning against a tree just beyond one of the torches. Meggie kept looking at him, trying to coax him forward.

He didn't budge. He was silent and angry again.

18

$\mathcal{H}$E WAS QUIET most of the way home. Mrs. Hutchins remarked that she hadn't once seen him dance, and he said he'd preferred to watch. Edan said he'd felt almost certain Richard and Meggie would be frequent partners in the dances and games. Instead Ned Morgan had been Meg's partner much of the time. No one responded to that.

"Ye half chased him durin' Drop-Glove," Edan remarked to Meg as the wagon bumped and creaked its way over a hill. "Ye could've caught the man."

"Easily," Mrs. Hutchins said.

"I didn't want a kiss from Ned," Meggie responded sourly. They shouldn't press her. In the end she'd been annoyed with herself that she'd scared Richard off. Brought up the subject of his mum and him going home when he'd asked her to drop him a handkerchief during Drop-Glove. In a roundabout sort of way, he'd been asking her for a kiss. In a roundabout *sweet* sort of way.

She wondered if he cared anything for her, or if he *was* using her as another excuse not to go home.

She didn't believe that, not really.

Ryan Darrow had hung behind for a while longer, having become interested in Effie, quite interested, thank goodness. Ian was sleeping with his head on Meg's lap, and Meggie noticed with interest that Edan had tucked Mrs. Hutchins's hand between his arm and his body. She tried to remember which of them had been widowed longer, and she couldn't. Edan, she suspected. Richard had control of the reins, and he held them loosely as he turned his sparkling gaze on Meg.

It had softened; it wasn't so cool as when he'd stood leaning against that tree, probably wondering if she meant to chase hard after Ned and demand a kiss. She hadn't because she hadn't wanted to—she had no desire to chase and kiss anyone but Richard. When she'd said those things about his mum and him going home, she hadn't meant to make him think she didn't care about him.

She did care. Too much. She cared about him, and about his mum, and she thought that if he ever went home he'd work through his guilt over Willy's death, and Mrs. Foster would work through her pain over losing a son. The knowledge that she still had at least one son would lessen Mrs. Foster's hurt.

As for Richard . . . he had to realize Willy hadn't been a boy when he marched off to war; that even if Willy hadn't followed him, he eventually would have been pressed into service. He might have died anyway, on another battlefield, far removed from his brother.

Meggie held Richard's gaze. She smiled at him, and he smiled back. She wondered if he'd realized that sharing his pain and his deepest emotions with someone wasn't such a bad thing; that sharing them released them, or at least lessened them and allowed the healing to start, or continue.

The night wasn't over for the two of them. Meg sensed that. He needed her, wanted her with him.

She didn't want to be an excuse for him not to go home, but she'd fallen in love with him, more than likely while bickering with him about her morning singing, and she couldn't turn her back on him when she knew he was hurting. She couldn't turn her back on anyone she loved.

He focused his attention on the horses again and on the path ahead. His shoulders were more squared, his back more erect.

Meggie began humming "Do, Do, Pity My Case," and when Richard cocked his head toward her, she hummed louder. He smiled—she was sure of it.

She sang the last two lines of the verse, adapting them as usual: "The stranger tumbled off the ledge, into the lady's garden."

Edan chuckled. Mrs. Hutchins snickered behind her hand.

Richard looked back at Meggie, lifting a brow and warning her silently and playfully. "Very funny," he said.

Meg laughed and hummed another verse.

Once the wagon reached home, Mr. Sardis came out to greet the group and to take the reins. Richard appeared at the side of the wagon, offering to take Ian from Meggie and carry him inside and upstairs to bed. Meg handed her son over, placing him in Richard's arms.

He spoke her name softly as he cradled Ian against him. "You're a treasure," he said. "A pot of gold."

Grinning, she tilted her head. "Now how can that be? Ye haven't yet reached the end of the rainbow. It's in Ohio."

"You don't intend to leave me alone about going home, do you?"

She shook her head. "Don't be thinkin' I don't care. Yer mum's hurtin' a lot worse than I'll be hurtin' when ye go."

"Meggie," he whispered again, "I've caught a leprechaun."

"Ooh . . . Ye don't want to be doin' that," she said, climbing over the side of the wagon. "All sorts of trouble can come from that."

"I've *had* all sorts of trouble these past months. Almost every morning, I'm forced awake at an ungodly hour. And just recently, I took a tumble into some lady's garden."

"Ha!" The man was funny. Playing on her own words, on the lyrics to the song! "It won't take long for Ian to get heavy."

"Changing the subject?"

She dropped to her feet. Smiling, she gave him a mischievous look from the corner of her eye, then turned away with a flip of her skirt.

She was teasing him, trifling with him—but she meant to make good on the teasing later. She'd wait until everyone settled for the night, then she'd go to him.

The wait took forever. Everyone went inside, and after they went their separate ways and Meggie put Ian to bed, she listened for the inn to settle down, for Edan to come upstairs and for his door to close; for Mrs. Hutchins to finish whatever she'd started in the kitchen.

She finally did finish, and Meg's heart raced as she listened to Mrs. Hutchins's boots tap their way up the stairs and down the upper hallway, fading and fading until her bedroom door finally shut softly behind her.

Meggie waited for a decent amount of time to pass, time for Mrs. Hutchins to prepare herself for bed, before she pushed her own door open an inch. She peered down the dark hallway, not seeing even a hint of light glowing beneath Mrs. Hutchins's door.

Drawing a deep breath of excitement, she stepped out into the passage, her lamp in hand, and eased her door shut. She closed her eyes as she did, willing the portal to latch quietly. It clicked, and Meg crept toward Richard's room, clad in only her shift and a thin wrap, her hair flowing freely.

Seconds later, she knocked softly on his door.

When he opened the portal, he still wore his trousers and shirt. The shirt hung loose, and it was open at the throat—he wore no neckcloth or stock.

He didn't exactly look surprised to see her; a grin twitched his lips as he opened the door farther and stepped aside, silently bidding her to enter.

Meggie slipped by him, waving a knotted white handkerchief and flashing him a smile. She dropped the handkerchief at his feet, and then she crossed the room and sat on the window ledge, gathering the loose material of her shift around her waist.

Richard shut the door and turned the key in the lock. He picked up the handkerchief. "This means I'm supposed to catch you and demand a kiss . . . ?"

"Aye, 'tis what it means, surely as I'm sittin' here," Meg said softly.

He stepped her way, his gaze intent on her. "You're not running, Miss Meggie."

"I've stopped wantin' to."

He neared one of the posts at the foot of the bed. There he hesitated.

"I'm afraid to love you, Megan McBride. I can make no promises. I have no idea what tomorrow will bring."

"A pity, isn't it?" she said lightheartedly. "Not knowin' what tomorrow'll bring. A cryin' shame. Perhaps it'll bring the end of the rainbow."

"Meggie," he scolded.

She clicked her tongue, rose from the window ledge, and sauntered toward the bed—and him. "Ye're wantin' to be serious an' I'm wantin' to jest. Well . . . I've no expectations, y'know. I put my nose where it didn't belong an' learned things I had no bus'ness learnin'. But I'm glad of it, even if ye're still miffed at me. I understand ye . . . mostly."

She slipped her hand beneath his. Her other hand gathered up the fullness of her shift, and she brought her left leg onto the bed. From that position, she gazed up at him, entirely serious now.

"I'm afraid, too. Of most ev'rythin'. There're times when I can't catch m'breath, I'm so afraid. But each step pushes the fear farther away . . . eases it."

She backed her way up onto the bed, bringing her other leg onto it as he stared down at her, love and desire shimmering in his eyes.

On her knees, she moved toward the middle of the tick, and Richard went with her, letting her pull him along. He was on his knees, too. He lifted his hands to her neck, slid them up into her hair, and turned her face up to his.

"You're a bothersome woman," he said, amusement lighting his eyes.

She laughed. "Ye don't mind as much as ye used to."

"You're right—I don't."

He kissed her softly, and then he kissed her again. His

tongue outlined her mouth, sweetly and gently, and Meg slid her hands around his waist and up his back, feeling the strength of him, closing her eyes and relishing it.

The backs of his fingers stroked the side of her face, and she turned her head and kissed them, one by one, as he gazed down at her. His clothes and skin smelled like the pine torches and the wind, and faintly of tobacco. His hands felt rough to touch, but they handled her so tenderly, they almost felt soft. Meggie loved the feel of them on her face and neck, on her shoulders and then on her breasts through the shift.

He cupped her breasts, and his fingertips massaged them; he ran his thumb over the nipples and made a sound of appreciation, a low growl in his chest that made her feel exquisite. He deepened his kisses, his tongue caressing hers as she pressed closer against him. Meggie lost herself in the pleasant tingling of her skin and the pounding of her heart.

A low throb began in the tender flesh between her legs, and his hand wandered that way, slowly drawing up her shift and baring her thighs. His fingertips caressed her buttocks. His hand slid around and between her legs.

He touched her wet heat, slid his fingers back and forth over it, gently pinched and rubbed her swollen bud until Meg's strength, her flame, seemed centered in that area, the rest of her body melting around her like a hot candle. She gasped and whimpered and clung to him; she rested her head against his chest while he continued the sweet torture, the pleasure.

The flame grew and finally exploded deep inside of her, and she tilted her face up to his, again welcoming the softness of his lips on hers.

He lifted her shift more, removed it, something Meggie couldn't have done by herself right then. She felt weak with pleasure, drained of energy. But when he tossed the shift aside and his hands returned to her breasts and teased her nipples into pebbles again . . . when desire flared through her again, she felt renewed.

She kissed him and slid her hands up beneath his shirt, raked her fingers through his chest hair and kissed his belly, relishing the salty taste of his skin. She dipped her tongue into his navel, ran her hand down his hard thigh, up and over his erection. She guided his hands, put them where she wanted them. She urged his fingers up into her; she led him, showed him the way. And he went along eagerly, clinging to her, whispering her name.

She worked at his trouser buttons as his hands played in her hair and his lips feasted on her neck. He whispered words about her strength and courage, and she drew his head down to her breast. He turned his ear to her chest, closed his eyes, seemed to listen to her heartbeat and her breathing. He drew her left nipple into his mouth and suckled.

At last she freed him. She curled her hand around his length, the throbbing hardness exciting her all the more. She bent and kissed it, drew the end of it into her mouth and swirled her tongue around it.

Richard gasped her name. He didn't know how long he could hold back if she continued. Not very long. Meggie . . . fiery Meggie. She refused to let him wallow in guilt and shame. She gave of her courage and strength, of her life and passion. He lost himself in her. God, how he lost himself in her.

He pulled away, shook his head when she glanced up at him, probably wondering why he didn't seem to enjoy what she was doing. But he did—that was the problem.

"I like it," he whispered, easing her onto her back. "Too much."

Her womanly scent filled his head. He inhaled deeply, loving the smell, loving her.

He came up between her thighs and slid into her heavenly heat. Her moist velvet caressed him and tempted him in deeper, and soon he rocked to the rhythm of her cries.

He buried his face between her breasts and rocked on, feeling a tingle build low in his groin. Nothing could feel better than this, than being inside of Meggie, than feeling her arms around him, her hands on his back, shoulders and arms, her legs curled around his waist. Nothing could sound better than her cries of pleasure as he filled her again and again. Nothing could bring him more joy than hearing her whisper that she loved him.

The words sent him over the edge.

She arched up to him, parting her legs more, and he flowed into her as she stroked his hair. She kissed his forehead; she spoke his name. She whispered again that she loved him. She brought his head down to rest on her breast.

Her heart pounded and lurched. It soon settled into an easy, soothing rhythm—and Richard settled with it. He shifted their bodies to one side. Then he reached down and pulled the coverlet up over them.

"Ye had only the one brother?" she asked softly.

Richard suppressed a groan of dread. "Lord, Meggie, you plan to make me talk about him, don't you?"

"His name was Willy, an' he died in battle."

"What if I don't want to do this?"

"He was eighteen when ye enlisted. Old enough t'know his own mind."

"You had no business reading my journal."

"An' if he hadn't enlisted, the President would've called 'im up. Thousands went off that didn't want to. Cowards hid out. Would ye rather Willy had been one of 'em?"

Hair bristled on the back of Richard's neck. "My brother was no coward. He fought hard and fast. He could reload in—"

"Mr. Lincoln would've called him. All men of fightin' age an' means had to go. Willy might've been killed anywhere . . . Antietam, Chattanooga, Vicksburg . . ."

Richard turned onto his back and stared up at the ceiling. "Gettysburg . . . he died at Gettysburg. He's buried there." He inhaled deeply. "I don't know which grave. They're lined up forever," he whispered. "The stones . . . you wouldn't believe how many markers. No names. More than twenty thousand fell for the North alone. I know what hell is—I've been there."

Meggie rose up on her left elbow and rested her right hand on Richard's chest. He was in hell again just talking about it.

She had to convince him that he wasn't responsible for his brother's death, that Willy would have ended up in the war one way or another, that he might have died on any battlefield.

"If he hadn't gone, he would have been called up," she said again, this time in a fierce whisper. "Gettysburg . . . Saints, ye drove Lee back across the Potomac! He didn't get to Washin'ton 'cause ye didn't let 'im!"

"Willy didn't see the retreat. Neither did I."

"But ye both helped make it possible. Ye, an' plenty of others who fell b'fore it happened. Willy's a hero. Ye're a hero. Don't rob yerself o' that."

"He didn't want to be a hero."

Meg scoffed. Sweet Jesus, he was determined to feel guilty and ashamed. "A humble hero is the better kind, to be sure."

He looked distant and pensive, more sad than she'd seen him look.

She shook her head at him. "'Tis over . . . ye've told me, an' I can't count the number o' times Poppa's told me the same. 'Tis over. The dead are buried, the prisons are emptied."

"The air is clear," Richard whispered. "There's no stench."

She was reaching him. God, how she prayed. "Ye didn't kill Willy. The war did."

He glanced at her. "Why did Kevin go?"

The question took her by surprise. She smiled sadly. "Boredom. An Irishman itchin' for a fight, an' the one between the states was a good one. Leastwise, that's what he said. Oh, he'd've told ye it was to preserve the Union an' free the slaves. But, truth be known, Kevin wanted a fight. He gave it his all, I've no doubt. Lucky for him, he had papers on 'im that said who he was. That's how he came to be buried at McBride's instead of somewhere else."

"You were lucky."

"I know."

Meggie laid her head on Richard's chest and closed her eyes. She remembered the day the wagon had come with Kevin's body. She'd thought she might never stop shedding tears. She'd thought she might never stop being angry with him.

The passing of time had helped. The passing of time and the realization that Kevin had gone voluntarily. She'd realized also that she wasn't the only person suffering, that she wasn't the only war widow, and that thousands of women had lost sons, the fruit of their wombs. Understanding those things had made her stop feeling so sorry for herself.

"Does yer mum know ye're alive?" she asked Richard.

"Guilt now, Meggie?"

She raised her head and looked him in the eye. "Lord knows ye've enough o' that. I'm curious, 'tis all."

He reached up and twirled one of her curls around his finger. "You never question without purpose."

"Ye're always suspectin' me of somethin'," she complained, affecting a pout.

Using the curl, he tugged her down to him and kissed her protruding lower lip. "What makes you think that?"

"The way ye look at me . . . watch me."

"You're usually up to something."

She turned her cheek to him. "I could bore ye. Then ye'd have reason to complain."

"I don't look twice at people who bore me."

"Then be happy with what ye have," she retorted.

Chuckling, Richard kissed the corner of her mouth. "Do I have you, Meggie McBride? I'm never too sure of anything where you're concerned."

She gave him a sly smile. "At present ye do. I'd have to cut my hair to get away."

"That's not what I mean."

"What're ye meanin', then?"

He nudged her onto her back. Meg rested her head on the pillow while he stared down at her, at her mouth, then into her eyes, looking serious suddenly. "Would you marry me if I asked you to?"

She caught her breath. Surely he wasn't asking. Surely not.

"Ye've . . . ye've no bus'ness askin' such a thing. Not when ye haven't been home yet. Go home, Richard. See yer mum. Let her know she has a son alive an' well. An' write to her. If ye plan to tarry here much longer, write to her."

His stare turned cool. She hadn't given him the response he'd wanted.

He turned back onto his back, withdrew from her. He fastened his gaze on the ceiling again. "I wasn't asking."

Meg shook her head. "Ye were. I won't be yer reason for stayin'."

"*I'm* my reason for staying. Stop saying that."

"I've said it only twice. Perhaps it should be said—"

"Twice is plenty."

He rose from the bed and strode to the window that overlooked her garden.

There he lit a cheroot and stood smoking, gazing out, his profile outlined by the moonlight.

Meggie suddenly realized that his limp had become more and more subtle. He'd gained strength helping Edan and Mr. Sardis with tasks. She wondered if that had been Edan's ulterior motive in proposing that Richard help them in exchange for board. Probably. It sounded like something Edan would do.

Meggie took the light coverlet with her when she left the tick. She wrapped herself in it and went to sit on the window ledge, where she could be close to Richard. She watched the shimmering water with him, then she spotted Caomh making his way along her garden paths. She'd take up the matter with the tomcat in the morning.

"Please understand," she told Richard softly. "'Tis not that I don't love ye an' want to be with ye. I jus' think yer mum has a right to ye first. She's gone years not knowin' if ye're dead or alive."

He reached out and caressed her face. He gave a slight laugh. "Damn you, Meggie . . . you won't let me hide or wallow in self-pity and cowardice." He said the words with such fondness, with such affection, she knew he was no longer angry.

"Nay, I won't," she said.

He brought her head to rest against his side. He stroked the side of her face, and as he smoked, they listened to the tree limbs brush together and Felan bark somewhere in the distance—the dog was forever roaming the countryside, irritating Meggie whenever she needed him to help with the sheep.

They watched the moon reflect off the river, and she told Richard of the first time she'd met Edan, when he and Kevin had come into her father's tavern, the night Edan couldn't stop kicking up his heels. Kevin had had to practically roll his pop home because Edan had drunk a little much. At least that was the story Kevin always told. Edan always said he'd danced all the way home. More than likely, Kevin's version was the truthful one. Edan never liked to admit when whiskey got the better of him.

Presently Richard tossed the stub of his cheroot into a nearby spittoon. Then he took Meggie's hand and led her back to the bedstead.

He laid her down and kissed her, and when she parted her legs, he slid into place and sank into her.

He filled her, and they arched and rocked together. She clung to him, kissed the droplets of perspiration from his brow. She wrapped her legs around him, drawing him closer.

Would she marry him if he asked?

In a heartbeat—if he returned from Ohio after he went home.

19

$\mathcal{F}$IRST THING THE next morning, Meg chased Caomh out of her garden.

The morning glories were wide open, stretching their necks toward the sunlight. Dewdrops clung to them, looking like tiny diamonds in places. Meg stooped and pulled weeds from beneath the vines. She hummed as she worked, and soon she began to sing.

"Tis on this rail-road bank I stand,
all for the love of a railroad man;
How I wish that train would come,
an' take me back from where I come."

"Mum, do ye think I could go downriver with Mr. Sardis this mornin'?" Ian asked, stepping up beside her.

"Goin' to see his kin, is he?" she responded.

"An' all the hundred children his kinsmen 'ave, too!" Ian's eyes brightened at that realization.

Meggie couldn't resist teasing him. "So 'tis not necessarily Mr. Sardis's company ye're wantin'?"

"Mum!"

"Ian!" She laughed. "G'on, then, an' mind yer manners. Ye've some strong arms on ye. Row that skiff for Mr.

Sardis." *An' no involvin' yerself in anythin' that'll get ye hurt, either.* She bit her tongue to keep from spilling that thought. If she said it, he'd get a sour look on his face and shuffle off.

Instead, he raced away smiling, and Meg went back to tending her morning glories and to singing.

> *"Love, oh, love, oh, care-less love.*
> *Love, oh, love, oh, care-less love.*
> *See what care-less love has done.*
> *'Tis on this railroad bank I stand,*
> *All for the love of a railroad man.*
> *How I wish that train would come,*
> *An' take me back where I come from."*

"A sad song this morning, Meggie?" Richard asked from the ledge. "Was your night so bad that you're sad?"

She smiled up at him, certain her face turned crimson. It felt hot suddenly. His hair was tousled. He wore a white shirt, opened at the neck and untucked. "Ye know better."

"I like to think I do."

"Ye're lookin' frowsy, Mr. Foster," she remarked as he lit a cheroot and drew from it.

He grinned. "Why do you look so perky after getting so little sleep?"

"I'm always perky in the mornin's. Doesn't seem to matter how much I've slept."

"Good thing."

Her face heated more. They really hadn't slept much. All of four hours at the most. By this afternoon she'd tire. She'd be ready to lie down in a bed of clover somewhere.

She plucked weeds while he sat on the ledge and smoked. She broke up the dirt around a row of boxwood, then began digging up onions in a patch on the far side of her garden.

"Where is your family, Meggie?" Richard asked.

"McBride's is my family. Edan an' Mrs. Hutchins an' Mr. Sardis. My own pop died over a tankard some six years ago. Jus' keeled over one night. Mum died a little before that. She fell sick one winter an' never recovered. Suffered for nearly a full year b'fore she succumbed. I've no brothers or sisters. McBride's really is my family."

"No wonder you're so devoted to everyone here."

She went back to singing, and he went back to smoking.

"Down in the valley, the valley so low,
* hang yer head ov-er, hear the wind blow.*
* Hear the wind blow, dear, hear the wind blow;*
* Hang yer head over, hear the wind blow."*

"I'm goin' into Havershill this afternoon for supplies," she told Richard. "Ye're welcome to go along if ye'd like."

He arched a brow in surprise. "Quite a change from when I volunteered to go along."

"Aye, well, a few things 'ave changed since then," she said, smiling up at him.

"I don't know how to feel, Meggie. You're being as gracious to me as you are to the guests."

She shook a handful of onions at him. "G'on now, b'fore I change my ways."

He laughed. "Your hair looks pretty."

Meggie tipped her head and considered him. She'd braided her hair to one side. The coppery plait hung nearly to her waist. Nothing fancy. "Ye're not 'bout to start goin' on an' on again, are ye?"

"Compliments from me make you nervous."

"Ha! They make me wonder if ye're still touched in the head."

"I never was. Say thank you."

"Thank ye," she said, dipping slightly. "Now I'd like to do my gardenin' if ye don't mind."

"I must remember that."

She sighed. "I'll be with ye again soon," she told the onions. "Remember what?" she asked Richard.

"That you're grumpy when the conversation doesn't go your way."

She huffed and turned away from him.

She went back to digging up onions, and soon another song spilled from her.

"I got a lad in the head of the hol-low,
hey, did-dle-dum dey.
He won't come an' I won't call 'im,
hey, did-dle-dum dey,
hey, did-dle-dum dey,
hey, did-dle-dum dey.
He won't come an' I won't call 'im,
hey, did-dle-dum dey . . ."

They traveled the river road, the wagon shifting and creaking beneath them, the water frolicking in the afternoon sunshine. Richard guided the horses, the reins held loosely in his hands.

He hadn't returned to Havershill since the afternoon he'd gone to the mercantile to purchase shirts. The townspeople had been cool at that time, and he wondered how he'd be received now. He'd met Mr. Dickson, the storekeeper, again the night of the play-party, and he'd met a number of other people who were from Havershill. Most everyone had been friendly, including Mr. Dickson.

As Mr. Hutchins had once told Richard, he wasn't a stranger anymore. The war and the troubles it spawned had made the mountain people distrustful and cool. But, once they became better acquainted with you, if you gave them reason to trust you, they put their misgivings aside.

Meg sat beside Richard, her right hand buried in her dress pocket. Her fingers were closed around the missive she'd penned this morning, folded, and sealed with wax. She'd then addressed it to Mrs. Foster of 810 Euclid Avenue in Cleveland, Ohio. When she'd asked Richard if he wanted to go into Havershill with her this afternoon, she'd forgotten about needing to take the letter to the post office.

How could she take it now, with Richard there? Saints. She went into Havershill only every few weeks. If she didn't take the missive to the post office today, it would have to wait until the next time she journeyed into town. That would mean another delay before Richard's mother could be notified that he was alive.

She had to find a way to post the letter without him

knowing. She had to busy him with something in the mercantile while she went to the post office. But with what?

She'd think of something, surely. They had another few miles to travel yet, and he was in a quiet sort of mood this afternoon. A contemplative sort of mood. She wondered what was going through his mind.

The town buildings came into view, the boarding house, the gray shanty that housed the post office . . . Not far away sat the mercantile and the Presbyterian church where Meg had attended many a service.

Mr. Dickson occupied the steps that led to his store. He was shucking the ears of corn that sat in a bucket at his feet. Nearby, Elijah Owens and Nester Ledbetter sat cleaning fish. Down Main Street a ways, some boys shouted as they chased each other between bed sheets that had been hung on a line to dry. Seconds later, several aproned women appeared to shoo them off.

"Afternoon, Meg," Mr. Dickson greeted. He grinned at her and inclined his head in greeting to Richard.

"Afternoon, Mr. Dickson," Richard greeted in return.

Meggie hopped down off the wagon seat and asked the storekeeper where he'd come by those fine-looking ears of corn.

"Oh, Almira brought 'em down to trade fer some cloth yesterd'y. I was gonna put 'em up fer sale. But they looked too good so I decided to put 'em in my pot instead. What can I get fer ya t'day? Usual things?"

"Aye, an' a few extras. Mrs. Hutchins's birthday's comin'. I'm thinkin' I'll make her a quilt for winter since she's always so cold when the snow comes. I've plenty of scraps from which to make squares, but I need a length of cloth for the backin'. I brought a list," Meggie said, pulling it from her dress pocket, making sure she left the missive to Richard's mother. "Edan's needin' tobacco, too, an' Mrs. Hutchins needs flour an' other things, like always."

"What can I get for *you*, Mr. Foster?" the storekeeper asked.

"I reckon he's just along for the ride," Nester said, not looking up from his work.

"Seems that way," Elijah commented.

"Actually, I thought I might look more closely at those boots you have for sale," Richard told Mr. Dickson. Then he added: "If you're agreeable."

"Well, why wouldn't I be?" Mr. Dickson rose and brushed the corn silk off his trousers. "C'mon. I've got more in the back room, too."

A woman rounded the boarding house, a small child on her left hip.

"Is that Annie Giles I'm seein'?" Meggie asked, shielding her eyes from the sun.

"Sure as shootin'," Nester said, still not looking up.

How he could do that, know who she was talking about without so much as a glance at the person, Meg couldn't figure. But it was Annie, all right, whose grandmother had died while sitting in her rocking chair. And now Annie was headed toward the Post.

"I'll gather these things, Meg," Mr. Dickson said. "Go talk to Annie."

"Y'know how women like to talk," Elijah remarked. "We've been cleaning for an hour. How much more we got, Nest?"

"Another bucketful over yonder."

Elijah grumbled that he might not get home before nightfall, as many fish as they had to clean and as slow as they were going.

Mr. Dickson chuckled. "Maybe if *you* talked more you wouldn't catch so many."

Elijah shot him a scowl.

"Be some good eatin'," Nester said as Mr. Dickson pulled open the front door of the mercantile.

"You coming to look at those boots?" the storekeeper asked Richard.

Richard nodded. He tipped his head to Meggie, who had already stepped away from the porch, just before he followed Mr. Dickson into the store.

Meggie's palm perspired as she gripped the envelope in her pocket and walked toward the Post. Richard might either have nothing to do with her once he found out about the missive, or he might be grateful she'd taken this step for him. She'd mentioned to him that he should write to his mother, and he'd balked. So she'd decided to take matters into her own hands.

Her first order of business would be to mail the letter. Then she'd visit with Annie.

The missive went on its way, and so did Meg and Richard after she had her conversation with Annie and after Mr. Dickson helped them gather their supplies and load everything in the wagon bed.

Some wild turkeys tore off through the undergrowth between poplars and cottonwoods. A few minutes later, Meggie spotted a raspberry bush and had Richard stop the wagon. She was hungry. As sour as they might be, the raspberries would settle her stomach until they reached home.

"Tell me, *do* ye intend to write to ye're mum an' let her know ye're alive?" Meg asked Richard as she plucked berries and popped them into her mouth.

"Meggie." His tone was stern—he didn't want to talk about whether he meant to write to his mother.

She gave him a look that was equally stern. "As ye know, it troubles me, an' when somethin' troubles me, I don't usually let it be."

"I'm finding that out."

"Well, do ye intend to write or not?"

He'd taken to picking up stones and skipping them across the water. "I don't know."

She huffed. "An' jus' how long b'fore ye know?"

"I don't know."

"Ye're a stubborn one," she said, scowling.

He grinned at her. "I know." He skipped another stone.

She made a sound of exasperation. "At least ye know *something*."

He laughed. "A few things, yes."

She plucked more berries and popped them into her mouth. "I'm thinkin' ye need to write to yer mum. Tell her ye're alive. Tell her where ye've been an' —"

"Meggie, it's my business."

"—that ye're doin' well. Tell her ye were injured an' that ye've recovered. Why, ye're stronger jus' since comin' to McBride's."

"Meggie, I don't want to write," he said, walking toward her. He didn't look happy. Not at all. His brows were drawn together in an unhappy line.

She backed away, not wanting to get too far from the raspberry bush but also not liking the look on his face. "Then let someone write for ye."

"It's my responsibility."

"Aye, that it is," she said, and she backed away more. He didn't look pleased—he looked as if he'd had enough of this conversation. She wasn't about to leave it alone.

"But if ye had someone write for ye, then at least ye'd know one way or another how yer mum feels. She couldn't be feelin' too good 'bout not knowin' if ye're dead or alive. If she blames ye for Willy, too . . . ye'd be better off knowin'. A person's always better off knowin' things."

"Meggie . . . you interfering little leprechaun." His hand shot out and grabbed her wrist.

He pulled her toward him, and Meg gave little resistance.

She stood within inches of him, and as he looked down at her, she saw a touch of humor in his eyes. She didn't know what he planned to do, but she took the initiative—she kissed him on the mouth and said softly, "Write to her."

"I have to settle this myself," he responded, and he gathered her close and kissed her back.

The kisses deepened. Touches began, building into caresses. They sighed and clung to each other and fumbled with their clothing.

They found a patch of soft grass nearby, shaded by the cottonwoods and poplars, and they sank down to it. They whispered and murmured sweet words, and joined bodies while the birds sang in the trees and the river shimmered in the pretty afternoon.

Afterward Meggie made certain her undergarments were in place, and then she splashed into the water.

She swam out a little ways, and when she surfaced, she

was surprised but pleased to see Richard venturing into the river—not with the enthusiasm she exhibited, but at least he was coming in.

She smiled and held her hand out to him. He smiled back a bit devilishly and submerged himself. Meg yelped, knowing he was coming after her, and she splashed down into the water and swam with all her might.

He caught her anyway. He grabbed her foot and then her leg. Finally his hands came around her waist, and he lifted her up out of the water. Laughing, he slid her down against him and held her close.

"I love you, Meggie McBride," he whispered against her lips.

She thought, *Ye can't love me so much that ye don't go home.* But she didn't want to ruin these moments—she didn't want to put another frown on his face—so she simply held him and kissed the droplets of water from his jaw.

They played more in the water. They made love again in the bed of soft grass.

"What happens to us when I go home?" he asked moments later as Meggie sat up to slip on her dress.

She glanced at him, unsure of what to say.

"I couldn't take you away from the inn. Or from this countryside," he said. But she could tell he wasn't certain of that; he was wondering what her reaction would be.

She'd go wherever he went, wherever they chose to make a life together—if they chose to make a life together. But she wouldn't say that.

She knelt beside him and took his jaw in her hands. "I love you, Richard," she said instead. "Go home. Do it b'fore winter sets in."

She stood and buttoned her dress. He watched her in silence. She remarked that if they got started now they would reach the inn before nightfall. The sun was melting, spreading its rivers of color across the western sky.

Her fingers trembled as she brushed the wrinkles from her skirt. He pulled on his trousers finally, then his shirt.

They'd share no more pleasant conversation today, Meggie could tell.

20

$\mathscr{A}$S THEY ROUNDED a bend, the inn came into sight.
So did a man trudging up the road with a knapsack thrown
over his bent shoulder.

As the seconds ticked by and Meggie stared at the man . . .
as realization dawned, her heart paused, and her breath
caught in her throat. She stood to have a better look at him.
She had to be sure. She had to be absolutely sure.

He was uncommonly thin. His dark hair was long and
scraggly, and he was dirty. Even now, after the beating the
Southern states had taken, he wore Confederate Gray. It was
tattered in places and just as dirty as he, just as defeated as
the South. But it was a good sight. A grand sight.

Meg cried out. She was aware of Richard talking to the
horses, halting them, asking her what was wrong. The man
was another soldier, he knew. But he didn't think the man
posed them any danger. The Reb looked too beat, too worn to
a thread.

"Zachary," she whispered, bringing her hands to her
mouth. "Saints be praised . . . 'tis *Zachary*!"

Seconds passed. Richard asked: "Mrs. Hutchins's son?"

"Aye."

Meggie gathered her skirts and scrambled down from the
wagon.

She tore off running up the road, shouting and waving her arms. "Zachary, Zachary! 'Tis Meggie McBride!" She thought of the joyous look that would pass over Mrs. Hutchins's face when she saw her son, and she thought of how the woman would fuss over him, too, because he was so thin and sickly-looking. He was alive, not buried on some battlefield in an unmarked grave or beneath a stone that proclaimed him an unknown soldier. He was alive, and he'd returned home, to the Kentucky hills . . . to McBride's.

Meg wondered how Richard, having been a Union soldier, would react to Zachary in his Confederate Gray. She wondered if Edan and Mr. Sardis would set aside the hostile sentiments they'd exhibited when Zachary announced that he'd chosen his side—that he was with the South. Mrs. Hutchins had cried the entire day. She'd cried more when Zachary and Edan had words, and even more when Zachary announced that he was going off to join the Confederate Army.

Meggie called to Zachary again, and this time he looked up. She'd almost reached him—not more than a hundred yards separated them.

He squinted at her. "Meg? Meggie McBride?"

"Aye, 'tis me! Zachary Hutchins, ye don't know how happy yer mum will be to see ye!"

She reached him at last and threw her arms around his neck.

He truly was ungodly thin, a skeleton. They'd not fed him well. But then, they couldn't have, at least not during the past year. The Confederacy had starved and burned.

She was crying when she pulled away from him. Crying for all the dead soldiers and their families. Crying because he was alive, and because he was nearly starved. Crying because he was seventeen when he left, and because now, five years later, he looked like a man of more than thirty.

"It's all right, Meg. Don't cry," he said, trying to soothe her.

"I can't help m'self," she sobbed. "Ye're home an' ye're alive."

His bony hand rubbed her back. He'd seen a lot of

misfortune; she could tell by looking into his dull brown eyes.

Richard had brought the wagon forward. It squeaked to a stop, and Meggie glanced at him, again wondering how he would react to a man who still wore Confederate Gray.

"I know you," Zachary told him, stiffening, holding Meg and staring at Richard suddenly. She felt tense. The two men surely wouldn't go to blows. The fighting was over. "I know you . . ." Zachary said again.

Richard studied him. "Then you have a sharper mind than I do, Captain. I made a point of not remembering the faces of the men I fought."

"A good thing. Libby Prison . . ." Zachary said. "I know you from Libby Prison . . . I helped escort you there."

Richard nodded slowly. That Confederate prison had almost killed him. Meggie knew that from reading his diary. How he must hate the men who had helped put him there.

She stepped forward, thinking to put herself between the two men. "It doesn't matter—"

Richard stretched out his hand and told Zachary his name.

Zachary hesitated. A moment later, he reached out and shook Richard's hand.

A former Union lieutenant and a Confederate captain, men who had enlisted in armies that had fought bitterly one against the other, now greeted each other in peace.

Meggie shed more tears.

Richard offered Zachary a ride the rest of the short distance to McBride's, and Zachary accepted. Brushing away her tears, Meg helped him climb slowly up onto the wagon seat.

Edan was the first to see them approach the inn. He and Felon, the dog, apparently had just brought the sheep in from grazing. Edan stood outside the gate, dropping the leather latch over the corner post. He stared at the wagon—at Richard, Meg, and Zachary. Then he mouthed something Meggie felt certain was a curse. He too couldn't believe his eyes.

He walked slowly in their direction, giving Richard a chance to bring the wagon up alongside the sheep pen.

When Zachary said, "Howdy, Edan," almost without a care, Meg thought her father-in-law would keel over.

"God in heaven!" he gasped. "Zachary. Let's get ye down from that wagon an' into the house. I'd giv'n up hope, I had. Not proud to be admittin' that, but I had."

"You sure you want me in your house?" Zach asked.

Meggie caught her breath. Things hadn't been good between Edan and Zachary when Mrs. Hutchins's son announced that he meant to join the Rebel forces. They hadn't been good at all.

"'Tis over," Edan said softly and meaningfully; he caught and held Zachary's gaze. "I won't be sayin' who was right an' who was wrong. 'Tis over—an' ye're like me own son. Let's get ye down from there."

Meg shed more tears. She had no control over them. They gushed from her eyes and flowed down her cheeks, and she could do nothing to stay them. Richard slipped his arm around her and pressed her close to his shoulder while Edan reached up and took hold of the frail Zachary.

"I ain't tipped a bottle in months!" Ryan Darrow said, running toward them from the landing. "I see Zachary Hutchins sure as my feet are on the ground!"

Edan tossed a squinted look at the ferryman, obviously expecting the worst—Ryan still made it clear at times that he'd sided with the Union. "We'll be havin' no trouble here," Edan warned the man. "He's welcome at McBride's."

Mr. Darrow blanched. "I ain't planning to cause trouble."

"Good."

Mr. Sardis came from the stable, hobbling toward the wagon as fast as he could, his eyes as bright as Meggie could remember ever seeing them. He'd heard the ruckus and knew what was going on—he knew Zachary had come home.

Meggie shot a look toward the inn, expecting Mrs. Hutchins, too, to tear outside at any moment. But the kitchen was located at the back of the structure, and if she was in that room she probably couldn't hear the commotion.

She was. The group of them—Edan, Richard, Nathaniel Sardis, Ryan Darrow, and Meg—escorted Zachary into the inn and took him directly to the kitchen. From the doorway, they peered into that room as Zachary stepped forward and said, "Ma?"

Mrs. Hutchins had her back to the door. She stood facing the table in the center of the room, working with a row of jars—she was making more jam. At the sound of Zachary's voice, she went still. Meggie wondered if she'd spin around, if she'd tear across the kitchen and snatch Zach into her big arms. But the woman didn't move.

Zachary took several more steps. "Ma? It's me, Zach. I'm home."

She turned around slowly, her eyes wide and glossy as they fastened on her son. She opened her mouth as if she meant to say something. She closed it, swallowed, and inhaled deeply. She gripped the back of a nearby chair, tipping it, then righting it.

"I'd given you up for dead," she whispered, and then the tears came, a river of them, rushing down her face. Despite her outward faith, she'd had fear in her that Zach was dead and that she'd never see him again. She'd put on a brave front, waiting all these months, never seeming to doubt that he'd come home alive and well. But she *had* doubted.

"My boy . . ." she said. "My boy, my boy, my boy . . ."

She toppled the chair in her haste to get to him.

Meg started forward, fearing Mrs. Hutchins would grab Zachary, fragile as he was, and crush him in an embrace, literally crush him. She felt a hand on her shoulder, Richard's hand, and when she glanced at him, he shook his head at her, silently telling her not to interfere. She wondered how the sight of the reunion affected him, if he considered his mother who waited in Ohio.

He shifted his gaze back to Zachary and Mrs. Hutchins. The muscles in his jaw worked, and emotion flickered in his eyes. But Meggie couldn't tell what it was—she couldn't guess at his thoughts.

Meg shed more tears as she backed up from the doorway, meaning to leave Mrs. Hutchins and Zachary to themselves.

"Praise the Lord," Mr. Sardis said, and he too wiped at his eyes.

"Why's he still wearing that Gray?" Ryan Darrow asked, quietly, thank God. "Somebody might've killed him along the way."

Edan took hold of the man by the back of his shirt and pulled him back farther into the hallway. "We'll be leavin' 'em be now," he told everyone, and Meggie felt certain that no one considered arguing.

The group made their way to the front door.

Supper was a joyous affair that evening. Meg served the meal, ordering Mrs. Hutchins out of the kitchen so she and Zachary could visit. Meggie sliced the roasted leg of lamb Mrs. Hutchins had prepared and put heaping spoonfuls of herbed potatoes on plates all the way around. Earlier, Ian had helped shell peas and cut carrots, and Meg served those vegetables, too, and later, slices of apple pie.

Several more guests had arrived earlier in the day—a Mr. Bartlett and a Mr. Rossiter. Mr. Bartlett kept to himself, going upstairs directly after supper, but Mr. Rossiter remained downstairs to talk and visit and join in the festive occasion of Zachary's homecoming. Edan played the harmonica, and everyone but Zach sang and danced. He had no energy; he was worn down from the fighting, and he'd walked all the way from Virginia to this part of Kentucky.

No one talked about the war, and Meggie was glad of that. Edan and Kevin had been for the Union, and Zachary had announced his support for the Southern states months before any military engagement. Arguments had ensued, and tempers had flared. The month before he signed up, Zachary hadn't stayed at the inn because he, Edan, and Kevin had disagreed so much. Having Edan and Zachary together in peace again was a refreshing thing.

Later, after Meggie had tucked Ian into bed and made sure the guests and Zach were comfortable, she and Richard walked alongside the river.

"'Twas good of ye . . . not bein' hostile toward Zachary," she remarked.

He looked out across the water. "You expected me to be hostile?"

"I don't know what I expected. Aye . . . Saints, he helped escort ye to that prison . . . he knew ye."

"As a soldier, he did his duty."

He'd been quieter than usual since they'd come upon Zachary. He'd apppeared deep in thought, turning things over in his mind. Clearly his unhostile stance toward Zach was a matter of honor between military men. Richard respected Zachary for his loyalty, for following orders—for "doing his duty." In turn, both men respected the fact that the war was over, that peace had been declared.

Meg and Richard walked on. Ryan Darrow had shut the ferry down hours ago. It rocked and creaked in the Ohio. Crickets chirped, and frogs croaked. In the distance, coyotes howled, one right after the other. Then a chorus of them began, a haunting sound in the night. The sheep stirred in their pen up near the stable, bawling at the sound of the predators. Mr. Sardis always slept in a room attached to the stable, his rifle never far away, so Meg didn't worry. Old as he was, Mr. Sardis seemed forever alert. If a coyote or a wolf came too close, a shot would be fired before the animal ever realized a human was near.

Richard squeezed Meggie's hand, which rested on his arm. "I've, uh . . . I've been thinking of going home."

She fought to keep from freezing in place. Her heart didn't want him to go, and yet she knew that going home would be the best thing for him and his family. He was nervous about his decision, that was obvious by his shaky tone and his broken speech. So was she, but she meant to be supportive of his choice.

"Have ye?"

"Yes."

She waited for him to say something else, to say, perhaps, when he planned to leave, and to state the reason he'd been thinking of going home. Had Zachary's appearance had something to do with his change of heart? Mrs. Hutchins's reaction to her son coming home, perhaps? The sight of the reunion?

"I have to settle things, Meggie," Richard said, halting his steps and drawing her close.

Smiling, she pressed her finger to his lips. "I know."

She kissed him and held him, wanting to remember
forever the feel of him and the warmth of his breath against
her neck.

During the ensuing days and weeks, Zachary ate little, as
much as his queasy stomach could stand. His appetite
increased slowly, and the passing of time began to put flesh
on his bony frame and color in his cheeks.

Along with his mother and the McBrides, he attended
church services in Havershill several Sundays in a row—
and he renewed his interest in a mountain girl. He even took
a job at a lumber mill on the other side of the settlement,
something that surprised McBride's residents given the fact
that Zach had had no purpose, really, before he'd gone off
to the war. For the most part, he'd run wild in the hills. Now
he put money back and talked about settling down on a
piece of land. He even talked about choosing a girl and
having a family.

August blazed into September. There was so little rain
and moisture, that Meggie brought buckets of water from
the Ohio to dampen her garden so her precious plants
wouldn't wilt. Richard helped her wet the kitchen garden,
too, soaking the tomatoes, beans, corn, and other vegetables. The growing season wouldn't last much longer—
October would bring cold and frost, fallen leaves and frozen
plants—but every year she helped the gardens survive for
as long as possible.

The changes in Zach delighted Mrs. Hutchins, and she
bustled around the kitchen and the inn cheerfully, full of
energy, always singing and chattering. It helped too that she
and Edan had a little something going under the eaves. They
were cute together, she beaming shy smiles at him, and he
finding a million excuses to go to the kitchen—when he'd
never bothered with the kitchen before. In the early afternoon, when he usually inspected the land and all of his
holdings, animals included, and did odd tasks, he now could
be found inside the inn. Wasn't it coincidence, Meg thought

with a big smile, that Mrs. Hutchins always did her first-floor cleaning during that time?

She didn't know why it had taken the two of them so long to match themselves to each other, or why she hadn't thought of matching them herself. It had truly never occurred to her. But then, the last five years or more had been consumed by threats of war, then the reality of it, and lately the recuperation from the horrible things the conflict had wrought. Who had had time for romance, or even thoughts of it?

While summer burned away, Meg continued to sing in her garden every morning, as always, and Richard continued to sit on the window ledge and listen to her and smoke his usual morning cheroot.

The chilled air of October would not be long in coming, and so Meggie harvested and dried herbs, and plucked and stored what vegetables would keep through winter. She filled her garden shed with stores, and she even filled the little underground storage that Edan had dug and built several years ago. She piled corn and potatoes and other vegetables into sturdy woven baskets and she and Richard carried the baskets down the ladder and arranged them neatly in the underground space.

Some afternoons she fished and swam with Richard and Ian, and countless times she and Richard made love in the moonlight on the damp grass in secluded spots on the riverbank. The end of summer passed peacefully and quietly.

Fall arrived, the maples turned red and joined the oaks and other trees in dropping their colorful leaves. Another season. A better season. All was well at McBride's—the war had ended earlier in the year, Zachary had come home, Ian had grown stronger, and business was good on the ferry and at the inn.

Meggie's only troubling thoughts were about Richard—her worry that he didn't intend to go home after all. They were happy together, too happy. Happier than they had a right to be considering the fact that his mother still sat in Ohio, probably almost convinced by now that the war had taken both of her sons. There'd been no word from her or from Richard's father, no acknowledgment that they'd received Meggie's letter, and Meg worried over that, too. Had the missive gotten lost along the way?

She worried that her and Richard's love kept him here, that she had made things too easy for him. There had been a day when she'd vowed not to do that. But she'd fallen in love with the man and she seemed to have little willpower to push him away.

Sometimes she lay awake at night wondering about her letter, if it would ever find its way to Cleveland, to Richard's family. She refused to dwell on her deepest concern: that the missive had been received and that Richard's worst fear had come to pass, that his mother blamed him for Willy's death and didn't care to restore contact with Richard.

Then one day Meggie learned that the letter *had* been received—and acknowledged.

21

$\mathcal{M}$EG, RICHARD, AND Ian went into Havershill for more supplies, and nearly as soon as they entered the mercantile Mr. Dickson informed Richard that a letter had come for him and that Halbert Covey, the postmaster, had brought it to the shop. Halbert knew Meg came there every few weeks, and he thought Mr. Dickson could give her the letter and she could give it to Mr. Foster. "But here you are yourself," Mr. Dickson told Richard, and he held out an envelope.

Richard's face tightened with a mixture of emotions—confusion and surprise—and Meg's stomach tightened with apprehension. She could lose him completely over this, over writing to his mother and mailing her missive to the address she'd found in his diary. Over informing his mother that he was alive and well, and that he blamed himself for Willy's death and feared going home and facing her grief. Meggie had made the decision to share Richard's deepest feelings with someone, thoughts she knew he'd shared with no one but her, and in doing so she had betrayed his trust in her. But at least his mother knew he was alive.

"Came from Cleveland, Ohio," Mr. Dickson remarked as Meg's face burned and her legs weakened.

She couldn't stand it. She was going to be ill. She crept off toward a row of plowing implements, needing time to gather her wits—and her churning stomach. As far as she knew, Richard hadn't written to his parents, and it wouldn't take him long to guess how they knew he was staying at an inn located just outside of Havershill, Kentucky.

She was right—it took him all of two minutes.

"Meggie," he barked in a harsh, scratchy tone. An angry tone. A tone of fury. Talking to him, trying to convince him through words to write home, was fine. But she'd gone too far. She'd overstepped him by miles, gone way beyond propriety; she'd taken advantage of finding that address in his journal.

Yes, she had, and if she could repeat the day she'd left that letter at the post office for his parents, her actions would be the same.

Ian blurted out questions, wanting to know who the letter was from, why Richard was angry, why he didn't open the envelope.

"Something wrong?" Meg heard Mr. Dickson ask Richard.

Richard growled, "Plenty," and then she heard boots hit hard and heavy on the oak floor.

At first she was afraid Richard was coming to thrash her, and she shrank back more. But when she peeked over the row of plowing devices, she saw him storming toward the door.

Ian said, "Richard, look at—Mum?"

Meggie raced toward the door, calling Richard's name. She had to make him understand that she'd written to his mother because her heart had been breaking for the woman, because she knew Mrs. Foster's heart must be breaking. Surely the woman had the right to know she had one son still alive and well. Considering that, whether or not Meg should have taken it upon herself to inform Mrs. Foster seemed irrelevant. Someone had had to—and no one else had been privy to the facts. Or made themselves privy to them, as Meggie had.

"Richard, please try to understand," she said, racing after him. But he was already down the mercantile steps.

He stormed across the dirt street, his right hand gripping the letter.

"I felt she had a right to know!" Meg called. "Think about it. Ye're her only son now an' . . . Richard, please, listen to me!"

He headed toward one of the two taverns down the way.

Recognizing where he was going, Meggie stopped short. If he was so angry that he meant to tip a bottle, he also meant to wallow in self-pity. Blast him! Let him go, then. Let his guilt and shame trap him forever. Let him drown in his cowardice.

She didn't mean it, not really. She knew her temper was getting the best of her, as it often did. She was frustrated by not being able to reach him, by not being able to convince him that he needed to set his guilt and shame aside and go home.

Meg turned back toward the mercantile and found Mr. Dickson and Ian staring at her from the steps, curious, worried looks marking their expressions. Other people stared, too, pausing on the walkways and in the street. Mr. Covey studied her from the door of the post office.

"What's the matter with Richard?" Ian asked when Meg stepped up onto the porch of the mercantile.

"Stubbornness," she muttered as she pulled out her list of supplies and held it out to Mr. Dickson.

He took it, shaking his head. "Long as I can remember, you've been in the middle of trouble, Miss Meggie," he said, trying to make light of the situation.

"Where's he goin'?" Ian demanded, looking more worried with each passing second.

"To pout," Meg said. "To feel sorry for himself. We'll gather our things an' be on our way."

"We can't leave him!"

"He's off to seek other comfort."

"What's the matter?" Ian asked, unmoving. "Why's he so angry? We'll see him again, won't we, Mum? *Mum?*" He whipped around to confront her.

"Ian—stop." Meggie set her jaw and checked her temper, which now flared at her son. Close as he'd become to Richard, Ian deserved an explanation.

"Come here," she told Ian, and she took him aside, down

the walkway a fair distance so they'd be out of earshot of Mr. Dickson. She'd tell Ian what was wrong with Richard, but she wouldn't have anyone else knowing unless Richard told them.

"I wrote to Richard's family," she explained to her son. "He didn't want them to know where he was because he feels terrible 'bout somethin' that happened . . . His brother died during the war, and Richard thinks he should've been able to save him. He has problems we can't solve for him, Ian—he's got to remedy them himself. He has to go home, an' he's afraid to."

"So he's angry b'cause he didn't want his family to feel sorry for him?"

Meggie took a deep breath. "He's thinkin' they might blame him for his brother's death. He's thinkin' they might also feel he should've been able to save his brother."

"But sometimes people, they can't be saved," Ian said. So innocent, so sweet. "I was lucky."

He was referring to Mr. Sardis pulling him from the burning stable. If Mr. Sardis hadn't done so, Ian would have perished, no doubt. Mrs. Hutchins had been petrified by the sight of the burning structure. Ryan Darrow had been stammering and stuttering when Meg arrived at the stable. Edan had taken the sheep out to graze. Mr. Sardis had raced into the blazing building and then raced out moments later, cradling Ian in his arms. A beam had fallen on him, he'd said. Ian had screamed over and over because he couldn't move, couldn't escape the fire.

"True," Meg responded. "Now, let's gather our things an' go home. Nothin' more will be said about Richard t'day. Understand?"

Ian twisted his mouth, pouting this way and that way. He dropped his troubled gaze to his boots, which he shuffled back and forth on the walkway. "Aye, Mum," he said finally.

They returned to where Mr. Dickson stood. The store-keeper reached out and ruffled Ian's hair. "There's stick candy inside if you're interested."

Ian shot him a reluctant smile. Then he hurried off toward the door of the mercantile with Mr. Dickson.

Meggie turned in time to spot Richard push open the door to one of the taverns. She didn't take him for a man who frequented such places, but given his mood right now, she guessed that he meant to have himself a drink or two, perhaps even an entire bottle.

Richard didn't come home that night, at least not back to McBride's. Meg knew in her mind that his true home was in Ohio, but he'd settled in so well at the inn, she thought of it as his home. He seemed to be part of the family.

She lay awake listening for him, for the sound of the front door opening downstairs, for the sound of boots on the floor and in the hall upstairs . . . for any sound at all that might indicate that he'd come home. She even listened for the sound of an approaching horse or horse and wagon. While McBride's wasn't such a far distance from Havershill, he could have rented a mount and even a wagon at the livery in that settlement.

She listened and heard only the usual creaks and groans of a house settling in for the night, the whine of wind that whistled beneath the eaves, the rattle of windowpanes as a storm brewed outside, the rumble of thunder, the patter of rain on the roof. She worried that he was outside somewhere in the storm, in air that grew cooler every day, that was right now chilled by the night.

She stood shivering at her bedroom window, watching lightning flash in the distance and listening to the horses whinny in the stable. They didn't like storms, but Mr. Sardis was there to calm them. The man was so old, Meg wondered how much longer he'd last. She gathered her wrap more closely around her body and turned away from the window.

Might Richard have crossed the river and headed toward home? Had the letter delivered good news? That his mother didn't blame him and was happy to hear he was alive? That she wanted to see him? If that were the case, would he have gone home? Without saying goodbye to her? To any of them—to Ian, Edan, Mrs. Hutchins . . . ? Had he been so furious with her for writing that letter to his parents that he would've done such a thing?

Meggie sank back against the wall to one side of the window. Not knowing something was horrible. Her heart cracked at the thought that he might've gone home without saying goodbye. Without sharing one last kiss with her.

More thunder rumbled and cracked. More lightning flashed, crooked, jagged lines against the black sky. Scarcely a star could be seen tonight. The rain became a torrent, driving and pounding. Ian cried out from his room next door.

Meg went to her son, crawling up onto his bed and curling her body around his. She smoothed back his soft hair, and she kissed his temple. He snuggled against her, sighing his way back to sleep.

She smiled. Funny how lately he wanted to feel big and half-grown, a little like a man, even to the point of not letting her ruffle his hair or kiss his cheek. But let a storm come along, and he welcomed the soothing hands and feel of his mother.

She was tired. But could she sleep?

She closed her eyes, tried to concentrate on the tasks she had planned for tomorrow. She meant to pick what would no doubt be the last of the wild berries for the year from the forest. She meant to make butter in the afternoon, and she meant to harvest more herbs and hang them to dry. School had started in Havershill, and while Mr. Sardis had volunteered to take Ian to school in the morning, Meggie fetched him in the afternoon, still refusing to let her son walk home alone. Ian didn't like that, and he fussed at her, but she didn't care. She was still protective, and while she had eased up some, she wasn't ready to ease up that much.

Ian was warm, and Meg eventually fell asleep snuggled close to him, her chin resting on the top of his head.

In Havershill the next afternoon, Meg caught herself glancing around for any sign of Richard. The school sat apart from the main settlement. Nevertheless, Meggie looked that way, hoping to catch a glimpse of him. If he'd gone back to Ohio already, that meant he'd left behind what belongings he had collected since being released from prison—and would he have done that?

"He's not comin' back, is he, Mum?" Ian asked as he climbed up onto the wagon seat.

"I don't know," she said quietly. That was the worst part, not knowing. Would they just have to wait for the days to pass, each day making them realize more and more that he wouldn't be back? Meg hated that thought. She hated it for Ian. She hated it for herself. They loved him.

Swallowing the huge lump in her throat, she took the reins in hand and gave them a shake, putting the horse into motion.

Ian sat quietly for the first mile. Then he sniffed and said, "Why would he jus' leave?"

What to tell him? She was angry and hurt herself, but she had to appear calm and mild-mannered for Ian.

"We must try to understand him," she said presently, and she spoke to herself as well as to her son. "If he went home . . . to Ohio, it's for the best. Ye know how Mrs. Hutchins missed Zach. Ye know how I worried that he was dead an' wouldn't come home. Richard's parents have spent years not knowin' if he was dead or alive. He fought at Gettysburg, a mess in itself . . . so many dead, there wasn't a way to identify who ev'ryone was. Richard ended up with a farmer who cared for him, then he went to prison for a time. Each side had their own prisons, an' the Confederates got him. His parents surely believed he was either dead, an unknown soldier buried in a grave on the battlefield, or missing. For them to know he's alive . . . 'tis best if he's gone home."

"But he didn't want to go home! Why do ye think he's gone home?"

"Because maybe the letter brought good news. But maybe he's angry with me for tellin' things he thinks I had no business tellin'."

"Why'd ye tell?" Ian's eyes were wide. He wasn't angry with her—he was simply trying to understand Richard's anger, why he might have left without saying goodbye, and why she'd felt compelled to write to Richard's parents.

"Because I watched Mrs. Hutchins worry over Zach, an' I couldn't bear the thought of Richard's mum not knowin' if she had a son left alive."

That quieted Ian. The rest of the ride home was spent in silence.

At the inn, Meg took the wagon directly to the stable, where Mr. Sardis waited. Edan was there, and he asked if she'd seen Richard. She told him she hadn't, and she made the mistake of avoiding his gaze when she spoke, which made him ask more questions.

"Somethin' happened between the two o' ye?" he queried, apparently unable to help himself. "A fallin'-out o' sorts?"

Meggie nodded. "He may have gone home."

Sighing, Edan walked to the stable doorway and glanced out, hands on his hips. "Well, if he has, God bless 'im an' his kin."

"Aye," Meg said, fighting tears. She handed the reins over to Mr. Sardis and then jumped down from the wagon. She grabbed a tin bucket, thinking she'd go pick those berries now. She was about to cry, and she didn't want Ian or Edan or Mr. Sardis to witness such a sight, such a weakness. She'd spend the rest of the day in the forest if she had to to prevent everyone from seeing her cry because Richard had left without saying goodbye, leaving her in an emotional mess.

Ian asked if he could go with her, and when she told him no, that she preferred he stay with Mr. Sardis or Edan, he presented no argument. Bless the child—he seemed to realize she too was having a hard time with Richard being gone.

Bucket in hand, she passed Edan in the doorway. He said nothing more, but she felt his sympathetic look and she kept going.

She didn't falter once until she was within the safety, the secrecy, of the forest, hidden by the many trees. Then she collapsed onto a soft bed of low-lying ferns and let the tears flow. Her heart hurt—she hadn't realized how much until now—and she let herself feel the pain. She didn't push it away, she didn't try to hide it. She let it go, too, and she let her anger and frustration spill.

When she finally brushed away the last tear and pushed her way up from the ferns, she thought a good amount of time had passed. At least an hour. She took up the bucket again and went off to pluck berries.

"He's here," Edan told her when she returned to McBride's. He was sitting at his desk in his study, and he called to Meg as she passed by the doorway.

She paused, her heart in her throat. "Richard?"

Edan nodded. "Aye. But he has plans to leave." He said the latter as if he regretted having to tell her, and even to say it. He didn't want Richard to go any more than she or Ian did.

"I'll not try to hold him."

"Ye could, lass, with a few words."

She shook her head. "'Twouldn't be right of me, Mr. McBride."

He sighed heavily. "I know, girl." He jerked his head to the left, in the direction of the staircase. "He's up there. Go see him."

No one had to command her to do that. Her feet would have taken her up the stairs and to his room even if she'd not wanted to go there. But she'd bite her tongue clean off if she started to urge him to stay.

She made herself deliver the bucket of berries to the kitchen. Mrs. Hutchins was absent, thank goodness, probably off walking with Zach or visiting friends with him, as was sometimes their habit in the afternoons.

Meggie hurried back to the staircase, her perspiring hands gripping the folds of her skirt as she lifted it and raced up the steps. She didn't know how she'd be received. She didn't know if Richard would greet her in anger or in sadness, in love or in hate. But she had to know.

The door to his room stood open. Meg slowed her pace as she approached, and she attempted to catch her breath, without success.

She stepped into the doorway and glimpsed him sitting on

the tick with Ian, his belongings cluttering the bed. Ian held the hatbox, turning it in his hands, inspecting it. Meggie wondered if Ian had told Richard what she'd shared with him—and if Richard was furious that she'd exposed his secrets to yet another person.

Ian saw her first. His eyes flared, and a grin broke out on his face. "Mum, look! He's back!"

Richard turned, and as soon as he caught sight of Meg standing in the doorway, he stood and faced her, gracefully, fluidly, forever the gentleman, his hands clasped in front of him. His head dipped in acknowledgment to her.

Meggie's breath lodged in her chest. She searched his eyes for anger, hatred, resentment, and she saw none of the emotions. She released her breath in a rush, so light-headed suddenly that she gripped the door frame to steady herself.

Her fingers were stained from the berries, and she lowered her hands and clasped them together to hide the marks. Her hair was a mess, too, and her smock also was stained. She'd eaten at least a handful of the berries—were her lips marked as well? She'd not considered her appearance before she'd flown upstairs.

She smoothed the loose strands of hair back from the right side of her face and smiled at her son, saying, "I know, Ian. Leave us now, love. We've some talkin' to do."

He knew better than to argue. He said, "Aye, Mum," very quietly, and then he headed toward her and the door. She thanked him as he passed her.

After he'd gone, she shut the portal, then turned about to face Richard.

She took a few steps in his direction and stopped there. He made no movement toward her, and there was no indication that he had anything to say. Well, she had plenty to say and she meant to say it all. Hands gripping the sides of her apron, she took a deep breath and began.

"I won't apologize for what I did. If I had it to do over, I'd do the same. I—"

"Meggie, you should—"

"Listen. *Please.*" She twisted the apron, forcing herself to stop seconds later. "Whether or not ye agree with what I did,

I felt I had to do it. I felt it needed to be done. As far as I knew, I was the only person besides yerself who knew of the burdens ye've carried, an' who knew yer family had probably given ye up fer dead after all this time. After Kevin came home in that box an' we buried him on that hilltop, I never believed Zach would come home alive, if he ever even came home. We received word of battles from travelers ev'rytime we went into Havershill or Ironton. We heard the numbers of dead an' wounded which we tried to keep from Mrs. Hutchins. We let her go on believin' an' sayin' Zach would come home. But I reached the point that I couldn't believe it an' let her go on believin' it anymore. Yet I didn't have the heart to say that to her outright—that Zach was surely dead, an' she had to go on. I wanted to tell her he was alive. She always said she believed he was, but she didn't in her heart. I saw the worry on her face, in her eyes, an' I wanted so much to tell her he was alive an' mean it. *Know* it. Other friends lost husbands, brothers, sons. I watched 'em grieve. I grieved with 'em, all the while wishin' I could tell 'em their loved ones were alive an' well."

She swiped at the irritating tears that dripped down her cheeks. She'd thought she had no more to cry. How embarrassing and frustrating that she couldn't stop.

"We fought our own battles at home," she continued. "We worried an' we prayed. We knitted socks an' underthings by lamplight an' sent them off to keep our men warm. We cried an' we buried our dead, an' we prayed more for the ones we knew nothin' about—whether they were dead or alive. I'll tell ye this—there was many a mum I wanted to deliver good news to. I couldn't, until a few months ago. So if ye're expectin' an apology from me, Richard Foster, ye'll not be gettin' one. I'll go to my grave knowin' I did the right thing."

That was all she had to say on the subject. She stared at him defiantly, all self-conscious thoughts about her appearance pushed to the back of her mind now. Her hands were tight, but they no longer perspired with nervous apprehension.

She turned to leave.

She placed her hand on the doorknob, but that was as far as she got. Suddenly Richard was behind her, his hand braced high up on the door. He didn't intend to let her open the portal.

His breath was warm in her hair, on her skin, against her ear. "You said we had some talking to do. So far, you've done it all, Meggie McBride." He chuckled. "I don't know why that surprises me."

She swallowed hard. He didn't seem angry. He'd laughed. He'd joked that she'd done all the talking. Was this the same man who'd stormed off from the mercantile yesterday after receiving that letter and realizing she'd revealed his whereabouts to his parents?

Slowly she turned around to face him. He brought his other hand up to the opposite side of the frame, closing her in, and he gazed down at her, a smile twitching the corners of his mouth. He brought down the hand he'd just lifted, ran his forefinger along her jaw, then twisted a thick curl around the hand and lowered his face to hers.

"You nosy, meddling, *infuriating* little busybody," he said. "I've a mind to—"

Meg yelped and tried to jerk away. But she'd lose part of her scalp if she went too far. He'd tricked her, playing nice when he was angry. He'd just wanted to get close enough to get a hand, or two, on her to ensure that she didn't escape.

"I'll not apologize," she said stubbornly. "I told ye that."

"You took it upon yourself to write to my parents—"

Three seconds more of this nonsense and she'd stomp his foot. "Let go," she ordered.

"—and their response was positive."

"Ye have about one— *What?*" A sound, like the squeal of a mouse, shot from her mouth. "What did ye say?"

He grinned. "You heard me. So positive a response, in fact, that they want to know more about you."

Meggie stared at him. A moment passed before she found her voice again: "Well, ye'll tell them . . . write an' tell them I'm not fond of leavin' Kentucky."

His brows shot up. "You're ordering me around again.

If you're so accomplished at writing letters, write them another."

"Positive? Richard, what does that mean? What did the letter say?"

He withdrew from her, moving back toward the bed. "Curiosity, Meggie. Will you ever learn to restrain it? Or contain it? Or something? It's damned irritating at times."

She followed close on his heels. "Stop scoldin' me. The letter . . . what did it say? Ye're welcome at home?"

From the tick he picked up a piece of paper that obviously had been folded three ways; the creases in the paper indicated that. "Let's see, among other things, she wonders about you, how old you are and what you're like, if you're of *marrying* age." He grinned at Meg. "It seems you've won my mother's favor before she's even met you."

Another stare. Another squeal. "Richard, it sounds like a pleasant letter."

His grin widened. He put the letter in her hand and told her to read it. "I am ashamed to say it took me all of last night and most of today to muster the courage to open the envelope and absorb the contents."

He went to sit on the window ledge, where he promptly lit a cheroot, affording Meggie space and time in which to read the missive.

Dying of curiosity, she nevertheless restrained it enough— taking to heart his suggestion that she learn to do that—to settle herself comfortably in the chair on the opposite side of the bed. There she arranged the letter on her lap and began reading:

My dear Richard,

I pray that you carefully manage your temper when you receive this. It is a temper I know well, and one Megan McBride does not deserve. She is a thoughtful girl, or woman, whatever the case might be. As you will undoubtedly surmise, she wrote to inform this mother that her eldest son was alive, and of where he could be located. She has a fine heart, and it is evident that she cares for you. I am curious to know more about her.

How old is she? Is she of marrying age? That is, if you have not already married. I should not carry on, therefore risk sounding like I am trying to arrange your life for you.

At this moment you cannot know my joy in simply knowing that you are alive. Megan suggests that I had given both you and Willy up for dead.

Months after the Gettysburg battle, army officials wrote to inform us that regretfully you and Willy were "unaccounted for." In other words, that you both were missing in action. I cannot tell you how often I prayed for your safe return. I did not give up hope until a few months ago. Now that hope, that belief, is restored, at least where you are concerned.

Come home, Richard. I do not blame you for William's death. Neither does your father. What a comfort and a joy to know that one of our sons is still alive! I know what Megan has told you about your guilt. I agree with her. William would have been called into service if he had not enlisted—any remaining men capable of fighting were indeed summoned. William also might have died on any battlefield. I am thankful, and grateful, that you were with him.

You are an uncle twice over! Your sister married three years ago and has two children, a son and a daughter. Come home soon and meet your nephew and niece, and be prepared to tell us about this Megan McBride. We all love you and miss you.

The letter was signed simply, "Mother."

Meg couldn't seem to stop crying today. She had to move the letter, hold it a safe distance away, to ensure that her tears wouldn't drip on it and smear the ink.

"Thank you, Meggie McBride," Richard said softly from his ledge. He drew deeply from his cheroot, and he smiled at her as smoke drifted up from his mouth and nose, forming a light cloud around his head.

The cloud dissipated. Meg smiled back and wiped away the last of her tears. Saints, but she was tired of crying!

She approached him, and she settled herself beside him on the ledge.

He took her hand in his and lifted it to his mouth, kissing the back of it. It was a sweet gesture, one that clenched Meggie's heart and made her want to climb onto his lap.

"I'm going home," he said quietly, looking serious suddenly.

She knew he had to go—and part of her silently rejoiced. She felt another pang in her heart and she braced herself.

She tipped her head and treated him to one of her mischievous looks. "Aye. An' well ye should—'tis about time, Lieutenant. An' when ye get there, ye'd do good to drop to yer knees an' beg yer mum's everlastin' forgiveness. Look how ye've worried her!"

He groaned lightly. "Meggie . . ."

She sobered. "I love ye. No one else could tolerate ye in the mornin's."

That drew laughter from him.

"When are ye leavin'?"

"In the morning."

"Hah! Not too early in the mornin'."

"As soon as you sing me awake."

"That'll be the middle o' the night then," she informed him, standing, flipping her skirt and heading toward the bed, where his belongings were strewn. "The sooner, the better."

He grabbed her by the elbow, turned her around, and pulled her close to him. He was grinning, and he'd deposited the cheroot somewhere, most likely in the spittoon that stood not far away.

"Forever saucy, aren't you? And forever disheveled," he teased. "Berry stains. What happened to your hair? It looks as though you got caught in the bush."

He reached behind her and pulled her hair free of the ribbon that bound it.

She tossed her head, and he brought his hands up her back to her neck, where he entwined his fingers in her hair and urged her face close to his.

He kissed her, and then he whispered against her lips, "I love you like no one else ever will. How could they, you impudent, stubborn, unpredictable, delightful woman? I'm coming back for you, Meggie McBride, so don't think about marrying someone else while I'm away."

Meg squeezed her eyes shut. She shook her head. "Don't . . . don't make promises ye might not be able to keep. Please, don't."

"I intend to keep this one," he murmured. "Will you marry me?"

She shouldn't answer him. She should wait and see what Ohio held for him, wait and see if he returned.

She couldn't.

"Aye. I'll marry ye," she whispered, and then she caught his lips with hers and put a stop to his teasing.

Epilogue

*T*HE AZALEAS HAD bloomed, turning the hillsides scarlet. Here and there moccasin flowers splashed pink, and hepaticas lent shades of lilac and violet blues. Tulip trees stretched their pillared limbs, coloring the countryside with pale yellow blossoms. The poplars and oaks and maples and the chestnuts had awakened from long winter slumbers, adding their own variations of green to those of the pines and hemlocks.

A freshness filled the air, a newness. Animals peeked from burrows and nests, from dens and holes, mothers looking out for offspring and the offspring peering out curiously, ready to wander from maternal protection.

Ian shed his clothes while Meggie gathered creeping wintergreen for brewing mountain tea and cut mushrooms to add to stews and other foods. She'd told him she didn't want him swimming—the water was still far too cold—and yet when she turned from the mushrooms, he and Russell were splashing in the Ohio, their clothing left in piles on the lush riverbank.

She opened her mouth to shout at Ian and Russell, to tell them to get out of the water and put their clothes back on.

But she snapped her mouth shut, shaking her head and smiling at herself in the end. They were already in the water—and boys would be boys. It wouldn't be the first time Ian and Russell had been exposed to cold water, and she doubted whether it would be the last. She'd let them swim for a little while, then she'd call them in.

She cut more mushrooms, the handle of the basket draped over her forearm. It had been a long winter for her, also. There'd been no word from Ohio, from either Richard or his mother, and she had simply tried to stay busy with tasks. She'd even taught for nearly all of January at the Havershill school because the schoolmaster had taken ill and had been confined to bed for weeks. The town committee might have had several other choices, but Meg had volunteered herself for the position, knowing full well that she might end up with a permanent position if the schoolmaster died. It didn't matter. The busier the better.

She finished gathering mushrooms and made her way to the edge of the water, where she pretended to be angry: "Ian McBride, ye're doin' what yer mother told ye not to do. Get out of the water!"

He hung his head as she knew he would. Impulsive child—he'd have fun and endure the consequences later. He slowly made his way to the bank, and Russell followed him, a long expression on his face as if he didn't know what to expect, either.

"We'll be takin' Russell home, an' ye'll have supper in yer room t'night," she told Ian.

His face fell another few inches. Ooh, how he hated eating alone, unable to share conversation with everyone. He loved taking part in the evening meal, in the discourse and the togetherness. Well, he'd had his swim—she'd given him that. But there was a price for disobedience.

The boys dressed, and Meg led the way to Russell's home. The walk was spent in silence, with Ian and Russell occasionally stealing regretful glances at each other. Doubtless Russell wondered if she meant to tattle on him to his mother. Meggie didn't, but she saw no point in telling him that. The twenty minutes he spent sweating and worrying and mulling over what he and Ian had done seemed punishment enough.

Once Meg had left Russell with his mother, she placed her hand around Ian's shoulder, assurance that she still loved him, that she always loved him no matter what, and the two of them set out together for the inn.

It didn't take them long to reach McBride's, and Meggie was just in time to see Coamh flickering his white tail on his way into her garden. He'd find his way into her morning glories, as he always did, and then she'd have to take up a switch and set off after him, as she'd done numerous times.

"Take this to Mrs. Hutchins, please," Meg said, handing Ian the basket.

"Ye'll not hurt 'im, will ye?"

"Ian, I'll not hurt 'im. But he'll know I'm angry. He digs up my vines an' shreds the leaves. I'll not stand for that." Especially not when her garden was so young. The oregano was just beginning to spread, and the many other plants and herbs had poked their heads above ground only a few weeks ago. They were at a tender age, even the hearty morning glory vines. Why, they were just now beginning to climb the trellis!

Ian shuffled off toward the front door of the inn while Meggie hurried toward her garden. She snared Caomh by the tail just as he spotted her and started to dash away. She tossed him out of the garden, and when he stood and stared at her, as if waiting for her to turn her back, she stomped at him several times. "Go!" she seethed. "Get. Now!"

"I see your temperament hasn't changed since I left," someone said from behind her.

Richard.

Meg stopped breathing. Sometimes in summer the heat made her a little dizzy and light-headed. But the air was still cool, another reason why she'd not wanted Ian swimming yet. There was no heat to make her dizzy or light-headed today, which also, in turn, often made her thoughts unclear. Yet she *was* dizzy suddenly, and her thoughts *were* unclear. Was it Richard's voice, or was her imagination playing tricks on her?

She missed him so much, missed their closeness, his touch, the love that had developed between them. Mrs. Hutchins and Edan had married last month, and the ceremony had made her long for Richard, too. He'd asked her to marry him, after all.

"As fiery as ever," he remarked.

She wasn't imagining. He was here. He'd returned just as he'd said he would.

Meggie turned around, her hands gripping the sides of her skirt. He leaned against a crape myrtle, its purple blooms a breathtaking backdrop, their sweet fragrance perfuming the air. His arms were folded across his chest, and one corner of his mouth lifted in a lopsided grin.

"I couldn't wait until morning," he said softly. "You're so fond of this garden, I thought planting myself here was a good idea. I knew you'd be along before long."

She couldn't help herself. She ran to him, almost tripping over her skirt.

She threw her arms around his waist and pressed her face to his chest. She listened to his heartbeat and the sound of his rumbling laughter.

"When this garden blooms fully, it will be a fine place for a wedding," he said. "Edan has already agreed to provide us with the corner room up there." He glanced up toward the window, the ledge where he'd sat so many mornings listening to her and watching her as he smoked.

She lifted her head and kissed him, the lips she'd missed so much. "Home . . . How was home?"

He smiled. "It was good. So good, in fact, that I brought people with me who want to meet you."

She stared at him for a moment. "Yer parents?"

"My parents."

Her hands immediately went to her hair. She couldn't meet his parents right now, disheveled as she must look. "I'll go in the back way. I'll hurry upstairs an' change my dress. I'll brush my hair an'—"

He caught one of her arms. "Meggie. I already told them about you. They know what to expect."

She bristled. That didn't sound good. "Oh? An' jus' what are they expectin'?" She plopped her hands on her hips.

He grinned. "You. Just you."

That didn't tell her a thing.

He pulled her close and kissed her. Meg sighed. It felt so good to be in his arms, to feel his breath on her lips again and his body pressed to hers.

"Ye're stayin'?" she had to ask. "Ye're really stayin'?"

"Of course I'm staying," he murmured. "And I expect you to sing to me every morning from your garden."

Laughing with joy, Meggie buried her face in his shirt.

FREE

Romance

(a $4.50 value)

Send in the Coupon Below

To get your FREE historical romance and start saving, fill out the coupon below and mail it today. As soon as we receive it we'll send you your FREE Book along with your first month's selections.

Mail To: **True Value Home Subscription Services, Inc. P.O. Box 5235**
120 Brighton Road, Clifton, New Jersey 07015-5235

YES! I want to start previewing the very best historical romances being published today. Send me my FREE book along with the first month's selections. I understand that I may look them over FREE for 10 days. If I'm not absolutely delighted I may return them and owe nothing. Otherwise I will pay the low price of just $4.00 each: a total $16.00 (at *least* an $18.00 value) and save at least $2.00. Then each month I will receive four brand new novels to preview as soon as they are published for the same low price. I can always return a shipment and I may cancel this subscription at any time with no obligation to buy even a single book. In any event the FREE book is mine to keep regardless.

Name _____

Street Address _____ Apt. No. _____

City _____ State _____ Zip Code _____

Telephone _____

Signature _____
(if under 18 parent or guardian must sign)

Terms and prices subject to change. Orders subject
to acceptance by True Value Home Subscription
Services. Inc.

12004-9